THE CELTIC STONE

The "Stone Collection" Book 5

NICK HAWKES

Hawkesflight Media

The Celtic Stone

A novel

by
Nick Hawkes

Chapter 1

Better keep the devil at the door
than have to turn him out of the house.
(Scottish proverb)

C hris plucked at his shirt, trying to unstick it from his back. The humidity was oppressive. Beside him, the water of the river flowed sluggishly. He slapped at a mosquito, and wondered why anyone would choose to live in the top end of Australia.

Not everyone shared his dour mood. Around him, tourists chatted eagerly, and pushed for a place near the railing of the tourist boat's deck. Chris stepped back to make room for a small boy who was determined not to miss out on the spectacle.

Toward the bow of the boat, a man held out a pole from which dangled a chunk of bloodied meat.

Everyone waited.

Chris felt his mobile phone begin to vibrate in his pocket.

His fellow tourists pointed excitedly and exclaimed in hushed awe as a brutal head emerged from the murky water beside them. Chris had a disturbing impression of two reptilian eyes, unblinking, focused.

The vibrating phone was insistent. Chris reached into his pocket.

Sixteen feet of heavily armored crocodile eased to the surface.

"Chris Norman speaking."

"G'day mate."

Chris recognized the voice of Jim Baxter, Chief Flying Instructor at the flying school where he was training to be a commercial pilot. "What's up, Jim?"

"How's the holiday?"

"Overrated."

"Why aren't you out fishing, catching lots of barramundi?"

"Because I'm watching a sixteen-foot reptilian killing machine. If you swim in the water here, they'll kill you. And if you stay on land, you've got to dodge the snakes. The inland taipan has a venom fifty times more deadly than the cobra."

Jim chuckled. "Sounds like you need to get back in the air where it is safe; and I think I can help. I've been asked to find a pilot to ferry a Scottish Aviation Bulldog from Darwin to Alice Springs. As you're already up there on holiday, I thought you'd like the gig."

"You're joking." Chris turned away from the noisy chatter going on around him to better hear what was being said.

"No, honestly. It's been bought by the Central Australian Aviation Museum. They've got a motley collection of World War II aircraft, and they've bought a Bulldog series 120 to make their collection more contemporary. It's fully aerobatic. Are you interested? Expenses only, I'm afraid, but the museum will send you back here to Adelaide on the Ghan."

There was a gasp from the people around him. Chris had a vague impression of the massive reptile leaping out of the water.

"By rail?"

"Gold class. Yes or no?"

The tour operator spoke through the loud speaker. "That's one ton of crocodile leaping out of the water as far as its back legs, folks. Unusually, it's managed to take the meat at the first grab. So that's it for today. Hasn't it been a great experience?"

Chris groaned. "You've just caused me to miss a one-hundred dollar spectacle, Jim."

"Yes or no?"

There was never ever any doubt. "Yes, I'll do it."

"Good. I'll email the details." Jim paused before continuing. "And Chris, it's a long flight for a small plane. Don't do anything silly."

"I won't."

It was only a small lie.

Chris checked the altimeter. *Five-thousand feet. Fine.* He stretched wearily, grateful to be near the end of the final leg of his flight to Alice Springs. He glanced at his flight plan to refresh himself on the approach procedures to the airport. As he did, he couldn't help but grieve the fact that the aircraft he was flying would shortly be shackled to the ground as a museum piece. She was a thoroughbred and deserved better. He glanced at the fuel gauge. *Fourteen gallons of fuel remaining.*

The beginning of an idea began to suggest itself. *It would be a pity to waste the fuel.*

Chris banked his aircraft and headed southwest to ensure clear air space. *Let's put you through your paces one last time, Old Girl. Let's see what you can do.*

Below him, the majestic ridges and gullies of the MacDonnell Ranges stretched to the horizon. Chris knew little about the area other than that the famous Aboriginal watercolor artist, Albert Namatjira, came from somewhere nearby. He shuddered. Namatjira could keep it. Nothing he could see of the Australian outback commended itself to him. It was hot and harsh, and he'd seen too much of it.

He tightened his five-point harness, checked that the airspace was clear, and then eased the throttle open.

The six-foot, two-inch diameter Hartzel propeller howled angrily.

Chapter 2

Let them care that come behind.
(Scottish saying)

The hunter stood on the cliff top, holding his spears. He was perfectly still, perfectly balanced. One of his legs was cocked sideways, allowing a foot to wedge against the opposite knee. Like an egret at a water hole, he watched for movement that would betray his prey. He knew that he was close now, but the long chase had brought him to a strange place.

He felt his strength begin to slip away like water seeping from cupped hands. Schooled by habit, he fingered the winged stone that hung around his neck. He wanted to draw out its strength, but it gave him no comfort. The fact remained: he had come to the edge of his country, his language group. Every step he now walked would take him further from the songs of his people, and the land that defined him.

He gazed east, across the unfamiliar rocky mountain ranges. This was *Warlawurr,* caterpillar dreaming, and he did not know its stories. As a man was only truly a man when he understood his songlines, he was ill at ease. Deliberately, he conjured in his mind a picture of his grandmother. She had come from the *Warlawurru* and could speak *Warlpin*. She would know.

"Sing to me, Grandmother."

A moment passed, then he was a child again…and the voice of her singing came low and faint to his ears. He strained to listen, and the chant became louder. She sang the stories of her childhood, of the giant caterpillars that had made the massive ranges, and of the emu feet of the sky god that had created the canyons that patterned its red flanks.

All too soon, the song ended.

"Please, Grandmother, sing me some more."

She smiled, "Aaah, hungry child." After a pause, her flat monotone began again. Her chant told him that the canyons he saw held pools of water left by the mother of the moon when she wept for her stolen child. When the story was told, the chanting stopped…and there was silence. "Now go to sleep, child."

But he would not sleep. Not yet. He searched the landscape, watching, for he was *kudaitja*—the assassin.

He'd been chosen by the elders to hunt Moketarinja for the crime committed against his sister. He had been hunting Moketarinja for five days, but each day had put him further from his people. He ached to be back among them. The hunter called them to mind, seeking their strength, and waited for them to come into his heart.

Aaah, he felt them now. He could see the men stalking kangaroo and wallaby. They were strong, silent, and deadly. He drew closer to his people's camp and saw the women using sticks to dig up yams, lizards and honey ants. The naked, tousle-haired children were helping by prizing witchetty grubs from the roots of the acacia. One woman shouted angrily as two young boys ran away from their work to throw heavy-headed play-sticks through the grass to see which one would slide the furthest.

The hunter reached for the winged pendant around his neck. It was a stone like no other. Even during his initiation, its mystery had not been revealed to him. He had simply been given it by his birth father who, in turn, had been given it by his father years before. It was the sacred stone of his tribe's medicine men, and was said to be more powerful than the magic *atnongara* stones of the medicine men to the north. Yet the winged stone held the secret of its power close. Even his grandfather did not know the story of its carved heart or its outstretched wings. He knew only that it was the symbol of a very powerful God—perhaps older, he said, than any dreaming he knew.

The hunter shivered and wished for the thousandth time that he did not have the burden of having to wear it. Laying his spears on the ground, he pulled at a bunch of dried grass and wove it crudely around the winged stone. It was best not to provoke the local spirit-beings by wearing it too openly as he crossed their land.

Looking east, he noted the dark, straight line at the base of the great wall of cliffs. He was getting closer to white man's business. Their straight tracks scarred the landscape, uncaring of whose land they walked on, uncaring of any dreaming.

The white man was strong, and his father had always insisted that his people have nothing to do with them. His people's culture was one thousand generations old and no generation was allowed to change it. You could not despise the ways of your ancestors. Their spirits guarded the waterholes—and without water, there could be no life.

It was hot. The old men had talked about the recent hot summers, and wondered about them. They had asked his father to inquire of the ancestor spirits.

The hunter flinched, losing his train of thought as he heard a distant sound. It was like that of a hornet seeking out its prey. He looked to the sky. The white man left his marks across the sky as well. How could he do that? How could he make smoke, straight as a spear, fly across the sky?

He glanced down at his own two spears. He had selected the wood with care and taken pains to straighten them well by heating the shafts over a fire, and bending them into shape before they cooled. He was proud of the result. His spears would fly true—and kill.

Killing. He'd seen death. Death was part of living. But to kill a man—that was different. Again, he grasped his pendant and felt the string of twisted grass fibers press into the back of his neck.

He turned these thoughts over in his head, knowing outwardly that he must show no sign of them. He must remain impassive, guarding his thoughts from any spirit-being that might be watching.

Flies fought to find what moisture they could from his mouth and nostrils as he scanned the landscape for signs of his quarry. The sound came again. It was the sound of a hornet. The insect sounded angry and agitated.

Chapter 3

Even God cannot make two mountains
without a valley in between.
(Scottish proverb)

C hris aimed the two-hundred-horsepower Lycoming engine at
the sky. He checked that his wings were level with the horizon, and waited for the aircraft to climb as high as it could before
stalling. With just the minimum of forward movement left, he
stamped on the left rudder bar, cart-wheeling the plane until it
aimed at the ground. Snapping the throttle closed, he kicked at the
right rudder bar to prevent the aircraft swinging like a pendulum.
No you don't, my darling. I've got you. Chris eased the joystick toward his
stomach, nursing the aircraft out of its vertical dive as the G-forces
started to crush him into his seat.

Using the momentum of his dive, he soared up toward the
heavens again. At the apex of his climb, he smelled it—the pungent,
acrid smell of burning vinyl. *No, no, no.* Something was horribly
wrong. *No, no. Don't let it be. Dammit. Something's shorted the busbar. Please,*

God—not a cockpit fire! Hideous images of the melted faces of Second World War airmen flitted across his mind.

In just a few seconds, foul smelling smoke filled the cockpit.

Chris flicked off the master switch, killing all the electrics. Coughing and retching, he reached above himself, and tugged at the yellow handle that released the hood of the canopy. It crashed backward, allowing the engine's slipstream to suck the smoke from the cockpit. However, the extra oxygen fueled the fire. Blinded by tears, Chris groped for the fire extinguisher that was clipped between the seats, and wrenched it free. Perversely, it slipped from his fingers. But instead of dropping to the floor, it smashed against his face and disappeared out of the hatch.

Dammit! I'm upside-down.

Chris looked through the smoke and saw patches of brown, scabby land above his head. He hauled the wings level and put the aircraft into a steep, spiral dive. *Land! Land before you burn, fool!* He fought to control his terror. *Where?* With savage bitterness, he realized that the West MacDonnell Ranges could, in no way, be construed as an ideal landing ground.

With no instruments, Chris could only guess his speed. *Don't stall. Please don't stall.* He tried not to panic as he reviewed his situation. *No parachute. No stall-warning alarm. No instruments. No flaps.* And now the heat from the fire behind the dashboard was beginning to sear his shins as his feet rested on the rudder bar. He had to get down as fast as possible. *No radio. No way to transmit a mayday call.* He was going to crash, and no one would know.

Dear God, dear God, dear God!

Chris looked for a landing spot. The only location he could see was a bald stone plateau on top of a rocky ridge. It was covered with tussocks of grass and low vegetation.

He rolled out of the spiral dive at what he judged to be four hundred feet above the plateau and drove the aircraft at the ground, screaming in agony as the flames licked at his legs. The carefully trained part of his brain continued to fly the aircraft. *No flaps. Too fast, too fast. You're too fast!*

Chris dropped the Bulldog down onto its main wheels. The

aircraft shuddered and skimmed across the uneven surface until both wheels hit a small, scabby rock ledge, throwing the nose-wheel to the ground with such force that it collapsed. The ruined plane skidded across the rocky plateau on its nose in a shower of sparks and dust.

Chris punched at the quick-release button on his harness. As he did, the plane flipped over onto its back, throwing him out of the aircraft before toppling off the plateau into a steep gorge. The aircraft exploded into flames.

It took only thirty seconds for the first of the flies to find his broken body.

The hunter had watched the roaring monster as it dived from the air and crashed to the ground like a bird killed in flight. The shock of the spectacle and the explosion that followed meant it was a few moments before he noticed that a man, a white man, had been spewed out of the monster before it had died. The fire caused by the explosion quickly burned itself out. Silence followed. Nothing moved.

Terror gave way to shock, and shock gave way to awe. The white man, the Eagle Man, had flown through the air. Amazing. But now he was dead. Perhaps he was not meant to fly. Had he angered a spirit-being? He looked carefully at the Eagle Man lying on the rock face. He looked dead. That was good. Here was spirit-magic he did not understand, and he wanted nothing to do with it.

High above, a wedge-tailed eagle soared on an air thermal rising from the sun-scorched, rocky range. "Aaieee, aaieee," it cried. The hunter looked up and considered its message carefully. It was very rare for a wedge-tail to call in flight. His grandmother's spirits were trying to tell him something. He reached for the winged stone and waited for understanding. Slowly, it came to him. The eagle was not afraid, so neither should he be. He felt the winged stone's assurance. It would keep him safe. But even so, he would have a spear ready. He edged toward the body on the rock face.

For a while, he watched the white man's shallow breathing. There was a terrible gash across his left eye. If the white man lived, he would always be blind in that eye. The man's left leg was also broken, and the bottoms of both legs were badly burned. He could see angry, charred-red flesh. The hunter gave the white man a prod with the end of a spear.

There was no response.

"Aaieee, aaieee," urged the eagle. Was the eagle urging him on, or calling for a mate? He searched the sky but could see no other bird. The hunter reflected. Perhaps it was time he too found a mate? He would ask his aunts. They would enjoy arguing and negotiating. Once they had chosen someone suitable, they would ask the elders. Seldom did the elders go against the women. The women were shrewd. They knew. But that was for later. Right now, the eagle was calling for him to help the white man, the Eagle Man. The man needed water and medicine. He would need to be carried into one of the steep chasms where there was water and shade.

The hunter assessed the weight of the Eagle Man. He was bulky and well-muscled, about the weight of a female red kangaroo. With a grunt, he heaved the Eagle Man across his shoulders. The white man's smell was strange, different from his own people. It was a bitter, sour smell, and he didn't like it. He squatted down to pick up his spears, and then began to pad across the rock face under his burden.

Chris had his hands in the fine, dry sand of a beach. He moved his fingers, luxuriating in the feel of its flowing softness. It was warm, and behind him he could hear waves pounding the shallows and hissing up the sand. His mother was calling him. He knew he should go, but it was so pleasant. Lying near the top of the beach, he could see white butterflies dancing among the flowering spurge and stat-ice. The balmy salt air, tinged with the musky, iodine smell of seaweed, delighted him. He loved it here.

Then someone threw water into his face, and he woke up.

He wished he hadn't. Only one eye opened. The pain on the other side of his head was horrendous. His legs felt as if they were still on fire. More disturbing was the sight of a black figure bending over him, staring at him with a dispassionate expression. He had a wide, flat nose, deeply inset eyes, and an untidy mat of woolly hair. A pendant wrapped in grass hung around his neck. The black man's lips were slightly parted to reveal a gap where his two front teeth should have been. Two hideous, horizontal scars deformed his chest.

It was all too much—so he surrendered to unconsciousness.

When he came to again, Chris found he was sitting on a patch of sand with his back against a rock. He could see that he was in some sort of deep canyon. The sand was comforting and still warm despite being in the shade. Without a word, the dark man he'd seen earlier produced a wooden bowl of water and held it to his lips. Most of the water dribbled out. The bowl was refilled, and he drank again with more success. The searing pain in his head and legs was overwhelming. He teetered again on the edge of consciousness, and allowed his head to loll back against the rock.

Chris did not want to come in just yet. But his mother was insistent. She had dinner ready. He should go. But there, above the beach, a wedge-tailed eagle soared. It was marvelous. He would stay a while, and watch it.

The hunter watched the white man's head sag backward. The man was delirious and obviously in pain. He bent down and felt along the length of the man's broken leg. With rough efficiency, he pulled the leg straight and tied it to a rough, wooden splint. He did not wash away the blood. Wounds needed to bleed if they were to heal.

Leaving Eagle Man beside the rock pool, he went searching for *pitjuri*, a bush that grew in the drier areas of the land beyond the canyon. He needed its powerful narcotic.

Eagle Man had regained consciousness and was groaning in pain when he returned. The hunter laid lengths of *pitjuri* on the back of his *woomera*, took out his knife, and cut the *pitjuri* into small pieces. He spoke to the man as he worked. He would have liked to sing, but it was too dangerous. Singing was good for pain, but he might awaken the spirits of the land and make them curious.

Having prepared the sections of *pitjuri* to his satisfaction, he picked up three short pieces and motioned to Eagle Man that he should eat them.

Eagle Man looked disoriented and puzzled. But then he seemed to understand. He took the pieces of *pitjuri* and began to chew them. The hunter watched and waited for the *pitjuri* to take away his pain. Gradually, the white man's head dropped. He was asleep. The hunter was pleased. This was a healing sleep.

He would now light a cooking fire, that would later be rebuilt to become a warming fire which stayed alight until morning. Night was when the bad spirit-beings came out of hiding. The two men needed a fire to be safe.

Taking a long, thin fire-stick from his bag of woven grass, he looked around for a log of hard wood with a crack in it. Having found it, he filled the crack with crushed, dried kangaroo droppings, and surrounded it with a halo of fine, dry grass. Wedging the fire-stick into the crack, he spun it back and forth, rubbing it between his hands until a thin wisp of smoke appeared. Bending low, he blew on it, coaxing the smoldering dust into a flame that set the dry grass on fire. He made the fire strong, feeding its adolescence until it died down into maturity and became useful.

When the white man regained consciousness, the hunter cooked grubs of the rain moth, and *anaty*, feeding them in small pieces to Eagle Man. Although it was easy eating, Eagle Man was not inclined to eat. But the hunter was insistent, and fed the Eagle Man like a child, ceasing only when he had pushed a final piece of *ahakeye* into the man's mouth. The white man would need food if he were to survive the day.

Chris found the food strange and his forced feeding slightly alarming. He nonetheless recognized its benevolent intent, and was curiously comforted by its intimacy. After the meal, he watched the firelight dance on the rust-red walls of the canyon. The color of the walls was curiously at odds with the bleached, pale rocks and sand at the base of the canyon. He wondered why.

The young Aborigine blocked out the firelight as he moved across to stand over him. It took several seconds for Chris to focus on him with his one good eye. The bushman looked away, avoiding eye contact, but remained in front of him. It took a moment before Chris understood. *You want to talk.* Sitting in silence, he waited apprehensively. Eventually, the bushman tapped his chest and said in a low voice, "Raberaba."

Chris understood that the bushman was telling him his name. "Reyba," Chris repeated.

The man tapped his chest again. "Raberaba."

"Rubbera."

In exasperation, the bushman put a hand either side of Chris's face, and forced him to watch his speech closely. "Raberaba," he said slowly. A mother might have done the same thing to a child.

Chris nodded and pointed to his own chest. "Christopher." For some reason, it was important to him that the man should know his full name rather than its shortened form.

The man considered the name for a moment before repeating, "Kritofer."

It was good enough.

As some stage, Chris fell asleep.

He woke in the middle of the night. The fire was no more than slow-burning embers. Leaning back, he gazed upward with his one good eye. Even in his pain, the sight he beheld took his breath away. Visible between the walls of the canyon, was the night sky. The stars of the universe shone with a brightness so intense that it hurt to see them. He reached a hand toward the heavens to collect the ice-cut diamonds.

His action caused Raberaba to wake. Chris saw his deep-set eyes glittering in the firelight as he looked up to where Chris was reaching. After a pause, the hunter said quietly, "Yiwarra," and rose to his feet to push a log further onto the fire. He then handed Chris some more pieces of plant to eat. As Chris chewed, he found the Southern Cross among the scattered jewels, and pointed to it.

Raberaba looked upward, and then crouched down beside him. "Waluwara." he said.

Chris frowned.

"Waluwara," he said again.

Chris had no idea what it meant.

Somewhere in the distance, a dingo howled. Chris leaned back against the rock and fell back to sleep.

———

Chris woke to find that he had slipped sideways onto the ground. He was on the sand next to some pale limestone rocks. Pain jarred him into full consciousness. "Oh, God!" In panic, he tried to sit up. "Aargh!" His cry echoed off the canyon walls.

Rough hands took him by the shoulders and sat him upright. Raberaba seemed to have been up for some time. A shingleback lizard was cooking in its skin on the embers of the fire. Chris balked at eating any of it, but did accept more bush yam, and mercifully, more *pitjuri*. With some alarm, he watched Raberaba eat all of the shingleback, including its heavily armored skin.

He fell asleep.

In what seemed only a moment later, he awoke and blinked cautiously as he took stock of his surroundings. Shafts of morning light streamed into the canyon, causing the towering western wall to glow a warm peach color. On the floor of the canyon, Chris was amazed to see some small palms growing near a pool of water under the base of a cliff. This extraordinary chasm in the middle of the desert evidently produced a microclimate that allowed plants— vestiges of a bygone tropical climate—to survive. It was incredible. Drunk with *pitjuri*, he again fell sideways next to the pale, limestone rocks. His one good eye could see fossils of long-extinct sea creatures visible on their surface. He tried to make sense of it. How could the limestone of an ancient ocean now exist between quartzite cliffs in central Australia?

Everything is so confusing.

Raberaba waded in the pool under the rock ledge of the cliff, feeling with his feet in the sand for freshwater mussels. He ducked under a rock ledge as he moved methodically through the water. Glancing up, he saw something that caused him alarm. Rock markings— markings that he was not meant to see. They were the business of another people. This was not his place. He must move on, fulfill his assignment, and return to his people as soon as possible. But now he had the encumbrance of a wounded man. It had become clear in the night when the white man had looked at the stars that he was indeed Eagle Man. His single eye had sought out Waluwara in the night sky, the eagle, whose bright talons always pointed to the south.

He climbed out of the rock pool, walked over to Eagle Man, and sat him upright again. As he did so, Eagle Man reached out to touch the winged stone hanging from his neck. Raberaba leaned back, putting it out of reach, and was silent for a while, thinking. There could be no more doubt about it. He was again being given the message to see the Eagle Man to safety.

He considered how he would do it. Eventually, he concluded that he would not need to go very far to achieve it. The big walking tracks of the white man were close at hand. He would simply find the nearest track, and leave Eagle Man there.

He had seen the track that he wanted from his vantage point the day before. It lay directly at the base of the rocky ranges on which he now stood. It was almost no distance. However, to reach it, he would need to carry Eagle Man down a long, exposed slope and then descend into another steep gorge. It was a perilous route, suited more for an eagle than a man. He sighed. So be it. He began to gulp down as much water as his stomach could take. Then he reached for the shallow, wooden dish in order to ply Eagle Man with water until he was satisfied he could drink no more.

Chris felt himself being hauled upright and manhandled over Raberaba's shoulders. His head lolled against the back of Raberaba's waist, bumping alongside the woven grass bag hanging there. Clutching his spears in his left hand, Raberaba padded his way out of the canyon into the full glare of the morning sun. Chris couldn't believe the difference in temperature. The sun heated the back of his thin, cotton, flying suit so that it became scorching hot.

It wasn't long before he began to appreciate Raberaba's wiry strength. They followed a zigzag course down the sparse, dry scrubland slope. Sometimes, Raberaba stopped to unburden himself and rest. At other times, he would leave Chris, and scout ahead for the best way down—but never for very long. All too soon, Chris was yanked upright and swung over the black man's shoulders—and the agony of the journey would continue.

Flies swarmed around the savage wound across Chris's eye and explored every orifice that offered moisture. His free arm swung uselessly, brushing against the grizzled, sun-bleached scrub. The scratches it gave him added to his litany of discomforts. Even in his half-drugged state, the journey was a nightmare. Every jolt caused agony in his broken leg and pounding head. The flies formed a black, moving scab over his wounds. Ants joined the torment whenever he was dumped to the ground—which happened with about as much ceremony as a farmer dropping a sack of wheat. In his semi-delirium, Chris examined the ants. There were so many. Big ones and little ones. *How many ants are there in Australia?*

The sun grew hotter, and the rest stops seemed to become more frequent. Chris sometimes had the presence of mind to look up and appreciate the view. As far as he could judge, they seemed to be walking to the edge of the world. A massive plain spread out underneath them, as flat as a billiard table for five or six miles until another multi-colored mountain range, jagged and intimidating, erupted from the plain.

Chris wanted to see something green. He wanted to go back to the canyon. He wanted the interminable bouncing to stop. He wanted...

Just when he thought he couldn't take any more, Raberaba

dumped him down again, and moved off to reconnoiter the steep climb down. The narcotic was beginning to wear off. The pain in Chris's head and legs was unbearable. Sweating and grunting, he gritted his teeth and fought the waves of agony and nausea.

After an eternity, Raberaba returned, his face inscrutable. Chris made an eating motion, begging for more of the plant to chew. To his dismay, Raberaba ignored his entreaty and heaved him over his back. Chris screamed in pain. Raberaba took no notice, and carried him to the end of a rocky ledge. There, he was dropped to the ground, and his companion went over the edge alone.

A moment later, two long arms came up, turned Chris over onto his stomach, and dragged him over the ledge.

Even through the agony of the maneuver, Chris was sufficiently aware to be appalled at the vertical drop beneath him. Unable to use his broken leg, he did what he could to help Raberaba ease him down the face of the cliff. Adrenaline was now helping him to cope with his pain. He realized that Raberaba had needed him to be alert and to assist in the dangerous descent. There would be no *pitjuri* until they were safely down.

They made slow progress. Raberaba would climb down a short way and then coax Chris down to him, shielding him from the chasm with his body whenever he could. Raberaba would then check that he was secure before climbing down a little further to repeat the process. It was interminable, agonizing work, and Chris's arms became desperately tired.

Chris was looping his hand around a rock, when he suddenly saw a snake. Its coiled, olive-brown body was exactly level with his head. Instantly, the snake reared up to strike. Chris gasped in horror. The snake hurled itself at his face, feinting an attack before darting back and slithering behind the rock.

Chris reared back instinctively, just managing to hang on to the rock face with one hand.

Raberaba, who was pressed up right behind him, stood no chance.

With his hands ripped from their holds, Raberaba began to fall backward into the canyon.

Everything seemed to happen in slow motion. Chris looked at him in horror as his arms flailed once in the air. For a brief second, Raberaba looked into Chris's eyes. Chris willed him to grab at his free hand and save himself, though it must surely kill them both.

Raberaba did not.

Flinging out his hand, Chris caught hold of Raberaba's pendant.

The grass string snapped as Raberaba fell backward into the void. Chris heard his long cry: "Aieeeeeeeeeeeeeee!"

It was the cry of an eagle.

Four hours later, a group of five university students trekking the Larapinta trail found the body of a young white man by the side of the track. He was at the mouth of a canyon. The man was unconscious and terribly wounded. Barely alive. In his hand was a stone, wrapped in dry grass. When they prized his hand open, it proved to be a carved Celtic cross.

Chapter 4

A blind man needs no looking-glass.
(Scottish proverb)

The tip of the dorsal fin sliced through the waters of the loch. Thin streams of water cut away on either side as the fin emerged taller and taller from the sea until it stood almost as high as a man. Breaking out of the water underneath it, a black back glistened with water in the moonlight. The huge body lifted gracefully before sinking back into the sea, instinct driving the Orca back into The Minch, where it would hunt for Atlantic gray seal.

Ach! Magnus felt a smile tug at the edge of his mouth as he watched it. He'd glanced through the window and caught sight of the formidable killer as it had risen out of the sea. After it had gone, he turned his gaze to the mountains on the other side of the loch. The coast of the Isle of Skye sat black and indomitable against the lingering twilight. Tiny pinpricks of yellow light dotting the shoreline indicated that some other crofters were still awake.

Magnus turned back to the task that had demanded his attention—overhauling the carburetor of an outboard motor. The engine had been hoisted onto two hessian sacks laid across the dining table.

A puff of smoke blew into the room from the peat fire that glowed in the hearth. He regarded it with a baleful glare. *Ach, wee laddie. You'd better move your arse right soon an' clean yon chimbley to get it drawing better.* Sighing, he reached for the bottle of whiskey and poured a generous amount into a tumbler. He was drinking too much, and he knew it. He also knew that his wife would be scandalized that he was doing repairs on the engine in the house. The ache of her loss, an oh-so-familiar grief, washed over him. *Cara, my sweet bonny lass.* He savored her memory and smiled sadly. *My, but weren't you a feisty one!*

Putting his head in his hands, he nursed his grief. *How I'm needing you now, ma lovely.* He looked at the dark stain of petrol seeping through the sackcloth to the table. *Though I doubt you'd be giving me a right laldy.*

He took another sip of whiskey to help him overcome a small pang of guilt. He couldn't work on the engine in the shed, he reasoned. The shed had no heating, and its rotting thatched roof seemed to hold in the damp. It would be bitterly cold. *Far better to be in the house. Besides, someone has to look after the boy.*

With a fresh wave of guilt, he looked across to his young son sitting on the bench at the end of the table. His chatter and endless questions had stopped about thirty minutes ago. His head had dropped onto the table, and he was fast asleep. The man leaned forward and ruffled the boy's unkempt hair. "Time for bed, young Ruan."

The boy reluctantly came to consciousness.

"I said, time for bed."

The boy grunted.

"Didn't I tell you to have a bath tonight?"

"Ach, I had a bath last week, Da. It's too cold for bathing."

Magnus sighed and pointed to the wooden stairs that went up to the two bedrooms above. "Full pajamas tonight, Ruan."

"All right, Da," said the boy. He gave his father a perfunctory kiss and trailed upstairs.

In the blackness of her bedroom, a woman dressed in leggings walked to a CD player and switched it on. Stepping back, she raised both arms above her head. She lifted her chin and waited for the music—upright and perfectly poised.

A skirl from a bagpipe announced an ancient Scottish reel.

In her mind's eye, she could see the piper dressed in the blue, green, and red tartan of the MacDonnell clan—and she could see herself too. Then she began to dance.

As she waited for the third reel to begin, her concentration was broken by the quiet, asthmatic purring of a Land Rover. She was familiar with the sound.

Damn. She switched off the CD player, and waited for the knock on the door. She knew her visitor. In truth, she reflected, he was almost the only one who ever dared to call. And he was the only man she'd learned to trust—at least to some degree.

Bess, her heavily pregnant German pointer, lolloped to the door, and began to bark. The woman ran down the stairs, pushed Bess away, and opened the door as far as the security chain would allow. Speaking through the crack, she asked, "Is it yourself, Murdoch?"

"Aye, Morag, it is. It's Sox, the Laird's chestnut. She's in foal and struggling to deliver. I need you to steady her while I turn the foal in her."

Morag nodded to herself. This was not the first occasion she had been called on for her skill. After a pause, she said, "Give me three minutes." So saying, she shut the door.

Murdoch was not surprised by this most un-Scottish treatment of a visitor. He turned back to the Land Rover and climbed back into the seat.

Sure enough, a few minutes later Morag opened the door. Murdoch saw that she was dressed in overalls and had pulled a woolen hat down over her luxuriant hair. Her feet had been pushed into a pair of gumboots. She closed the door behind her and stepped toward the Land Rover.

But then the woman paused, turned in apparent irritation, and reopened the door of her house to fetch a large, canvas carryall. When Murdoch saw it, he grunted his approval and stepped out of the cab to escort Morag to the passenger door.

"Don't fuss me, Murdoch. I may be blind, but I can find your vehicle easy enough."

"It's to speed you, not to fuss you, woman," Murdoch growled, telling only half the truth. "You've nae got your stick."

"Humph!"

They bumped and jolted their way up the glen along the rutted dirt track.

He noticed a light in Magnus's cottage as they drove by, but said nothing. *Up late, and like as not, drinking too much.*

Morag broke the silence. "Does the horse know you well?"

"Aye."

"Then lend me your jacket when we get there."

Murdoch grunted his assent and steered the Land Rover over a cattle grid before swinging left to park in front of a stable block. Morag climbed out of the vehicle and waited for him to lead her into the stable. As he did so, she paused at the entrance and sniffed the air. Murdoch had no idea why, only that it was telling her something.

He looked anxiously at the chestnut mare tethered against the wall. The mare had her back legs apart and was sashaying back and forth in obvious distress. Her ears were pricked back, and her eyes rolled upward in fear. Frothy saliva ringed her lower lip.

After donning Murdoch's jacket, Morag delved into her canvas bag, and poured some dried herbs from a jar into one of the jacket pockets. When this was done, she said, "Take me to the side of her so she can see me well. Stand with me for a minute then back away."

Murdoch did what she asked. He stepped away from her and watched.

Morag allowed the horse to see her clearly, and smell the calming aroma hidden in her jacket pocket.

The chestnut tossed her head.

Morag seemed to be listening intently, feeling the mood of the animal. Very slowly, she stepped away from the horse. The horse watched, beginning to appreciate that she was no threat, and that the new pleasing smell was leaving with her.

Murdoch had seen this scenario before. "She's turned to you," he murmured, watching as Morag bent down slowly and retrieved a block of what looked like beeswax from her carryall. As she did, the mare's ears pricked, and her nostrils flared with interest. The horse edged toward Morag, who turned away. Then, very softly, Morag began to sing a plaintive Scottish lament. The horse stepped closer. Morag turned slowly, stopped singing, and began to speak ancient endearments to the mare. She spoke in Gaelic, gentling the horse with strange, archaic words unknown even to Murdoch. Handing the mare the block to bite on, Morag was soon stroking the horse's giant, sweat-flecked head.

Murdoch nodded in admiration. "You have the way of your mother, sure enough, Morag."

Morag breathed gently over the horse's nostrils before murmuring, "Do what you have to do, Murdoch."

He moved over to the wooden bench along the sidewall, stripped off his shirt, and soaped his right arm before washing it in a bucket of tepid water. Returning to the mare, he lifted its tail, inserted his arm into the birth canal, and felt for the foal. The mare's muscles crushed his arm in contraction, but he persisted in pulling the head of the foal around so that it lay along its front legs—taking care that the umbilical cord remained free. Hoping he would not have to resort to using the rope to pull the foal from the tiring mare, he called quietly to Morag. "I'm ready, lass. I need her to push."

Morag whispered to the mare and then lifted the animal's head upward.

He grunted as the contraction again crushed his arm, then he pulled the tiny front legs of the foal.

All of a sudden, the foal slipped out, causing Murdoch to fall backward. The foal was almost on top of him, fighting to free itself of the last of its enshrouding membrane. Murdoch rolled sideways to avoid the stringy afterbirth, which plopped down beside him. He got to his feet, grabbed a handful of straw, and began to rub the mucous from the face of the young foal.

The tiny animal was already rocking backward and forward, trying to stand on its spindly legs. Murdoch put a hand underneath it and helped it up onto its feet. It wobbled unsteadily, and then took its first tentative steps.

Morag released the mare's head as it turned to lick the face of the foal. This was a ritual Murdoch had seen many times, but it was one that never failed to move him.

The foal staggered under its mother, butting her gently in the belly until it found the teat, and began to suck greedily.

"We've got ourselves a bonny, wee colt, Morag. My heartfelt thanks, lass."

Two hurricane lamps hanging from hooks on the roof beam cast yellow light over the scene. The light lent fiery highlights to Morag's rich, auburn hair. Long strands of it had escaped from under her woolly cap. Morag's face was delicate and beautiful, pale as fresh cream. Her sightless eyes seemed to be looking into the distance at something infinitely sad. Murdoch was puzzled. *How can a birth make a soul so sad?*

Murdoch began to rub the sweaty flanks of the big mare with a brush. He chided the animal gently when it turned toward Morag, obviously hoping for more of the mysterious food stick she had tasted earlier.

When he had finished, he washed himself in the bucket of water and dressed himself. "Will you take a strupack with me, Morag, before I take you home, or maybe a wee dram?"

"Thanks, Murdoch." She handed him back his jacket. "But no doubt you have things to attend to here. Just run me home."

Ruan woke, coughing at the smoke, wondering at the strange heat in his room and bewildered by the roaring sound beneath him. He slipped out of bed. The rough boards beneath his feet were uncomfortably hot. With a rising sense of panic, he ran to the bedroom door. Unlatching it, he jerked it open, only to be faced with the awful sight of flames licking up through a pall of smoke.

"Da! Da! Help, Da!" he screamed, before breaking off in a fit of coughing. He slammed the door shut and ran back to bed—the floorboards even hotter than before. Ruan reached the bed with his eyes streaming.

It was now difficult to breathe. In desperation, he made a dash for the dormer window, and pushed it open. As he did, a thin finger of flame reached through the smoke from under the door, searching for the fresh air he'd let in through the window.

Ruan climbed onto the sill and ducked through the window. Feeling for the gutter, he swung himself over the edge. His feet found the corrugated iron roof of the woodshed. He dropped from its roof to the ground.

Ruan turned round and was appalled at the spectacle he saw. Flames were arching out of the two downstairs windows. Terrified, he ran past the byre, where the milking cow was bellowing in panic. Ruan leaped over the stile in the dry stone wall and sprinted up the road to the large white house where he knew he would find help.

His small fists pummeled the front door. "Morag! Morag!"

Chapter 5

Your feet will bring you to where your heart is.
(Celtic proverb)

C hris sat up, half delirious, and pushed away the nurses who were trying to keep him on the gurney. "I've got to find him. He fell. I've got to find him!"

A pinprick in the arm.

Oblivion.

An eternity later, Chris woke to find himself being inspected by a thin, middle-aged doctor. Chris studied him. He was graying at the temples, and his eyes looked infinitely tired. Chris tried to piece together what his subconscious was trying to tell him. Then he remembered. His friend, the one who fell... He screwed up his eyes in anguish and groaned.

The doctor pulled a chair up beside the bed and sat down. "Hello, Christopher. How are you feeling?"

"I've got to find someone."

The doctor held his hand up. "Christopher, you've been here for two days, and every moment that you've been conscious, you've mentioned the need to find your friend. You've been saying that he fell into the canyon where you were found—an Aboriginal friend, I understand."

Chris nodded, and then wished he hadn't. Pain exploded in his head.

The doctor continued. "Let me fill you in on some details, and then perhaps you can help us fill in some of the information we need. But first let me ask, do you know where you are?"

"No."

"You are in the high dependency ward at the Royal Adelaide Hospital."

"Doctor, my mate...have they found him? He's got to be dead, but we've still got to find him."

The doctor pursed his lips. "Can you tell me his name?"

"Raberaba." *How could I forget?*

The doctor continued, "And where does he come from?"

"I don't know."

"Well, where did you meet him?"

"In the ranges where I crashed—I think." It hurt to talk.

"You think?"

Again, Chris said nothing. The oxygen tube in his nostrils was pulling uncomfortably to one side.

The doctor took a deep breath. "So you've not known him long?"

"No."

"Let me see if I've got this right. You have a friend who comes from a place you don't know; whom you met at a place you are not sure of; and whom you have known for only two days." The doctor paused before saying, "Is there any chance you might have imagined it?"

"No. Why?"

"Because State Emergency Services and police from Alice Springs have searched the canyon where you were found, and have found nothing. No body. No blood. Nothing." The doctor paused and reached across to adjust the oxygen tube on Chris's face before continuing. "We alerted the police two days ago, when you first told us of the possibility that someone else was with you."

Chris was dumbfounded. How could no evidence of his body be found? Had it all been a dream, a nightmare? Then he remembered. "Wait. He had a pendant. I grabbed it off him when he fell." With just a hint of desperation, he asked, "Where's the pendant?"

The doctor leaned sideways, opened the top drawer of the bedside cupboard, and took out a Burgundy colored stone cross. "Is this it?"

"Um... I think so." Chris reached out and fingered the broken length of rough two-ply string still looped through a hole in the end of the pendant.

Very deliberately, the doctor placed the pendant into Chris's hand. "Mr. Norman, this is a Celtic cross. What Aboriginal man would be wearing a Celtic cross?"

Chris said nothing. The string was real. The pendant was real. He hadn't imagined it.

The doctor continued. "Don't you want to know about your own injuries?" There was just a hint of acerbity in his bedside manner.

"I suppose so." Chris eased his head back onto the pillow. Most of his head was swathed in bandages, and he could feel that his upper leg was encased in some sort of brace. There was a cage over his legs, presumably to protect the burns.

The doctor paused and took a deep breath. "Christopher, I'm sorry to tell you that you've lost your left eye. We couldn't save it. I'm afraid the laceration it received was too severe." The doctor allowed time for the enormity of this information to register, and then continued. "You have a compound fracture of your left femur. We've reset it and put a medullary nail inside to hold it together. We're actually very pleased with how it's worked out."

Pleased? Chris felt his mouth drop open in horror.

"The good news is that the burns on your shins only needed minor skin grafts, which we've taken from your upper arm and the side of your stomach. The burns will nonetheless take a while to heal." The doctor unhooked the observation chart and inspected it.

"You're also fighting an infection. I'm afraid you will be here for at least another two weeks, probably three."

But... but... Chris turned his head away.

"I'm very sorry—but at least you have one good eye left." The doctor swallowed. "In time you'll be fitted with an artificial eye. They're very good these days." He cleared his throat and continued in an upbeat tone. "Whilst we couldn't do anything for the eye, there's no reason why the rest of you won't mend and be as right as rain in about six or seven weeks." He paused. "You've actually been a very lucky man."

Lucky! A pitiful, mewing escaped his throat as Chris gave vent to his despair.

"Is there a particular problem?" asked the doctor.

There was a long silence. "I can't fly. I was training to be a commercial pilot. It's all I ever wanted." He closed his one good eye. "It's all I've ever lived for."

The enormity of the loss finally seemed to register with the doctor. "I'm sorry." After a moment of uncomfortable silence, he got up and left.

He was replaced an hour later by a nurse. "Mr. Norman, can you help us with our records." It was a no-nonsense statement, not a question. After checking Chris's full name, address, and medical history, she asked, "Who is your next-of-kin?"

Chris was rapidly developing a hearty dislike of hospital officialdom. "I don't know." He tried not to sound as truculent as he felt.

"Come on, Mr. Norman, do co-operate. I've only a few more questions to ask. Do you have a wife, a father?"

Chris turned his head away from her. "No wife. And my father died two years ago of a heart attack." He didn't add that his father had been a workaholic who had chosen to spend his life living in the deserts of Australia as a mining engineer.

"A mother?"

"She walked out on me and my father when I was seven years old. I've had nothing to do with her since." He barely concealed his bitterness. "I suppose she is technically my next-of-kin. She lives somewhere up in Queensland, on the Gold Coast, with a property developer."

"Do you have her address?"

Chris gave a snort of derision. The thought of his mother, the one who had walked out on him, being his next-of-kin was absurd. Wasn't 'next-of-kin' meant to be those who were closest to you, who would care about you most and make decisions about you if you were dead or incapable? Her abandonment of him, and her subsequent divorce from his father, had come as a complete shock. She had left them both just after they had all enjoyed a holiday at Second Valley. Up until then, it had been his favorite holiday spot—a place of happiness. The beach, cliffs, coves, and jetty had entranced him. The water was typically crystal clear, and there was often a pod of dolphins or a seal to be seen. Since she'd left, he'd never visited the place again.

His father, a taciturn, forbidding man of Scottish descent, hadn't been much better. He'd placed Chris in a boarding school, and headed for the desert, where he worked himself into an early grave. Chris could remember school holidays spent in sterile, utilitarian mining towns. When he'd first arrived at the mining town where his father worked, neither of them had known what to do. Eventually, his father hit on the idea of taking Chris with him to the work site. There, Chris helped out doing menial jobs until he was fourteen. From then on, he'd simply been left each day in the care of the foreman of the building site. Chris was grateful. His new workmates were better company, and they taught him how to build houses in desert conditions.

The best parts of his holidays were the flights to and from the places his father worked. He soon became adept at inveigling himself into the co-pilot's seat of the planes that ferried people to the outback. He remembered his first experience of flight. The sensation had captivated him. From that moment, there was never any doubt what he wanted to do with his life. He started to save the money he earned on the building sites, putting it away to pay for flying lessons.

But it was all gone now. His dreams were shattered. He was a cripple with nothing left to live for.

The nurse prompted him again. "Do you have her address?"

Chris fought back his irritation. He had no wish to give it. His mother meant nothing to him. She'd sent him a birthday card each year, but it never contained more than two or three lines. It was as if she couldn't find the words to explain herself. He never replied to them. The cards had nonetheless told him where she lived. Pretending a grace he did not feel, he gave the nurse what she wanted.

"Thank you, Mr. Norman." The nurse gave his bed sheets a perfunctory tug. "A Dr. Mullins will be seeing you this afternoon. He's a specialist in ophthalmology, and is visiting from Sydney. We're making use of his expertise."

Chris said nothing, and was glad when she finally left.

At some stage during the day he felt himself being moved to another ward. The booth he had occupied in the high dependency ward had no natural light, and no darkness in which to hide. His new room had the same white ceiling, the same unforgiving fluro lights, the same utilitarian hand basin, and the inevitable white Venetian blinds trying to block out the glorious vista of Adelaide's botanical gardens. Chris was nonetheless grateful for its peace. He looked briefly out of his fifth-story window and judged that he was about sixty feet high. *Just a few seconds from touch-down. All gone. Just a dream.*

A young man in a white coat stood in the doorway of his room. "G'day, Chris. Can I come in?"

Chris grunted his assent, surprised that he should ask.

The man came in, and flopped into a chair. He looked at Chris and said without preamble, "You're lucky to be alive, mate."

Chris, not feeling lucky at all, glared at the stranger through his one good eye.

"I'm John Mullins from the New South Wales School of Medical Science. I'm researching regeneration of eye tissue." He paused briefly, and then delivered the final death-blow to any lingering hope Chris might have. "Not possible in your case, though.

33

Something blunt, jagged, and horrible poked into your eye, and destroyed it convincingly. Fortunately, it didn't penetrate the orbit, or you would be dead."

"Your bedside manner sucks." Chris was surprised to find that the doctor's candor put him at ease.

"Aah. That's the thing with us research guys, we rarely have to deal with people."

Chris couldn't bring himself to smile. "I suppose there's no chance of getting a donor eye?" He tried to keep the desperation out of his voice.

"Nope. None at all." Warming to his subject, Mullins smiled. "When we talk of eye transplants, we are really only talking about transplanting the cornea. In fact, I'm currently researching how to re-grow the old cornea for people who can't have corneal transplants. We've had some great breakthroughs. But in your case, you've mashed your whole eye."

"But don't people donate eyes? Surely you can replace an eye."

"No, we can't. Not a whole eye. We only re-use bits of donated eyes. You'd need a whole eye, and sewing together the million optic fibers that run from the eye to the brain is even beyond me, brilliant as I am." Mullins's smile widened. "I'm afraid your eye is consummately knackered."

He reached across to the tray table and helped himself to one of Chris's biscuits. "I understand that losing your eye means your career as a pilot is stuffed."

"Yes." Chris felt surprisingly grateful for Dr. Mullins' brutal honesty.

"Hmm." Mullins chewed his biscuit. "You know what the Arabs say about a one-eyed person?"

"No."

"Treat them with care. They see too much."

"The Civil Aviation Authority doesn't seem to think so."

Mullins dusted the crumbs off his hands. "Your life isn't over, Chris. In fact, I'll give you this challenge. Give me a ring at the School of Medical Science in Sydney one year from now, and I promise you will be telling me that life is worth living." He burrowed his hand between the buttons of his coat, retrieved his wallet, and extracted a business card. With a flourish, he slapped it down on the top of Chris's bedside locker, and got up from his chair. "I'm off to correct the lamentable impression some of your South Australian doctors have that you have a football team worthy of the name. I'll pop in tomorrow and talk to you about future options for your eye. See ya later."

Chris smiled in spite of himself. "Your bedside manner still sucks…but I'm grateful."

Dr. Mullins waved dismissively and was gone.

Chris was quiet for a long time, battling conflicting emotions. He reached over the top of his locker, picked up the Celtic cross, and stared at it. *Is life worth living?* He had lost his eye; the career he had lived for; and the job he loved. And yet, somewhere in central Australia, a man he didn't know had died trying to save him. *How does that make sense?*

He desperately needed to grieve his loss, the loss of a future he had worked toward for most of his life… and yet his loss was insignificant compared to the price a stranger had paid so that he could have a future.

He turned his head away, trying to block out the harsh neon light above him—and raged inwardly against the God who had allowed him to live instead of his rescuer. *Why?* He squeezed the Celtic cross in anguish as a disturbing conviction began to take shape. A man who owed him nothing had died trying to preserve his life. As such, he was not free to waste it. *Dammit!* It was an impossible dilemma. Death was denied him…and yet life was so hopeless. He raved bitterly against God until he had no strength left.

Then he wept until exhaustion overtook him.

Next to visit Christ was Jim Baxter, Chief Flying Instructor at his flying school. Three of Chris's fellow students came with him. It was not an easy visit.

The students tried. They tried hard.

"You'll get better." Awkward silence.

"No more sweating over FAA flight checks."

"Yeah. You can get a real job." Forced laughter.

Chris knew they were seeing their own worst nightmare. Jim Baxter asked the students to leave so he could have a word with Chris in private. They left quickly. Jim drew his chair closer to the bed. "I've been talking to Keith, the flight mechanic."

Chris waited for him to elaborate.

"Evidently, you've been spending a bit of time with him on the flight line helping him do the maintenance schedules of the aircraft." He paused before continuing. "It seems you've managed to impress him—and that's no mean feat. He reckons you're good with your hands."

More silence.

"He thinks you should retrain as an aircraft mechanic." Baxter looked up at Chris. "I checked your grades at school and they're excellent. Some of the units you've already covered would also count toward the mechanic's course."

Chris closed his eye, trying to fight off the specter of working among aircraft he could never hope to fly. Jim Baxter cleared his throat. "Anyway, think about it. I'd have no hesitation in recommending you."

As he got up to leave, Chris managed to say, "Thanks Jim. Thanks for...trying."

The flying instructor nodded and left.

The long, tedious days began to pass. Chris lost muscle tone despite the best attentions of the physiotherapist. Graduation from bed to a wheelchair only gave him easier access to the canteen, and he gained extra pounds eating comfort food.

John Mullins, the Sydney research doctor, continued to visit to discuss options for an artificial eye. A friendship of sorts, albeit an unconventional one, sprang up between them. It was the rough pastoral care of John Mullins that prevented Chris from becoming a full-blown food addict. One day, Mullins popped his head around the door to Chris's room. "Hey, fatty, do you want another game of chess tonight? You only won the last one because I was sober. I get off at seven. That should give you enough time to practice." Taking acceptance for granted, he walked off, calling, "See you then."

Sure enough, Mullins returned later that evening. "Here's the deal," he said without preamble. "If I win, you have to get out of the hospital every day this week in your wheelchair."

"And if I win?"

"A two-hundred-gram block of milk chocolate."

"It's a deal."

Chris lost.

"You're a cunning blighter, Mullins."

The doctor responded with a beatific smile of innocence.

Chris found his first foray outside the hospital an emotional trial. It wasn't so bad in the immediate grounds of the hospital where groups of patients in unflattering hospital gowns puffed at cigarettes, sabotaging the healing process their doctors were desperately trying to stimulate. Everyone there looked weird. It was only when Chris ventured further afield into the botanic gardens and along North Terrace, that he became acutely self-conscious of his encased legs and his bandaged eye. He was also desperately afraid that the rug over his knees would slip off to reveal that he was wearing only boxer shorts underneath. However, as time passed, he became more and more confident. The physical exercise of wheeling himself about at least stopped his weight gain, even if it didn't actually reverse it.

With the increase in activity came a growing conviction that he needed to find out about the Aboriginal man who had saved his life, particularly as he was finding it difficult to convince people that the man had even existed. Guilt at being the unwitting cause of his death added to the conviction. Chris reflected on the snatches of memory that he still retained. Whilst they were just snatches, they were nonetheless very real. Raberaba, who had fed him like a child; Raberaba, who had taught him to speak his name; Raberaba, whom he had killed. *My friend.* Yes, as brief as the time was that he'd known him, he knew him as a friend. *But who was he?*

It occurred to Chris that the South Australian Museum stood almost next door to the hospital, and that it contained one of the finest collections of Aboriginal artifacts in the world. Someone there must surely know where he could begin to find some answers. He rang the museum from a hospital payphone, and was eventually put through to a Professor Evans. The professor agreed to see him at the museum in two days time.

Chris had to plan his visit carefully in order to fit it in between doctor's visits and the lengthy time it took for the nurses to bandage his legs. On the appointed day, he skipped lunch and made his way to the hospital foyer, where he engaged an 'Access' cab capable of taking wheelchair patients.

"Where d'you want to go, mate?" asked the driver.

"The South Australian Museum."

"The South Australian Museum! Are you crazy, mate? It's just a few hundred yards away!"

Look at me, you idiot. I'm in a wheelchair. I hate it. I hate having to call an Access cab. I hate having to explain myself. "I know."

The taxi driver wasn't happy, but deposited Chris at the museum. Chris wheeled his chair up to the front desk and asked for Professor Evans. A series of lifts and corridors eventually led to the untidy office of the professor. Chris discovered the plump sixty-year-old chewing at the end of an unlit pipe.

Polite introductions completed, Chris recounted the story of his crash and rescue by a native Australian bushman. Chris asked if the professor could help in identifying who it was that saved him. "I need to know so that I can honor him in some way."

Professor Evans sat in silence, listening. When Chris had finished, the professor sat still for a long while, before nodding slowly. "Extraordinary; truly extraordinary. Hmm." Sucking noisily on his unlit pipe, he began to rummage inside a cupboard for a map of inland Australia that was marked with the territory of different Aboriginal language groups. Laying it on top of his desk, he said,

38

"Now, show me where you were when you crashed, and where you were found."

"I'm not sure of the exact position, but I know I was in the West MacDonnell Ranges, not far from the Larapinta walking trail."

"Aah." The professor traced a section of the map with the stem of his pipe. "The Larapinta trail runs from Mount Sonder to Alice Springs. That would put you about here, which is pretty much slap bang in the middle of the Arrernte language group of the Aranda people." He jabbed at the map. "Look, you can see their territory here."

Chris leaned forward and peered at the map. The Aranda people occupied a small area in almost the dead center of the Australian land mass.

"Can you tell me anything about how this young man was dressed?" Professor Evans asked.

Chris sifted through his jumble of recollections. *What was real? What wasn't?* He began carefully, "A bunch of feathers covered his crotch, and he had a red peg through his nose." He remembered the abrasive feel of... what was it? "He had a grass bag tied around his middle...and was carrying a couple of spears." Chris paused. "That's it. He wasn't wearing much else that could be described." His voice trailed off, leaving him feeling as if he'd said little that was useful.

"Did you notice anything else about him?"

Chris silently reviewed the scattered dog-ends of memory, some just impressions. Cliffs, water, ants—lots of ants—and of course, that dark, dispassionate face. He would never forget that.

"He had two front teeth missing and two scars across his chest, and he couldn't speak English."

"No English at all?"

"No."

"Hmm. That may mean he came from a subgroup of the Aranda, quite possibly from the desert plains to the southwest. Most of the Aranda living nearer Alice can speak at least a bit of pidgin English."

"Do the scars and the missing teeth mean anything to you?"

"Aah, yes. The missing teeth are an indication that he has been through adult initiation, and the scars would be mourning scars for someone who has died. Sometimes they are also given in initiation rites." The professor seemed to go off into some internal reverie of his own. "Unusual. Most unusual."

"Why unusual, Professor?"

"Yes, yes. Unusual, but quite possible. The thing is: the Aranda people usually get about quite naked. It is really only special people in the group who wear the decorations you describe—people such as the medicine man." The professor tapped the stem of his pipe against his teeth again. "How old was this man?"

"Difficult to say. Probably about eighteen or twenty. Maybe younger. He looked very fit, and his skin was smooth."

"Hmm. It is possible that this young man was the son of the medicine man."

Chris nodded. "Just one more thing, Professor. He was wearing this." Chris handed over the Celtic cross. The professor took it and looked at it with bewilderment. Chris held up his hands in acknowledgment. "I know, I know. It's weird. I don't understand either. It was hanging around his neck."

The professor turned the stone around in his hands and examined it carefully. "Celtic history is outside my area of expertise." He bent over and looked closely at it. "I think the stone may be carnelian." Looking up, he explained, "It's a semi-precious stone that's found in many places of the world, including Scotland."

Professor Evans opened his desk drawer, took out a magnifying glass, and examined the cross closely. "It's well-worn in places, but the relief of the carving can still be seen quite clearly. It's been protected from wear by the beading on its rim. There's an usual pattern weaving around on the arms, that looks as if it's got tangled in the center."

"I know," Chris said. "I've been looking at it for days."

The professor sat back in his chair and began to suck on his pipe again. After two minutes of noisy silence, he got up, made his way to a bookcase and, after running his hands along a shelf, extracted two books. He opened up one of them, examined the index, and turned to the section he was looking for. The professor began to read.

Chris was at the point of thinking that the professor had forgotten he was in the room when the man spoke. "I think I know what might have happened."

Chris started in surprise.

"The cross is likely to have come from a missionary. Only two groups of missionaries were active in this area. One lot was the Lutherans based at Hermannsburg." The professor stabbed at the map just south of the West MacDonnell Ranges. "They founded a mission center there in 1877. A bunch of them travelled up all the way from Bethany in the Barossa Valley."

Chris tried not to look dubious. "Would Lutherans carry Celtic Crosses?"

The professor again tapped his teeth with the pipe stem. "It's unlikely, but not impossible. However, I think it more likely came from one of those working with Dr. Flynn. Some of his missionaries worked with Aborigines."

"You're not talking about the bloke that started the Flying Doctor Service?"

"I am indeed." The professor consulted the page in front of him. "The Presbyterian Church established the Australian Inland Mission in 1912 to reach those—and I'm quoting here— 'beyond the farthest fence' with God's word. The first Superintendent was none other than Rev. Dr. John Flynn." The professor searched the page in front of him again. "His vision was to see that hospital and nursing facilities were provided within a hundred miles of every spot in Australia where people lived." He looked up at Chris. "Being an aviator, he also understood that only aircraft had the potential of allowing rural people access to the medical facilities centralized in the cities, so he founded the world's first air ambulance."

"Impressive. But how does knowing that help us?"

"Because, according to this book, only one of Flynn's missionaries worked in this area. His name was Rev. Arthur Daniel." The professor turned a page and read some more. "Evidently, he kept a meticulous diary of his work with Aborigines, which later became an invaluable asset to those studying their anthropology."

Chris's head was now beginning to ache. He had been out too long, and the strain was beginning to tell. He sighed. "I wonder where those diaries are now."

"Not in Australia, I'm afraid. He died in 1969, and it says here that all his diaries were eventually returned to his relatives in Scotland. Evidently, he came from the Isle of Skye."

"Do we know where he came from on Skye?"

"No. But I shouldn't think it would be too hard to find out. All you would have to do is look for records of the Daniels family there. Why do you ask?"

"Because my father's family is from Skye. In fact, my grandfather still owns a small croft there."

Dr. Evans grunted polite interest.

"Thanks, Professor. You've been a great help." Chris's head was now in agony. "May I use your phone to call for a cab to take me back to the hospital?"

Chris was relieved when he finally graduated from a wheelchair to a walking stick, and was allowed to return home. Not that it was much to come home to. The ex-government Housing Trust home, built in the 1950s, had received very little maintenance in its lifetime. The new owners had bought it with the long-term aim of knocking it down and building two courtyard homes in its place. In the meantime, they were milking it for all it was worth by renting it to students. Chris was currently sharing it with two students from Malaysia who were studying at the University of Adelaide. They kept fairly much to themselves, which suited Chris. His social life was centered on the flying school at Parafield Airport nearby. Or rather, that's where it used to be centered, he reminded himself.

No one else was in when he arrived. Chris moved slowly around the flat as if seeing it for the first time. There wasn't much to see. He hadn't amassed much in the way of worldly goods, reasoning that once he'd finished flying school, he could end up living anywhere. Chris didn't own much other than a motorbike, a computer, and some books. He'd spent most of his money on flight training.

He looked around at his forlorn, threadbare home. It was difficult to think of a more soul-destroying place in which to convalesce. A nurse had been organized to come each day for the next two weeks to change the dressings, and he was booked in to go to physiotherapy twice a week. Beyond that, he had nothing else to do, but catch up on his administration. There was a modest pile of mail waiting for him on the telephone table. Neither of his two housemates had thought to bring it to him in hospital. With a sigh, he began to sort through it.

He was surprised to see that one letter was from a firm of solicitors in Inverness, Scotland. Intrigued, he opened it and read:

Dear Mr. Norman,

We are acting on behalf of Jason Haines, Laird of Dunvegan on the Isle of Skye. Mr. Haines is the landlord of the croft your grandfather, Joseph Angus Norman, worked, before his death last month on July 27.

I am instructed to tell you that under Scottish law, you as next-of-kin have the option of taking over your grandfather's croft. If you do, it must be understood that you will not only be taking on the croft but that you will also be taking on debts of unpaid rent that are owing: currently estimated to be five-hundred-and-thirty-two pounds.

The croft contains six acres of agricultural land, previously subleased to a neighbor for growing potatoes. The croft also has rights to the common land shared with the other local crofters, which is used for rough grazing of cattle.

I am required to tell you that if you take on the croft, you must work it yourself, or sublease it so that it is farmed to the satisfaction of the Scottish Crofters Commission.

Whilst the land of the croft is rented from my client, the building and maintenance of the house is the sole responsibility of the person leasing the croft. Your grandfather's croft currently contains a small, two-bedroom stone cottage and a small agricultural shed, both of which are in need of repair.

If you do not take on your grandfather's crofting lease and work it within six months of his death, my client, as lessee, has the legal right to repossess the croft. This will include the house and all other improvements that have been added, as these are tied to the land.

Please understand that Scottish law allows my client to object to the sale of the lease to anyone other than a close relative of yours. I am instructed to tell you that my client fully intends to exercise this right.

My client wishes you to know that he is prepared to buy your grandfather's lease from you at the current market price, as determined by the Scottish Crofters Commission, plus five per cent.

I think you will agree that this is a very generous offer, given the circumstances.

We are writing this letter to comply with legal requirements, but we obviously do not expect you to take up your grandfather's croft, as you have a life in Australia.

We look forward to your agreement to my client's proposition and await your reply.

Yours sincerely

James MacHenry (of Abbots and MacHenry, Solicitors)

Chris felt shocked. He had not even known that his grandfather was ill, let alone dead. Why had no one seen fit to tell him? This fact more than anything else grieved him, for although his grandfather had not enjoyed a good relationship with his son, he and Chris had corresponded regularly. A letter from him never failed to come on his birthday. Chris always looked forward to reading them. The letters were typically brief and formal, and talked mainly of the seasons of the agricultural year, and fishing. Every letter also contained some sort of moralistic admonition. This advice varied from the need for thrift, the merits of hard work, and what to look for in a wife. Whilst these letters manifestly failed to foster a loving relationship, Chris nonetheless treasured them as links to his past, as threads tying him to his story—a story he knew very little about.

He searched through the other unopened letters, hoping to find any more from Scotland that might have details of his grandfather's death. Sure enough, there was one that had arrived just after he set off for the Northern Territory—a lifetime ago. It was a brief letter from someone called Murdoch Caig, informing him, with a masterful economy of words, that Caig was acting as the executor to his grandfather's will. As such, he was writing to inform Chris that he was the sole beneficiary of his grandfather's estate, except for the house cow, which had been willed to a neighbor. Murdoch warned Chris that his inheritance didn't amount to very much other than a ragtag collection of old furniture. If Chris wished, he could instruct Murdoch to disburse it as he thought fit among those who would benefit from it. There followed a few details about his grandfather's funeral, designed to assure Chris that all had gone well. He had then signed off simply, "Murdoch Caig."

Chris sat thinking for a long time, trying to make sense of it all. He looked around at the grimy, cream walls of the hallway and through the front door to the breeze-block porch. It was all so depressing—as was his immediate future. He watched a fly bounce against the window in a futile attempt to get inside. Chris understood its frustration.

In the end, it was the house cow that decided him. *In what sort of place do people will their house cow to a friend?* He was suddenly aware that he wanted to find out. *Why not?* His father was Scottish, which meant that Chris held dual citizenship. There were therefore no passport problems. He was free to go to Scotland as soon his health allowed. A trip to the Isle of Skye would also give him the chance of tracking down the diaries of Rev. Arthur Daniel.

At the very least, it would allow him to see the croft that was now technically his...and perhaps teach him more about a community in which a house cow could feature in someone's last will and testament.

Chapter 6

He who has water and peat on his own farm
has the world his own way.
(Celtic proverb)

Murdoch normally liked cemeteries. Over time, the Atlantic storms had washed the tears from the headstones to leave the whisper of stories—stories fondly told of those who had once belonged. Among the grass tussocks and sedges, lichen-covered headstones leaned drunkenly. Given the amount of whiskey some of the islanders had consumed before they found their way under the peaty sod, it was probably entirely appropriate. Murdoch was not, however, enjoying the cemetery at the moment. Whilst the funeral of his friend, Joseph Norman, three weeks ago had been fine, this funeral was raw and full of grief. A huddle of umbrellas protected those standing by the grave. Further back, the baggy tweed jackets of the crofters steamed slightly in the still, damp air. They did not have umbrellas, and they stood in the rain, stoic and grim. None of them were strangers to an untimely death, but even so, this one was more tragic than most.

Murdoch's feet squelched in the mud as he shifted his weight. In front of him, Morag had her arm around Ruan's tiny shoulders. The boy pressed against her, his tiny face stricken with incomprehension and horror. The fact that Ruan had not yet cried concerned Murdoch. It would take both time and love to help him work his grief out. Murdoch sighed as he held the umbrella further forward, the better to protect them both.

The crofters' sympathy for the boy was almost tangible. His father had been one of them. In fact, he had been something of a leader within their tiny community. Now his boy had no parent at all, and would be fostered out—goodness knows where.

Morag, Ruan, and Murdoch formed a small knot of people who stood slightly apart from the rest of the mourners. Murdoch knew this was not just out of respect. Quite the reverse. Whilst the rough sympathy of the crofters was with young Ruan, the ancient antipathy they harbored for Morag and her family meant they kept their distance from her. Murdoch shook his head in irritation. *If yon Scots could maintain their wits as well as they could maintain their feuds, they'd be ruling the world.*

Around him, he could hear snatches of conversation. Islanders were never shy of talking whilst the preacher was speaking. Murdoch, himself a lay preacher, knew that well enough. Few preachers could hold a group of islanders silent. If the preacher came from the mainland, as this one had, there was no chance at all. Murdoch had been asked to conduct the funeral but had declined, citing his need to attend Morag and the boy. He contented himself with watching and listening.

"We are also here, of course, to share the sorrow of those who mourn, and to offer them our love and support. Let us hear the word of Scripture, that we may all face the future with hope."

"Is there much of him in there, then?"

"Not much. It was a very hot fire."

"Aye, there was lots of wood when the ceiling came down on him. 'Twas a grand pyre."

"Eternal God, our heavenly Father, your love for us is everlasting. We acknowledge that you alone can turn the shadow of death into the brightness of the morning light."

"The pollis and the fire engine were quick enough, considering they had to come from the other side."

"Aye, but too late, as usual. We'd been fighting it for fifteen minutes afore they came."

"Ach. Not that we did much good, despite there been a muckle crowd of us."

"Aye, Magnus would have liked to have seen that. Pity he's dead."

"In strength and in weakness, in achievement and failure, in the brightness of joy and the darkness of despair, we remember him as one of us." The preacher droned on.

"Ee were fixing the outboard, inside the house, then?"

"Aye, that's the way of it. Silly blighter."

"We now commit his body to the ground, confident that he is in the loving arms of his Lord and Savior, through our Lord Jesus Christ."

"The wee mannie escaped without hurt?"

"Aye: as nimble as a ferret, that one. Slipped out the window and ran to the Daniel woman." The crofter spat on the ground.

"Why her? Didn't he know to keep clear?"

"I mind the laddie would run errands for her and collect the things for her potions."

"She's a weird one, that."

"Ach, haud yer whist. Don't begrudge the wain a wee bit of mithering. Lord knows he's no' had much."

"Aye. It's been an unlucky family—both parents and grandparents gone. The devil's singled them out, right enough."

Murdoch heard the mutterings and allowed his own thoughts to wander. *What am I to do?* He lifted his gaze to the distant mountains. Their tops were shrouded in the same gray clouds that leached what little color there was from the sad spectacle. *Aye, storm's coming.* He glanced past the stone church out to the sea. It was choppy and fretful, as if it too was uncertain of the future.

At the funeral's conclusion, the crofters and villagers shuffled past Ruan and nodded to him, unsure of what to say. Some muttered a well-meaning cliché or put a rough, calloused hand on his shoulder before moving on. A few nodded to Morag, trying to express their gratitude that she was providing a temporary place of safety for him. Her sightless eyes did not see them. She heard only the silence, a silence that she was well used to.

Morag knew that the death of Magnus had thrown the social norms for island funerals into disarray. Normally the family of the deceased would host a wake afterward to which everyone would bring their sweetmeats and a voracious thirst for whiskey. But in this case, Ruan had no one else. His grandfather had died three weeks earlier, and there were no other family members who could take charge of such things. However, the crofters would not be denied a chance to have a 'wee crack' and a drink. She heard them making their own arrangements. She and Ruan were not expected to attend.

She turned to the gamekeeper standing beside her. "Will you be taking us back now, Murdoch?"

"Aye lass. Give me your arm." He turned to Ruan. "Come, Ruan. Let's away."

The ancient Land Rover bumped its way down the rutted road to the scattering of houses around the bay below them. Morag was deep in thought. In the two weeks Ruan had been living with her, her life had changed a good deal. She remembered the first night when he had banged on the door. The boy had run into her arms in terror, stammering his urgency and horror, trying to explain the inexplicable. They had never hugged before. Only once had Morag's light fingers danced over the boy's face, giving her a mental picture of him. Beyond that, there had only been brief, appreciative squeezes of his shoulders when he found the ingredients she needed for the remedies she liked to make—both for herself, and for the animals she was sometimes asked to attend.

·   ·   ·

Tears came to her eyes. These last few, terrible days had forced her to acknowledge that her relationship with Ruan had aroused in her the oldest of human needs—the need to love and be loved. She had found herself looking forward to his visits, and the guileless stories he told of life beyond the darkness. In return for his services, she had told him the stories she knew—the old stories of the islands, of seafarers, feuds, and heroism. She had begun by telling these stories like a teacher, but had ended up sharing them like a mother. Ruan had broken through the defenses she had raised against the hurts of life. Morag tightened her arms around the boy squeezed in beside her, and smiled sadly.

She knew he had run into her arms that night because instinct had told him he was safe there. *You ever will be, mo ghaoil.* She held him close to her, remembering his terror as he had stammered out the appalling news. Without thinking, she had hugged him fiercely...before ringing Murdoch on her mobile phone. He had answered, stolid and reliable as ever, and told her to keep the boy safe until he came.

It had been a terrible night. At its conclusion, Ruan had been put into the spare bed at the end of the hallway. However, when Annie, Morag's housemaid, arrived next morning, she had found Ruan fast asleep at the foot of Morag's bed, encircled in his quilt.

Morag raised her voice above the engine noise. "It's an awful whiley since you've been into my house, Murdoch. Will you take a strupack with me?"

It was a slight evasion of the truth. However, if Murdoch picked up on the fact that she'd never before invited him inside her house, he gave no hint of it. "Thank you, Morag. I'd welcome that."

She felt Ruan squirm beside her, obviously uncomfortable in his borrowed clothes. Murdoch also noticed, for she heard him say, "Afore I do that though, I was thinking I'd go with Ruan down to the shore an' maybe get a wee bitty dulse. The tide's right for it now." He spoke to Ruan, "Will you change out of the fancy clothes and come with me, Ruan?"

"Aye." Ruan's voice was barely audible.

Morag was grateful. "They'll be some fresh baked girdle scones waiting for you to get back."

Ruan and Murdoch collected two buckets from the side of the house and made their way along the shoreline to the rocky end of the cove. Murdoch began to fill one bucket with dulse whilst Ruan filled the other with whelks. Murdoch said nothing for a long while as they clambered over the rocks, Ruan in his bare feet, seemingly impervious to the early spring chill. A cormorant was standing on a rock ledge, holding its wings out to dry, looking as if it was posing for someone painting a heraldic design. Ruan picked up a stone, crept forward and threw it hard at the bird. He missed.

"If I'd still got my ding, I'd have got Morag a skart."

"A ding?"

"My catapult. It got burned wi' everything else."

Murdoch grunted. "I'll fetch you back some inner tube, and you can make yourself another."

Lapsing into Gaelic, the boy replied, "*S math sin!*" before continuing, "Do you have a piece of leather I could have a lend of too?"

"I'll see what I can find." Silence followed. Taking a deep breath, Murdoch asked, "Did your dad teach you to use a ding?"

"Nae. It were Mr. Hamish." Ruan thought for a while before he continued. "Da give me a right laldy when I bust a chimney-pot with me first ding, but he was pleased enough when it fetched him some skart. That's when he showed me how to skin one."

"You can skin a skart?"

"Aye. Better 'n Da."

Murdoch sat down on a rock and dug into his coat pocket for his pipe. The boy sat with him. When the pipe was alight and emitting its sweet, pungent smell, Murdoch nodded. "I mind the time when your Da was with me taking some mainlanders fishing." He drew on his pipe. "The fishing was good, and the mainlanders were all excited—it being the first decent bit of fishing they'd had. It was getting late, and your dad said he had to get back so he could look after you. But the tourists didn't want to stop. In the end, your dad motored across to the skerries, promising them even better fishing." Murdoch laughed. "They got so tossed about in the tide race, they got seasick and asked to be brought back." He took another puff of his pipe. "He was a wily one, your Da." He paused. "He may have been rough in his ways, but he loved you right enough."

Ruan sniffed and looked away. Then he dropped his head and started to weep. Murdoch let him get well into his tears before he put an arm around him. "Aye, cry your tears, boy, cry your tears. The whole community's been crying tears for your dad. It's time to add your own." He gave Ruan's shoulders a squeeze. "It's good for the healing of the heart."

Back at the White House, Morag was in the kitchen setting the ingredients in place to make her scones, when the kitchen door was pushed open with a bang. Morag knew who it would be. "Annie, it's the afternoon. You've done your morning's work here."

Morag was treated to a scornful 'humph' as Annie hung up her coat. She eased Morag away from the kitchen bench. "So now you're telling me when I should come and give you a hand, are you? You canna cook to save yourself, and you've the boy and Murdoch to cook for."

Morag acknowledged that Annie claimed ownership of her kitchen with some justification. It wasn't that she couldn't cook; it was just that she forgot to. Annie continued to grumble. "'Tis rare enough to find another body here to cook for. What do you think I'm going to do, being as though I'm looking at you through my window from only eighty paces away?"

Morag conceded it was true. Annie and her husband were her nearest neighbors. And, in truth, Annie was so much more than a domestic help. She was her friend, confidant, and secretary. She also kept her informed of all the village gossip, passing praise or scornful judgment with uncompromising certainty.

Annie continued to grumble. "Ach, you live so far inside your head that the cooking of things is quite beyond you anyway. You'd forget summat." Annie banged a mixing spoon on the side of the bowl. Morag could feel the accusation in the taps.

"Do you know how many half-drunk cups of cold coffee I found around the house this morning?" Without waiting for an answer, Annie continued. "Four! That's got to be a record, even for you. One was no' even started."

Morag spared herself any more berating by holding a finger to her lips, urging silence. She cocked her head to listen to the noise that had disturbed her. When Annie stopped speaking, Morag heard the pitiful whine of a dog in pain. She nodded to herself and walked into the hallway to retrieve her canvas carryall. After checking its contents, she made her way out the back door, around the house to the stone water tank that stood next to the chimney. Because the space underneath the tank stand was kept warm by the chimney, it had made an ideal kennel for Bess. Morag did not need eyes to tell her that Bess was finally whelping. She crawled under the tank stand and cradled the dog's head in her hands. "Aah mo ghaoil, mo ghaoil, you're being a mither at last." Then she reached into her canvas bag.

Five minutes later, Murdoch and Ruan joined them by the tank stand. Ruan was not to be denied a ringside seat. He ducked through the entrance and sat beside Morag, watching in wonderment as the last two puppies were born. Four puppies were born alive, one dead. Bess nuzzled and licked the lifeless form until she too was convinced that it had died. The living puppies, blind, fat, and almost helpless, clambered over each other searching for their mother's teats. Murdoch watched Morag's hands flutter with the lightest of touches over the dogs, keeping her in touch with what was happening. Her fingers discovered Ruan's hand helping the final puppy find its mother's teat. After a moment's hesitation, she said to him, "Ruan, would you like to keep that puppy for yourself when it's old enough to leave its mother?"

Ruan, in obvious disbelief and wonderment, simply stammered "Y…y…yes. Yes, please." He reached over and began to stroke the tiny, pink stomach of his puppy as it fed.

When all the puppies were settled and cleaned, Ruan and Morag crawled out from under the old tank stand. As Murdoch helped Morag to her feet, she said, "Ruan, will you bring the dead puppy. Perhaps you and Murdoch could bury him."

Murdoch picked up his cue and said matter-of-factly, "Where shall we bury him, Ruan?"

The boy glanced at him with an uncertain frown, and then looked around the garden. "Over there," he said, pointing, "under the juniper bush where it's pretty."

"Good choice."

With deliberate care, Murdoch dug a hole with the garden spade and asked Ruan to lay the dead puppy at the bottom. Then, unhurriedly, Murdoch filled the hole as Ruan watched.

The sun gave up on a gray, sad day and began to sink below the sea, leaving the two of them staring at the bare patch of soil.

Eventually, in a voice barely more than a whisper, Ruan said, "Why did the puppy die?" Tears were trickling down his cheeks.

Murdoch reached for his pipe and set about lighting it. Leaning back against the stone wall, he watched a flock of geese fly north in a ragged V formation. They, at least, seemed to know where they were going. He sighed and said carefully, "Ruan, you have lived long enough to know that there are beginnings and endings. When a puppy is born; when a flower bud blossoms; we are seeing a beginning." He drew on his pipe, "And when you see an empty sea shell, a fallen autumn leaf, and a dead puppy, you are seeing an ending. There are beginnings and endings. That's the way of it, and it has always been so. There are beginnings and endings—and living is what we do in between. Some get to live a long time; others only a short time. But you know summat? It's not the length of time that matters; it's what you do with it." He paused. "Your father loved you and gave you a good start in life. You can now live on and live well because of him."

"I don't like it. I don't like dying."

Murdoch dropped a hand on his shoulder. "Neither do I, boy. Neither do I. But you need to understand, Ruan, death is not the end. It's just a place you wait until God makes all things new, and turns endings into beginnings." He took Ruan by the shoulder. "But in the meantime, dinna waste a single minute of living, Ruan. Live well. You hear me?"

Murdoch was pretty sure Ruan didn't understand, but saw him nod anyway. He pointed to the kitchen door with the stem of his pipe. "Now, let's go in and try some of Annie's girdle scones."

***

Murdoch was pleased to return to a life of relative normality. He was keenly aware the rhythm of the seasons waited for no man, certainly not for a gamekeeper. He needed to be up in the hills with his hunting scope, checking on the roe deer and the red deer. People from the mainland would soon be coming to hunt them. He particularly wanted to check on the well-being of a giant red stag, a royal, well past his prime, who was bothering the younger stags on the mountains. He would have to be culled this season. *A pity.* Murdoch sighed. *He's a noble one, right enough.*

There was also a need to check the coverts. Shooting parties would begin arriving in two weeks. Some would hunt grouse, woodcock, pheasant, and partridge; whilst others preferred to head down to the estuary and try for duck and snipe. Whilst these bird habitats did not require any management, they did need protection—and that meant controlling the foxes. The vixens would be having their litters about now and be out looking for food. They were voracious hunters, and he wanted to get on top of them early this year.

Murdoch leaned back in his office chair and stared at the wall calendar. Next month he had a party of anglers coming for fly-fishing lessons before they tried their luck on the rivers. Most would then go off and fish the Sligachan, Brittle and Snizort rivers, but some would try the small stream that ran through the estate. It was now in spate following the winter rains. There should be plenty of brown trout, and perhaps even a sea trout. Although the season would not start for another month, he knew that Hamish would have already poached a few. Murdoch had seen the telltale scuff marks on the riverbank where Hamish had set his nets. Hamish and Murdoch had been matching their wits for many years. By Murdoch's calculation, the score was about even.

He rose from his chair and traced a stubby, dirt-ingrained, finger along the current month's engagements. He had some mainlanders coming next week to try for salmon. He'd told them that the big runs wouldn't start until the end of June, but the inflexibility of city ways had forced some fishermen to come early. Murdoch shook his head. Their ways were a mystery to him. He was, however, confident of being able to give the fishermen an experience to remember. If the river fishing were poor, he would organize some sea fishing, and take them within sight of the cliffs where the gannets roosted. Seeing them dive into the sea when a shoal of fish was near the surface was a sight to behold. With any luck, they would also see a puffin or two. He always enjoyed seeing their comical, dumpy bodies skimming across the surface of the water.

Murdoch sighed. *The seasons show no respect for human tragedy.*

"Ms. Daniel, we want to thank you for looking after…" The social worker paused to look at her notes. "…Ruan, over what must have been a very difficult time."

Morag heard the well-practiced phrases slipping out, and wondered if Ms. Eden had any idea what a 'difficult time' meant. Was she aware of the long nights she'd held Ruan until he'd wept himself dry? Did she know what had been required to navigate him through the awful bouts of depression that sapped his energy and stopped him eating and laughing? Did she understand the bursts of destructive anger, and then the heartbreaking contrition he showed when he said sorry?

The social worker continued to speak. "We'll need to take him into temporary care until we work out what to do with him."

Lapsing instinctively back into cultured, mainland English,

Morag said, "Miss Eden, you make him sound like a misplaced parcel. I can assure you that the best thing for Ruan is for him to stay here in the midst of the community he knows. He's lost quite enough without having to lose that too."

"Ms. Daniel, you will find that young children are surprisingly adaptable..."

Morag interrupted. "Ma'am, do you come from the islands?"

"No. Glasgow."

"If you came from the islands, you would know that you can't easily take the island out of a boy. His whole way of thinking and imagining is set by the islands. His place is in this community where everyone knows his name, where any mother will feed him, where every man can tell tales about his father. To take him from that would be to rip his heart out." She forbore from adding, *and rip mine out, too.*

"But he has no family here."

"The village is his family. I am his family."

"Then describe to me, if you please, your history with Ruan's family. Are you closely connected to him—that is to say, more than other people in the village?"

"No, not exactly."

"Did your families join together for meals, maybe share Christmas together?"

"No."

"Did you babysit or care for him when he was younger?"

"No."

"Then what did you do that gives you any claim to care for the boy?"

Morag could hear the steel in the social worker's voice. "He ran to me."

"Why do you mean by that?"

Morag wasn't sure she could voice the answer. "And I used to tell him stories."

Ms. Eden remained eloquently silent.

Morag put her hands up to acknowledge the seemingly ridiculous reply. "Yes, I know it sounds stupid. But it's true. I told him stories."

"You told him stories?" The social worker was obviously struggling to understand. "Fairy stories? What do you mean?"

"No, I told him stories of the island—the history, the dramas, the heroes and the villains." Morag dropped her head. "I studied history at Aberdeen. I am..." She corrected herself. "I *was* an amateur historian of Scottish history, about to start a Master's degree." She didn't want to go further. And even as she sought to list her academic credentials, she knew it was irrelevant to why she told Ruan stories. The truth was that stories were important to islanders. They loved them. Stories defined them and gave them their identity. Telling them had nothing to do with it being an academic discipline.

"Were these history lessons part of his schoolwork?"

Morag realized that Ruan's best interests would probably not be served by admitting that many of these stories had been told whilst he should have been at school. In fact, it would not be unfair to suggest that Ruan viewed school as an optional activity to be undertaken only if it was too rough to go fishing, or too wet to explore the coves.

"No. It was in payment for small errands that he used to run for me."

"Don't tell me Ruan labored for you!"

"You make me sound as if I was employing him as slave labor to clean Victorian chimneys." Morag bit her lips. "No, I used to ask him to find ingredients for me from the hedgerows and pastures. I use them in medications, usually for animals."

There was silence.

Morag hurried on. "Things like St John's wort, parson-in-the-pulpit, digitalis, and shepherd's purse—the medicinal herbs."

Morag could feel Ms. Eden's disbelief in the silence that followed.

"Perhaps, Ms. Daniels, I could have a word with Ruan. Is he about?"

Morag called down the hallway to the kitchen but got no reply. "I think I know where he might be." She walked down the hallway and, to her dismay, the social worker followed her. They went through the kitchen, out of the house, and around to the tank stand.

Morag called gently, "Ruan," and bent down. It was unfortunate that Ms. Eden bent down at the same time. She was rewarded by a view of a German short-haired pointer suckling four young pups. Lying fast asleep alongside them was Ruan. He had curled himself up to conserve warmth, but his bare feet were still in plain view. Bess wagged her tail, and began to lick the flank of one of her puppies. However, she extended her proprietorial care to Ruan, and licked him on his face. Ruan, roused only slightly awake, simply edged closer to the body warmth supplied by Bess.

It took a while for Ms. Eden's outrage to subside.

In the end, it was Ruan's theatrics that went some way toward restoring the social worker's faith in Morag. When the possibility of being removed to a place where he could be better cared for was mentioned, Ruan ran to Morag's side, beseeching her not to let anyone take him from her. "I'll live here. Morag, I'll be good. Don't let them take me!"

Morag said with a calm certainty, "No one will ever take you from me, Ruan, or take you anywhere you don't want to go—as long as I live and breathe."

The social worker stepped toward Ruan to reassure him, but it was all too much. Ruan bolted for the door and ran from the house.

An uncomfortable silence followed. Eventually, it was broken by Morag. "Perhaps you'd like to see the bedroom where Ruan really does sleep. I think you'll find it very warm, safe and comfortable," she said evenly. "After that, I will introduce you…"

She was interrupted as the kitchen door was pushed open by Annie, who said with characteristic brusqueness, "A stramash, is it? And who'd be causing that then?"

Morag, seizing on the good fortune of Annie's arrival, addressed her in a tone of calculated innocence. "Annie, I was just going to bring Ms. Eden, Ruan's social worker, to meet you. She isn't sure Ruan is being cared for well enough here."

Knowing there was little that would raise Annie's ire more than suggesting her housekeeping was anything less than perfect, Morag waited for the inevitable. She heard Annie splutter before exploding, "And what blithering eejit would dare suggest such a daft thing?" There was silence. Morag dropped her head, leaving Ms. Eden to accept blame.

Annie continued with a passion, just shy of a nuclear blast. "Lassie, I cook for Morag and Ruan... an' there's no one that gets better cooking on this island." Morag could picture her glaring at the social worker, daring her to say otherwise. "An' my housekeeping is better 'n any fancy place you have on the mainland, an' I'll tell you for why. It's because I look on them as my own. That's why." She slapped the table, "So you can stop wi' your eejit questions."

Morag was never more proud of Annie than at that moment.

That evening, Ruan did not return for supper. Morag was deeply concerned and began to fret. Instinct told her he would be back once he felt the threat from the social worker had gone, but there was always the nagging doubt. Nothing in life was certain except the inevitability of having to deal, occasionally, with its cruelty. She replayed the events of her meeting with Ms. Eden over in her mind yet again.

The only comfort she was able to take from the day was her delight at hearing Ruan voice his desire to stay with her. She had never heard him say it before, and she found part of her heart rejoicing at the memory of it. Someone wanted her, needed her, and perhaps even loved her. It was wonderful.

Morag trailed down the hallway to her desk in the library and switched on her computer. It was an advanced model that had a program enabling her to access a voicemail box via the Internet. It was a system she chose in order to preserve her privacy.

She listened to her calls. The last one was delivered in a strong Cockney accent, an accent she instantly recognized.

"Allo darlin', Wozza here. Still calling yourself Raggie Dan? Wot'cha doing? We need some more of yer magic, sweet-heart. The guys are planning to

record in London in mid-July. We'll need abaat fifteen songs for the new album.

Wiv your vicious take on the worst of humanity, can you give us twenty song lyrics wot we can choose from? Because, my darling, you do it so well. If ya give us the songs as ya write cem, we can get a head start.

Why don't yer come down when we record so we can meet ya in person? The band would really like ta meet the writer of their lyrics. We could organize a bit of publicity for ya which would earn ya enough work to keep ya legless for as long as you like.

Anyway, I 'ope you spent the dosh from the last album really badly.

Tell me when you want to come down to London, and we'll 'ave ourselves a booze up."

Despite the grim drama of the day, Morag smiled. The message was from Wozza D, lead singer of the band, *Clinically Dead*.

Five years ago, she had sent Wozza some savage lyrics born from her anger and anguish at being blinded. She'd been amazed when two of them had been accepted and used on their next album. This proved to be the start of a perfect marriage. The fact was; *Clinically Dead* were better musicians than they were lyricists. Their style was angry, raw, driving rock. It was great music, but they needed a lyricist who could do justice to their harsh musical style. Morag supplied it, but always insisted on maintaining her anonymity. She only communicated via the Internet, and always used her pseudonym, 'Raggie Dan.'

Royalties from the lyrics had paid well, and Morag was, in fact, a wealthy woman. The extent of her income was not known by anyone else in the local community, and the modest way she lived meant that everyone thought she was living on insurance or compensation money from the incident that had caused her blindness. The house she now lived in was rented from the local laird. She would have preferred to live in the house of her childhood, but her parents had sold it when they moved to Edinburgh. Her father had once been a schoolteacher on the island.

Morag sat in front of her computer for a long while, allowing the bitterness and anxieties of the day to wash over her. She matched her mood with the germ of an idea for a song, and began to type:

Just kill me now before we fall in love
　'Cos you know that I am merely male
　Let's skip the fights, the push and shove
　Just kill me now before love fails.

Love ain't all that it's cracked up to be
　It's a trick pulled on us by our genes
　So we'll copulate and grow the family tree
　Before we find out what commitment means.

Just kill me now before we fall in love
　For I couldn't bear the aching pain
　Of us not fitting like a perfect glove
　And my failings staying still the same…

Her creative flow was interrupted by the purr of Murdoch's Land Rover. It was curious how her savage bitterness seemed to evaporate when Murdoch was around. His gruff, kindly manner seemed incompatible with the thoughts that she was trying to cultivate, driving them away.

When Morag opened the door, Murdoch said without preamble, "I see that the welfare girl is nae about."

"No, she left four hours ago," Morag said.

"Then I think I have something that belongs to you." Turning around, he called out, "Come, Ruan. All's well."

At that, Ruan jumped from the side door of the Land Rover and ran to Morag, hugging her around the waist in fierce desperation.

Morag bent over him protectively. "Ach, mo ghaoil, my bonnie bairn. Do you think I'd let a social worker take you from me? Fie, mo ghaoil." She stroked his hair until he had his emotions back under control. When the time was right, she held him at arm's length. "Now, give Bess and her pups a feed, then feed yourself. You'll find Annie still in the kitchen with a pie warming for you in the stove. Have your supper whilst I speak with Murdoch. I'll join you in the kitchen for a hot chocolate later." With the rhythm of normality firmly re-established, Ruan scampered off.

Morag turned back to Murdoch. "Come away in, Murdoch, and help me. I've lost myself in my thinking over Ruan."

Murdoch sat down. "The boy was at my cottage waiting when I came in from the glen. He'd had a fair walk to find me. So what's been amiss to give you both such a fright?"

Morag shivered. She knew it was delayed shock and relief at having Ruan back, but hoped Murdoch would ascribe it to the chill air. "I knew he'd come back, Murdoch, but I was afeared."

"Dinna fash yerself, lass. All's well. Get yourself settled. The worry will wait for a cup of tea, and we'll both be thinking the clearer for it." Murdoch got to his feet. "I'll go make it."

An aggrieved voice boomed down the hallway from Annie in the kitchen. "You'll do no such thing, Murdoch. I'll make the tea. You sit with Morag and sort her. She's bin' moping around, driving me crazy."

Murdoch sat down again and waited for Morag to speak.

She paced up and down in front of him, full of restless energy. "The social worker came after lunch." Morag opened and closed her fingers. "She was after going on about her rules and regulations." Morag went on to recount the visit from Ms. Eden.

Murdoch listened without comment. When all was told, he remained silent for some time. Eventually, he spoke. "Morag, I can see you've grown to love the child, but more is afoot here than you think."

Morag lifted her chin, showing more than a hint of defiance.

"I canna fault the welfare girl's concern. You've only recently grown fond of the boy, and long term care means long term commitment. You're blind, and you've been antisocial ever since you came back to the island to live. None of this bodes well for you being able to care for Ruan." Instinct must have warned him she was about to round on him angrily because he concluded in a gentler tone. "I only tell you this for your own good, y'understand."

Morag sighed. "Aye, Murdoch, I ken that right enough." Feeling for an armchair, she sat down and tried not to look as forlorn as she felt. Tears came unbidden to her eyes, and she lowered her head.

Murdoch sighed heavily. "I don't know what can be done legally, lass, but as I see it, only one of the factors I've listed is really under your control. Can you stop being a recluse, and take your place in the community? Raising a child is a community thing, just as you told the welfare lassie."

Morag said nothing for a long while. Eventually she sniffed and reminded him with bitterness, "You forget, Murdoch, I'm a Daniel of the MacDonalds. I'm a pariah around here."

"Ach, lass. That was a long time ago. All right-thinking folk would not recall it, if you'd only open yourself up to 'em. They're basically good folk. Look at me." He paused. "I'm Murdoch Caig of the MacLeods. We MacLeods have been feuding with the MacDonalds for half our history on these islands, but they accept me right enough. These are modern times, Morag. It's time to let the ghosts of the past go."

"You're a preacher man, Murdoch. I don't share your faith in humanity."

"It's nae my faith in humanity, lassie. It's my faith in God who loves us in our humanity."

Another lengthy silence followed. Morag could hear sounds of murmured conversations, occasionally punctuated by laughter, coming from the kitchen. Morag used the sound of it as an excuse to end the conversation. "It's ower late for Ruan."

But Murdoch would have none of it. "Annie will attend him."

Silence hung between them for some time. Murdoch eventually cleared his throat. "I think it's time to stop hiding, Morag. Perhaps it's time you told me why you're running scared of people? What happened to you before you came back here to live four years ago?"

Morag sniffed, lifted her head, and said crossly, "I was blinded; that's what."

Murdoch's silence made it clear he was not accepting her comment as any sort of explanation.

Morag shuddered as if an evil wraith had passed in front of her. Dropping her head again, she started to speak softly. "I was in the second month of my Master's degree at Edinburgh. One night, I worked late in the university library and was walking from the bus stop to my parents' house, when I was attacked by two men." She breathed in deeply, sucking in strength. "One sprayed ammonia into my eyes and blinded me before pushing me into the back of a van. He sat on top of me and started hitting me in the face until the van stopped in a warehouse on an industrial estate. There they dragged me out and raped me." Tears started to course down her cheeks. "They took turns in raping me again and again. I was screaming from the pain...and the pain in my eyes. They hit me until I fell unconscious."

The nightmare played itself out again in her memory.

"They didn't kill me, although I wished they had. A security patrol disturbed them, and they ran for it. They were caught within a month as a result of DNA tests. Both had records of violence." Morag lifted her head. Her voice dropped to a whisper. "When the judge asked why they blinded me rather than simply covering my face to stop me seeing them, they said they wanted to see my face as they...as they...as..." She broke down and wailed heart-rending tears that went on and on.

Minutes passed before she was able to take a deep breath and continue. "They were like animals." More soul-shuddering sobs followed as she shared the final tragedy. "They used...things, and... and it's not at all certain I'll ever be able to have children."

For a long time, only the wind moaning over the rooftops could be heard. Eventually Murdoch said quietly, "And so you're bitter at life, at people, and at men in particular."

Morag said nothing but sat with her head bowed.

After another long silence, Murdoch said, "Morag, as a man, I see you as someone sacred to God and therefore someone very special." He paused before adding in an oddly formal way, "I apologize for the foul wounding you've had at the hands of men."

She heard his hand rasp across his whiskery face. "I didna' know that was the way of it, and it must ha' hurt to tell it. So thank you for trusting me wi' it, lass."

Murdoch heaved himself out of his chair. "I'll away now, but before I go, Morag, can I lay a hand on your shoulder and tell you sommat?" Morag stiffened slightly but nodded. He laid a hand gently on her shoulder and said, "As true as I'm here, Morag, I will do all I can to honor you, lass. You'll never need to be afeared of anything from me."

Morag wrestled with a storm of emotions, but understood enough to know that the last few minutes had, in some way, been significant. The power of something had been broken, but she was under no illusions that it was only one step on the long path to healing.

"Thank you, Murdoch."

"Ach, I've done little enough." He made to go but turned back. "Two more things, Morag. The first is, I think you'd make a good mother for Ruan."

Morag reached out a hand and placed it flat against the lapel of Murdoch's jacket. It was a simple gesture of thanks. She hoped Murdoch would understand that the gesture had a significance that went well beyond words.

After a moment, she prompted, "And the other thing?"

"The grandson of old Joseph Norman—that's the son of his firstborn who went to Australia—he's coming to stay wi' me."

"What's he coming for?" Morag didn't understand.

"He wants to have a look at old Joseph's croft, I doubt."

"But why is he staying with you?"

"Because I invited him."

"Why?"

"Because he's Ruan's cousin, once removed, and as such, he might just have something to say about Ruan's future."

Morag felt her mouth drop open. Anger stirred once more. "Does this Australian mannie even know about Ruan?"

"I doubt it. The Norman men were famous for falling out with each other and not speaking."

"Then how do we know he'll make the right choice for him?"

Murdoch chuckled. "Ach, lass, why else do you think I invited him to stay wi' me?"

Chapter 7

You canna hurry a crofter...or his cow.
(Scottish proverb)

The soft, subdued light of the northern latitudes was in sharp contrast to the harsh Australian light. Scotland's ambience was like a Harris Tweed jacket—full of tans, dark greens, grays, and blues. There was nothing outlandish, just the colors of scrubby heather, distant blue mountains, and storm-tossed lochs. Even the signage of the village shops was understated and demure. It was almost as if God had written on the gray sky overhead, "Please don't shout here."

A twenty-eight-hour flight from Australia, plus six hours on British trains, had taken the edge off Chris's first experience of Scotland. However, all this travel had only got him as far as the Kyle of Lochalsh. From there, he needed to catch the twelve-thirty bus to Portree—another three-and-a-half-hour trip. It seemed that the Scots did nothing in a hurry. Once in Portree, he had to wait a further ninety minutes before the bus took him the final hour's journey to Dunvegan. He arrived as the light was starting to fade, exhausted and aching with pain.

Chris had limited his luggage to one shoulder bag and a small travel case, since he needed a hand free to hold his walking stick. Even so, he didn't find it easy hauling his luggage along. He trailed his case behind him as he limped across to the hotel where he had organized to meet Murdoch Caig.

Chris left his case in the foyer and made his way through to the bar. Three locals sat at one end. Two wore dirty, heavy-knit woolen jumpers and the third a shapeless jacket, shiny in places from grime despite its coarse weave. One of them still had his yellow water-proof trousers on, having evidently come into the pub straight from his fishing boat.

At the other end of the bar, a young man was chatting with the barman—a portly figure who sported an untidy gray beard. The young man was dressed in jeans, walking boots, and a smart tweed jacket. Chris noticed that the fingers around his whiskey glass were long and artistic. With his face glowing from the whiskey, he was in full flight, telling a tale.

"So there I am with five unmarked, illegal lobster pots tangled around my keel, and this irate islander in his boat chugging along-side me, swearing at me, threatening to report me to the police."

Chris addressed the group of three men standing nearest to him. "Excuse me, but I'm looking for Murdoch Caig."

The three men looked him up and down and immediately began to speak in Gaelic.

Chris didn't understand what was being said, but the snub was clear enough. The pain in his head was murderous, and he desperately needed to sit down. He turned to the young man at the other end of the bar. "I don't suppose you are Murdoch Caig?"

"My dear chap, I'm not sober enough to be Murdoch Caig. Have you planned to meet him here?"

Relieved to be hearing at least some civility from someone, Chris sighed, "Yes."

"Then, I'd sit down and wait." The young man looked Chris up and down. "You do look rather knackered. Don't worry, Murdoch will be here soon enough if he has promised to meet you."

Turning to the barman, Chris said, "I've left my travel case in the foyer. I hope that's okay."

The barman shrugged. "Buy a pint of heavy and we'll call it even."

Unsure what a pint of heavy was, Chris simply nodded his assent before sitting down on a stool at the bar. It was a profound relief to be off his feet.

The young man's gray eyes regarded Chris with continued interest. "You don't look as if you've come here for the game. It's a bit too early in the season yet for the best of it, anyway. So what brings you to Skye?"

Chris rubbed his forehead to try and manage the pain in his head. "Just having a look."

"Aah, a tourist. It never ceases to amaze us locals that people would want to come to the Isle of Mists, except for the whiskey, of course." He smiled as he lifted his glass. "*Slainte Mhath.*"

Chris regarded him with his one good eye. "You don't sound like a local."

"Oh; what do I sound like?"

"Like a character invented by P.G. Wodehouse."

"Aah, blame an English boarding school, and four years at Oxford for that."

Despite his headache, Chris's interest was stirred. "What were you doing in Oxford?"

"It was where I dedicated myself to unbridled revelry and all things Bacchanalian, thinly disguised as the pursuit of a degree in English literature."

Chris smiled. "So what are you doing now?"

"You are sounding distressingly like my literary agent, my dear fellow. She is continually asking me the same thing."

"You write books, then?"

"I write books of brilliant, penetrating insight and piercing wit about the romantic places I travel to." He took another sip of his whiskey. "Alternatively, you might like to believe my agent. She says

I simply sponge off my privileged upbringing to travel, and write mildly amusing travelogues that her expertise alone is responsible for getting published." The young man looked speculatively at Chris. "What about you? What do you do? Do I detect an Australian accent?"

Momentarily, Chris's heart gave a lurch. What did he do? Nothing. What could he do? *Very little.* "Yeah. I come from Adelaide." Realizing that more information was expected of him, he followed lamely, "My ancestors came from these parts, so I thought I'd take a look."

"Good God, I hope you're not related to my family. We have a terrible genetic make-up—probably the inbreeding. My ancestors have been here for hundreds of years."

Chris recognized the opportunity to ask a question about the Scottish missionary to inland Australia, Rev. Arthur Daniel. "I don't suppose you know a family from around here by the name of Daniel?"

The young man looked at Chris with renewed interest. "Yes, I do. Mr. Daniel was the schoolteacher here. His wife was from the Outer Hebrides and was considered to be a wee bit fey. Some thought she talked with the fairies." He chuckled, emptied his glass of whiskey, and pushed the glass across to the barman for a refill. "They left for Edinburgh and have been gone for quite a few years now. But their daughter is still here. She was blinded in an accident, and came back here to live about four years ago." He reached for his refilled whiskey glass. "She doesn't live very far from Murdoch, actually. He'll show you where she lives."

Chris nodded his gratitude for the information. "I must say; I didn't expect to find an Oxford graduate on the West coast of Skye."

"Ach, didn't Voltaire say, 'We look to Scotland for all our ideas of civilization'?" He grinned, "We're positively awash with academics. My, it was just 1700-and-something when Dr. Samuel Johnson, the greatest man of letters of his time, came to visit us."

Chris laughed despite himself. "Seriously, why does an urbane sophisticate choose to live here?"

"Well, quite often I don't live here. I'm away in France, or traveling and glad-handing literary people in some city or other." He cocked his head sideways and considered the question for a few moments. "I live here for three reasons: First, to get away to a quiet spot and write. Second, to sail among the islands—it's great sailing if you know what you're doing. And third," he held up his whiskey glass, "for the Talisker. There's not a drop like it."

"You can buy Talisker anywhere."

"Hmm, how perspicacious." The young man smiled. "Well, the truth of it is, once you've lived in the islands, you never really feel you belong anywhere else."

At the other end of the bar, Chris had the vague impression of the barman pouring a glass of nut-brown beer. As the barman turned around to reach for a dishcloth, Chris returned his attention to his new companion. "How do you cope with the weather?"

Behind him, the fishermen guffawed briefly.

His companion ignored the question and frowned over Chris's shoulder. All Chris could see was the barman bringing his beer over. He was surprised when his companion leaned toward him and whispered, "Someone just spat in your beer. Don't drink it." He looked embarrassed. "I'll get you another." He hailed the barman. "Another pint of heavy, thanks Angus. Charge the other one up to Willie. He's already claimed it for himself."

The fisherman in the yellow pants stood up from his stool and protested belligerently. "I'll no' pay for any drink for a Daniel person."

As he spoke, there was movement in the doorway behind him.

"If yer brain was as big as yer balls, Willie McHugh, you might amount to something." The voice came from an older man who had just entered the snug. He was dressed in walking boots, tough trousers, and a large green hunting jacket. His tanned face seemed ageless. Chris could only guess he was somewhere between fifty and sixty-five years of age. While the four-day stubble and short gray hair made the man look intimidating, his muscular frame and thick legs made him look downright formidable. The newcomer continued to growl at Willie. "I can either speak to you as a brother of the kirk, or as a gamekeeper well able to crack your head. Take your pick."

The belligerence of the fisherman quickly faded. The newcomer continued. "Now let's see you do the right thing."

With ill grace, Willie took out his wallet, pulled out a five-pound note, and placed it on the counter.

The young man with Chris smiled at the newcomer. "Good evening, Murdoch. Your arrival, as always, is timed nicely to restore the reputation of islanders with displaced Antipodeans." He gestured toward Chris. "I think the wee mannie here is the one you want."

Murdoch shouldered his way past the fishermen and held out a calloused hand. "Welcome to the island, Mr. Norman. I'm Murdoch Caig."

"G'day. Please call me Chris."

"Right, Chris it is." He also shook the hand of the young man with Chris. "Alsdair. You're at the drinking early tonight. Are you celebrating?"

"As much as every day, Murdoch." He turned to Chris, "How remiss of me. Let me introduce myself. I'm Alsdair Haines."

Chris shook his hand. "G'day. I'm Chris Norman. Thanks for looking out for me just now." Even as he was speaking, Chris was searching his memory. *Haines.* Where had he heard that name before? Then he remembered. The letter from the Scottish solicitor had referred to a Haines. "You aren't any relation to a Jason Haines, are you?"

"I'm afraid so. He's my older brother. He's one of the Lairds hereabouts, and occupies the ancestral pile."

"He's the Laird here in Dunvegan, then?"

"No. Dunvegan is the MacLeod's home seat. They live in the castle just north of here. They're obviously quite fond of the old place, as it's the longest continually occupied castle in Scotland. No, my family's land is next door."

"Does this mean you also live in an ancestral pile?" asked Chris with a smile.

Alsdair shuddered. "No, thank God. It's as cold as hell. I live in a small house on a croft by the coast. I sublease the land, so all I have to do is sleep, eat, and write—which, if you add drinking, is a fair summary of my hierarchy of needs." He took another gulp of whiskey, then cocked his head. "You're not related to old Joseph Norman, are you?"

Chris nodded. "He was my grandfather, although sadly I never had the chance to meet him."

Inexplicably, Alsdair chuckled. "My, my. This could get very interesting."

Murdoch interrupted. "I apologize for being a few minutes late, Chris. I took the opportunity of stopping by a house to check someone was available to be a gillie this season." He looked Chris over. Chris had the uneasy feeling that very little was escaping his attention. Murdoch nodded briefly and said, "Let's get you to a warm fire, a meal and a good bed, Chris. You look fair puggled."

Chris remembered very little of the fifteen minute drive to Murdoch's cottage. Through the pain and the tiredness, he had a vague impression of hills and narrow laneways, of small, white, pebble-dashed houses and squat, stone cottages perched beside a rocky coastline.

Sitting beside him in the Land Rover, Murdoch said, "I didna' know you were so broken up by your accident. Why didn'ya say?"

"I hadn't come to terms with it, myself."

Murdoch nodded and said with equal candor, "The islands are not kind to people wi' disabilities. It's a wee bit hard to get around."

A long silence followed. It was eventually broken by Chris. "Why would a man spit in my beer because I was asking about the Daniel family?"

Murdoch's face became grim, and he hauled the big steering wheel of the Land Rover with slightly more force than was needed to guide it through a corner. "We islanders are over fond of our quarrels. I'm afraid you bumped into a feud that should have ended a hundred years ago. Think nae more about it."

Chris woke next morning at ten o'clock, having slept longer than he had for a very long time. As he woke, the fresh, cold air of the morning seemed to scald his lungs. He found that he was breathing out clouds of condensation from his mouth. He experimented for a while like a child, making cloudy patterns in the air.

Chris was appalled at the cold and couldn't imagine how anyone could live in a house that was so frigid. He remembered the warmth of the hearth the previous evening and wondered how it could be so different now in the morning. Chris had been given Murdoch's bedroom. It opened straight off the parlor, which pretty much constituted the rest of the house. Not that there was much to it. The room contained a hearth, two armchairs, and a kitchen complete with a much-abused table.

Murdoch had slept in his office that was accessed via an outside door adjacent to the back entrance. Chris had been shown inside it briefly and been surprised to see a large and overflowing bookshelf. His host was obviously a reader. Murdoch had set up a camp stretcher for himself opposite his desk.

The cottage itself was made of stone, and the ceiling had exposed beams. The floors were paved with flagstones covered with a few threadbare rugs. It was unmistakably a bachelor's home. Chris reluctantly got out of bed, slipped on his walking boots and anorak, and made a pilgrimage to the outside toilet. He was staggered to observe a gap of at least one inch under the back door where generations of feet had worn down the flagstones. The concept of thermal insulation appeared to be quite foreign to Murdoch.

The man himself came scrunching up the path behind Chris as he made his way back into the house.

"How are you feeling?" Murdoch asked.

"Cold, but otherwise okay."

"We'll warm you wi' breakfast."

Murdoch was as good as his word. In quick succession he made tea, porridge, scrambled eggs, and oatcakes. Chris was surprised when Murdoch sprinkled salt rather than sugar on the porridge, but made no protest.

"Breakfast like a king, lunch like a prince, and sup like a pauper," Murdoch intoned as they began to eat.

"How long have you been up for?"

"I get up at six. I've been down the stables. The stable hand has had to be away quite a bit these last two months to look after his sick mither. I deputize for him, feeding the horses and exercising 'em."

Chris had a vague memory of passing a neat-looking stable block about four hundred yards away from Murdoch's cottage.

Murdoch continued. "If you've a mind to, I'll take you down to look at your grandfather's croft. You take the quad bike and follow me in the Land Rover. I'll leave you there, as I need to get up to the fells to check some fox baits. Supper will be at six o'clock. D'ya ken how to drive a quad bike?"

"If you show me the basics, I expect I'll be fine. I used to ride a motorbike."

Murdoch nodded. "That's good, then." He scratched his stubble. "Christopher, I need to chat to you tonight about some things concerning your family which you ought to know. But for now, explore the village and the croft. Enjoy yourself. You'll find a wee store in the village which sells most things, including the makings for lunch." He smiled. "If you call in there first, it will save you explaining who you are to the locals. It will be blethered around the village in no time at all."

Murdoch showed Chris the fundamentals of riding a quad bike. It was simple enough. As Murdoch was getting into the Land Rover, he turned and said, "Christopher, take some time to be still today. You need to mend. Let the island speak to you. You'll find it has something to say." Then he drove off.

Chris finished strapping his walking stick to the front parcel rack, and followed a few seconds later. The quad bike bucked and slithered along the dirt track. With the chill Atlantic air blowing into his face, he found it exhilarating.

They emerged from the hills into a small community of scattered crofts that dotted the rocky foreshore. Murdoch led the way along a track that was just out of reach of the highest tide. At one point, he pointed to a small white painted house, which Chris correctly surmised was the local store. There was little to indicate it was a store other than some lettering on a window and a notice board affixed to a wall. Murdoch drove a little further; passing a house that had been destroyed by fire. It was a pitiful sight, and the ruins seemed greatly at odds with the bright spring day. A fresh southwesterly wind had stirred up a fractious sea that pounded the rocks along the shoreline. Spray and spindrift blew across the track.

Four-hundred yards further on, Murdoch's Land Rover squeaked to a halt. Chris motored up beside him, killed the engine, and unstrapped his walking stick. A small stone building stood behind a dry-stone wall. It was hunched down, as if trying to avoid the worst of the elements. Both of its end walls leaned inward slightly. One sported a chimneybreast that rose up toward a squat chimney-pot.

As the two of them pushed through the front gate, a jaunty middle-aged man wrapped in an old trench coat came into view, trundling a wheelbarrow in front of him. On seeing Murdoch, he affected pleasurable surprise. "Ach, if it isn't Murdoch himself."

"Aye, it is so," said Murdoch slowly.

The man put the wheelbarrow down and swept a hand expansively to indicate the sunny vista. "It's beautiful, just."

Murdoch again nodded slowly. "Aye, it's a braw day." Chris had the impression of two long-term combatants circling each other in an age-old ritual. Murdoch continued, "And what would you be doing wi' Joseph's wheelbarrow, Hamish?"

"Did you no hear? Three months past, Joseph promised me his wheelbarrow."

"Is that so?"

"Aye, true as I'm standing here."

"Why would Joseph give you his wheelbarrow just weeks before he died, d'ya think?"

"He were a good neighbor."

"No doubt he promised you his stack of peats under the back shed, too."

"Aye, that's the way of it."

"Now there's a thing. Why would Joseph give you his peats when he was struggling to get enough warmth into his own bones?" Murdoch did not wait for a reply. "You're an old rascal, Hamish. And thieving, even from the dead, is a sin. Put the wheelbarrow back." Murdoch waved a finger under Hamish's nose. "I'm having a look round, and if I see anything else missing, I'll ask for it back on Sunday at the kirk in front of everyone. D'ya hear?"

Hamish did not look greatly put out. "Ach, Murdoch, you have a suspicious mind. But to keep you easy in your thinking, I'll donate the wheelbarrow back to Joseph's kin."

"I'm right pleased to hear it," growled Murdoch.

Hamish walked past them out of the gate, touching his cap as he did. As he walked down the track, he called back. "Someone's done a fearful amount of wrecking in there. There's not a thing worth salvaging. "'Tis a crying shame what some folks will do."

This comment caused Murdoch's brow to furrow. He walked up to the front door and gave it a push. The door simply fell back, swinging on one hinge. Inside the house was complete devastation. The internal stone wall separating the two bedrooms from the parlor had been pushed over. The rocks had completely smashed the thin wooden wall that separated the bedrooms. In the parlor, the kitchen bench had been prized loose from the wall and split into pieces. The old ceramic sink had been smashed, and the tap that fed water in from the rainwater tank pulled loose from the wall.

Murdoch looked around in obvious dismay. It was understandable. The calculated savagery of the vandalism and the senseless, wanton destruction was shocking. Murdoch turned to him and said softly, "Christopher, I'm right sorry for what's been done here. 'Tis mischief, sure enough, the like of which I've not seen afore." He shook his head, "I canna think who would do such a thing."

Chris was no stranger to vandalism; he had seen plenty of it in the northern suburbs of Adelaide. But even so, he was appalled. "It wouldn't be that old man, Hamish, would it?"

"Ach, no. He's a rascal, right enough, but moral in his own way. This is not the work of a local. They're a tight-knit community that squabble and fight, but in the end, they look out for each other."

Chris put his hands against the thick outside walls, and

notwithstanding the destruction around him, was surprised to feel a sense of wonderment. His father had been born within these walls...and his grandfather had written to him from here. In a very real sense, his story had begun in this house. A strange, warming emotion welled up within him. He allowed it to last only a moment. Chris suppressed it by reminding himself that there was nothing here for him. He would look at the land of his ancestors, be grateful for the experience, and then return to Australia...and become what? An aircraft mechanic? Deep grief overwhelmed him, crushing any delight he felt at being in his ancestral home.

Murdoch laid a hand on Chris's shoulder. "I'm away off now, Christopher. I'll let the pollis know what's happened here, but they'll nae do much." He paused. "I'm right sorry I have to go, leaving you like this, but I've a meeting at the estate, and then I'm away to the high country for the foxes. I'll be seeing you at supper." With that, he stepped over the shards of broken tiles and through the back door.

Chris was left inside amidst the destruction and gloom, watching the dust motes in the shafts of light dance stories of what might have been. After a while, he pulled himself together and began a desultory search through the rubble for anything that might shed light on the life of his grandfather. Murdoch had already disbursed all furniture and any useful domestic items within the community, but Chris still hoped to find something of his grandfather hidden in the wreckage. There was little enough to search. The bedrooms resembled a quarry, but the shell of the building remained sound. He marveled at its simplicity. There were no skirting boards or architraves, no paneling, just stone walls and flagstones.

He grimaced with pain as he bent down to explore a crack between the flagstones and the wall. As he did so, his finger jabbed into something sharp. Chris jerked his hand away and sucked at his bleeding finger. Cautiously, he felt again in the crack, and located the object that had pricked him. He prized it loose and lifted it out.

It was a large pin, shaped like a miniature sword. A silver thistle entwined with leaves sat where the hilt of the sword would normally be. Chris recognized it at once, as his father had a similar one. It was a kilt pin. It must have fallen behind a dressing table years ago. He took it to the window and turned it over in his hand. The pin had probably belonged to his grandfather. Unbidden, tears came to his eyes. He blinked them away and stared out the window. There, beyond the byre, his grandfather's crofting land rose gently toward the heather, which, in turn, led up to the mountains. He could see the croft's boundaries clearly. It had been enclosed by sections of dry-stone walls and old wire fences. Some of the land looked as if it had been cultivated, probably for potatoes, but most of it seemed to have been used for grazing.

Chris turned and made his way out of the house, through the wreckage and back to the quad bike. His wounded finger was still bleeding, so he decided to return to the village store and try to buy a Band-Aid. He parked the bike beside the store, and limped over to the door. As he opened it, a bell tinkled above him. A moment later, an indecipherable stream of words was directed at him from behind a magazine stand.

"I beg your pardon?"

A steely haired woman with bright eyes and a smiling face peered around the stand. "Ach, d'ya no have the Gaelic, is it?"

"Er, no."

"And who would you be, then?"

Chris smiled at the priority given to information in these parts. Almost anywhere else, he would be asked, "What do you want?"

"I'm Chris Norman." Understanding this was as good a time as any to explain himself to the local community, he added: "I'm Joseph Norman's grandson, come from Australia to look at his croft."

"Well now, there's a thing. Fancy that. Joseph's grandson." The woman, who wore a slightly less-than-white apron, ran her eyes over Chris. "You look as if you've danced with the devil and come off second best."

"I'm recovering from an accident. I was a pilot, and my plane crashed."

"Ah, is that the way of it?" The woman noticed Chris's bleeding finger. "Ach, and now look at your finger. You're bleeding. I've a bandage for that." She went bustling off, searching for it even before Chris could confirm that was why he had come.

The woman applied the sticking plaster to Chris's finger herself and then invited Chris to stay for a cup of tea. He sat on a stool at the shop counter and watched her heft a large kettle onto the stove. "Och, I'll forget myself. I did'na tell you my name," she called over her shoulder. "I'm Jessie Collins. I run the store, and my husband Henry does bitty jobs around the place. He takes the tourists out in his boat in the summer."

After a few minutes, Jessie placed a mug of tea in front of him and perched herself opposite him behind the counter. Chris suspected that such an action was not uncommon in Jessie's shop.

She continued to chat. "Ah, Old Joseph. He were a good man, if a dour one. I never saw him dance at a ceilidh. He said he couldna' dance." She scoffed. "He just didna' like dancing."

Chris caught himself smiling, enjoying the sense of being included in the gossip of the village. The fact that he was Joseph's grandson seemed to grant him the right to share in it, despite having lived his life on the other side of the world. It was a strange sensation—like being wrapped in a blanket he'd not seen since childhood.

"An' what's to become of yer grandfather's croft?" Jessie asked. "No doubt you'll be back in Australia afore long, and no' be working it."

Chris nodded. "That's probably right. But I'm not sure what to do now that I can no longer fly."

"An' why can't you fly any more?"

The brutal, straightforward questioning again awakened the demons of grief. Chris pinched the top of his nose and said, "You need two good eyes to be allowed to fly."

"Pah," she said dismissively. "Plenty of one-eyed seagulls stay fat enough."

"It's a bit different with the Civil Aviation Authority."

"Where are you staying?"

"With Murdoch Caig."

"Aah. He's a good man." She smiled. "I made a play for him

once when I were young, but I think his heart was elsewhere. Still an' all, he never married."

Chris finished his tea and left, saying he would return later to buy lunch. Jessie promised to have a hot potato in the oven waiting for him when he came back. "I'll fill it with cheese. It will fill your belly and warm your hands into the bargain."

He puttered back up the dirt track on the quad bike to his grandfather's croft. Instead of entering the house, he hobbled down to the foreshore, along a path that his grandfather and father must have helped to tread down. Chris sat on a rock and looked out to the loch in front of him. The sea was looking beautiful. He luxuriated in the peace of the place. The only sound came from the wind and the waves, and the mewing of gulls. He glanced around. Cliffs lined the shore. They formed rocky promontories that pushed out into the sea. Chris could see beaches of sand and shingle between them. Tussocks of grass and heather sat on top of the cliffs like icing on a birthday cake, and way out to sea, he could see the hazy blue silhouettes of islands. Chris leaned back, letting the sun fall full on his wind-chilled face.

Two hours later, after a long, painful hobble along the beach, he returned to the village to collect his lunch. Chris had not seen any other person in the village all morning and yet Jessie greeted him with, "I hear tell the vandals have been at yer grandfather's hoosie."

"I'm afraid so."

"Hamish was after telling me that it could have only happened last night. He were saying nothing was amiss in the cottage yesterday." She shook her head. "Tsk, tsk. I dinna know what the world's coming to. Who could've done such a thing?"

Chris accepted the hot potato filled with cheese and relish, and drove back to the beach. He made his way across the sand, settled himself against a rock, and began to eat. From his position, he was able to watch unobserved as a small boy jumped from rock to rock, stopping occasionally to throw stones into the water. Despite the cold, the boy was bare-footed, but seemed perfectly happy.

Chris's memory took him back to another beach, in a warmer

place. He remembered hearing his mother calling him in…and him choosing to stay on the beach…and never seeing her again.

An excited, high-pitched barking brought Chris back to the present, and alerted him to the fact that the boy had a young puppy with him. As the boy sat on a rock to brush a piece of shell from his foot, the puppy tried to jump up and join him. However, it was not successful. The puppy fell backward off the rock-face in an untidy heap. Undaunted, it tried again.

The boy laughed at the puppy's antics, reached over, scooped it up, and tucked it inside his jacket. There, the puppy scrabbled to turn itself around. As the boy began to prize a crab out from under a rock, it started to bark in excitement. This prompted the boy to push it further down into his jacket, but it fought to emerge again, to watch bright-eyed before struggling forward to smell the crab now resting in the boy's hand.

Finally the boy saw Chris resting against a rock, eating his lunch. Chris received a friendly hail. "Ach Jimmy, you gi' yourself a *foileag*, is it?"

Chris deduced enough to show the boy his potato. "And you have a devoted companion, I see."

"Aye." The boy plucked the puppy from his jacket and held it out. "This is JJ. She's my dog." His pride was evident. The puppy dangling from his hands wagged its tail and fought to get free so it could get to Chris. "She's forever in a hurry to find mischief."

"You can let her go if you like. I don't mind dogs." The boy did so. The puppy bounded over to Chris and jumped up onto his chest, licking him with unbridled enthusiasm. Chris fought to protect his face from the worst of the onslaught. But as he did so, the cheese potato fell to the ground. The puppy immediately pounced on it and started to devour it.

The boy lunged forward, appalled at the disaster. "Git 'ere, JJ. Ach, I'll gi' ye laldy."

Chris was not greatly troubled. "Don't worry, mate. I had a big breakfast, and I need to lose weight." As the boy reclaimed his errant puppy, Chris asked, "And what's your name?"

"I'm Ruan Norman."

Chris was momentarily in shock. He sat upright as Ruan continued blithely, "Hamish says it will chuck it down tonight." He sighed. "It will, right enough. He aren't never wrong. Wouldn't it be grand if it could stay like this, just?" He paused, and cocked his head sideways. "What's wrong wi' your eye?"

Chris didn't answer the question. Instead he pointed to the cottage behind him. "Did you know the old man who used to live in there?"

"Of course. He were my great granddad. He's dead now. Died a few months back." The boy dropped his head. "Just before me Da. He died in the fire."

Chris was speechless. He looked at the urchin in front of him, trying to comprehend the significance of what he had just learned. "I think I'd better tell you who I am."

Chapter 8

M urdoch returned from the hills to his cottage much later than he expected. The Laird had called in contractors to do some blasting in the quarry so they could get some more building stone. Murdoch had had to wait for two hours before the wildlife he was monitoring settled down again. Heavy rain in the late afternoon had further frustrated his plans for the day.

Murdoch had long since learned to be philosophical about the weather, and was content enough as he stamped the mud off his boots. He pushed through the back door to find Chris sitting at the kitchen table, huddled in his coat, fiddling with the bread toaster. The arm of the spring that held its side flap shut had broken off years ago. In recent years, Murdoch had kept it closed using a book-end, which he kept on the table for that purpose.

Chris had unwound some coils of the spring to fashion a new spring arm and was just finishing putting everything back together. Murdoch shook the rain off his cape and hung it up. Then he picked up the toaster, and tested the repair. "Ach, you're a handy one, sure enough, Christopher." He smelled the air appreciatively. "And what's that I'm smelling?"

"I've put a shepherd's pie in the oven. It should be about ready to eat."

Murdoch nodded his thanks. Seeing Chris huddled against the cold, he stepped across to the hearth, pulled a few peat turfs off the smoldering fire, and replaced them with wooden logs. "And how did you fare today?"

"It had its share of surprises." Chris pushed his hands deep into his jacket pockets. "I met a young boy on the beach..." he trailed off.

Murdoch sighed, realizing the significance of Chris's hesitation. "You've met Ruan, is it?"

Chris nodded. "Why didn't you tell me about him?"

"Ach, I would have soon enough. I was hoping to give you a day or so to settle in first." He sat down on one of the wooden chairs, and reached inside his jacket for his pipe. Blue smoke was soon curling up into the age-blackened roof beams. "His father died in a fire a few weeks after your grandfather. His mother died in a car accident three years ago, so Magnus was raising the bairn on his own. He was a good enough father, but rough in his ways. I'm afraid Ruan has grown up a wee bit wild."

Chris furrowed his brow. "I'm just amazed that I didn't know about him. My grandfather told me about the fishing and the pota-toes. Why didn't he think to tell me Magnus was married and had a child?"

Murdoch waved the stem of his pipe dismissively. "Ach, it was the curse of the Norman menfolk to be ever taking offense, and not speaking to each other." With brutal candor, he continued, "Even your father was a dour one." He looked at Chris through a haze of pipe smoke. "I'm sorry, Christopher." He paused and tried to think how much he should say. "I expect there are many things you're about to discover on this island."

Silence hung between them for some minutes. Eventually, Murdoch slapped his thighs, got up, and went out of the back door. He returned a moment later, carrying an old-fashioned suitcase that he'd fetched from his office. "Hopefully, this is a better surprise for you. I kept some of your grandfather's personal things in here for you."

"Um. Thanks." Chris weighed the suitcase in his hands for a few moments before putting it down beside the wall. "I reckon dinner's ready."

During dinner, Murdoch chose to continue their earlier conversation. "Y'understand, Christopher, that you are Ruan's next-of-kin, don't you?"

Chris spluttered on his food. "Surely not." He looked at Murdoch with a puzzled frown.

Murdoch loaded some more shepherd's pie on his fork, electing to say nothing in order to allow Chris to digest the significance of what he'd said. He ate unhurriedly, trying to work out what Chris's relationship with Ruan was. *What do you call the son of a cousin? A cousin once removed? A second cousin?* He had no idea.

"What about his grandparents?" Chris asked.

"His last grandparents died in the car accident with his mother."

Chris sat silently, ignoring his food. Eventually, he looked up at Murdoch. "Then who is looking after him now?"

"That would be Morag Daniel, the woman you're wanting to see about your history things." He paused. "She's a good woman, and she and Ruan have grown ower fond of each other—though, no doubt, she finds him a handful."

Murdoch could see that Chris was in shock. He sympathized. It wasn't every day a man discovered he was the nearest relative of an orphaned child. He'd be beginning to understand that his connection with the island was a lot more significant than he'd ever imagined. Murdoch sighed. "No doubt you'll be wanting the Land Rover this evening to visit Morag?"

Chris roused himself from his reverie. "Er. What? Um… Do you think I should? Yes. Um. I suppose I must. Thanks."

"You'll be going to the White House. That's the big double-storied house about five hundred yards up from the shore. D'ya ken seeing it?"

After a brief pause, Chris nodded.

Two hours later, Chris was standing in drizzle on the step leading to the front door of the White House. It was in total darkness. Tentatively, he knocked on the door.

A moment later, Chris could hear footsteps coming to the door. The safety chain rattled off the latch. As the door swung open, he heard a woman's voice say, "It's yourself, Murdoch? Come away…" She got no further. A large dog came bounding out of the door barking. In its exuberance, it knocked Chris's walking stick, causing him to lose his balance and fall onto the wet flagstones. This excited the dog even more. It barked in a frenzy of excitement and lunged at Chris.

"Get it off me!" yelled Chris in alarm.

"What's happening? Bess! Come here. What's happened?"

"Can't you see? Your wretched dog has knocked me down."

"No, I can't see! Who are you?"

Chris was appalled. He had forgotten that Miss Daniel was blind. "I'm sorry. I forgot…" The dog grabbed Chris's stick and started prancing around him with the trophy in her mouth. "Oi! Give me my stick!"

"Why? What stick?" The woman's voice rose in alarm.

"Because I need it to walk."

"Oh!" An instant later, the front light switched on.

Chris had the impression of a petite, well-shaped woman with a cascade of fiery, auburn hair falling around her shoulders and hiding much of her face. He caught a glimpse of clear pale skin, two half closed eyes, and an elegant neckline. The woman was dressed in jeans and a soft, woolen sweater with a floppy, rolled neck. Chris blinked. *She is certainly… what?* he thought. *Striking? No, compelling.*

Feeling ridiculous lying on the wet flagstones, he introduced himself in a way he hoped would give some sort of assurance. "I'm sorry to alarm you. I'm Chris Norman, er…Ruan's relative from Australia."

"Oh," the woman said. "I'm Morag Daniel. You'd better come in." She held out Chris's stick with one hand whilst holding the collar of the dog with the other. Chris took the stick and levered himself up from the ground. Slowly, he followed her in and, at her invitation, stepped into the lounge. She switched on an electric fire then left, saying that she would make them both a cup of tea.

Chris stood in the semi-darkness and reached over to switch on the light. She had forgotten to do so.

The dog, which had been introduced to him as Bess, sniffed at Chris briefly before flopping down on the carpet in front of the electric fire. The dog rested her muzzle on her paws and watched Chris with limpid brown eyes.

The room was still very cold. Chris found himself wishing he could have followed Morag into the kitchen where he felt sure it would be warmer, and where he would feel more at home.

Morag eventually returned with a tray carrying two mugs. "Your voice is that of a young man, but you walk with a stick. How old are you?"

Chris was momentarily taken aback. "I'm twenty-four. I'm…" He corrected himself. "I used to be a pilot, but I recently had a plane crash in which I lost an eye and broke a leg."

"Oh. I'm sorry."

"Yeah. Life's a bummer." He looked at Morag. She was using her hair to hide as much of her face and blindness as possible. "You'd know a bit about that yourself," he added.

She nodded, and they both sat for some time without talking.

Chris broke the silence. "Thanks for taking Ruan in, and looking after him. That was a pretty amazing thing to do."

"No, it was natural," snapped Morag. She lowered her head and continued in a softer tone. "We've become…good friends." She busied herself with milk and sugar. Chris could see the tension in her. Her jaw was rigid.

Morag handed Chris his mug of tea, paused, then blurted out, "Mr. Norman, what are you going to do with Ruan?"

Her question caught Chris completely off guard. It had never occurred to him he would be doing anything with Ruan, or have any say in his future. Two days ago he didn't even know the boy existed.

He cleared his throat. "Hmm, if I asked you to call me Chris, can I call you Morag?"

She nodded.

Chris began slowly. "Morag, I didn't even know about Ruan's existence until today, so I think it would be most unfair for me to insist on anything." Silence hung in the air. Bess got up, padded across to Morag, and put her head on her lap, as if sensing her distress. Chris continued, "I reckon the best thing for the moment is for him to stay here with you until we understand what the options are, and what will be best for him."

Morag dropped her head, allowing her hair to again hide her face again. "Can I show you the house and where Ruan lives so that you can get an idea of how he's being looked after?"

Chris raised his eyebrow but accepted the offer out of courtesy.

He was taken to the kitchen, where Morag explained that Annie came in most mornings to cook and clean. "She's brilliant."

Chris looked at the clean kitchen and the cooling racks laden with pies, and could well believe it. Morag then took him upstairs to Ruan's bedroom. She pushed open the door. Light from the hallway fell across the boy's sleeping form. The careless peace of innocence was displayed in all its beauty. Chris stared at Ruan's face, softened by sleep, and was conscious of something stirring deep within him. Was this family? Was this what it looked like? Chris shook his head. He was this boy's nearest relative. It was amazing.

As Chris looked on, he spotted a slight movement under the covers near the boy's chest. "Excuse me," he whispered and stepped over to the bed. He gently drew back the covers, and discovered a furry face, featuring two bright eyes, peering back at him. Chris lifted the puppy out of the bed and replaced the covers. As he did so, his fingers brushed against the cheek of the sleeping child. It was accidental...incidental...but it evoked an extraordinary sensation within him.

He turned to Morag. "I think this furry beast might be a stow-away." The puppy lunged forward in Chris's arms, trying to lick him. Morag started to apologize, but Chris held up a hand. "Morag, relax. You're obviously looking after Ruan really well." He gestured to the boy, intending to say that he was grateful, but remembered that she couldn't see. Chiding himself, he remained silent, allowing himself to look briefly at Morag.

He turned his eyes away from her with a pang of guilt. *Stupid thoughts at the most inopportune moments.* But she really did have the most fantastic figure...and such a beautiful mouth, even when compressed with anguish.

Back in the front parlor, JJ romped over to join her mother. Chris watched as Bess mechanically moved her head away from the puppy's first assault. JJ then rolled on to her back and reached out a paw to scratch at Bess's sleeping form, trying to provoke a response. Unsuccessful with this ploy, she got to her feet, padded forward and bit her mother on the ear. Bess pulled her head away and put out her massive paw, pinning the puppy to the ground, causing it to yip and back way from underneath it. Rolling back on to her side, the mother was soon back asleep. The puppy sat back on her haunches, and regarded the prostrate form of her mother balefully. Then it started to scratch itself. In the process, JJ noticed her own tail, and tried to pounce on it—only to find that it disappeared with her own movement. Following a few fruitless twirls, she gave up and chose instead to flop down against her mother, nuzzling her contentedly before closing her eyes in sleep.

Morag sat down opposite Chris. He watched as she began to

wring her hands in her lap. Her opening words betrayed a rehearsed speech. "Mr. Norman..."

"Chris, please."

"Oh, er, Chris..." She swallowed. "I showed you round the house because I want to make a case for Ruan to continue to live here with me." She hurried on. "He belongs here in this village... with people who care."

Silence hung between them. Chris understood that they had finally come to the issue playing on Morag's heart. He cleared his throat. "Morag, I don't know how these things work. All I know is that Ruan is being well looked after here."

A thought suddenly occurred to him. "Ruan's upkeep must come at a cost. I'd like to reimburse you to make sure you're not out of pocket."

This was too much for Morag. She burst into tears. Chris was both bewildered and appalled that he should have caused such a reaction. Morag eventually regained some control. "I don't look after him for money. Finances have nothing to do with it." She dabbed at her eyes between sobs. "He ran to me after the fire. He ran to me, don't you see?"

Chris didn't see at all, but realized that Morag's commitment to Ruan ran very deep indeed. "Morag..." He took a deep breath. "Please give me time. I'm very new at all this, and have no idea of what is right and wrong." He searched for the right words to say. "It's obvious that you care for Ruan very much. And there's little doubt that you've been a godsend for him." He paused. "If I had to say anything now, I would simply ask if Ruan could stay with you for the time being, and perhaps for the future too." He shrugged. "I just don't know enough yet."

Morag digested his comments in silence for a long while. Eventually, she gave a shuddering sigh. "Yes, yes, of course. Do forgive me." She dropped her head.

Thinking that he'd inflicted enough psychological trauma for one day, Chris said, "I reckon both of us have had enough surprises for today." He looked at the light dancing from the highlights in her hair. "I'll, er...get out of your..." He wanted to say *hair*. "...way."

Morag didn't move. It was as if she hadn't heard. She seemed to be lost in her own thinking.

Desperately hoping that he'd said enough to give her some sort of assurance, he waited.

"Your, er…voice," she said eventually, "is not what I expected."

Chris had no idea what she meant. He stood up to leave. Morag also rose and surprised him with a last question. "Does your blindness mean you can't fly any more?"

"Yes."

Morag nodded.

For some reason, Chris added, "I'm wearing an eye patch over my left eye until they decide what to do with it."

Morag reached a hand forward and, with the lightest touch of her fingertips, explored the contours of Chris's face, and the edge of his eye patch. Then, as if startled by her own forwardness, she dropped her hands back down to her side.

Chris affected a normalcy in his voice that he did not feel. "May I come to see you and Ruan again tomorrow, perhaps in the afternoon?"

"Er, yes. Of course."

The touch of her fingers remained with him for a very long time.

———————

The wind moaned and shuddered outside the kitchen window before it subsided to gather strength for yet another onslaught. Splatterings of rain dashed against the roof. Chris looked outside at the dark, stormy day, and grimaced. If he stayed in Scotland, he'd have to get used to the dismal weather. It certainly didn't offer much good flying weather. *Quite appropriate, really,* he thought.

Murdoch was laying some peat turfs over the fire to damp it down, and keep it alight during the day. "And what will you be doing with yourself today, Christopher?"

"Thinking, mostly. I'm meeting up with Morag and Ruan this afternoon."

"This weather will blow itself out during the morning, so this afternoon will be the best of it." Murdoch took his cape off the hook and shrugged himself into it. "How did you fare last night?"

"It wasn't easy. Didn't know what to say; and when I did, I made Morag cry." Chris balled his hand into a fist at the memory of it.

Murdoch looked up sharply, his brow furrowed with obvious concern.

Chris hurried on. "I think...I hope...it all ended okay." He paused. "It's just that we both had a few surprises.

Murdoch grunted. "Morag's a mite sensitive to some things. She loves Ruan, and doesn't want to lose him."

Chris nodded. "That's quite evident. But I also had the impression that there was something else..." He paused. "Something deeper." He recalled how Morag had hugged herself protectively. "She was very fearful of me initially."

"Initially?"

"Yes."

"Just initially?" Murdoch persisted.

"Yes."

Murdoch's look changed to one of approval. "Then you've done well, laddie."

"What on earth do you mean?"

Murdoch sighed. "I'm telling you this in the strictest confidence, Christopher. But I think it may help you to understand, if I tell you that Morag lost her sight in Edinburgh when she was mugged and raped. Two men threw ammonia in her eyes and abused her so violently that she may not be able to have children of her own. So, you'll understand why she is a wee bit fearful of people, and of men in particular."

Chris was appalled. "Good grief!"

"She's mending, Christopher, but it's a slow thing." He put a rough hand on Chris's shoulder. "Just be careful."

"Of course," Chris stammered. "Of course I will."

After lunch, Chris pulled on his anorak and walked outside to the quad bike. The rain had gone, and bursts of sunshine occasionally peeped out between the fast-moving clouds. However, the wind was still powerful enough to lift the edge of some poorly secured sheets of corrugated iron. One banged repeatedly against a stone wall. Chris placed a rock on top of it to stop the noise. As he did so, he noticed some spring flowers peeping out from grass beside the wall. For no reason he could think of, he began to pick a collection of them. During his search, Chris discovered a sleek kayak leaning against the side wall of the cottage. It looked as if it hadn't been used for a while, as weeds and wildflowers had nearly engulfed it. Murdoch was obviously a man of many talents.

Having gathered a ragged posy of wild flowers, Chris placed it inside a plastic lunchbox and placed it in the quad bike's carry tray.

Five minutes later, Chris was knocking on the door of the White House. He listened to the sound of an internal door shutting on Bess's barking. Then Morag opened the front door.

Wanting to reassure her quickly, he said. "Hi, Morag. It's Chris." He thrust out his bunch of flowers. "I found some spring flowers, so I've brought a few to remind you of life outside." He suddenly remembered that she couldn't see them, so he brushed the end of a flower against the back of her hand. Morag gave a brief start of surprise. For a while, she did not move. Then she lifted her chin to smell the fresh lime smell of the newly picked flowers.

Slowly, Morag reached out and took the flowers and ran her fingers over them. As she did, she named them aloud. "Narcissus, primrose, bluebell, and celandines." As she raised her head and smiled, her beautiful face was fully lit by the afternoon sun. Chris noticed how extraordinarily long her eyelashes were over her closed eyes.

Morag quickly suppressed the smile, and a small frown appeared on her brow. "Giving a blind girl flowers is perhaps a little unusual. Why?" she asked guardedly.

"Because I suspect you will see them better than a sighted person."

"Oh!" she said weakly. She paused. "Well, come on in."

They were soon ensconced in the kitchen. Chris saw that she had wheeled her office chair to the kitchen table so she could work on the computer next to the warmth of the stove. A pot of freshly made tea sat beside the computer. Morag put the flowers into a glass tumbler and placed them in the middle of the table. After primping them into shape, she poured him a cup of tea. He was intrigued by how she did this. She poured the tea into a mug, leaving a finger hovering over the lip so that the temperature change told her when to stop pouring.

"Was there any particular reason why you wanted to see me?" she asked.

"Yes. You're Ruan's carer, and I want to learn more about him...and what may be best for him." Chris was aware this was probably not the whole truth, but he didn't let himself dwell on it.

Morag remained standing, hugging herself with her arms, cupping her elbows in each hand.

Chris could see that Morag was still very much on edge. He sighed. "Morag, the last thing I want to be to you is a threat. Murdoch told me in strict confidence how you came to be blinded." He shrugged. "The flowers were my pathetic attempt to push back against the nasty things of life."

"Oh." Morag uncrossed her arms and sat down in her chair.

Slowly, the conversation began to flow. Chris was aware, however, that it was a fragile thing. One moment, she would ask questions, express sympathy, and even occasionally laugh. Then, as if surprised at her abandon, she would retreat, bending her head forward so that her hair hid her face.

Chris risked asking a question he'd wanted to ask for a while. "Morag, what would be the right reasons for a foreigner like me to stay and live on Skye?"

"Is it even a remote possibility?"

"Remote is about right."

She thought carefully before answering. "Living on the islands is not for everyone. In fact, I suspect it is not a good option for most people. You need to be comfortable with isolation and the culture of island life. In small island communities, everyone knows everyone else. There is a dense web of interrelationships which makes anonymity impossible." She paused to collect her thoughts. "Most islanders live modestly. There's not much to generate wealth. Everyone has at least two jobs. Certainly, ninety-per-cent of crofts are too poor to be economically viable by themselves." She leaned back in the chair, her face now fully visible. "Islanders are socially incestuous. They don't look outside the island for much, and can fail to keep up with possibilities in the outside world. In fact, they can look on the outside world with some disdain." She smiled. "On top of that, the weather is lousy, and you need to live here for three generations before they consider you to be a local."

"You make it sound irresistible."

"I'm simply being honest. Mainlanders come here with all sorts of ideals and notions. Most leave within two years. The truth is: any romantic idea of a 'sea change' needs to be balanced by an understanding that ours is one of the stormiest seas in the world. It may look like an idyllic, rustic lifestyle, but it requires you to endure harsh, primitive conditions. So the ideal of peace and tranquility has to be balanced by the reality of isolation and, um..." she dropped her head, "a lack of social sophistication."

"Yet you choose to live here."

"I'm an islander. It's difficult to get the island out of an island girl."

"But that's not the entire reason, I suspect."

"No." She paused. "The isolation suits me."

"Hmm." Silence hung between them for a while. "If those are the reasons a person shouldn't stay, what are the reasons a person should stay?"

Morag blanched. A troubled frown appeared momentarily, until she composed herself. "You would need to feel fulfilled in your work. You would need to feel that this was a place where you could see a future, and raise a family." She shrugged. "You'd need to develop good, social connections."

Chris noticed a streak of color showed along her elegant neck. "Thanks, Morag."

"What about Ruan?"

"What about him?" Chris asked, slightly off balance at the new direction of the conversation.

"I've got the social worker, Ms. Eden, coming to see me next Wednesday morning to discuss his future…and I hate talking with her." She paused. "I'm afraid I find her very difficult."

"Then I'll just have to be here with you to back you up. What time is the appointment?"

"Oh," said Morag weakly. "Ten o'clock."

"Okay, I'll see you then."

"Um, thanks."

"No worries. Any chance of seeing Ruan?"

Morag nodded. "He'll probably be down the boatshed with Hamish. His croft is next to your grandfather's."

"Aah, my grandfather's subleasing tenant, and new owner of the cow." Silently he added, *and doubtless many other things from my grandfather's croft that were not actually bolted down.*

"Pardon?"

"Forget it."

"Chris."

"Yes?"

"Thanks for the flowers."

Chris parked the quad beside the stone wall and walked through the farm gate to Hamish's cottage, and its untidy collection of outbuildings.

He could hear Hamish's voice before he reached the first of the sheds. His invectives were being delivered with heat enough to singe the hairs off a highland cow. "Damn and blast you, pig! The sooner I turn you into bacon the better, you…"

Chris watched as Ruan shepherded a large pig out of the boat-shed with the assistance of JJ. "Come on, Mr. Percival," urged Ruan. On seeing Chris, he smiled.

Chris pointed to the pig. "That, I presume, is Mr. Percival?"

"Aye," Ruan said. "He butted Hamish while he was hammering. He hit his thumb."

Chris put his head inside the boat-shed. Sure enough, Hamish was sucking his thumb while looking darkly over his shoulder at the pig. In front of him, a business-like wooden fishing boat sat on its chocks. Hamish had been repairing holes in its hull with small patches of copper.

"This is probably not the best time to remind you that you owe three months of agricultural lease payments." Chris waited for Hamish to give him his attention. "If you're happy with the current arrangement, let's keep it going and we'll negotiate something that's acceptable to us both later."

Hamish nodded.

Chris jerked a thumb at Ruan outside. "Mind if I borrow your helper for a bit?"

"Ach." Hamish was still sucking his finger. "He's after telling me you're some sort of cousin. Is that right?"

"Yeah. I'm actually his next-of-kin."

Hamish digested the information, and waved dismissively at him. "Off ye go. Get him home to Morag by six."

Chris smiled at yet more evidence of how this community cared for its own. He called out to Ruan. "Oi, Half-Pint. Have a walk with me back to Morag's and tell me why you like living with her."

"I aren't no half-pint," protested Ruan. "Is it true you've flown airplanes? Morag told me."

"Yeah. But I crashed the last one. Blinded myself in one eye and busted a leg. I'm not allowed to be a pilot any more."

"But you flew." Ruan's voice was full of wonder. "Like, you flew a lot?"

"Yeah."

Ruan thought about it. "That's better'n anyone else around here. You're lucky."

"I'll try and remember that."

They strolled down to the foreshore, sat on a rock, and watched the waves pound onto the shore. Ruan said, "I'm hungry. I hope we've got tatties and crowdie for tea."

"Crowding?"

"Crowdie."

"Croody."

In exasperation, Ruan turned and held a hand either side of Chris's face, forcing him to watch his lips closely. "Crowdie."

The image of an Aboriginal bushman swam into Chris's consciousness. He'd made the same gesture, holding Chris head, forcing him to watch him as he said, "Raberaba."

"What did you say?" demanded Ruan.

Unaware that he had spoken out loud, Chris leaned back with a sigh. "Nothing. Let's get you home."

Later that night, Chris lay awake in his bed, pressed down by the weight of bedclothes. It had been an extraordinary day full of images that would stay with him forever. *But what do they mean?* Even as he thought it, he knew the answer. A shaft of moonlight appeared from between the clouds and shone through the ill-fitting window to illuminate the stone wall of his bedroom. The suitcase Murdoch had given him stood against the wall. He had explored its contents before going to bed.

The first thing he'd found was his grandfather's kilt. He had lifted it out and been amazed by its weight. He'd fingered the heavy folds of the yellow and black tartan of the MacLeods, the Norman clan. Underneath it had been a folder containing some old photographs. There were old black and white pictures of Chris's father as a child, standing on a beach with his younger sister. There were also pictures of his sister as an adult, with baby Magnus in her arms. He even found a colored photograph of himself in the collection. His father must have sent it. But what truly amazed him were the contents of a large manila envelope. On opening it, he discovered his grandfather had kept every one of Chris's letters.

Chris knew that he had come to the island with no idea about his future, where he would live or where he belonged. However, the rugged beauty of the island had begun to suggest an answer. His grandfather's tiny stone cottage had reinforced it. But he knew that it was feeling the skin on a child's cheek that had finished it. He resolved to explore the possibility of staying on the island.

Chris did a mental review of his finances. He was fairly well off —even if it was for all the wrong reasons. The 'loss of license' insurance that he had only recently taken out, as well as his life insurance policy with its disability clause, meant he was now assured of a steady income. He was actually in a good financial position to consider rebuilding his grandfather's cottage. The building should, of course, rightly be demolished, but he knew he could never bring himself to get rid of the ancient stone walls that had nurtured his family for generations. Was it possible to keep them? He booted up the CAD software on his computer and set about designing what might be possible. Even as he fell asleep, he was mentally listing the companies and products that he would begin to research next day.

Next morning, Murdoch offered Chris the use of the Land Rover. "I need to check the marshes and the reed beds to see what's about, so I'll take the quad." He paused. "Tomorrow I'm off into Portree to pick up a water pump, if you want a lift."

Chris looked up from his computer. "Thanks Murdoch. That would be great."

Murdoch grunted. "You've a wee bit of energy about you today. 'Tis good to see."

By the time Chris drove down to the village, the sun was well up in a soft blue sky. It was good to feel the spring warmth on his shoulders. He arrived at the village store and found Jessie Collins sitting on her stool behind the counter. She put down her newspaper as he came in. "Ach, it is yourself, Christopher. Now what would you be needing?"

"G'day Jessie. I need a long tape measure and a notebook. Can you help?"

"Aye, it's just a question of finding them. Look along that shelf."

Chris found the items easily enough, and brought them to the counter. "Murdoch tells me you handle the post here, Jessie."

"Aye. Are you planning on getting any?"

Chris nodded.

"Then I'll include it in with Murdoch's."

Chris drew a deep breath. "I've decided to stay and take over my grandfather's croft."

Jessie cocked her head and regarded Chris with her bright eyes. "If that's the way of it, I've no doubt you'll want the postie to send your mail there."

"Yes, please."

"I'm right pleased to hear that you're staying, Christopher." She smiled. "We need young folk here, particularly folk what's got their heads screwed on right."

Chris went back to the Land Rover and idled his way slowly along the foreshore track, passing along the front of the stone cottages on his way to his grandfather's house. As he did, he saw a familiar figure sitting in a chair in front of a cottage, enjoying the sunshine. Chris brought the Land Rover to a stop and slid back the side window. "G'day, Alsdair. I didn't recognize you without a glass of whiskey in your hand."

"I can fix that," Alsdair said.

Chris laughed. "So this is your literary hideaway."

"Aye. It is one of the cruel ironies of life that the place I write best is a hideously damp little cottage on a rain-soaked island off Scotland." He sighed theatrically. "All my colleagues find they can't write unless they are in Southern France or the South Sea islands. It's very unfair."

"You're just a home-loving type of guy who wants to surround himself with the certainties of youth."

"Bollocks. It's the whiskey. Come on in and let me make you a coffee."

Chris was pleased to accept.

The inside of the cottage was comfortably furnished with quality items. Prominent on the kitchen bench was a chrome coffee-making machine. Alsdair pointed to it. "One of the few luxuries I insist on, when sobriety is called for. It makes a mean cup of coffee."

Chris wandered over to a desk that Alsdair had positioned under the front window. It had an expensive-looking computer on it. The window itself was covered in condensation, making it impossible to see anything outside clearly. "Blimey!" Chris said. "Have you Scots got a masochistic aversion to warmth and clear visibility?"

"Oh." Alsdair shrugged. "You live with it long enough, you get used to it."

Chris sighed in exasperation and walked back out of the cottage to the Land Rover. He returned a minute later with his tape measure and measured the width and height of the window. Accepting a mug of coffee, he limped back outside into the sunshine. Alsdair followed him, carrying a kitchen chair for Chris to sit on.

The two of them sat outside on the chairs, leaning back against the sun-warmed stonework of the cottage, and allowing the peace of the loch and the emerald green of the grass above the cliffs, to soak into them. For an Australian starved of the sun for many days, it was a welcome experience.

After twenty minutes of undemanding companionship, Chris took his leave and drove on to his grandfather's cottage, where he set about measuring distances and making notes. He found a rusted spade against a dry-stone wall and used it to dig holes around the outside of the cottage to search for the presence of bedrock. When he'd finished, he came back inside, and took out his computer, well pleased with what he'd discovered.

Chris began to draw on his experience of building super-insulated houses in central Australia and began searching the Internet to explore different building options. His familiarity with using geothermal technology in house building led him to make a phone call to St. Andrews University in Fife. He was finally put through to Professor Ewen Edmondson of the Department of Earth Sciences. After listening to Chris for five minutes, the professor's interest changed from reserved caution to curiosity. He invited Chris to visit him. "Mid-term break for Candlemas term has just begun. If you can be here first thing in the morning in two days' time, I can give you an hour."

Chris was delighted. As he returned the phone to his pocket, he realized that it was now important for him to put a priority on getting his own transport.

Next morning, Murdoch dropped Chris off at a car yard in Portree.

Forty minutes later, Chris drove out with a second-hand Jeep Cherokee, and headed south along the coast road. Before long, he was crossing the bridge that linked Skye to the mainland.

It was early evening by the time he drove down the A91 from Dundee into the university town of St. Andrews. He had booked into a 'bed and breakfast' on North Street, which according to the landlady, was just past the New Picture House. When he got there, it didn't look new at all. The double-storied stone houses lining the street reeked with history. He parked his car and walked across the street to his lodgings.

After washing away the weariness of travel, he re-emerged onto the street, determined to explore the town as much as he could before nightfall. He limped east along North Street toward a tall clock tower. In front of the gateway below the tower, two co-joined initials, "PH," were embedded in the cobblestones. A young man surprised him by saying; "I wouldn't walk on the initials if I were you."

"Why?"

The man was leaning against the wall, smoking a cigarette. "Because it will bring you bad luck in your exams."

"I'm afraid I've already stepped on it. Am I doomed?" Chris feigned concern.

"Not necessarily. But you will have to wait until May Day for the May dip. Then you'll be required to have a swim in the North Sea to wash off the curse." He smiled. "On the plus side, you will be encouraged in your ablutions by a choir singing madrigals from the shore."

"You Scots are all mad, you know that." Chris laughed. "What's the significance of these initials?"

"They are the initials of Patrick Hamilton, a protestant martyr who was burned to death on that spot in 1528."

Chris whistled. "How come you know all this?"

"I'm reading history here, but most students at St. Andrews would know about Patch." The student smiled. "We're a superstitious lot."

"It all looks very old." Chris looked at the buttresses and Gothic windows of the building that stood next to the tower.

"It's the third oldest university in the English-speaking world, my friend. A charter was given to the Augustinian priory in 1413." He pointed east up the street. "If you go up there, you'll see the ruins of St. Andrew's Cathedral."

Chris pointed to the Gothic windows. "I thought this was a cathedral."

"No, this is St. Salvator's College." He jerked his thumb at the archway. "Go through and take a look if you want."

Chris did so. It was the start of a fascinating evening that concluded in a local pub. There, he pondered all he'd seen. As he did, his thoughts turned to Morag, and he reflected sadly on all that was denied her because of her blindness.

Next morning, he located the Earth Science Department and the untidy office of Professor Ewen Edmondson. Fifteen minutes later, the Professor canceled the rest of his morning's appointments in order to continue his talk with Chris. They pored over geological maps, and explored websites for the next three hours. Before he left, Chris was taken down to the sheds behind the building where a mobile drilling rig was parked. A man was washing the mud off a massive auger bit with a high-pressure hose.

"This is Cody," the professor said. "We hire his services so often that he finds it easier to keep his rig here."

Cody, a dour-looking man of few words, listened to Chris and the professor as they outlined their ideas.

By the time Chris got back into his car, his head was spinning.

He began threading his way through Scotland—going back the

way he'd come—until he reached the town of Kyle of Lochalsh. After spending another evening at a clean, but very tiny, bed and breakfast, Chris found his way to the industrial estate that housed the Scottish Crofting Federation.

Chris explained his business.

He was then handed the necessary form to transfer ownership of the croft from his grandfather to himself. The young man at reception chatted with Chris as he helped him navigate his way through the form. He proved to be a mine of information. Chris learned that there were still eighteen-thousand working crofts in Scotland, two-thousand of which were on Skye. Sensing an interested audience, the young man kept talking.

"More people are now moving to the highlands than leaving them, and we've got a waiting list for those wanting a crofting license." He grimaced. "A lot of disenchanted businessmen from the south are wanting a change in lifestyle. The trouble is, most of them don't know how tough crofting really is."

During a pause in the conversation, Chris broached the subject of rebuilding his grandfather's cottage. However, when he began to mention the latest innovations in low-temperature hydrothermal technology, the young man was out of his depth, and went off to fetch the manager.

The manager turned out to be a ferocious-looking man with a bushy beard and a keen intelligence. Chris shared with him his ideas for building his house and the technology he wanted to employ.

The manager expressed interest, saying that any innovation which improved the quality of life of crofters was important. At the end of their discussion, Chris was persuaded to fill out an application form for a grant from the Scottish Community and House-holders Renewables Initiative to help put his ideas into practice.

The conversation turned to the subject of building regulations and building plans. Chris was pretty sure the vandalism of his cottage was designed to dissuade him from taking up his grandfather's croft, and there was no reason why it wouldn't happen again. As his building project was vulnerable to malicious damage, he wanted to complete it as quickly as possible. When he mentioned this, he was advised to visit an architect in a nearby building, with whom the Crofting Federation worked closely.

The Federation manager also put through a call to Lionacleit High School on the Isle of Benbecula, which, he was told, ran courses on crofting. The principal of the school promised to email a letter supporting Chris's application, since he too saw its potential benefits.

Chris expressed his heartfelt thanks. He'd done better than he could have hoped.

Four hours later, dog-tired, he headed back across the bridge to Skye.

Next morning, Chris watched Murdoch unlock his gun cabinet and take out his shotgun. Chris guessed it was not going to be a good day for foxes.

Murdoch stuffed a box of cartridges into his jacket pocket. "I understand you're seeing the welfare woman with Morag this morning?"

"That's right."

Murdoch nodded slowly as if searching for words. In the end, he simply said, "I hope it goes well," and strode out to the Land Rover.

Two hours later, Chris pulled up at the White House. The presence of a Volkswagen Golf told him the social worker had already arrived.

As he knocked on the door, he braced himself for an onslaught from Bess. It did not eventuate. The dog had obviously been banished from the house. Morag opened the door to him. She was dressed in beige slacks, a white shirt and a tartan sleeveless jumper. At her throat was a jeweled Celtic choker. Chris thought she looked amazing.

It was obvious, however, that she did not feel that way. "Thank goodness you're here. I've come close to losing my patience with her already."

"Morag, take a deep breath. Relax. Let's keep our cool and

work together on this." Chris sought to calm her down. "Let me take the heat, if there is any to take."

Morag unclenched her fists, straightened herself up, and took a deep breath. Chris was amazed how those few movements transformed her into a woman of extraordinary poise and presence.

He was introduced to Ms. Eden, and discussions about Ruan began. However, they were interrupted when Annie barged into the room. Chris did not fail to note her brusque manner, or the combative glint in her eye. "You'll all be having tea then?"

"Thank you, Annie," Morag said. With a dismissive sniff, Annie left the room. Chris and Morag set about making a case for Ruan to stay in the village.

After asking a few introductory questions, Ms. Eden gave a brutal summary of their situation. "As I understand it, you, Mr. Norman, don't have a job or a home, and didn't even know of Ruan's existence until this week, despite being his closest relative." She turned to Morag. "Ms. Daniel, whilst you have undoubtedly formed a strong emotional attachment to Ruan, you are not only blind, but a single person living on your own." She looked down at her notes. "A report from Ruan's school tells me he has less than a twenty-five per cent attendance record and that, I'm afraid to say, will greatly mitigate against him being able to stay with you. He needs to live in a place where his education can be assured."

Chris could see Morag's chin rise in a way that made her look extraordinarily regal. Anticipating her blistering retort, he interrupted.

"Ms. Eden, I quite understand your concern. In fairness, I have to say that Ruan's pattern for truancy was well-established before he came into Morag's care." It was difficult not to notice scuffling noises outside the door where Annie was doing a poor job at being discreet with her eavesdropping. "While both of us have shortcomings in our ability to care for Ruan, I feel that together we can do it very well. Morag, with Annie's help, has proven to be a dedicated carer, and I plan to be a…significant male figure in his life. I've chosen to live in my grandfather's cottage just half a mile away, in order to do so." He shrugged. "As for his education…"

"We can teach him what he's missed out on," Morag broke in.

"Er, yes. Both of us."

"Together."

Silence hung in the room for a very long time as Ms. Eden considered their proposal. It seemed like an eternity before she spoke. "Very well. I will let Ruan stay with you for three months, after which he will be assessed to see if he can stay longer." She pursed her lips. "This means you have until the end of the summer holidays to bring him up to speed. If you do, I will make a case for him to stay with you. However, I cannot guarantee it will be possible."

Morag sighed with obvious relief. Chris nodded his gratitude. "Thank you, Ms. Eden. I'm sure you won't be disappointed."

Annie pushed open the door and addressed Ms. Eden. "You're leaving, is it? I'm sorry you won't be staying for yer tea."

A few minutes later, Chris followed Morag and Annie into the kitchen. Ruan was already there, dressed smartly. His hair was brushed and his shoes were on. He was finishing a mug of hot chocolate and working his way through one of Annie's oatcakes. He grinned at Chris. "Ach, if it's not my cousin-something. 'Ave you come for one of Annie's oatcakes?"

"That I have."

Turning to Morag, Ruan pleaded, "Can I take me shoes off now?"

Morag ruffled his hair. "Yes, off you go."

Grabbing another oatcake, Ruan ran out of the kitchen and bounded up the stairs. Annie yelled after him, "Don't you go giving my oatcakes to that animal of yours."

Chris turned to her. "G'day Annie. I'm Chris Norman, Joseph Norman's grandson. I've heard a lot about you. Thanks for all you've done in looking after Ruan."

Annie still had a combative air about her. She put her hands on her hips. "Well, isn't he the weird one, speaking like he does."

"It's called an Australian accent, Annie. It's about as weird as your Scottish one."

"Ach, the cheek of you." She looked Chris over as he sat at the table, holding his walking stick between his knees. "Well, you're not much of a catch, are you? Look at the state of you."

Chris smiled tiredly. "I crashed an airplane and busted myself up."

Annie sniffed, "I don't hold wi' flying. It's not natural." She turned away and began to pour out the tea. "I suppose you'll be going back to those fool contraptions when you're mended."

"No. They don't let people with one eye fly."

"Hmph. Then they've done you a favor."

The three of them settled around the table to discuss how to best organize Ruan's home schooling. "We'll need a curriculum that will tell us what Ruan needs to have learned at his age. They must have one in Portree," Morag said.

"I'll pick it up tomorrow, so we can go through it together." Chris turned to Morag. "How about you and I share the teaching each morning, and give Ruan his freedom in the afternoons?"

"If you don't, he'll think his throat's been cut," Annie said. "It's going to be hard enough getting the wee bairn to agree to the mornings."

Chris nodded. "Annie, you're the only person Ruan stands in awe of. Would you mind if we taught Ruan in the kitchen here? It's warm, and it's his favorite place. If we just used one end of the kitchen table, we could keep out of your way. And you could bribe him with your cooking."

"Lord, help me." Annie rolled her eyes. "Now there's another man sweet-talking me for my cooking." She gave another of her sniffs. "Ach, it's fine with me."

"I can hear him read and tell him his history," said Morag. "But I won't be able to do much more than that." Tears filled her eyes, but she blinked them away.

The movement was not lost on Chris. "I suspect that if you cause Ruan to love reading and to love stories, you will have achieved something pretty amazing." He paused. "I can teach him writing, basic math, and science."

Morag sat up in her chair. "Can you do that? I mean, can you really...?" she trailed off.

Chris saw her anxiety and replied with more conviction than he felt. "Yes, Morag I can. You can't train to be a commercial pilot without getting good marks at school. I'll keep my end up. Don't worry."

Morag lowered her head. "Oh, I'm sorry. I didn't mean to…"

Anxious to move on, he asked, "When do we start? Is Monday week too soon?"

"I suppose it will take that long to sort out what we will teach." Morag chewed her lip. "Monday week is fine with me. What about you, Annie?"

"Aye, tis fine wi' me." She sighed. "Someone had better tell Ruan the way of it, I suppose. Poor wee mannie."

Chris looked out of the window at Ruan dragging a tree branch to the kindling bin beside the back door. JJ was running around in circles in a fever of excitement, pausing occasionally to bite at the foliage. Chris eased himself off the chair. "It's time I pulled my weight. I'll do it." He limped to the kitchen door, opened it, and stood on the back step. "Oi, Half-Pint. Come and sit with me here. I've got something to tell you."

Ruan gave the impression that he was not at all sure he would like what he was about to hear. Nonetheless he sat down beside Chris.

"Okay, mate, here's the deal. The social worker wants to take you from Morag, move you to the mainland, and put you in a home in order to make you go to school."

Ruan started to protest.

Chris held up his hand for quiet. "But Morag and I, as your next-of-kin, don't want that to happen. We'd like you to stay here."

"I'm not leaving," Ruan said, defiantly.

"And you don't have to, provided you let Morag and me teach you here every weekday morning for the next three months. And that means all through the summer holidays."

Ruan protested. "I don't like schooling. There's no dampty point in it." He picked up a stone and threw it at the peg bin. "It don't make you fish any better, milk a cow any better or cook a skart any better. You just learn British history and things you'll never use."

Chris lifted his head back and gazed at the view in front of him, seeking inspiration from the land. Beyond the croft, the land rose upward to the gorse-covered hills. A lot was riding on what he said next.

"How much money do you get if you pick five buckets of whelks?" He didn't wait for an answer. "If your boat was heading east at eight knots, and the tide was taking you south at three knots, how many degrees will you have to turn the boat to counteract it?" He paused. "If building stones weigh twenty-two pounds each, how many tons of stone will I need to build a wall, that's thirty by ten feet in size?"

Chris went on remorselessly. "If you wanted to buy a boat for two-thousand pounds and you save one hundred pounds a week, how long will it be before you can buy the boat? Why do palm trees grow in Scotland when in other places this far north it is too cold for them to grow? Where do the birds go in winter; and what causes the aurora borealis?" Chris reached over and tickled JJ behind the ear, giving time for the questions to do their work. Finally, he said, "You okay to start Monday week, nine o'clock sharp?"

"Aye. I suppose so," said Ruan sulkily.

"Good man." He collected his walking stick and stood up with a grunt. Chris looked down at the disconsolate boy. "Ruan, I'm rebuilding my grandfather's house, and I'm going to live in it. You're welcome to help me in the afternoons if you want." He smiled. "And here's something else: If I teach you how to build a house, will you teach me how to fish?"

"Aye." Ruan spilled JJ off his lap as he stood up. He stuck out his chest. "It's easy."

Half an hour later, Chris idled the Cherokee along the foreshore toward his cottage. Before he started work, he wanted to call in on Alsdair. He pulled up behind a champagne colored Mercedes-Benz parked in front of his house. Chris opened the rear door of his car, extracted some overalls, and pulled them on. He then picked up a pane of glass, which had had its edges sleeved with a plastic sheath, and walked to Alsdair's front door. When he arrived, he found that the door was ajar, and that a fierce argument was raging inside.

A mystery voice shouted, "You have no sense of responsibility. Why won't you invest in the development? For goodness' sake, every dollar we invest now will save us ten later." "It's not as if you haven't got the money, dammit!"

The languid, unruffled voice of Alsdair drifted out to Chris. "I don't want to invest in the project because I think it stinks."

"Rubbish. It's your moral responsibility. It's good for the island."

"You mean, it's good for you because you're desperate to recoup the money you lost on your dodgy Malaysian investment scam."

"You impudent little turd!"

Chris judged this to be an opportune moment to interrupt. He pushed through the door, smiled and said, "Don't mind me."

A large, florid man was standing over Alsdair as he lounged on a kitchen chair. The big man spun around and growled, "Push off. We're busy."

Chris smiled. "That's a shame. Y'see, I'm on a tight schedule." He put the pane of glass down carefully on Alsdair's desk, and then limped back outside, without bothering to close the door.

As Chris went to retrieve his toolbox and walking stick, he could hear the stranger rounding on Alsdair again. "The island needs your support, and I demand it."

"The crofters will never allow it."

"They don't know what's good for them. You leave them to me."

Chris picked up his toolbox and walking stick and returned to the front door.

Alsdair's voice was becoming louder and louder. "Don't you dare bully the crofters! It was you who trashed the Norman cottage, wasn't it?"

Chris, who was about to enter through the door, remained rooted to the spot.

"It had to be you," Alsdair shouted. "You were the only one I told about Chris coming to see if he wanted to live there. The coincidence is just too great."

The beefy man grabbed Alsdair by the lapels and snarled, "You keep your mouth shut, you weak little turd. You haven't got the balls to do what's necessary for the good of the island."

The big man gave Alsdair a backhanded slap and began shaking him like a rag doll. "If I have any more obstruction from you, I'll…"

The man got no further. Chris stepped inside, lifted his walking stick, and whipped it against the back of the man's legs. As he fell, Chris smashed the stick down on the man's shoulder.

The stick broke, and the man yelled in agony.

Chris stepped over him and jabbed the broken end of his walking stick against the man's Adam's apple.

Whilst Chris knew himself to be dangerously angry, he also knew that he was close to toppling sideways because of his weak leg. He hissed savagely at the man. "Move, and I'll pin you into the ground like an insect."

The beefy man did not move.

Keeping his eyes on the man, Chris spoke to Alsdair, "Who is this dirt-bag?"

Alsdair readjusted his jacket collar with elaborate dignity and cleared his throat. "This is Jason Haines, acting Laird of these parts, and my older brother." He gave a delicate cough. "He's also your landlord."

Chris pushed the broken stick harder against the man's throat. "Listen carefully, maggot. My name is Chris Norman. I will be taking over my grandfather's lease. If I trip over anything, catch a cold, or am in any way upset, I will go with Alsdair to the police and report you. It is only because of my regard for Alsdair that I'm not doing so now." Chris lifted the stick off the man's throat. "Now, get up and move your fat arse out of here."

Haines winced as he rolled over onto his knees and got to his feet. He glared at both Chris and Alsdair before lurching out of the cottage.

Chris watched him go. "Geez!" he said, sinking thankfully into a chair.

Alsdair rubbed his cheek. "Well, that was interesting." He

smiled. "You certainly put the wind up him. Not many people manage to do that. I think the eye-patch helped. You looked very convincing."

Coming off his adrenaline high, Chris put his head in his hands. "Did I push him too hard?"

Alsdair shook his head. "Nah, it will do him good. He's always been a bully—made my life a misery as a kid. I was glad to go to boarding school so I could get away from him."

"Are you serious about him being my boss?" Chris asked.

"Yep. He's acting Laird for my father, who is now very frail. For the last two years, Jason has taken over the management of everything except Murdoch's gamekeeping, and the stables. Father still attends to that." Alsdair walked over to a kitchen cupboard and extracted a bottle of whiskey. "Jason doesn't understand the land much. His skills are more in the area of accounting." Pouring two generous glasses, he handed one to Chris and smiled. "Purely medicinal."

Chris took it and drank gratefully, spluttering as the fiery liquid coursed down his throat. He put his head back into his hands as a fresh wave of anguish swept over him. "My landlord? Dammit!"

"Relax." Alsdair raised his glass to Chris in a toast. "You are merely continuing the ancient crofters' tradition of thumbing your nose at authority."

Next morning, Chris drove to Portree. After checking the map, he found his way to the local primary school on Blaven Road. The school buildings were painted with the inevitable white paint, and roofed with slate colored tiles. What attracted Chris's attention, however, were the solar panels he saw on the roof. Someone, at least, was being innovative.

Chris was received courteously and was soon ushered into the office of the deputy principal, an efficient-looking woman called Mrs. Wilks. Chris explained that he'd come to formally notify the school that he and Morag would be doing an intensive three-month home-school program with Ruan. He also asked if it was possible for him to have the current year's teaching syllabus, and a list of learning outcomes that a boy of Ruan's age should have achieved.

Mrs. Wilks rose to the challenge, and Chris was soon furnished with scores of photocopied sheets and a list of website addresses containing educational resources designed for children doing distance education.

Forty minutes later, he was back in the village, pulling up in front of the White House. He found himself looking forward to spending time with Morag, particularly at a time when there wasn't high drama. He told himself that it was merely because he wanted an opportunity to question her about the diaries of her relative, the Rev. Arthur Daniel. Reaching inside his shirt, he fingered the Celtic cross hanging around his neck. As he reflected on it, he discovered that he liked the idea of the cross being linked to Morag. The thought brought him up short. *Why? Certainly, she is a complex and compelling woman… and beautiful,* he admitted. Alarmed at his thoughts, he forced himself to be rational. *Be careful. Long-term relationships don't work. They inevitably lead to betrayal.*

Having got his thinking back under control, he eased himself out of the car, mounted the steps, and knocked on the door. Annie opened it. She had her coat and scarf on and was about to leave. "Ach, it is yourself—the bird man. Come away in. She's in the kitchen. I'm off. But if I'm spared, I'll be back tomorrow with a salmon." She peered at him. "Just in case you're anywhere near at lunchtime."

Chris divined that he had somehow been successful in winning Annie's approval. However, as he watched her squelch across the pasture toward her cottage, he had the disquieting thought that Annie's thinking was a step or two ahead of his own. He just wasn't sure where it was headed.

He discovered Morag in the kitchen. Music was playing loudly, and she was dancing. The sight of her caused him to hold his breath. With a pang of guilt, he realized that he was being a voyeur, and so he took two steps back. "Morag, it's Chris. Are you in the kitchen?" When he entered, Morag was sitting at the kitchen table with her hands folded demurely in her lap. Chris smiled to himself.

"I've brought the teaching syllabus for Ruan."

Morag cleared her throat. "Good. Let's go through it, but first let me make you a cup of tea."

Chris volunteered to get the milk from the fridge. When he opened it, he found the remote control unit for the music player sitting on one of the shelves. He took it out. "Is there any reason why your music center remote should be in the fridge?"

Morag dropped her head in embarrassment. "I did wonder where it was. I can get a bit absent-minded sometimes."

Chris laughed. "I'm actually amazed by what you do manage to do."

Morag smiled, and they were soon deep in discussion about the curriculum, working out a three-month learning plan for Ruan. It became apparent to Chris that he would need to do the lion's share of the teaching. Morag could hear him read and test him with his multiplication and spelling. However, Chris would need to do the rest. He glanced at Morag. Even though she had turned her head away, he caught a glimpse of a face pinched with anguish. She excused herself, walked quickly out into the hall and into her study where she half-closed the door.

Chris still had a clear line of sight from the kitchen across the hall into the study. He saw her bunch her fists on her desk and weep in frustration. Heart-breaking sobs escaped her. It was a good five minutes before she was able to get herself back in control, repair the blotchiness on her face, and return to the kitchen. Her face was hidden by her hair. "Right. Let's do what we can, starting Monday week."

"Morag, do you mind me asking who your eye doctor is? I need a doctor who understands my, ah, own circumstances."

"Oh, um, yes." Morag gave him the name of a doctor in Edinburgh. "He's very good, but I'm afraid he's not local. It's just that Edinburgh was where I...lost my sight."

"Oh, really." He paused. "Perhaps you're right. I might ask around for someone who is a bit closer. Thanks anyway." Silence hung between them for some time. Chris cleared his throat. "I need some guidance from you, Morag. But I can see you're a bit emotional right now. I can come back later."

"No, no. Stay." Morag dabbed a handkerchief to her eye and sat upright.

"It's just that I've been looking for a chance to chat with you for a bit, to ask you about someone I think could be a relative of yours. He was a missionary in central Australia."

"Of course, of course. I am sorry you've needed to wait so long —with all the drama." She sniffed. "You would have to be talking about Joseph, my great-uncle."

"Gee. I didn't even know for sure whether he was a relative of yours. I just knew he was a Daniel."

Morag's tone took on a touch of harshness. "All of the Daniel family has left the island, except for me. I came back here after I was blinded, so that I could get out of everyone's way." She laughed bitterly. "Despite everything, I felt safe on the island, because I'd grown up here. Ironic, really."

Her reply begged a number of questions, but instinct told Chris now was not the time to ask. Instead, he leaned his head forward and took the Celtic cross from around his neck. "Morag, I'm going to tell a story—my story—and invite you to tell me how it might end." He recounted the events of his crash, and the research he'd done at the South Australian Museum. "So I'm hoping to find the diaries of Rev. Arthur Daniel and perhaps discover who might have worn the Celtic cross." He paused. "If you hold out your hand, I'll put the cross in it."

Tentatively, Morag did so. As she did, Chris noticed that Morag's eyes were again full of tears. She said softly, "I had no idea that you had been through so much. I'm so sorry." She caressed the Celtic cross in her hand.

"There are stories that I have heard about such a cross," she said, slowly. "But I suppose there were a number of crosses made like this. You'd need to check."

She paused.

Chris saw that she seemed to be struggling with some sort of inner conflict, and wasn't sure what to make of it.

As if sensing his confusion, she gave a half-laugh of apology. "I'm sorry. It's just that my father…" She petered off and sighed. "My father used to tell me amazing tales of the islands. He was a schoolteacher. He taught me to love their history so much that I began a Master's research thesis on the subject. But I gave it up when I was blinded."

She forced a smile. "I'm telling you this so you will not be surprised that I'm able to tell you exactly what happened to Arthur's diaries—because of my research. They were sent to my father, who, after keeping them for some years, gave them to the library at the abbey in Iona. Arthur Daniel was a brother of the community there." She looked down. "So if you want to see the diaries, you need to go to Iona."

The late afternoon shadows were beginning to lengthen in the hills. Murdoch was in the high country trudging his way up a glen, trying to keep out of sight behind the shoulder of a bluff. It was nearly time to go home. His mind was not entirely on the job. He was trying to work out the implications of Chris's altercation with Jason Haines. Chris had recounted the tale the previous evening. The event itself was disturbing enough. However, it was Jason's reference to possible coercion of the crofters that particularly concerned him. What should he do? Because he was the local preacher, he was the one to whom the tiny community looked for care and consolation. He did not find it an easy responsibility to bear.

A movement eight hundred yards up-wind caused him to sink instinctively to the ground. Lying on his stomach in the grass, he brought a telescopic sight to his eye, and swept it carefully across the glen. *Nothing… Nothing… There it is! Got you!* He smiled as the blurred form of a red deer, a stag, swam into focus. Even as he watched, it lifted its head—heavy with its spread of antlers—to smell the air.

The evening sun highlighted the stag's rusty brown flank. He was magnificent.

"Ach, I'll be keeping an eye out for you this season, my bonny prince."

Refreshed by what he'd seen, Murdoch eased himself to his feet, and retraced his steps down the glen.

When he arrived at his cottage, he discovered that Chris had screwed a draft excluder to the bottom of the back door, and was fixing the light socket in the outside toilet. He voiced his gratitude. "I've a rabbit hanging in the garage, and some carragheen pudding that was given to me by the cook at the manor. Let's set about it."

Over dinner, Chris told him that Morag was related to the Rev. Daniel he was researching, and that the man's diaries had been sent to the abbey on the island of Iona.

"Iona, eh? Now there's a thing." Murdoch sat quietly, lost in his own reverie as Chris collected the plates and took them to the sink. Eventually, he picked up a tea towel and helped Chris with the washing up. "I think it's time I had a chat with Alsdair, in company with yourself, Christopher. We need to figure out what trouble Jason might be bringing on the crofters." He lifted two plates onto the kitchen shelf. "If I phone Alsdair to check he's in, will you come with me to see him for a wee crack?"

"Of course."

An hour later, Chris was seated in front of the fire in Alsdair's cottage. Murdoch was next to him. It was apparent when they arrived that Alsdair had already managed a significant start on the bottle of whiskey they were now sharing.

"Tell me again, Alsdair," Murdoch growled. "What exactly did you hear Jason say, and what do you suspect it means?"

Alsdair was clearly embarrassed for his brother. "Jason has got some harebrained scheme for developing a tourist complex, with ghastly condominiums and suchlike. The trouble is: he wants to build part of it on the crofters' common grazing land up by the

Bluff because it has the best views." He shook his head. "He would have to get a vote of approval from the crofters, and I can't see them ever agreeing to it." He sighed. "Nonetheless he seems pretty sure that he will get his way."

"When was all this going to become public knowledge?" growled Murdoch.

Alsdair shrugged. "No idea. Pretty soon, I would guess. I had the impression that he was keen to get going on the project as soon as possible."

Chris didn't understand. "What's all this about the crofters' grazing land?"

Murdoch stared into his glass of whiskey. "As well as having their own wee bitty piece of land, every crofter has the right to common grazing land for their cattle. The land is protected by law, and nothing can be developed on it without the crofters consent."

Chris nodded. There was so much he had yet to learn about the ways of the islands. The three of them sat in silence, staring at the fire.

"I think the crofters might be needing a little bit of help from someone they respect, someone who understands them." Murdoch looked up at Alsdair. "When Chris talked earlier this evening about going to Iona, it gave me the idea of inviting Brother Peter to the island early this summer. What do you think?"

"My old sailing buddy. Excellent idea."

"Who is Peter?" Chris was mystified.

"Brother Peter lives at the Abbey in Iona. He usually comes here to take over the kirk during the summer months when I'm too busy to lead it. We put him up in the old manse." Murdoch nodded at Alsdair. "That's how Alsdair got to know him. It turns out they both like sailing their wee boats."

Alsdair held up his glass and inspected the color of his whiskey. "Yes. He's quite handy on a boat for an old codger. Way too respectable, of course, but otherwise an excellent fellow. The villagers respect him hugely. Some think he's a saint. He probably is."

Chris was amazed that such a magnanimous verdict should come from someone who was normally so cynical.

Murdoch grunted. "Let's give him a ring." He paused. "And you, Chris, might use the opportunity to speak with Peter about visiting the abbey's library." He walked to Alsdair's desk and picked up the phone. Chris noted that he did not need to look up the number. They were obviously well used to talking with each other.

As Murdoch murmured into the telephone, Alsdair began to talk enthusiastically about the merits of sailing the Hebrides. Chris admitted that he had never been in a sailing boat.

Alsdair seemed genuinely appalled. "Not ever?"

"Never."

"Not even a small one?"

"No." Chris grinned at Alsdair's shocked face. "You make me sound as if I've got a communicable disease."

"Dear boy, you have. It is simply dreadful. Sailing has been the basis of our rich heritage of rape and pillage. You're completely disconnected with it. No, no..." he shook his head, "...such ignorance can't be tolerated." He pulled himself upright in his chair and signaled to Murdoch.

The gamekeeper raised his eyebrows.

Alsdair grinned at him. "I've just had the most brilliant idea. Tell Peter we'll pick him up in *Wanderlust*." He turned back to Chris. "How do you feel about sailing down to Mull with me in my boat to pick up Peter?"

That night, Chris pulled his laptop onto his knees, and began to type an email to his chess-playing nemesis, Dr. John Mullins from the New South Wales School of Medical Science.

Dear John,

I still regard your chess playing antics as reprehensible and totally consistent with anyone who supports the Swans.

You bored me silly with explanations of your research in Sydney, but I've remembered enough about it to think it might possibly be relevant to someone I've recently met. As you were no use to me at all with my damaged eye, perhaps you might be to her with your newfangled ideas.

I'll give you her doctor's name and address, and you can spy on her using doctor's privilege to see if there is any hope. I simply ask one thing. Do it quickly. Use email. There's quite a lot at stake.

Go the Adelaide Crows!

Chris.

P.S. Don't let cost be a problem. I'll cover it.

Chapter 9

Dear God, be good to me.
The sea is so wide,
And my boat is so small.
(Celtic prayer)

It was evident to Chris that a hangover was working its way inexorably through Alsdair's system when he arrived next morning to pick him up. They set off together and headed inland, before turning north to skirt the base of Beinn Bhreac, which rose steeply to their left. The clouds hanging in the valley turned the countryside into a mystical fairyland. However, it wasn't long before they were enveloped in cloud themselves, and the view was lost. They continued to climb higher through the cloying mist until they broke through the top of it into bright sunshine. An early shower of rain had left drops of water hanging like diamonds from the wire fences, and glistening on the leaves of wizened oak trees. Their gnarled, lichen-covered branches were flung out sideways, fleeing from the prevailing wind. Chris was enchanted.

By the time they trundled down the hill toward the village of Stein, Alsdair's irrepressible humor was starting to return. "I keep *Wanderlust* moored here for two very good reasons. First, because it provides a safe anchorage." He pointed ahead to a white building which had 'INN' painted in black, six-foot high letters on one end, leaving its function in no doubt at all. "And there's the other. That pub can serve no less than ninety different whiskeys. I'm told it also serves wonderful seafood meals, but honestly, they could serve what they like." He grinned. "I mean—who'd know after the tenth whiskey?"

They parked the car and made their way down to the foreshore. A pretty, blue-hulled sloop lay at anchor forty yards offshore. Chris was alarmed at its size. "How big did you say your boat was?"

"It's an Ericson 28; big enough to look after me, and small enough for me to handle on my own." He grinned. "Don't worry, she hasn't killed me in the six years I've been sailing her."

Chris was far from comforted by this revelation.

Alsdair retrieved an inflatable dinghy that had been tethered upside-down above the high-water mark, and rowed Chris out to the boat. When he climbed on board, Chris was mortified to discover that *Wanderlust* was even smaller than she'd looked from the shore.

Alsdair rowed back to collect the last lot of baggage from the shore, then they both set to, stowing the gear and getting the boat ready to sail. The mainsail cover was removed, and the sail winched up to the top of the mast. The foresail was then unfurled, and joined the main in shaking and banging in the wind. Alsdair asked Chris to pull in the anchor line as he started the boat's engine.

A moment later, the noise of the engine shattered the peace of the loch.

As *Wanderlust* edged forward, Chris pulled in the anchor chain until he was able to lift the anchor onto the foredeck. Alsdair winched in the mainsheet and the jib until both sails caught the wind, causing the boat to heel at what Chris thought to be an alarming angle.

Alsdair reached through the cockpit hatchway, flicked a switch, and killed the engine. Soon, only the gentle swishing sound of the boat moving through the water could be heard. Chris could feel the wind driving the boat forward like a living thing. It was an enjoyable sensation.

Alsdair pointed to two islands ahead. "We'll pass south of Isay and Mingay, and then aim for Dunvegan Head. If I've timed it right, the ebb tide will carry us south." He glanced at the sky. "With this northwesterly wind, we'll make good progress."

Chris didn't really understand what was being said, but nodded anyway.

Alsdair continued. "Why don't you slip down below and pour out some soup from the vacuum flask? You might also rustle up some cheese sandwiches. You'll find it easier doing it now than once we've rounded the heads. It'll get a bit bumpy then."

Not greatly encouraged by Alsdair's comment, Chris went below and busied himself making cheese and pickle sandwiches. He was staggered at how difficult it was to do even the simplest of tasks. Even pouring the soup, with the boat pitching and heeling, was an effort. His gammy leg made it even harder.

As he lurched against the oven, Alsdair looked down the hatchway and saw him. "Don't worry, Chris, we'll make a sailor out of you yet."

"Forget the sailor thing. I'll just be happy to survive!"

When they rounded Dunvegan Head, the seas became larger, but with the wind coming from behind them, they surged down the west coast of Skye at great speed. Chris watched the coastline with awe. It featured sheer rocky cliffs for mile after mile. Above the cliffs, green pasture led inland to a line of bracken and heather. This, in turn, gave way to the sparse upland vegetation of the mountains. When Chris pointed out the obvious dearth of safe anchorages along the coast, Alsdair simply smiled. "Yep, there's nothing safe until we pass MacLeod's Maidens, the rocks near Idrigill Point at the entrance to Loch Bracadale." He beckoned Chris to come over and sit beside him. "Now, come up here and get your first sailing lesson."

Chris affected an Oxford accent. "You misunderstood me, my

good man. I came on this voyage on the understanding that I would be balancing a Pimms delicately in my hand whilst looking out for porpoises and sea maidens."

"Move your bloomin' backside." Alsdair made room at the tiller and waited until Chris had settled beside him. "Sailing is easy. The further away from the eye of the wind you sail, the further out you ease the sail to catch it. Simply let it out until the front edge starts to blow in the wrong way, then pull in the sail until it flattens out again."

Chris was not at all comfortable taking the helm, but he did enjoy feeling the energy of the boat through the tiller. He sat alongside Alsdair on the high side of the cockpit, bracing his feet on the opposite seat. Both of them were now dressed in oilskins. Chris realized that it was as much for protection against the wind as the water. Just occasionally, *Wanderlust* dug her bow into a big sea, causing spray to sizzle through the air and drench them.

Alsdair reveled in it. "There's really only one rule to sailing the Hebrides."

"What's that?"

"Don't bump into anything. This isn't the east coast of England with its soft mud and sands. Here, it's all rock, and it's as hard as hell."

"I think I'd rather not know that."

"Well, you better know it because you have the rocks of An Dubh Sgeir a mile up ahead waiting to sink us."

Chris applied himself to the task and, although he would not admit it out loud, began to find sailing exhilarating. They sat in companionable silence, watching the endless parade of cliffs. Alsdair seemed relaxed and watched lazily through half-closed eyes, obviously very much at home on his boat.

Chris found the rugged beauty of the Hebrides touching a chord deep within him. The wild vista seemed to speak to him. He noted that the sea was greener here than the blue waters of Australia.

They had just passed the wide entrance to Loch Bracadale and were abreast of a particularly rugged piece of coastline when

Alsdair stood up, removed his woolen hat and formally saluted the coastline. Chris could see that a wide, green valley swept down to a shingle beach, beyond the craggy headland,

"What on earth are you doing?" asked Chris.

Alsdair did not respond straight away. He kept his pose for some time before deigning to answer. "That, my ignorant friend, is Talisker Bay, the home of the finest whiskey in the world."

Chris laughed. "May I congratulate you on the sobriety you've exhibited so far in this voyage, and venture to inquire how long I can expect you to maintain it?"

Alsdair staged affront. "Are you, in your coarse, antipodean way, casting aspersions on my proclivity for imbibing fine whiskey?"

"Yes."

"Aah." Alsdair favored him with a grin. "It may interest you to know that I don't drink whilst I sail. Only once we're safely moored."

"Then may I suggest you take a world trip: it might mean there is some whiskey left on Skye for the rest of us to tipple."

It was intended as humor but, after a lengthy pause, Alsdair said, "I do drink too much."

Chris said nothing.

Alsdair sighed. "And I'm drinking earlier and earlier, damn it."

"Is it beginning to get you worried?" Chris inquired carefully.

Alsdair passed a hand over his mouth. Chris was not sure if it indicated that he wanted a drink, or if he was trying to stop himself saying what he knew. "There are more alcoholics per square mile in the Hebrides than anywhere else in the world." He turned to Chris, his voice sounding harsh. "Did you know that?"

Chris shook his head.

Alsdair grunted. "I'm not in a hurry to join them."

There was a lengthy pause. Eventually, Chris asked, "What do you think you need to do to get the beast back under control?"

"Dunno." Alsdair forced a grin. "With any luck, it will be too late."

Chris didn't allow himself to be fobbed off. "Seriously?"

Alsdair sighed. "I imagine it would involve a lot of very tedious things."

"Such as?"

Alsdair said, irritably, "Oh, being accountable, I suppose. Doing something physical with my hands in the afternoons rather than just sitting with a bottle while I'm writing." He paused. "Afternoons and evenings are the worst."

"Well, mate, I reckon you're half way to getting it under control by admitting it." Chris slapped him on the shoulder. "All you've got to do now is put into practice what you said."

"Yeah. That's all, dammit." Alsdair reached down the hatchway, picked up some binoculars from the shelf and used them to study the sea ahead of them. "There's a nasty, rocky island just off Loch Eynort." He pointed, "See? Just below that peak, An Gruachin. Keep to the right of it. Once we've passed it, we'll alter course a few points to starboard and make for Kinloch on the Isle of Rum. That'll be quite enough sailing for one day."

"Right ho, skipper."

Alsdair busied himself taking transit readings between prominent objects on the shore, which he then plotted on the chart. Chris was bewildered as to why it was necessary. "Wouldn't it be simpler to take compass bearings?"

Alsdair pointed to the formidable mountain peaks on their left-hand side. "Do you see those mountains, oh ignorant one? They are the Cuillin Mountains, and are famous for two things. First, they kill poorly prepared hill-walkers. Second, they are magnetic—so compass bearings get totally stuffed."

"Oh!" Chris felt somewhat humbled. After a moment, his thoughts turned to their destination. "And what's the Isle of Rum got to commend it?"

"Very little. It's the most sparsely populated island in the Hebrides. For much of its history, it was simply a sporting estate where the over-privileged and over-indulged hunted red deer."

Two hours later, Chris could clearly see the white sand beaches of the north coast of Rum. With the last of the ebb tide beneath them, they made their way down the coast keeping far enough offshore to avoid the disturbed wind blowing over the top of Mullach Mor. Eventually, Alsdair gybed the boat, and they tacked up the dark green waters of Loch Scresort. They anchored just off the ferry terminal serving the tiny settlement of Kinloch. Once the sails had been furled away, Alsdair went below and returned with a whiskey bottle and two glasses.

"Good idea," said Chris. "But why don't we use the last hour or so of light and explore that place?" He pointed to an impressive castle built of red stone, which was decorated with turrets and colonnades. "What is it?"

Alsdair pursed his lips. "I hate the wretched thing. It's the folly of an Edwardian industrialist who had more money than sense. He built it in 1897 using a team of three-hundred craftsmen." He shook his head. "It cost eighteen million pounds in today's money—and that didn't include the cost of importing a quarter of a million tons of soil for the garden."

Chris looked on at Alsdair's outrage and burst out laughing.

"What are you laughing at?" demanded Alsdair.

"It's you," Chris said, struggling to stifle his mirth. "There you are: someone from one of the most privileged families on Skye, and yet you still manage to sound like a parsimonious Scot."

Alsdair pointed a quivering finger at the inflatable dinghy they had taken off the cabin roof and launched over the side. "Get in the dinghy, you profligate, hedonistic Aussie, and I'll show you what I mean. The blighter even built himself a huge automated organ."

When they finally got back on board *Wanderlust* after inspecting the estate, they cooked an evening meal, drank a single glass of whiskey, and wriggled into their sleeping bags. When the cabin light was switched off, Chris said in the darkness, "Alsdair, you know I'm about to rebuild my grandfather's cottage." He was rewarded with a grunt, so he continued, "If it will help, I'd be happy to have your company at the cottage in the afternoons."

For a long time, there was no answer. Chris was beginning to think he had not been heard, but Alsdair eventually said, "Thanks. I'd like that. I'll write in the mornings and work with you in the afternoons." He paused before adding, "Chris…"

"Yes."

"Don't let me off the hook."

Next morning, they set sail at seven-thirty, again catching the ebb tide that carried them south. Ahead of them, the forbidding bulk of the Isle of Eigg began to rise out of the sea. "What's your favorite place in the Hebrides?" asked Chris as he handed a cup of cocoa up to Alsdair.

Alsdair nodded his thanks. "For the most majestic cliffs, go to the Isle of Mingulay. For the best birdlife—particularly puffins, go to the uninhabited Shiant Islands between Skye and Lewis in the Outer Hebrides. However, if you want the prettiest island, go over there." He pointed to a dark shape on the horizon to their right. "That's the Isle of Canna. It's known as 'The Garden of the Hebrides.' We'll try and stop there on our way back."

Chris picked up the binoculars and weighed them in his hand. *It was designed for two eyes.* Experimentally, he put them up to his one good eye. The lens-piece banged against his eye patch. Eventually, he managed to focus them on the distant island. "And what's the nastiest place?" he said, with just a touch of bitterness.

"The most frightening sea is the Corryvreckan, the giant whirlpool off Islay. But the saddest place to visit is that island dead ahead, the Isle of Eigg."

"Why's that?" Chris swung around to study the island through the binoculars. "I can see beautiful white beaches."

"That's the 'singing sands' of the Bay of Laig. The quartzite sand squeaks when you walk on it. Kids love it."

"It doesn't sound too bad to me."

Alsdair pointed to the mountain peak toward the south of the island. "That volcanic plug is An Sgurr. It rises to a height of thirteen-hundred feet and it's sheer on three sides. But you can actually get up to it quite easily on the remaining slope. If you look due east from the top, you will see the town of Kildonnan, and the remains of the monastery built by St Donnan. He and his monks were slaughtered by a Pictish queen in 617AD."

"Yeah, I guess that would make it pretty sad."

"And if you look south-east to the coast, you'll see the place where the entire population of Eigg, some three hundred people, were murdered."

"Blimey! What happened?"

Alsdair sighed. "It was one of the many bloody sagas in the interminable feuding between the MacDonalds and the MacLeods. Some visiting MacLeods became too amorous with the local MacDonald women in 1566, so their men captured the MacLeods, tied them up and cast them adrift. Fortunately, they were rescued, but they returned eleven years later to kill everyone on the island. The locals saw them coming and hid in a cave called 'the Cave of Frances.' Its entrance was tiny and hidden behind a small waterfall. I've been in it. You have to crawl for about seven yards before it opens up into a huge cavern. Anyway, the MacLeods couldn't find anyone to kill, so they sailed away thinking the place was deserted. But an overenthusiastic MacDonald climbed a cliff to watch them sail away. He was spotted. The MacLeods returned and followed his footsteps in the snow back to the cave. They then blocked off the burn and built a fire at the cave entrance, killing almost everyone inside. Only one family escaped."

Chris was appalled and remained silent for a long time. "There's a lot of pain in the islands, isn't there?"

"Aye."

"Why would a man spit in my beer merely because I was planning to visit Morag?" He shrugged. "I asked Murdoch, but he wouldn't tell me."

"Forget it."

"Why?" insisted Chris.

"Why do you want to know?" Alsdair's tone was edged with aggression.

Chris closed his eyes to suppress his frustration. "Because..." He checked himself before saying in a more measured tone. "Because...it may impinge on me?"

Alsdair busied himself taking a compass bearing on An Sgurr. Eventually he said, "You're not thinking of getting romantically involved with Morag Daniel, are you?"

"No. We simply have..." he paused, searching for the right word, "a partnership."

"A what?"

"A business arrangement. One that will help look after Ruan."

"Oh." Alsdair relaxed slightly and said nothing for a long while. Finally, he pointed to a little island that was climbing from the horizon ahead of them. "D'you see that island?"

"Yes."

"That island rejoices in the singularly unfortunate name of 'Muck.' In the early nineteenth century, it had a population of five hundred. They were crofters for the most part, who made a living from cattle, fishing, and collecting kelp which they burned down to extract potash for the munitions industry." He paused to take a drink from his mug. "The land was always understood to be collectively owned, even though it technically belonged to the local Laird. Not much money changed hands for the simple reason there wasn't much around. Anyway, in the late nineteenth century, the Lairds and landowners discovered that their land would be much more profitable if they got rid of the crofters and replaced them with sheep. Whole villages were forced to emigrate—many to Canada, and the population of Muck fell to sixty." Alsdair passed a hand over his face. "It happened all over Scotland. It was called 'the clearances.' As you can imagine, feelings ran high."

"I still don't see what this has to do with..."

Alsdair held up his hand to forestall Chris. "The same thing happened in Skye. The Sheriff of Portree had to import fifty policemen from Glasgow to confront an angry group of men, women and children in the Trottenish who defied them with sticks. The protesters were soon overpowered, and five of them agreed to be taken to court for a token trial. This eventually led to the government passing the Crofter's Act of 1866, which gave crofters some protection. But by then it was too late. Generations of families had been forced off the land."

"But..."

"Morag's great-great-grandfather plotted with a local Laird, Angus Crenshaw, to dispossess the local crofters of their land.

Evidently, he did it for money." Alsdair grimaced. "It didn't do him any good, however, as Daniel killed Crenshaw when the two of them fell out." He shook his head sadly. "Daniel himself died in a fire just afterward. He'd probably lit it himself to camouflage his suicide." He shrugged. "The Daniel family has been hated ever since."

"But that was over a hundred years ago!"

"That is but yesterday to a Scot. We take our feuding very seriously."

Not much was said for the next two hours.

Alsdair edged *Wanderlust* around the cliffs of Ardnamurchan and entered the Sound of Mull—the narrow stretch of water that separated the island from the mainland. Mull's north coast was characterized by similarly rugged cliffs to those of Skye. The only difference Chris could see was the presence of some pine plantations.

As the last of the ebb tide gave out, they crept into the little port of Tobermory on the northeast coast. As they prepared to anchor, Chris asked, "How come you know all this stuff about the islands?"

"Because my first book was about my meanderings around the Hebrides in this boat."

"Really! What was it called?"

"Promise you won't laugh?"

"No."

Alsdair looked skeptical. He straightened himself up and said with exaggerated dignity, "It was called *Notes From Some Quarrelsome Islands*."

"Given what I've learned, I think it's a brilliant title."

"Really?"

"Yes, but I've just about had my fill of mournful Hebridean tales." Chris looked around at the delightful harbor, and the colorful splash made by the different colored houses crowding the foreshore. "At least you haven't regaled me with a jaundiced tale of this place. It's beautiful."

"Oh," Alsdair said, brightening. "I can fix that."

Chris groaned.

"Yes, indeed. It happened like this. In 1588, a Spanish galleon, the *Florenica*, fled north to escape being ravaged by Sir Francis Drake. Unfortunately, it was ravaged by a storm instead and had to put into Tobermory. The captain negotiated with the locals for provisions to allow them to sail back to Spain. However, the local Laird promised he would give them provisions only if he could borrow some Spanish soldiers to help him rampage around the island, stamping his authority. But once that was done, the captain discovered that the provisions were still not forthcoming, so he captured a local dignitary and held him to ransom. When the provisions were finally delivered, he let the local go, but not before the resourceful man had set a fuse alight in the ship's powder magazine." Alsdair chuckled. "The locals had the satisfaction of lining the cliffs to watch the *Florenica* get blown to smithereens."

"Geez, mate! What is it with you Scots?"

Alsdair grinned. "Word is, the ship was loaded with three-hundred-thousand pounds worth of gold bullion. The locals have been looking for it ever since."

Chris laughed in disbelief. "Why on earth would an invasion ship be carrying three-hundred-thousand pounds worth of gold bullion?"

"Don't spoil a perfectly good story."

Alsdair chose to anchor *Wanderlust* within easy reach of the town's pier. Once all was secured, he grinned. "Now, let me tell you about the local distillery."

Next morning, they woke to discover that the wind had veered to the northeast, straight off the Russian Steppes, It was bitterly cold. They set sail in a fresh breeze, stormed out of Tobermory harbor, and headed for the narrow gullet of the Sound of Mull. The mountains of the mainland loomed to the left, and the heights of Speinne Mor on Mull looked down at them on the right. Alsdair pointed to Mull's coastline. "Up there somewhere are the Bronze Age 'standing stones' of Ardnacross."

"Never heard of it." Chris was huddled low to keep out of the wind.

"You truly are a cultural desert, Christopher. But on this occasion I'll forgive you, as there actually isn't very much to see. There are plenty of better ones around. The islands are positively littered with them. The best are the Callanish Standing Stones on the Isle of Lewis. They're four-thousand years old."

Wanderlust suddenly heeled over sharply. Alsdair snatched the mainsheet out of the cleat, spilling wind out of the sail to bring the boat upright again. Chris lay sprawled in the bottom of the cockpit.

"Sorry about that," said Alsdair. "The Sound acts a bit like a wind funnel, so these gusts are not unusual. Grab the binoculars and see if you can spot Eileanan Glasa. It's a tiny island up ahead, and its worth avoiding."

They sailed on for three hours, but Chris found it exhausting work. The lively motion of the boat, and the constant need to play the mainsheet in and out, had taken its toll. His leg had stood up to the rigors of the last two days surprisingly well, but it was now beginning to ache.

Alsdair steered *Wanderlust* between a line of islands that straddled the Sound. One of the islands sported a lighthouse. Up ahead, Chris could see the stolid gray form of Duart Castle sitting on its rocky headland.

Alsdair pointed to a tiny rock in the distance off the port bow. "If you look over there, you will see a tiny rock with a squat little navigation light on it. That's Lady Rock."

"Unusual name," commented Chris. He realized too late that he had provoked Alsdair into another travelogue. "Oh no!"

"Oh yes. A scandalous tale, this one." Alsdair was almost salivating. "Lachlan MacLean married the Earl of Argyll's daughter, Elizabeth, but she failed to provide him with a son, so in 1523 he marooned the unhappy woman on that rock, knowing it would be covered at high tide and that she would drown. As luck would have it, she was rescued by some fishermen from Tayvallich who took her up Loch Fyne to her father's castle." Alsdair rubbed his hands together.

"The villainous husband, dressed in black, then visited his father-in-law bearing a weighted coffin containing, he said, the body of his wife who had died of disease. He was received with dignity to the great hall where he was shocked to see his wife in remarkably good health, sitting next to her father." Alsdair grinned. "Not wishing to fracture the Scottish code of hospitality, Argyll at least waited until Lachlan completed his journey to Edinburgh before having him murdered."

Chris shook his head. "You are all quite mad."

Alsdair edged *Wanderlust* toward the village of Craignure. The town, thinly spread around the bay, boasted no outstanding feature, but nonetheless looked inviting. Alsdair pointed to the shore. "There's a narrow gauge railway which runs from Craignure up to Torosay Castle beyond that point. You can just see it." He screwed up his face in distaste. "All very touristy."

Alsdair guided *Wanderlust* past the modern terminal where the Oban ferry docked and edged her over to the old stone pier. Chris could see lobster pots littered along the top of it. They looked for all the world as if they'd been discarded in haste by fishermen anxious to get across to the Craignure Inn that stood above the foreshore. Alsdair dropped the mainsail, and switched on the engine. As Chris stood on the cabin roof, lashing down the mainsail, he noticed an elderly man with long white hair walking across toward them from the inn. He arrived as they breasted gently against the old stone pier. The man caught the bow line that Alsdair threw to him and, once he'd made it fast, he stepped aboard the boat.

"Hello Alsdair," he said, shaking his hand. "Good to see you again. How was your trip?"

"Remarkably civil, thank you Peter—notwithstanding a troublesome lack of whiskey. In fact, I've never had such an abstemious voyage, due largely to this chap, Chris Norman, an Australian. I was always led to believe the felons of the antipodes could be relied on to engage in all things riotous and alcoholic." He turned back to Chris.

"Chris, may I introduce Brother Peter, theologian, sometime sailing companion, and full-time mind reader. Be careful."

Brother Peter shook Chris's hand. "Welcome to Mull. It's good to meet the voice on the phone. I must say: your story about the

Celtic cross intrigues me. But come. Let's get you to Iona where you can have a warm bath, and a hot meal."

After *Wanderlust* was made secure, they squeezed into Peter's car and set off west. Chris was hard-pressed not to doze off inside the well-heated car. He came awake only when Peter provided occasional commentary.

"We get a lot of hikers and bird-watchers in the summer. They come to spot our golden eagles and, believe it or not, our owls." Chris tried to express interest but soon slumped back in his seat, half asleep. Alsdair was fully asleep, snoring quietly in the back seat.

Chris was jolted awake when Peter had to brake hard to avoid hitting a stray sheep. Peter smiled apologetically. "And how are you going, Chris?"

Chris was surprised at the question. No one had asked him such a thing before. With rather more honesty than he intended, he replied, "Not real good."

Peter nodded. "Then I hope your stay with us will help. Do you know much about Iona?"

"Um, no. Sorry!"

Peter gave a deprecating wave. "Please don't apologize. I don't expect it's on the curriculum of many Australian schools." He paused before continuing. "Iona has been a key center for Christianity in Scotland for about fourteen centuries."

Chris was hard put to imagine how any place so obviously remote could be key to anything, but he said nothing.

Peter drove along the beautiful shoreline of Loch Scridain until they arrived at the village of Fionnphort. There, they were ushered down the slipway onto the ferry that took them across the one-mile stretch of water to the island of Iona.

They rolled off the ferry, and drove up into the village. Peter continued his commentary. "The island has a population of just one hundred and seventy. We don't really cater for tourists. Most come here to be refreshed spiritually."

They drove along a narrow street lined with tiny stone cottages nestled together in an untidy line. A Post Office sat on the downhill side of the road, identified only by a round red sign. A red Post

Office pushbike leaned against its wall. Chris thought it was probably a fair indication of the leisurely pace of life on Iona.

They turned north past Bishop's House, with its serried rows of chimneypots and dormer windows, and drove out toward the Abbey. Sheep grazed as they had done for centuries in pastures bordered by dry-stone walls.

The buildings of the Abbey complex soon appeared.

Peter pointed out its features. "The whole place was renovated in 1938." He pointed to what looked like a stone barn that stood a little apart from the main building. "That's Oran's chapel."

Chris's attention, however, was focused on something else. There, set casually on the neat, grazed grass, stood a number of tall, stone Celtic crosses. He shook his head. *These have to be the real deal.*

Peter seemed to pick up on his interest, for he said, "We have a number of Scottish kings buried here." He pointed to one of the crosses. "That's the replica cross of St John. The real one is inside the Abbey museum. All the others are authentic."

The car came to a halt, and Chris shook Alsdair awake. Peter led them into the main building. "I'll take you to your rooms so you can leave your bags, then I'll take you to meet the warden. Later on, we'll eat in the refectory. You'll be joining a group that is here for a retreat." He turned to Chris. "After that, I'll take you to the library. Oh…" he paused. "There's a brief service of *compline* in the Abbey at eight if you want to join us. It's entirely up to you."

A short time later, Peter conducted them through the cloisters toward the Warder's residence. A bronze monument of what looked to be a giant lotus bud sat in the middle of lawn at the center of the cloisters.

A short time later, they were chatting with the Warden, a genial man who simply introduced himself as David. The Warden handed each of them a glass of sherry and said, "I understand, Chris, that you have come to use our library; and that you, Alsdair, have come to kidnap Peter, and take him back to Skye by rather unconventional means."

"'Tis true," said Alsdair. "We thought we'd keep up the noble tradition of Viking pillaging—something, I understand, you have been well used to over the years."

The warden laughed. "Look after Peter for me. He's our chaplain, and I want him back in good order." He settled back in his chair and looked at Chris. "Do you know what we do here?"

"Not really."

"We are a community that offers spiritual retreats and resources for the wider church. Anyone can come."

"Anyone?" Chris said, surprised.

"Yes. It means that we have to sit delicately in the middle of a number of groups that would like to take ownership of us. First there are the fundamentalists who have commendable zeal but can lack a bit of grace. Then there are the liberal revisionists who want to strip Christianity of everything that gives hope, in order to pursue their pluralist agenda. And finally, there are the New-Agers who want to mug our Christian heritage, and re-badge our cultural symbols so that they become pagan."

Chris was not sure he understood all that he heard, but he got the gist of it. The Warden reached over to his desk, picked up two CDs and gave one each to Chris and Alsdair. "Let me give you a copy of our latest CD. It contains songs of prayer and meditation—simple stuff, mostly unaccompanied. There's even one to pray whilst you are milking a cow." He smiled. "Celtic Christians are a pretty earthy lot."

When Chris finally had a moment to himself, he elected to walk across the grass to take a closer look at the ancient Celtic crosses in the field outside. As he began to inspect them, he was conscious of a faint stirring deep within him. It was as if he was remembering something he had forgotten long ago. It had something to do with... what? He sighed. It was something to do with identity and meaning, but he wasn't sure. Whatever it was, he wanted to embrace it, but it was elusive and kept slipping away...leaving him only with a profound sense of sadness.

His reverie was disturbed by Peter, who wandered across the grass to join him. He stood beside Chris in silence for some. Then, without any introduction, he began to speak.

"Long ago, there was an Irish prince, a man driven by fierce ambitions and a fierce temper. In fact, his temper provoked a war with a neighboring king in which many men lost their lives." Peter paused before continuing. "This young man then discovered the love story of the Christian gospel, and heard about a God who died on a cross to win him back to himself. Mortified at his past behavior, the prince vowed to lead to faith at least as many men as he had caused to lose their lives in battle. He took twelve men with him and sailed to this island, where he built a monastery." He turned to Chris. "The man's name was Columba, and his monastery was responsible for spreading Christianity throughout Scotland and much of England." He reached out and touched the old stone cross.

Chris said slowly, "I had no idea."

"Hmm. In those days, Christianity was locked into a titanic battle with druidism. This was not the garlands-in-the-hair, tree-hugging, nature-worshippers that are portrayed today. It was grim stuff involving human sacrifices and a lot of fear. Christian kings would ride out and do battle against druidic kings. When they lost, they would come to Iona, lick their wounds, and then sally forth again and continue the fight. Eventually, the great druidic kings, Penda and Cadwallon, were defeated in the seventh century."

"I didn't know that Christianity was so old here. I sort of assumed it came much later."

"No." Peter traced the patterns on the stonework with his finger. "Christianity came to England very early. It was carried here by Christians from the monastic tradition. St. Ninian was one of them. He lived on the Isle of Whithorn in the Solway Firth during the fifth century." Peter smiled. "Come on. Let me take you to the refectory."

As they moved off, Chris asked, "Why did you tell me the story of Columba?"

"Because this ambitious firebrand became so changed as a result of his faith, that he later earned the nickname, "The Dove." Peter placed a hand on Chris's shoulder. "Nothing has to stay the same, Chris."

After dinner, Peter conducted Chris to the library. When they arrived, he pointed to three piles of diaries stacked on the end of a long oak table. "Arthur Daniel was a brother of this community, and those are his diaries." He smiled. "I hope you find what you are looking for." Then he left.

Chris sat down on a chair and stared at the diaries he had traveled so far to see. These were the writings of Morag's great-uncle, a member of a disgraced family who fled to Australia to escape the demons of his family's past. These could also be the writings of the man who had owned the Celtic cross now hanging around his own neck.

Chris had learned from his earlier research that Arthur Daniel probably had contact with the Aranda people in 1965. He began to search through the pile of diaries. Most of them had the same battered blue cover on them. It was obviously a style he liked.

Extracting the diary for 1965, he opened it and began to read. It was very soon apparent why these diaries had been so prized by those studying Aboriginal anthropology. Alongside Arthur's neat cursive writing were careful pencil drawings of headbands, necklaces, belts, and weapons used for hunting. They were extraordinarily detailed.

Chris flicked through a couple of diaries quickly to see if any section looked particularly promising. In the end, he found what he was looking for when searching through the diary for 1967. It came in an account of Arthur Daniel's tussle with the medicine man of a tribe of the Arrernte-speaking people. He described with obvious frustration how he would arrive at camp to discover that the medicine man would immediately order the tribe to break camp and move elsewhere. Or he would call a meeting of the tribe's elders to discover that the medicine man had called a meeting at the same time. This continued until the medicine man's son became critically ill with an infected wound. None of the medicine man's herbal remedies or incantations managed to heal it. Finally, in desperation, the medicine man asked for Arthur Daniel's help.

Arthur gave the boy a huge dose of penicillin and followed it up two days later with another. It was enough to turn the tide, and the boy lived. The incident caused the medicine man to ask about

Arthur Daniel's God. When told about him, he simply nodded and said, "I have always known of his existence. But now I know his name."

Arthur Daniels wrote joyfully, *"Even though my father had told me never to part with it, I gave him my Celtic cross, and said to him, 'Give this cross to your son, and instruct him to give it to his son. Never let this day be forgotten.'"*

Chris sat back in his chair. So there it was. The riddle was solved. Arthur Daniel had been the owner of the cross. And now the cross had come full circle, and arrived back home. As he sat there wondering at the vagaries of history, the faint sound of singing could be heard coming from the abbey. Looking at his watch, he realized that *compline* must have begun.

Chris got up and made his way outside, but instead of going into the abbey, he walked out into the moonlit night and across the pasture, until he was again standing beside one of the ancient crosses. The sound of singing could be heard clearly. A moon shadow, cast by the cross, touched him gently on his shoulder.

At breakfast, Chris learned that Alsdair had elected to spend the previous afternoon walking over to the west coast of Iona to inspect the 'spouting cave' and to admire the white sands of the beaches. This uncharacteristic behavior was the result of a conversation he'd had earlier with the raven-haired beauty who had served them dinner.

"Her name is Elizabeth," Alsdair enthused. "She's a doctor's daughter from Abingdon, doing voluntary work as a cook before she begins teaching next year. I've persuaded her to show me the sights."

"You're a cradle-snatcher who needs your backside kicked."

"She's only six years younger than me."

Eventually, it came time for them to leave. The Warden drove Peter, Chris, and Alsdair back to Torosay where *Wanderlust* bobbed in welcome at her mooring.

Chris remembered the rigors he'd endured on the voyage down, and was concerned whether Peter would cope aboard *Wanderlust*. He held out a hand to steady Peter as he clambered aboard.

Peter smiled. "Don't worry too much about me, Christopher. I've been sailing boats off and on for most of my life…" He nodded to Alsdair, "…sometimes with this reprobate here." He chuckled. "The only thing I might need to request occasionally is that we heave to so that I can use the heads. I'm not as gymnastic as I once was."

Chris considered his weak left leg and wished he'd thought of asking Alsdair to do the same on the voyage down.

The return voyage to Skye was fairly much a repeat of the voyage down. The only difference was that they needed to set sail later in the day to catch the flood tide that would carry them north. This gave them the opportunity to explore their ports of call in the morning before they set off. The wind had obligingly backed around to the southwest, giving them a favorable point of sailing that enabled them to make good progress.

Alsdair chose to return by a similar route, except that he elected to put in to the small island of Canna rather than Rum. Chris's growing confidence in *Wanderlust*, caused him to believe that he might actually survive the voyage after all—and perhaps get back to the village in time to begin teaching Ruan. His home schooling program was due to start in two days' time. Surprisingly, he found himself looking forward to it.

Chris watched the basalt cliffs of Canna deepen in shadow as the sun began to set. He shivered, and wondered at the wisdom of sailing a small boat near rocky islands at night. He was pleased to discover, however, that navigating at night was actually easier than navigating during the day. The waters seemed to abound with navigation buoys. Each had its own distinctive color and flashing pattern, which made identification simple.

As they crept through the darkness into the tiny harbor of Canna, Alsdair parodied a tour guide.

"Welcome to Canna, ladies and gentlemen, one of the few rat-free islands in the Hebrides. To the west, you will find the remains of Bronze Age round houses, and to the south, the tiny island of Sanday. It has a beautifully restored Roman Catholic church that has probably the most bizarre tower in all of Scotland. Perched precariously on a magnificent plug of stone to the east, you will find the ruins of An Coroghon castle. An eighteenth century Laird imprisoned his daughter in it to preserve her chastity." He pointed to the north. "Over there, you will find Magnetic Mountain, which has been playing merry hell with my compass for the last two hours. Enjoy your stay."

Chris woke late next morning, refreshed. After a leisurely break-fast, Alsdair announced that he would stay on board and draft a literary masterpiece for Elizabeth. Peter invited Chris to walk with him to see the remains of an old stone cross that stood in the grave-yard of the old church of St Columba. They took the inflatable to the shore and hauled it up the beach.

Together, they walked across the pasture, scattering sheep as they went to inspect the church.

Peter looked up at its thin pencil-like tower. "This is actually a relatively recent building modeled on an ancient Celtic design." He pushed through the door, and the two of them stood for a moment soaking in the building's tranquility. "Columba brought a particu-larly beautiful Christian faith to Scotland. It accommodated the culture of the time, but remained authentically Christian." He smiled. "It was something that our later missionaries might have done well to emulate."

"Perhaps it is a good job they didn't have to be missionaries, then."

"But they were. They sent missionaries from here to England, Germany, and as far afield as North Africa. Their simple lifestyle and scholarly wisdom made them very effective."

"How come I've never heard of them?"

"Sometimes the real history-makers leave their marks in ways we don't see. Did you know that the Book of Kells—so prized by the Irish, was actually written in Iona? It was only later that it was smuggled to Ireland to keep it safe from marauding Vikings."

Chris did not own up to the fact that he'd never heard of the Irish Book of Kells.

As they turned to go, he was amused to see that the offering plate at the door was actually a collection tin for the Royal National Lifeboat Institution. He commented on it.

Peter smiled. "An eloquent testimony to the link between the church and the sea in these parts."

They trailed up a path behind a lonely phone box and made their way up a narrow laneway toward an elegant, two-storied guesthouse. As the path wound through a belt of trees, Peter ventured, "I imagine the last few days have prompted a bit of thought, Chris."

Chris limped behind him. "Yes... but I'm not sure that I can make much sense of it. I've never had to think much about God before. I always thought we were masters of our own destiny."

"Hmm. If there is nothing bigger than us to believe in, we are indeed destitute."

"Why couldn't the universe just fluke itself into existence?" said Chris defensively.

"To believe that the universe came from nothing, is maintained by nothing, and means nothing, takes more faith than I'm capable of."

Chris shook his head. "No. I think that life just *is*, and you just have to get on and make the best of it."

Peter remained unruffled. "I think life is an invitation to seriously think about why we exist. To lazily shrug your shoulders and say it is all too difficult, is a totally inadequate response to the miracle of existence. If there is meaning to life, then each of us is accountable for how faithfully we have sought it out. So don't be lazy." He paused and pointed ahead. "There, take a look at that."

The remains of a Celtic cross stood within a wooden fence, presumably erected to keep the sheep from rubbing against it. Only the right arm of the cross was left in place. It stuck out from the central column as if pointing the way. Chris moved forward and began inspecting the carving on the stem. A tangle of horses and other animals had been carved into the stone.

Peter said, "This guy obviously thought his faith important enough to live for."

"Or was he just a fool living in a time when superstitions were rife?"

Peter smiled and said nothing.

The old man's calmness in the face of the cruel realities of life caused Chris a flash of irritation. "Why did God allow me to be blinded in a plane crash, so that I can't fly? And why did an innocent man have to die trying to rescue me?"

Peter nodded slowly, then he drew a deep breath. "There are no easy answers to the question of suffering. There's much that remains a mystery."

"There you are, then. Life is just a cruel joke."

Peter shook his head. "Not quite. There are some things we can know. God has, for example, given us free will to accept him or reject him; to care for his creation, or mess it up." He sighed. "Unfortunately, we've rather messed things up."

Chris nursed his hurts and said nothing. He saw Peter looking at him, and had the disturbing impression that he was seeing into his very soul.

Peter continued. "The good news is that God will not put up with the imperfect state of things forever, and has set a time when he will make all things new. In the meantime, he promises to be with us in our suffering to give us strength, and to empower us to do something about it whenever we come across it." He ran his hand over the arm of the cross. "It's not the whole answer, but it's the best one around."

Chris looked at the battered cross and didn't know what to think.

He did, however, feel a strengthening resolve to carry out the absurd plan he had in mind.

Chapter 10

Marry an island woman and you marry the island
(Celtic proverb)

The biting east wind rippled the shaggy coats of the highland cattle. Chris was amazed by their stolid indifference to the Hebridean weather. Three of the long-horned cattle were grazing fifty yards in front of him as he leaned on the stone wall that marked the end of his croft. Beyond him was the common grazing land. It rose up to the gorse and heather-covered hills.

Chris had walked to the end of his property early that morning to inspect the dry-stone walls and check their condition. To his delight, he discovered that they were not only sound but had been superbly made.

His musings were interrupted by the sound of loud banging. Hamish's wife, Elspeth, was summoning her two house cows for milking by belting a saucepan with a wooden spoon. Chris wondered which cow had belonged to his grandfather. He limped back along the low stone wall until he was adjacent to Hamish's byre. Chris climbed over the wall and walked over to the old stone building. By the time he got there, Elspeth had just finished milking the first cow. Its calf was tethered to the wall outside, cavorting in frustrated excitement at the prospect of drinking some of the milk from its mother. Elspeth came outside with a bucket, and the calf was soon sucking from it greedily.

She nodded to Chris before returning through the door to milk the second cow. Chris followed her inside. Steam rose from the flanks of the cow as it stood with its head pushed through the bars of the manger. Elspeth sat on her stool, pressed her forehead against the cow's side and, with a skill honed by decades of practice, began milking. Thin, high-pressure squirts of milk dashed against the bottom of the metal pail. At the far end of the byre, Chris could see the somnolent form of Percival the pig, dozing in his pen. Elspeth gave no indication that she had noticed Chris's arrival until she had finished milking. Without turning, she said, "So, it is yourself, Christopher. Now what would you be wanting?"

"G'day Elspeth. One of these days you'll have to teach me to do that."

"You can take this job from me any time you want." She laughed as she turned to inspect Chris as he leaned on his new walking stick. "Will you not come in for a strupak? I asked Hamish to put on the kettle afore I did the milking." She gave a tired smile. "He's after hearing everything I say, but once he's in his armchair, he pretends to be deaf. No doubt but I'll have to do it meself. Come away in."

Chris looked at the lowering clouds that were beginning to spit with rain, and accepted gratefully. Inside, they found Hamish snoring in the armchair in front of the hearth. Chris wondered what he might have been up to the previous night that had made him so tired in the morning.

Drops of water began to drip down from the chimney onto the stovetop in front of him, sizzling and dancing for a few seconds before vanishing. A sharp prod in the shoulder from his wife soon had Hamish awake. Ten minutes later, they were enjoying a strong brew of tea and companionable, if slightly careful, conversation.

"I was glad to see that the dry-stone walling on my grandfather's croft is all in good condition," Chris said.

Hamish sipped his tea and smacked his lips. "It'll be in a darn good state fifty years from now, I doubt."

"Hamish repaired most of the walls," Elspeth explained. "He makes the best walls hereabouts."

"Aye, my father were a hard man. He pushed down the first wall I made...and I vowed he'd never be able to do it again." Hamish fished into his jacket pocket for his pipe. "I build strong walls."

Chris was thoughtful for a while. "Hamish, my guess is that you've not got a lot of spare money to pay for leasing my grandfather's croft."

Elspeth caught her breath, and Chris realized he'd guessed correctly.

Hamish watched him with a guarded expression. Chris kept his expression carefully neutral. "If you help me build three yards of wall in my remodeling of my grandfather's cottage, we'll call it quits. What do you reckon?"

Hamish drew on his pipe and regarded Chris through the haze of smoke. "Mebee." He stabbed the stem of his pipe at Chris, "If we do, we work together mind. I dinna want to do all the heavy lifting myself."

Chris nodded. "We work together. I'm mainly looking for your skill, not your brawn. I'll do as much of the heavy work as I can."

Hamish looked at Chris's walking stick and frowned. Chris smiled. "Relax. The leg is getting stronger each week. I reckon it'll be pretty right in a month or so, with all the exercise it's getting."

Hamish grunted.

"I've got another proposition for you."

Hamish looked at Chris with a frown.

"If you give me some of the potatoes, milk, and the occasional poached trout, you can continue to farm my land for no rent at all, as long as we're both happy."

Hamish took the pipe from his mouth. "By poached, you'd be meaning how you cook it, I suppose?"

Chris looked him straight in the eye. "Of course."

Hamish nodded slowly. "Christopher, I'm thinking you'll make a fine islander."

Chris smiled, looked at his watch and saw that he was due to take over Ruan's lessons from Morag in ten minutes. He thanked Elspeth and Hamish for their hospitality and made his way back to his car. Pausing, he surveyed the beauty of the loch and the patterns on the water left by scuffs of wind. The guillemots were wheeling and calling just off the cliffs, having been disturbed by a distant, muffled boom from the quarry. It was, he decided, an extraordinarily beautiful place. But could it be home?

He had given some thought to his first lesson with Ruan. The previous evening, he'd searched through the discarded debris of the estate that was hidden behind the stables. There were two rusted car bodies overgrown with a tangle of weeds, and a collection of antiquated electrical items. He'd managed to salvage twenty yards of enamel-coated wire from an electric motor, an old telephone handset, and a discarded TV antenna. It was most of what was needed to make a crystal radio set. Chris was confident the project would capture Ruan's imagination, and hopefully motivate him to undertake more mundane tasks such as learning his multiplication. He wanted to reward Ruan with an interesting project every time he achieved a learning goal.

Even so, he was quite apprehensive when Annie opened the door, and ushered him down the hall. He saw Morag cross quickly from the kitchen into her study. Before he called out to ask how the morning had gone, Annie whispered, "Storm warning, laddie."

Chris stepped into the study. "How's the schoolmistress?"

Morag rounded on him. "Don't you 'schoolmistress' me!" Her hands were on her hips. "What on earth do you think you are doing, meddling with my life?"

Chris took an involuntary step back. Morag glared at him. The fiery red hair flowing over her shoulders, reminded him of a painting he'd seen of Joan of Arc leading her troops into battle. She looked sensational.

"Er, anything in particular?" he ventured.

"I've had a phone call from a Dr. Hardy at the North East England Stem Cell Institute based at Newcastle University."

"Aah, that." Realization dawned.

Morag clenched her fists and held her arms down by her sides as if trying to stop herself from exploding. "He has invited me to Newcastle next week." She clenched and unclenched her fists. "Next week!" she shouted indignantly. "He said he'd learned about my case from you, via a research doctor in Sydney."

"That would be true," Chris admitted slowly.

"How dare you! And what about Ruan's schooling? How dare you meddle with my life?"

"Morag," Chris said, seeking to placate her. "I'm half blind. Of course I'm looking at new advances in eye research. And of course I'm going to explore it for people who... I will be working closely with." There was a strained silence. He tried again. "Look: if it were Ruan who was blinded and you heard of a possible technique that might restore his sight, you'd move heaven and earth to explore it, wouldn't you?"

"That would be different."

"In what way?"

"I love Ruan, and I'm his official carer," she shouted.

Chris swallowed. "Then at least allow me to...care, if only for Ruan's sake. His ability to stay with you might depend on you getting some of your sight back."

A storm of emotions played across Morag's face. All of a sudden she dropped her head and started to weep. "Don't you think I'd love to see again? It's taken four years to get used to not seeing, to stop hoping. I...just haven't got the courage to hope any more."

Chris stepped forward, drew Morag to his chest, and stroked her hair as she sobbed in anguish. He desperately hoped she wouldn't push him away. "Yes, it will take courage to hope." He felt her warmth against him. "If you can't bring yourself to hope, will you at least allow me to?"

After a few minutes, she pulled away from him, turned around and leaned both hands on the desk. Chris watched as her slim body begin to shudder and heave as she wept.

Instinctively, he laid a hand on her shoulder. She waved him away. Chris recognized that it was as much an act of apology as a plea not to fuss.

He watched on helplessly as she struggled to regain some sort of composure.

After a moment, she said, "What about Ruan's schooling? I would have to be gone for at least a week."

"I'll organize someone suitable to deputize for us both. The best way of getting you to Newcastle will be in my car, so we both need to go." He shrugged. "Having caused you this trauma, I owe it to you to help you through it."

Silence hung between them for some time. At last, Morag said quietly, "Go and teach Ruan."

Two hours later, Ruan was experimenting with the crystal radio he had just made with Chris. Ruan carefully moved a nail up and down the flanks of a wire coil that had been wound around a plastic bottle. Chris watched as Ruan listened into the telephone receiver. Suddenly, the boy bounced up and down with excitement. "I can hear something!" Ruan listened again. "It's music."

Chris breathed a sigh of relief, and explained: "This was the sort of radio that prisoners-of-war made secretly in the Second World War. It doesn't require any power, so it was pretty handy."

"It's grand, is this," Ruan enthused.

"That's the end of your first science lesson, mate. I've got to go now."

Morag did not come out of her study when Chris left the house.

Morag sat hunched over in her office chair, thinking deeply. Conflicting emotions flittered through her heart. All of them disturbed her. Seeking solace in work, she dragged the keyboard toward her and began to write another song for Wozza. She'd entitled it "*Wild Woman*," and it came surprisingly easily.

I'd learned to hate, but you spoiled my day.
  You've made me see there is a better way.
  All this, of course, has been a pain,
    'Cos it's easier to hate than to hope again.

Wild woman…you've kinda spoiled my life
  And laid me open to your loving strife.
  I wish I was strong and could walk away,
  But now I wouldn't have it any other way.

Wild woman…

Chris felt he needed some safe, undemanding male company to get over the emotional challenges of the morning. He bought some fish and chips from Jessie at the village shop, and made his way to Alsdair's cottage. Chris was treated to an irreverent welcome.

"Hello, scabrous, scurvy knave. How's me old shipmate?"

"Recovering." Chris held up the package of fish and chips. "Lunch for two. Put the coffee on."

"Brilliant." Alsdair bounded over to the kitchen and began to fiddle with the coffee machine.

"You're looking pleased with yourself."

"I am, dear boy, I am." Alsdair twirled around, doing a few waltz steps with an imaginary partner. "Love is in the air."

"Oh dear. Tell me the worst."

"I refer, of course, to the dark and deliciously sultry Elizabeth." He twirled once more. "We were star-crossed lovers, destined to meet that day in Iona."

"More moonstruck than star-struck, I'd say. Do you have any evidence that she feels as loopy about you?"

"She has been responding to my emails." Alsdair grinned.

"An email does not 'a match in heaven make.'"

"You are being uncommonly boorish, old chap," Alsdair said. After a pause, he smiled, almost shyly. "Actually, I do think she's pretty terrific. She's actually..." He struggled to find the word. "... so very good." He waved in frustration. "You know... wholesome, and, um, totally captivating."

"Good! Wholesome! Is that the best you can come up with? Fie! And you a wordsmith!"

"I know, I know," Alsdair protested "But we got on so well." He grinned sheepishly. "I hardly needed to show off at all."

"Then it must be love." He paused. "Have you got any tomato sauce?"

"On fish and chips?"

"Yes."

"Peasant." Alsdair was quiet for a moment. "The thing is: I'm trying to find a way of inviting her here, but I can't think of how to do it without frightening her." He smiled. "You know: by making her think I'm a dirty old man devising a cunning plot to seduce her."

"Don't tell me you don't want to."

Alsdair gave Chris a withering look, and handed him the tomato sauce.

Conversation turned to Chris's altercation with Morag that morning. Chris rubbed his forehead. "I wish I was certain I was doing the right thing."

Alsdair patted him on the shoulder. "You sure play for high stakes, Chris. I'll say that for you."

Chris grunted.

Alsdair looked thoughtful. "How would you describe Morag's life now? Is it good or bad?"

"Pretty awful, I think."

"Do you think she likes it like that?"

"No."

"If that's the case, she has to change her situation. Simple."

The brutal logic of Alsdair's reasoning was undeniable. Chris thought about it for a while and then said wearily, "Thanks mate. But the problem is: I don't want to change it for the worse."

Alsdair munched on his chips in silence. However, after a minute, a grin creased his face. He thumped the arm of his chair. "Did you know that Elizabeth is a teacher?"

"Um, I think you did mention it."

"Well then, why don't you ask her to teach Ruan for the week you're away? If she stayed in the White House with Annie and Ruan, it would all be kosher—and she and I could spend some time together." Alsdair walked over to his computer and brought up his emails. A few seconds later, he was stabbing Elizabeth's phone number into his mobile phone.

"Whoa, whoa. Wait!" Chris protested. "Give me a moment to think."

"No way!" Alsdair said, grinning. "I've got a vested interest in this." He turned away and was soon in animated conversation. After a few minutes, he nodded and handed the phone to Chris. "She wants to speak to you."

Chris cleared his throat. "G'day, Elizabeth."

Half an hour later, Morag heard a knock on the door. Annie must have heard it too because she shouted, "Can you get that, Morag? I'm up to me elbows in pastry."

"You should have gone home two hours ago, Annie," Morag yelled as she got up from her desk.

"For why would I be home when there are things to be done here? My home is dampty empty when my man's out fishing in his boatie. Dinna fash yourself."

Morag pushed Bess out of the way with her knee, and opened the door slightly.

"Morag, sorry to bother you again."

It was Chris. He sounded tentative. Chris continued to speak. "I've got Alsdair Haines with me. I suppose you two know each other?"

She nodded. "He used to pull my hair at primary school."

"In revenge for you being better at schoolwork than me. Hello, Morag." Alsdair paused. "My, but seeing you now, it's difficult to imagine you were ever a gawky kid."

Morag recognized Alsdair's voice. "Oh, Hello. Come in. Mind the dog." She opened the door fully.

As they walked down the hall to the study, Annie called out to them. "Ach, and how is it men know to come when biscuits are in the oven? You'll need to wait ten minutes."

Inside her study, Morag leaned on her desk and tried not to allow the anguish of her last encounter with Chris to resurface. She was only partly successful. Implicit in Chris's initiative was a level of care, the possibility of…what? Ruan was, of course, the main reason for Chris's caring, and yet…she remembered how he'd touched her hair.

She tried to hide her stormy emotions behind a composed face, and waited for someone to speak.

Chris spoke; giving a brutal summation of the situation. "Alsdair's fallen in love with a girl called Elizabeth who's working as a volunteer at Iona. She's filling in time before she begins teaching in September. Elizabeth may be interested in coming here to teach Ruan and, in the process, to check that Alsdair really is too old and lecherous for her to be interested in him."

Morag could hear Alsdair's sharp intake of breath preparatory to a protest, but Chris continued. "However, she won't even contemplate the possibility until she's had a word with you." He paused and then added in a gentler tone, "If Alsdair and I take ourselves off to the kitchen, will you ring Elizabeth and see what, if anything, you are both comfortable with? Alsdair will tell you her number."

"It's not as it sounds…" Alsdair began.

Morag held up a hand to forestall him. "What's the number, Alsdair?"

Alsdair told her.

Morag then ordered the two men into kitchen.

She picked up the phone and dialed.

A young, fresh voice answered. "Hello. Elizabeth speaking."

Twenty minutes later, Morag made her way into the kitchen. Alsdair immediately began spluttering, trying to talk, probably with a mouth full of biscuit. She waved him into silence. "Elizabeth sounds lovely."

"She is," enthused Alsdair.

Chris shushed him into silence.

Morag cleared her throat. "And we had an honest girl talk about things I will not divulge." She reached forward and searched for the mug of tea she'd heard Annie place on the table. Chris guided her fingers to where it stood.

"And?" demanded Alsdair.

Picking up the mug, she announced, "Elizabeth arrives mid-afternoon in two days' time to check us all out. She'll be staying with me."

Alsdair gave a whoop of triumph.

Even as she said it, Morag was aware of a small pang of anxiety. She'd been on her own so long. She dropped her head forward to hide her face and hugged the mug of tea to her chest. It was therefore both heart-warming and mortifying to feel Chris brush against her hair and whisper, "Don't think for a moment that I don't appreciate what this decision is costing you, Morag. Thank you." His breath on her cheek...

Further thoughts were interrupted by Annie. "So it's a houseful we're getting at last, is it?" She banged her beefy hands together in approval. "Ach, but it's a sad house with only women's knickers on the line."

Morag aimed an exasperated look at her, not that she had any confidence Annie would heed it.

No one seemed to notice, and Morag was content to allow the ebb and flow of conversation around the kitchen table to ease her into a world of new possibilities. It had been a very long time since she had been part of anything like it.

She heard Ruan come bursting into the kitchen, followed inevitably by the skittering of JJ's feet. Amidst the clatter and banging, she heard Chris bark at Ruan, "Three times seven."

"Twenty-one."

Chris shot back, "What could you use for a crystal radio aerial if you couldn't find one from a TV?"

"A long bit of insulated wire. The longer, the better."

Ruan countered Chris's questions with one of his own. "When's the best time for shore fishing?"

"Sunrise or sunset on a high tide," said Chris. "A full moon or new moon makes it even better."

"You're catching on." Ruan scampered off, banging his way through the back door.

She heard Chris exhale slowly. "Cheeky blighter."

"Cheeky!" said Alsdair. "And this from a man brazen enough to enter my house and beat the crap out of my brother with his walking stick."

Morag caught her breath in shock. Alsdair continued on blithely. "He was magnificent. Crude; certainly. Effective; absolutely." He grinned. "But probably not the first choice of anyone seeking a model for civilized behavior."

"What went on?" she asked with alarm.

Alsdair was only too willing to tell her. He reported the altercation between Chris and his brother Jason with, what she hoped, was a liberal dose of poetic license.

Chris felt the need to interject occasionally to correct the worst of his exaggerations. Even so, she was shocked by what she heard.

She toyed with her empty mug. *There's certainly more to you, Chris Norman, than flowers.*

"I would love to know what the blighter was really planning," Alsdair said.

"Ach, the young Laird is ever wanting more than he's got. His pockets never seem to be big enough for his dreams." Annie sniffed. "Mind, he's been pretty good this year at not insisting we pay our rent on time."

This comment was met with silence. Annie appeared not to notice, for she sighed and said, "Well, I'm away off home. Don't forget your supper this time, Morag."

Morag nodded her thanks, but was slightly alarmed to hear

Annie whisper, "And you, Christopher, try to let your feet catch up with your shoes."

Annie banged the back door and clumped off to her house.

"I, um, am not always sure what…" began Chris…

Morag suspected that she understood Annie's allusion only too well. She quickly interrupted. "What do you think Jason is up to?"

"Yes," said Alsdair. "My thumbs are pricking. Something isn't right. I can't believe that Jason's apparently casual attitude to rent is accidental."

After a moment of silence, Chris said hesitantly, "Do you think Jason is letting crofters get in debt to him so that they will be forced to vote him the rights to develop the grazing land on the Bluff?"

Alsdair didn't answer.

Morag dragged her thoughts to the issue at hand, pondered things briefly, and said, "Being casual about rent is not in Jason's character. I should know. I rent this house from him, and I've always found him to be a stickler for prompt payment." She paused. "However, I find it difficult to believe he would do something like this. It would be a terrible abuse of the island traditions and the crofters' trust. I simply can't believe he'd do it."

"He trashed my cottage," Chris said.

"He damn near trashed me," complained Alsdair. "In his defense, I think he's got some fairly big money problems. That probably means he needs this project to work."

Silence hung between them for some time. Eventually, Morag said, "Chris, I think you should tell Murdoch about what might be occurring. If he can warn people not to get into debt to Jason, it might all blow over and come to nothing."

Chris cleared his throat. "Yes. Of course."

"Meanwhile, I'll make some inquiries of my own, and ask Annie to winkle some more information out of her husband." She was surprised to feel Chris give her hand a quick squeeze of encouragement.

It was a good feeling.

Next morning, Morag taught Ruan his eight times tables, and had him read from a book of legends from the Western Highlands. Although she enjoyed the stories as much as Ruan, she couldn't prevent her thoughts from wandering and taking her to places she hadn't dared to visit for years. She found that she was looking forward to Chris's company when he came to take over the teaching from her. He had such crazy ideas that, whilst impossible, did at least show a level of care. She told herself that this care was directed more toward Ruan than herself. Nonetheless, she was content to live in its shadow.

Twenty minutes later, she caught herself sitting at her desk with the study door open, eavesdropping on Chris and Ruan in the kitchen. She loved how their talking was so often punctuated with laughter.

Her musings were brought to a halt when the computer in front of her beeped, telling her that a new message had been stored on her voicemail message bank. It was from Wozza.

I like it, darlin'. You've gone a bit nice in this one, but I fink we'll do it. It's got sumfink special. So, whatever you're doin', keep it up…as I'm tryin' to do whenever I get the chance!

Wozza

Morag smiled. She knew that, in reality, Wozza was not as wild and promiscuous as he affected to be. He was devoted to his girlfriend.

She turned her thoughts to the task at hand. It was an unfamiliar one—and a surprising one given the way she'd been treated by the local community. She pondered the irony of it. So much had changed in the last few weeks. She sighed and began to apply herself to the task of how she might best protect the welfare of the crofting community. After some minutes of careful thought, she picked up the phone and put a call through to the Crofting Law Group at the University of Strathclyde.

Morag heard Elizabeth arrive in the afternoon of the following day. Elizabeth's restrained knocking might well have gone unnoticed had it not been for Bess' barking.

Morag opened the door, smelled a pleasing perfume and felt a confident handshake. She then surprised herself by saying, "May I hug you? I so enjoyed our phone call, and I will know you better if I do."

Elizabeth stepped forward and embraced Morag gently. As she did, she said, "I have long black hair, brown eyes and olive skin."

Morag continued the description. "And you are about five feet six inches tall, size twelve and have boobs that probably attract too much attention."

"Close enough," Elizabeth laughed. "Now tell me, am I a complete lunatic for coming here?"

"No," said Morag. "You're a much-needed fairy godmother, and you ought to check out the man who is besotted with you. What did you do to him to wreck him so quickly?"

Elizabeth's laughter was deep and husky. "I think it was because I didn't actually do anything at all—didn't have the chance. We had less than a day together. I just found him incredibly easy to talk to." She paused. "It may not come to anything, but I think I'd regret it if I didn't take the chance to check him out." She put her hands on Morag's shoulder. "Promise me you'll tell me anything you feel a girl should know about him—however vile."

Morag laughed. "I can honestly say I know of no dark secrets. Alsdair is basically a good man, great fun and, I suspect, very clever. But if I discover anything, I'll tell you."

"Great. I've brought some pâté, cheeses, and a bottle of red wine. I hope that's okay."

"Thanks. That's lovely." Morag smiled. "Come on, let me show you to your room and then I'll make a cup of tea."

As they climbed the stairs, Elizabeth asked, "Tell me about Ruan. How are you getting on with teaching him?"

She got no further. The kitchen door banged open, and Ruan hurtled into the hallway with JJ scampering and barking behind him. "Morag! Morag! Can I go fishing wi' Hamish tomorrow? He says I gotta ask you first, so I…" He skidded to a halt.

Morag could tell by the silence that Ruan was appraising the stranger.

"What fish are you trying for?" asked Elizabeth.

Morag smiled. In an instant, her misgivings about how the two of them would relate evaporated.

Chris had spent a tedious afternoon driving around Portree, searching out every building site he could find. He had a simple question for the men at each location: "Who are the most reliable, quality-conscious builders in town?" He quickly discovered that he needed skill and tact to frame the question so that he received a truthful answer. Chris needed to negotiate the usual human vices of suspicion, impatience, self-interest, and a natural tendency to 'take the mickey' out of a foreigner. After visiting five building sites, the name of a father and son building team cropped up on three occasions.

"The McCormacks. They're both ower religious and won't work Sundays, but they do good work," said the elderly foreman of the last site he visited. "They're not cheap, mind."

Chris stopped at the Post Office and looked up the McCormack's phone number. Mrs. McCormack answered his call and invited him around to the house. If he came at six, her menfolk would have returned by then. Chris kicked his heels for an hour at the docks, watching the boats come and go until it was time to visit Jack McCormack and his son Tom.

When he finally met them, he discovered that father and son looked extraordinarily alike. Both were stick-thin and dark-haired, and both wore the same expression that bespoke a serious Protestant work ethic. In the next twenty minutes, Chris used his computer to introduce both of them to a totally new way of building houses. They were intrigued. Chris had anticipated a brief initial visit, but he was asked to stay for tea. As a result, he didn't get back to Murdoch's cottage until late.

Chris walked into the parlor to see Brother Peter and Murdoch deep in conversation by the fire. Occasional downdrafts caused puffs of wood-smoke to curl into the parlor and mix with the pungent smell of Murdoch's pipe.

Chris made them all a fresh pot of tea, and then drew up a kitchen chair to join them by the fire. He turned to Peter. "How are you settling in at the manse?"

"I'm very comfortable, thanks. The parish have provided a new mattress mercifully, and hung new curtains in the kitchen." He accepted the mug of tea from Chris with a nod. "Murdoch has supplied me with wood for the fire, and I've been given the use of an old Land Rover from the estate."

"'Tis little enough, considering you offer your services for free," growled Murdoch.

The three of them sat in companionable silence, content to be mesmerized by the flickering flames of the fire.

Chris broke the silence. "Murdoch, can I share with you a concern that Morag, Alsdair, and I have about Jason Haines?"

Murdoch lifted his head sharply. "Aye."

"Morag has asked me to recruit your help to ensure that the interests of the crofters are protected." Chris went on to outline the suspicions of Morag and Alsdair, and the reasons for them.

Murdoch regarded Chris with his gray eyes and listened intently. At the end, he nodded. "Tell Morag I'll do what she's asked."

"Murdoch, there's something else."

"Aye?"

"It concerns my fight with Jason. Jason will know I'm staying with you, and he is the Laird of the estate you work for. I don't want the consequences of my behavior to wash up on your shore. So, I want to move out of here and find rented accommodation in the village."

As Murdoch digested this, Peter asked what had happened.

Chris briefly recounted the incident in Alsdair's cottage.

Murdoch sucked on his pipe. "Dinna fash yourself, Christopher. My job's safe enough."

Peter shook his head. "That's as may be, Murdoch, but there would be no harm in you being seen to be more independently positioned. It could even be useful." Peter turned to Chris. "Why don't you stay with me and use the other bedroom in the manse?" He smiled. "In truth, I'd welcome the company."

Murdoch leaned back and, after a few moments, nodded his approval. He jabbed the end of his pipe toward Chris. "No one in the village would be compromised if you stayed with Peter. It's a good plan." He smiled. "Besides, you've just about repaired everything that's needed repairing around here." He got up and kicked the fire into life. "And you'll find Peter a fine host. I should know."

"How's that?" Chris asked.

"Because Murdoch stayed with me when he was studying for the ministry."

Chris's mouth dropped open in surprise.

"Yes, indeed. He was a student at the theological college I lectured at." Peter smiled. "Quite why I lost my best student to gamekeeping is a mystery I've never been able to solve."

As neither Peter nor Murdoch volunteered any more information, Chris didn't pursue it. He simply said, "Thanks Peter. I'm grateful. I'll go and pack my things."

The Cherokee purred along the narrow bitumen road that wound its way over the top of the moors to Loch Snizort Beag and Portree. Chris could see the network of deep drainage channels between the peat hags and the occasional straight channel that marked the crofters' peat diggings. In the distance, clouds boiled around the mountain peaks of Creag a'Lain on the Trottenish peninsular. They looked spectacular. He stole a glance at the woman sitting beside him, and wished with all his heart that she could share the experience.

As the hours went past, they threaded their way through the

Scottish mountains toward Edinburgh. Chris had booked two rooms in a bed-and-breakfast just outside of Edinburgh. It would give them an easy journey to Newcastle the next day.

He had not expected the level of intimacy he felt sitting next to Morag in the car. Indeed, he was a little overwhelmed by it at first, but by the time they had passed Invergarry, he was comfortable enough to chat freely. And once they had passed Dalwhinnie, he was content to sit in the silence, enjoying her presence.

However, he knew the peace could not last. He'd got this outrageous idea. The issue that now plagued him was whether or not he should share it. He moved restlessly in his seat until Morag confronted him.

"What's on your mind, Chris? You've been squirming in your seat for the last twenty minutes."

The moment had come. Would he dare broach the subject, or forget it? He took a deep breath. "Sorry Morag. It's just that I've been trying to work out how to tell you about a crazy idea I've got." He was silent again for a few moments as he thought how he could broach it.

"For goodness sake, what's on your mind? Tell me. I won't bite."

Chris sighed and wished he could be as sure. Seeking to gauge the amount of room he had to maneuver, he asked, "What do you think of men?"

He saw the impact of his question on Morag from the corner of his eye. Her mouth opened in shock, and her hand instinctively began reaching for him. A puzzled look of uncertainty creased her face. Then she compressed her lips together, pushed herself back in her seat, and hugged herself with her arms.

For a moment, Chris thought she would not answer, but at length she said, "I have difficulty trusting them."

Chris swallowed, and pressed on. "You've no ambitions to marry and have a family?"

In a chilling voice that broke his heart, she replied, "I'm damaged goods, remember."

"I'm sorry Morag. I didn't mean to hurt you. I just...I just wanted to know if you had any, um…ambition to be married. You are still…very beautiful."

Chris could see that his questions had caused Morag to retreat into her old self.

He heard her say harshly, "Marriage! No, of course not."

Silence hung between them uncomfortably. Finally, Morag appeared to soften because she added quietly, "Although, of course, friends like you and Murdoch will always be important to me."

"Friends?"

"Yes."

Chris nodded and was silent for a while, before continuing. "My mother walked out on me when I was twelve. I don't think long-term, happy marriages are actually possible." He looked at Morag and lied, "I don't think I want to get married either."

It would have been a true enough statement three weeks ago.

Morag shook her head in irritation. "What are you getting at, Chris? Spit it out."

Chris sighed. "Okay. You want Ruan to stay with you. If he does well in his education assessment—you at least have a chance. And if you get your sight back, it will improve your chance." Chris licked his lips. "But only one thing will guarantee your custody of Ruan."

"What's that?"

"If we get married."

"*What?*"

Chris hastened on. "Of course, we wouldn't really be married. You'd keep your own name, and we'd live in separate houses, and there would be no wedding rings or anything, but legally we could be married." He paused. "It would solve your problem, because you don't really want to get married, at least not properly, and neither do I. So let's get married and make your custody of Ruan certain."

The idea was absurd. Chris realized it the moment Morag burst out laughing.

She shook her head. "No ring, no honeymoon, no loving, no shared home? Oh, you sweet-talking thing. Your proposition is irresistible to a girl."

"But we'd be friends."

"Friends?"

"Friends."

Silence hung between them for several long minutes. Eventually, she said, "Surely people would find out?"

"Not if we got married in the registry office in Edinburgh, with their staff acting as witnesses."

"Don't you have to give notice of these things?"

"Yes. I've researched it. If we call in to the registry office, we can fill in a marriage notice form, and leave it with them. We will need to come back between fifteen and ninety days later for the ceremony. Hopefully we can co-ordinate that with another visit to the eye specialist in Newcastle."

Morag nodded slowly. "So this was why you asked me to bring my birth certificate? It was for the marriage notice, not the doctor."

"Yes."

They bypassed Perth on the ring road and were soon on the M90, speeding south to Edinburgh. Morag reflected on the tousle-haired boy that always fell asleep on her lap before she'd finished telling him his bedtime story. Then her mind returned to Chris. She could feel him beside her—the edge of his coat brushed against her thigh. *His idea is absurd, insane, yet...yet...tempting—for Ruan's sake. Yes, Ruan—it is for Ruan. Chris would never be far away. Oh, it's madness! But it's attractive—very attractive. I just don't want to lose...* She took a deep breath and said quietly, "You'll find the registry office on Victoria Street, just off the Royal Mile between St Giles Cathedral and the Castle."

By anyone's definition, Dr. Hardy was rotund. He was also genial, and had obviously enjoyed the unconventional way Morag had been brought to his attention. Chris and Morag were seated in front of the desk in his office. It did not look like a consulting room—more like the study of some academic.

Chris could see the folder containing copies of Morag's medical records lying open on the doctor's desk. After rifling through it, Dr. Hardy closed the file, put his hands together, and began to explain.

"Miss Daniel, before I can say that we have any chance of returning at least some of your sight, I will need to anesthetize your eyes and examine your damaged corneas with an eye microscope. If what I see looks promising, I'll probe the rim of your corneas and scrape off some tiny samples in order to examine them. Do you have any questions?"

Morag shook her head.

Chris watched as Dr. Hardy guided her through the door into the eye surgery. She was looking pale and forlorn. He put his head in his hands in a storm of emotions, and waited.

Twenty minutes later, the door opened and the doctor escorted Morag back to her seat. Chris looked at her anxiously. Her face was expressionless. Dr. Hardy walked around the desk, eased his bulk into the seat and put his hands together, as if in prayer. His hands nodded as he spoke. "I'm pleased to say that I've managed to find a few live stem cells from the edge of Miss Daniel's cornea."

"What does that mean, doc?" asked Chris.

"It means that her cornea is not completely dead. However, the question remains as to whether we can find enough stem cells to give ourselves a chance. That will be the crucial thing." The doctor leaned back. "What I am hoping to do is to harvest any remaining stem cells from the cornea and grow them in the lab in a solution of insulin, hydrocortisone and some of Morag's own blood. If all goes well, these cells will grow on a thin sheet of amniotic membrane which I will transplant onto the surface of her eye." Unable to repress his enthusiasm, Dr. Hardy continued, "The amazing thing we have discovered is that the new layer of stem cells seems to trigger the eye's natural regeneration of its damaged surface, so that it grows new, robust cells of its own."

"Will this work for Morag?" Chris found it difficult to contain his impatience.

"Possibly. I've found a live stem cell. What I now need to do is give Morag another local eye anesthetic and shave off some more stem cells."

"When will you do this?"

"Now, if Morag will let me."

There was a stunned silence.

Morag nodded her assent and stood up. Chris stood up beside her. "What happens afterward?" He hardly dared to believe there was hope.

"Morag comes back in three weeks, I apply the amniotic membrane to her eyes and bandage them up. And," the doctor said, smiling, "with any luck, when I remove your bandage eight weeks afterward, Morag will be able to see."

Chris felt Morag shudder. She turned around, clung to Chris's lapels and sobbed and sobbed as if her heart was breaking. Chris held her against his chest and allowed the grief of years to be brutalized by hope.

He held her for a long time, nuzzling her hair, relishing the feel, and hating the cause of her tears. Eventually, he helped her back into her seat so that she could compose herself.

It was evident, however, that Dr. Hardy was not yet finished. Chris saw the doctor extract a file from under Morag's that, he was amazed to see, had his name on it. The doctor cleared his throat. "I'm afraid you don't escape, Christopher. My colleague in Sydney, Dr. John Mullins, has sent me your file. So, whilst I attend Morag here, you have an appointment at the ophthalmic hospital…" He looked at his watch. "…in twenty minutes. They are waiting to measure you up for a prosthetic eye." He smiled. "You'll discover that we've made quite a few advances in the area of ocular prostheses as well."

Chris's mouth dropped open in shock.

Dr. Hardy continued. "So, leave Morag here with me and pick her up in two hours' time." He paused. "Dr. Mullins has also instructed me to say something rude to you about crows. I've no idea what that means."

Chapter 11

Twelve highlanders and a bagpipe make a rebellion
(Scottish saying)

C hris wasn't sure whether he loved it or hated it. The small, capped pipe sticking up from the ground looked innocuous enough. It certainly didn't look much, considering it had cost him eleven thousand pounds. Cody and his massive drilling rig had driven off the previous day, leaving this tiny, capped bore-head in the middle of a muddy quagmire behind the cottage. Nonetheless, it did represent a significant triumph, considering that the project had only been given a seventy-five per cent chance of success.

Professor Ewen Edmondson had warned Chris that, although South Australia was a 'hot rock haven,' the same could not be said of Scotland.

Chris had heaved a huge sigh of relief when Cody managed to find a hot aquifer in sedimentary rocks two-hundred and twenty feet deep. The water in the aquifer was heated to a balmy twenty-two degrees Celsius by an underlying layer of volcanic rock.

170

Chris knew he'd been very lucky. Warm water could now be pumped up and fed through a network of pipes embedded in the concrete slab of his new house to provide heating.

In the past two weeks, he and Alsdair had carefully removed all the slate from the roof of the old house so that it could be resold. Then they had taken the stone gables from the top of the end walls and dismantled either end of the front wall, leaving the middle section standing vulnerable and unsupported. The two of them were now building a temporary bracing for the wall with lengths of timber.

"It doesn't look much like a renovation to me," said Alsdair, sucking a bruised thumb. "More like a demolition. What, exactly, are you planning to do?"

"What I'm effectively doing is surrounding the old cottage with a new house. Three sides of the old outside wall will now become internal walls. I'm building a new external wall three and a half yards out from the old stone wall." He patted the bulky wall. "The mass of the enclosed stone wall will act as a heat regulator, keeping the temperature constant inside." He pointed with a hammer. "The floor space of the old cottage will become the new living/dining area, and this will be extended to a big window in the new front wall to allow more light. A study, bedroom, and bathroom will be added to the eastern end. An entrance porch, kitchen and store room will be built at the back, and the main bedroom and en-suite will be at the western end."

Alsdair slapped his neck. "Blast it! That's the first cleg this summer."

"Cleg?"

"Horsefly. Wretched things. They terrorize you in early summer; then the midges take over in midsummer." He fingered the insect bite carefully. "Early evenings on still days are the worst, and if you wear dark clothing—the midges really go for you."

"I can't help thinking you might have told me this before I decided to stay in Scotland."

"My dear chap, you have not even begun to learn the dark

secrets of this place. They have caused the Scots to flee and become the flotsam and jetsam of the world."

Two weeks of intense physical activity followed. It was long enough to impact on the physique of both men. Chris was now free of his walking stick, and the excess weight he had carried since his time in hospital was falling away. Alsdair, already quite lean, was beginning to bulk up—a fact that delighted him. Not that he admitted it. Instead, he complained at length of tiredness and thirst, and of being driven like a slave.

Chris showed no sympathy at all. "Your pathetic whining is absolutely symptomatic of the malaise that caused you Scots to be consummately thrashed by the Wallabies this season."

A watery sun broke through the clouds and began drying the puddles left by the recent rain. The two men set about pegging out string lines to mark where the new wall foundations would go. It was just as well they did. The contractor arrived before lunch in a low loader carrying a mechanical digger. He unloaded, and immediately set about digging the trenches, expressing confidence that he would be finished by nightfall. Chris hoped he was right as he had planned to work with Tom and Jack McCormack next day to lay down insulation for the slab and footings. Everything was now moving fast. Chris sighed. For better or worse, his building project was under way.

"Would either of you gentlemen care for some tea and a bit of Annie's shortcake?" Chris turned around at hearing Elizabeth's purring voice. She was not alone. Morag was arm in arm with her, carrying a basket.

Chris had rarely seen Morag venture outside her home. He was conscious of feeling instant delight. Her trim figure was again squeezed into jeans and a high-waisted tweed jacket. *She really does look fantastic. Delicate yet strong; demure yet regal; fiancée yet not fiancée.* He was aware of a bitterness that surprised him. Ever since the emotional turmoil of Newcastle and their decision to enter into a marriage of convenience, conversation between them had been strained and careful. Chris shook his head. It was as if each was waiting for the other to say something important.

Alsdair, in contrast, was full of enthusiasm. He gave a whoop of delight, bounded over to Elizabeth, kissed her roundly on the cheek. Then he took the basket from Morag and began unpacking its contents.

Chris rested a plank between two trestles, and the four of them ate their lunch in the sunshine.

"Where's Ruan?" Chris asked.

"Helping Hamish paint the bottom of his boat. He's asked me to find out when he can help you start building your house."

"He can start tomorrow. We'll be laying the plastic membrane over the foundation trenches, and then we'll start wiring in the reinforcing rods." Chris found himself looking forward to having Ruan with him in the afternoons. Other than joining him in a couple of fishing trips with Hamish, he'd not spent much time with him outside his teaching time.

Morag smiled. "Ruan's dead keen. You'll have your hands full."

"I'll manage." Chris turned to Elizabeth. "I thought you were meant to be going home today."

Elizabeth dropped her head. Morag spoke up for her. "Elizabeth doesn't need to begin teaching until September, so she's decided to stay a bit longer and play things by ear. I certainly love having her with me…and her help with Ruan is indispensable."

Chris detected something slightly conspiratorial between the two women, but didn't comment.

"And of course, she can't drag herself away from my charms." Alsdair draped an arm around Elizabeth's shoulders. He'd aimed at bravado but sabotaged the effect by the softness of his voice.

It wasn't lost on Chris.

Elizabeth regarded Alsdair from under her long eyelashes. "Hmm. We'll see," she said enigmatically.

"Anyway," continued Alsdair, "you can't go yet. I've invited my mother, Marianne, over to meet you. She's flying over from Paris just as soon as she can."

"I take it your mother doesn't live with your father, the old Laird, then," Chris said.

"It's a bit complicated. They've never actually divorced, but for the last fifteen years Marianne has chosen to live in her family's château in Champagne-Ardenn. She's French."

"Sounds pretty exotic."

"Tragic, more like," Alsdair said, grimacing. "She married my father when he was in his mid-fifties. She was twenty-four years old at the time, and recovering from a broken engagement. They should never have married."

"Are you fond of her?" asked Elizabeth.

"Very much," admitted Alsdair. "She chose to move back to France only after I'd started at boarding school. I go across and stay with her when I can."

"You'd better tidy up your place before she arrives, then," warned Chris. "It's singularly 'bachelor,' at present."

"No need," Alsdair said. "Crofters' cottages aren't really the thing for beautiful French socialites. She'll be staying in her room at the manor. She only visits occasionally, but it's always kept ready for her."

"When will she be coming?" Morag colored slightly as she continued. "Chris and I will be away in Newcastle again seeing medical people in five days' time. I wouldn't like to miss her. I saw her once when I was little. She was the most beautiful person I'd ever seen."

Alsdair looked at Elizabeth. "Are you able to stay for another three weeks?"

Elizabeth searched Alsdair's eyes. "Yes."

Chris could smell the smoke from Brother Peter's pipe in the still air as he opened his car door. Walking around the manse, he found Peter seated on a wooden bench on the front porch. He was looking at the view down to the village and the coast. The silhouette of distant islands could be seen in the gathering twilight. Above them, stars glittered like jewels in the night sky.

Awakened from his reverie, Peter looked up. "You look dog tired, Chris. Have you eaten?"

"Not yet. I've brought back some sausages. What about you?"

"I've already eaten. Why don't you sit here and let me get dinner for you? By the look of you, I think you could do with a wee rest." He took the sausages and busied himself inside. Fifteen minutes later he emerged with a plate of fried sausages, potato, and tomato.

"Fantastic," Chris said. "Thanks."

When the meal was over, they were both content to nurse their mugs of tea and look out across the spangled night sky.

Chris said, "It's hard not to wonder about the universe when you see the stars like this."

"Aye. True enough."

"But it's all just the product of chance, evidently—we're one of an infinite number of universes."

Peter shook his head. "Ach, have you never read the famous physicist, Stephen Hawking?"

Chris frowned.

Peter continued. "At the start of his book, *A Brief History of Time*, he tells of a woman who interrupts a scientist, saying, 'You are wrong, young man. The universe is not as you describe it. The earth is really a large plate resting on the back of a giant turtle.' 'And what is the turtle standing on?' asks the scientist. 'Young man,' the woman replies, 'You can't trick me. It is standing on another turtle. There are turtles all the way down.'"

Chris smiled and nodded his understanding. "She doesn't answer the question. There's always the mystery of what the last turtle is standing on."

"Precisely." Peter drew on his pipe. "You can't explain the existence of our universe simply by saying that there are an infinite number of them. The potential for life and the laws of nature must originally have come from somewhere." He jabbed the stem of his pipe at Chris. "Life is the journey of making sense of it."

Chris looked down and saw the dirty dinner plate by his feet. Bachelor food. Would he still be a bachelor in a week's time? The thought that he might soon be technically married was surreal. What did he feel about it? He pondered the question. He certainly didn't feel that he was throwing his life away. In fact, he had to admit, the idea had an appeal that he couldn't fathom. It was all very strange. He shook his head to clear his mind, but couldn't stop thinking about Morag. He wondered for the millionth time what she felt about it all. *Am I being fair to her?* Surely someone as lovely as Morag should be allowed to have a real marriage.

He conjured up a mental image of her from the previous night. He had watched as she wrapped a warm towel around Ruan, hugging him to herself as he stepped from the bath. She deserved someone who would hold the towel for her and wrap her in it and… Again, he shook his head. Seeing Peter sitting calmly beside him, he blurted out the thoughts that pressed on him: "Pete, would it be wrong for me to enter a marriage of convenience in order to allow Morag to continue having custody of Ruan?"

There was a moment's silence. "Perhaps you'd better tell me the details."

Chris drew a deep breath, and did so.

When he'd finished the story, Peter said nothing for a long while. He then recharged his pipe and leaned back. "Let me tell you another story." The end of his pipe glowed in the dark as he sucked at it. "Have you heard the story of Huckleberry Finn and Tom Sawyer—and how they agreed to become blood brothers on the banks of the Mississippi?"

Chris nodded. "I think so."

"You might be interested to learn that the blood brother ceremony has a basis in history. In the Bronze Age, the strongest bond that could exist between two people in the Middle East was something called a 'blood covenant.' During the ceremony to become a blood brother, you exchanged coats, signifying that you would share everything. You exchanged sword-belts, signifying that you would protect each other. An animal was cut down the backbone, and you walked between the two halves in a figure-of-eight pattern, signifying unity. You even shared names so that you incorporated your partner's name in your own. Finally, you cut your wrists and let your blood mingle together. This signified that there could be no covenant without a cost."

"Why are you telling me this?"

"Because thousands of years ago, God entered into a blood covenant with humankind through a man called Abram." Peter shrugged. "Of course, God didn't have a coat or sword-belt, so he simply told Abram that he would protect him. He then told him to change his name to incorporate a syllable from his own name, Jehovah—the 'ah' sound."

"So he became Abraham."

Peter nodded. "That's right. And the shedding of blood was the ceremony of circumcision." He drew on his pipe again. "You see: the meaning and obligations of a blood covenant were clearly defined. It was the strongest bond possible between two people. Both were duty-bound to share everything and to help each other. It was an arrangement that could only be dissolved by death."

Chris was bewildered. "And the relevance of this is...?"

"God considers marriage to be a covenant." Peter smiled and eased himself up from the bench. "Goodnight, Chris." He placed a hand on Chris's shoulder. "You're a good man. I'm sure you'll work it out. Sleep well."

"Aye, it's happening, sure enough." Murdoch growled as he seated himself at the kitchen table in the White House. Morag, Chris, Alsdair, and Elizabeth sat in the other seats, while Annie moved behind them, pouring cups of tea. "Jason's called a meeting in the community hall in four weeks' time. He's trying to make it popular by organizing a bit of a ceilidh after, wi' dancing." He passed a hand over his forehead. "By my reckoning, there are thirty-one crofters who can vote. At least twenty of them have been allowed to get behind in paying their rents."

"Daft fools," Annie said. "All as dim as my man. Ooch. You'd a thought it bleedin' obvious no Laird was going to let you get behind in your rent without good reason." She sighed. "But there it is. You'll nae find a Scotsman refuse a whiskey, or a chance to delay a payment."

"The worst in debt is Hamish," growled Murdoch. "I've lent

him a wee bit just now so he doesn't get further in with Jason. But I'm afraid it's too late. He'll not be in a position to oppose Jason in any vote."

Chris raised an eyebrow at Murdoch. "I thought you and Hamish were sworn enemies."

Murdoch shook his head. "Nay, not enemies." He turned his mug of tea in his hands, and tried without success to think how he could explain the dense network of relationships, understandings and obligations of the islanders to a foreigner. "It's more complicated than that."

"I don't know if it's a good fisherman or a daft one that puts the fish back just so he can catch them again," Annie scoffed. "Maybe Hamish does it right."

Murdoch ignored the comment. "Hamish and the rest are a wee bit sheepish at being outwitted by Jason. Each thought he was the only one Jason was giving latitude to." He paused to scratch his stubbly chin. "I told him we were meeting to see what we could do. But there doesn't seem to be much hope. Jason has got them over a barrel."

Alsdair said, "Surely there are some legal avenues that we can explore? I'm prepared to write an exposé for the local newspaper. They'd love it."

Murdoch shook his head, and heaved his shoulders forward. "Thank you, Alsdair, but it's nae so simple. Nothing is written down, ya'see. You'll just be opening yourself up to a lawsuit—which would only help fund Jason's project." He sighed. "No, we need something altogether different."

Further conversation was prevented by Bess barking and bounding to the front door. A minute later, Annie led Hamish into the kitchen. He had his rough tweed jacket on. It was speckled with red anti-fouling paint and the grime of years. He was holding his cloth cap in both hands, alternately wringing it tight and unwinding it.

"You'll be having a strupack, Hamish?" Although technically a question, coming from Annie, it was a command.

Hamish nodded. Morag and Chris moved up on the wooden

bench to make room for Hamish to sit down. He began to speak as he sat down.

"Word's out that many of us crofters have been fools for the Laird's generosity."

Annie banged a mug of tea in front of him, spilling some of its contents. Hamish winced, but he continued to speak. "We'll nae be in a position to vote against the Laird."

"Aye. True enough," Murdoch said.

"But a group of us have had a wee talk. We may not be able to vote agin' the Laird, but we don't have to vote for him either."

Murdoch felt a stab of alarm. "Hamish, I appreciate you trying. But you know you can't just abstain, or fail to turn up—least not without a good excuse."

"Aye. Well, that's just it, y'see. We'll find an excuse."

"It had better be a good one," Murdoch said. "Jason is nae stupid."

"Ach, it will be." Hamish smiled. "The Laird knows we islanders take dying very seriously."

"What are you talking about?" asked Chris.

"Nothing. Just leave it to me." Hamish took a swig from his mug of tea and lumbered to his feet. "There'll be eight of us missing from the voting." He put his cap on his head and nodded solemnly. "Good day to ye."

Murdoch nodded to Hamish as he turned and left. He was not at all sure what to make of Hamish's information, but knew when it was wise not to inquire further.

Chris stood up, saying he needed to rejoin Ruan and the McCormacks at the building site. Murdoch held up his hand. "Afore you go, Christopher, I'd better tell you all…"

All faces turned to him.

He continued. "I've been asked to chair the meeting. Not being a crofter, I'm seen to be independent; and as their lay preacher, I'm seen to be acceptable." He looked around at each of them. "So, just know that I will be fair in all I do—even if it means we lose the day."

Five days of intense building activity followed for Chris. Once the reinforcing had been wired into place, the network of plastic pipes to take the geothermal water was laid on top. On the final day, the concrete was poured. The long boom of the concrete pump splashed out tons of concrete—its voracious appetite fed by a succession of cement trucks. A damp mist hung in the air, which persisted all day. Jack McCormack sniffed the air appreciatively. "It's a good slow-drying day. The concrete will set strong."

The last of the trucks finally rumbled away, and Chris looked at the thick pad of concrete, with three stone walls of the old cottage standing forlornly in the middle of it. Alsdair walked up beside him and surveyed their handiwork. "It's not much to show for a month's hard work."

Chris slapped him on the shoulder. "Mate, we've done at least a quarter of the build. Cheer up. We've done well to get this far so quickly." He looked around for Ruan and spotted him curled up in the back of the Cherokee. The boy was fast asleep, exhausted from the day's work. Turning back, he saw Hamish climb the wooden style over the stone wall to join them.

Hamish nodded at the concrete pad. "Where would you be wanting your wall then?"

Chris pointed. "I want to extend the eastern side wall to the front of the house, and stop it four feet before the front of the slab."

Hamish nodded.

Chris looked at the tough islander. The thought of him struggling with debt to Jason did not sit well with him. He cleared his throat. "I'll be away from tomorrow for five days. I'm going to Newcastle to try to sort out my eye. If you want to make a start on the wall—perhaps with Alsdair's help—please do. Leave a doorway against the old wall for access to the bathroom and study, and then build it straight out from there." Chris scribbled the dimensions on a piece of paper and handed it to Hamish. "I'll leave you two-thousand pounds to cover concrete expenses. Treat the remainder as a bonus for yourself."

Chris knew it was a lot of money—more than was strictly needed.

Hamish looked up sharply and searched his face. Chris remained inscrutable. After a moment, Hamish nodded. "That should do it."

"I'll best get Ruan home," Chris said.

Alsdair interrupted, "I forgot to tell you. Morag has invited us both round for supper. She thought we might appreciate it after a long day. She's assured us that we can come dressed as we are."

"Sounds good."

As they drove the short distance to the White House, Alsdair stretched wearily in the seat beside him. "I'd hoped to spend some time alone with Elizabeth tonight, but I'm too knackered to think of going out."

"Love has its trials," said Chris, unhelpfully.

When they arrived, Elizabeth was beginning to oversee Ruan's tea, bath, and bedtime. As it transpired, they all agreed to have a late supper. Annie had left a stew in the slow cooker, so they decided to postpone dinner for an hour.

Mindful of Alsdair's wish to spend at least some time with Elizabeth alone, Chris offered to take Morag out of the house for a twilight drive.

"Right, where shall we go?" he asked as he climbed into the car beside her.

Morag, rugged up in long white scarf and a warm jacket, leaned back with every appearance of contentment. "I'd like you to see the Bluff, where my great-great-grandfather lived. It's beautiful."

"Is that where Jason wants to build his condominiums?"

"Yes."

"Good. I'd like to see what all the fuss is about. How do I get there?"

"Assuming everything has remained the same, take the Portree road for one mile. Turn off down a dirt road opposite the entrance to the manor house; then turn left two hundred yards later over a cattle grid. You'll find a track that will take you across the grazing land up to the Bluff."

Ten minutes later, the Cherokee pushed its way uphill, threading its way across the rough grazing land. Chris breasted a hill and then braked to a stop near the edge of a spectacular cliff. "Wow!" he said as he took in the view. It was spectacular.

"Tell me what you see," said Morag.

"There's an amazing view across the loch and the islands offshore to the west. The sun is low, about to set. Shafts of light are spilling out behind the clouds on the horizon and they're being reflected on the sea." He looked around. "Twenty yards away to the right is a slight depression with a few grass-covered mounds and some rocks. There's also a row of bushes."

"That's the remains of old Lachlan Daniel's home. He was my grandfather's grandfather, and the estate manager for the Laird, Angus Crenshaw. Evidently, it was once a lovely house. The bushes are junipers. They tolerate coastal conditions well. He'd made a hedge of them around a garden."

"Would you like to go for a walk and tell me about it?"

Morag nodded, and they both got out of the car. Arm in arm, they walked through what little remained of the old house. Chris felt her body warmth through his coat and unconsciously drew her closer to him. "How do you feel coming back here?"

For a moment, Morag said nothing. Eventually she spoke, her voice low. "I'm glad you're here with me. I used to come here alone as a child. It's a very sad place. I suppose it's a shameful place, but I've never felt that. I used to come here when I needed a quiet place to think." She held on to Chris's arm with both hands. "I had just begun to research what happened here all those years ago, when I was blinded."

Chris said nothing, content simply to savor her company.

Morag breathed in the air and sighed. "At first I thought it was just wishful thinking, but as I began my research, some things about the circumstances surrounding the death of my great-great-grandfather didn't add up."

"In what way?"

"I started to research the oral tradition of the old people of the island and was beginning to get a rather odd impression. According to the old crofters, they always thought that their local Laird, Angus Crenshaw, was sympathetic to the crofters. And yet, evidence at the inquest pointed to a letter which suggested that he and his estate manager, Lachlan, were conspiring to evict the crofters." She shook her head. "This came to light after Lachlan murdered Angus in a fight over the payment of hush money. As Angus had no heirs, the crofters all voted to come under the management of the neighboring Laird, Haines." Morag sighed. "It didn't do them much good, though. Most of the crofters ended up being forced off their land anyway."

Chris looked at the grassy mounds. It was all that was left of the violent story. "What happened to Lachlan?"

"His dagger was left at the scene of Angus' murder, together with a note from Angus to Lachlan saying that he was not going to be blackmailed any longer. When a posse of locals came to this spot to confront Lachlan, they found his house on fire. Lachlan and his wife were dead inside it." Morag shrugged. "Whether the fire was an accident or the aftermath of a murder-suicide, the locals didn't care. They simply believed God's will had been done. So they contented themselves with cursing Lachlan for his duplicity, and for murdering Angus. Then they plundered what was left of the ruined cottage, and voted that his land be absorbed into the common grazing land of the crofters he had sought to betray. Poetic justice."

Chris gave Morag's arm a squeeze. "It must have been difficult to live with such a history."

They walked to the edge of the cliff and listened to the booming waves hundreds of feet below. Chris described what he could see. "It's all so dramatic and sheer."

"Looks can be deceiving. Can you see a bent old rowan tree right by the cliff edge, to the left?"

"Yes."

"Go over and take a look beside it. You should see some stone steps. Not many people know about them. They go all the way down to the wave-cut platform at the bottom." Morag gave him a gentle shove to encourage him. "The steps are actually well made, but you still need to be careful. Until quite recently, crofters used them to harvest gannet, fulmar, and guillemot eggs. They did that all the way along this cliff by hanging over the edge, suspended on the end of ropes."

Chris shook his head. "You'd have to be mad. It's crazy."

Morag took Chris by the lapels and shook him gently. "Are you calling me crazy?"

"Don't tell me you've done it!" he said in disbelief.

She smiled. "I did—the season before I went away to university. It was fun."

Chris shuddered and walked away to explore the cliff edge beside the bent and tangled rowan tree. He got down on his stomach and pushed himself through the grass until his head was over the cliff edge. To his surprise, he discovered the steps. They had been cut into a natural diagonal fissure in the rock that led down to the bottom of the cliff. They looked terrifying. Edging back, he got to his feet and rejoined Morag. "I wouldn't like to climb them on a dark night."

"A pilot scared of heights!" Morag teased.

"My anorak doesn't quite have the same Bernoulli effect as an airplane wing."

"Lachlan and his son used to climb up and down those steps all the time. They used them to reach lobster creels which they threw into the sea off the rocks."

Morag then surprised Chris by placing her hand on his chest so that it covered the Celtic cross hanging around his neck.

"Chris, I hinted to you that I might know a little about the history of your Celtic cross." She hung her head. "I was reluctant to tell you at the time because it involved, well…my family's shame."

Chris bent his head so that his lips brushed the top of her head. It might have been a kiss. "You don't have to apologize. What is it you'd like to tell me?"

Morag sniffed. "What you don't know is that Lachlan tied the Celtic cross you're wearing inside one of those lobster creels, presumably for his son to find. It was almost as if he knew that he might soon die." Morag leaned back to look up at him with sightless eyes. "I'm convinced that there is more to this saga than we know. Lachlan took considerable care to conceal the cross. He had tied it onto a piece of slate on which he'd scratched, *Never lose this*." She paused. "We didn't speak about it in our family. Dad only told me about it when he learned that I wanted to research it as part of my thesis."

Morag rested her forehead on Chris's chest. It was an intimate gesture that caused him to hold his breath. She went on quietly, "That's all I managed to find out before I lost my sight."

She lifted her hand and fingered the edges of the cross under his anorak. "It's extraordinary isn't it? This stone cross has come half way round the world, back to the place where its journey began." She paused. "I don't believe that to be an accident."

Chris didn't know what to think. All he knew was that his feelings for the woman standing in front of him were intense and deeply disturbing.

That night, Morag danced in the darkness of her room, hoping that physical weariness would result in the sleep that she knew would otherwise elude her. She would technically be married in just a few days. Technically.

She danced and danced until she was exhausted.

Morag remembered the India Building in Edinburgh as a distinguished, four-story building of gray stone that exuded respectability and stolid Presbyterian values. She'd walked past it often when she was at University. But never in her wildest dreams did she imagine herself getting married in it. It was such a severe place. She blinked back a tear, threw back her head, and allowed Chris to lead her inside.

She reflected bitterly that the marriage ceremony she was about to be part of could in no way be construed as typical.

"How many guests will be attending?" asked the marriage celebrant.

"None," Chris said.

"Who will be the witnesses for the marriage?"

"We arranged last time for two of your staff to witness our signatures."

"Ah, yes." The marriage celebrant looked down at his file. "Will there be an exchange of rings?"

"No," said Chris.

"Any special requests? Any poems, music, or readings that you want read to make the occasion special for you?"

Chris didn't answer.

Morag couldn't bear it. She just wanted it over and done with. "None," she said. "We'd appreciate it if the ceremony was over as quickly as possible, with the minimum of fuss." Even as she said it, she knew it was a lie. She wanted a real wedding. She wanted something worthy of the truth that she had finally admitted to herself. She wanted to hear Chris declare his love for her. She wanted church bells to ring and for people to know. She wanted a long honeymoon. She wanted so many things.

How had she let herself fall in love with this man who dreamed such big dreams and saw such possibilities?

She wiped away a tear. *Why was it that blind eyes still cried?* She loved Chris's gentleness and energy. She loved him bringing her flowers. She loved that he was safe, and had turned her kitchen into a place where a community of friends loved to linger. Morag sniffed. *Perhaps he might learn to love me, at least a bit…with time.*

"I normally invite the bride and groom to hold hands when I pronounce them married. Are you happy with that?" asked the celebrant.

Morag answered rather more curtly than she intended. "We would prefer it if we didn't."

"Then I'll simply invite you to kiss the bride, Christopher."

She felt Chris, who was holding her arm, stiffen. *What is he thinking? Is the idea too terrible?* She lowered her head. "No," Chris said. "We'll do our own thing afterward. Please leave that bit out, too."

There was an awkward silence. The celebrant cleared his throat. "Ah, right then. I suppose we can begin."

The ceremony was over in ten minutes. Its formal proceedings were interrupted only once—at the point where the bride and groom normally exchanged rings. "Wait," said Chris. "I do have something that I want to give to Morag." He pulled the Celtic cross out from under his shirt, and hung it around her neck.

She fingered it lightly and felt the warmth in it that had come from his body. She slipped it inside her shirt so that she could feel it between her breasts.

"I now pronounce you man and wife. Please step forward and sign the register."

Chris seemed very withdrawn as they walked back into the waiting room in front of the celebrant's office. The two of them stood there in silence.

Chris cleared his throat. "Please forgive me, Morag, but I need to spend some time phoning a few people about a shipment of windows and doors."

She swallowed. "Fine."

"Let's find a quiet coffee shop or pub." Chris walked away to settle the account with the celebrant. Morag took the opportunity to put a call through to the National Museum of Scotland. After getting through to the right department, she told them she was in possession of an old Celtic pectoral cross. Could they have a look at it to determine if it had any historical significance? After a brief conversation to determine the age of the cross and something of its provenance, the museum assured her that they would like to look at it. She finished the call as Chris returned to escort her from the building.

While they walked along the pavement outside, she said, "Chris, as we're in Edinburgh, I'd like to take the opportunity to speak with someone at the National Museum about my Master's research.

187

You'll find it on the intersection of Chambers Street and George IV Bridge. The Greyfriars pub is just opposite. You can make all the calls you need from there. I will give you a ring you when I'm ready for you to pick me up from the museum."

Chris grunted his assent. As he helped Morag into the front seat of the car, he held on to her hand. "Morag, I suspect that what's just happened was not something you enjoyed very much. Thanks for your courage in going through with it and…" His voice faltered. "…thanks for your friendship."

Morag reached up and laid a hand on his cheek. "You'll always have it."

They drove in silence to Newcastle. When they arrived, Chris dropped Morag off at Dr. Hardy's clinic where she was due to undergo the delicate procedure of having a membrane of cells laid over both corneas. He could feel her tension in the car, and his heart ached for her. Chris desperately wanted to hold her to himself and protect her from all things cruel and hurtful. As it was, he was summarily dismissed and told to come back in two hours.

Chris trailed off to keep his appointment with the ocular prosthetic department and have his false eye fitted.

He found the experience extraordinary. The ophthalmologist chatted to him cheerfully and told him that artificial eyes used to look more sunken than normal eyes, but with modern technology they now looked normal. He was right. When Chris looked at himself in the mirror, he was shocked to see himself staring back with two apparently good eyes. The match was perfect.

The ophthalmologist chattered on. "There's no real feeling in the ocular cavity, but it will still take you a while to get used to it. See how you go, then come back after a month and we'll see how you're going."

"Can I come back in eight weeks?" asked Chris.

"I suppose so. Ring for an appointment when you know the

date. Don't forget what I've told you about maintaining the hygiene of the ocular cavity."

When Chris returned to Dr. Hardy's clinic, a nurse conducted him to the surgery room. As Chris entered, Dr. Hardy was surveying the bandage he had just wrapped around Morag's eyes. The doctor nodded in evident satisfaction. "How do you feel, young lady?"

"I feel as if I'm playing blind man's bluff," replied Morag.

"And so you will for eight weeks, my girl. The bandage has to stay in place all the time—vanity or no vanity. Change the sterile pads over the eyes every second day and re-bandage them into place. I've laid a thin film of cells over both corneas. They must be allowed to graft onto the eye and stimulate the cornea to grow healthy cells. Ideally, I should keep you here in Newcastle but, as you insist on returning to Skye, you'll need to find someone to dress your eyes for you."

Chris cleared his throat. "I'll do it, Doc. Show me what you want me to do."

Dr. Hardy did so, and finished by saying, "As I said: come back in eight weeks' time. But ring me any time before then if there is any discomfort, discharge or sign of infection."

Morag reached out a hand for Chris and took his hand. In a tremulous voice, she asked, "And is there a chance I might see in eight weeks?"

"I think 'might' is being a bit pessimistic. We've grafted on a good layer of cells. If, as is likely, there is no infection, and the graft takes, I fully expect you to see in eight weeks' time."

"Oh." Her voice was a whisper.

That night, he lay down in the hotel bed that he'd booked and wondered what the future might bring. The girl in the next room was his wife. She was the one he loved—but could never get close to.

Next morning, they sat together for breakfast. As they finished eating, Morag placed a hand on Chris's wrist. "Let's stay with my parents in Edinburgh tonight. I'd like you to meet them."

He nodded. "Okay. Are you sure that's what you want?"

"Yes."

They returned to the car and headed north toward Edinburgh on the A68. As they passed the ruined abbey at Jedburgh, Chris asked, "Why didn't you go to live with your parents after you were blinded?"

"They were protecting me rather too much, and I felt I needed to get away to a place that didn't have social obligations." She paused. "I needed to be alone."

"Did it work—being alone?" asked Chris.

Morag smiled. "It was working pretty well until you came along."

He drew a deep breath. "Do you regret it?"

There was a long silence. Eventually she answered. "No."

A wave of relief coursed through him.

"Why do you want to stay with your parents tonight?" he asked.

"Well, right or wrong, Chris Norman, you are now a big part of my life, so I thought it was time they met you."

The tone of her reply gave Chris the impression that he wasn't quite being told everything. Morag seemed to realize it too, because she hurried on. "Dad is a wonderful man. He taught me to love Scottish history, particularly of the islands. And Mum, she's..." Morag paused, "...very special. She's an island girl from the Outer Hebrides."

Three hours later, they pulled up outside a narrow but elegant four-storied house in the Edinburgh suburb of Marchmont. A thin man with intelligent eyes and an unruly mop of gray hair answered the door. He shook Chris's hand and introduced himself. "I'm James, Morag's father."

Chris lifted their luggage out of the car and shook him by the hand. "G'day James. I'm Chris. I've been riding shotgun on Morag whilst she's been getting some treatment to..." He wondered how much he should say. "...to make her eyes more comfortable."

James picked up Morag's suitcase. "Yes. So I'd heard. Thanks for looking after her."

"Oh, I've done little enough." Chris shouldered his rucksack. "It's Morag who has done the work. On top of everything else, she's had to look after young Ruan…and teach me what a foreigner needs to survive on the Isle of Skye."

"I think," James said with a smile, "that would be a predilection for whiskey and a love of quarrels."

Chris admitted to having already become acquainted with both.

James laughed. "Come and meet Ailise. She's waiting for you."

The bags were dropped in the hallway, and he and Morag were ushered down to the kitchen.

Chris could see Ailise standing in the center of the kitchen watching them as they approached. He could also see jars of preserves stacked on the end of a bench, and bunches of herbs drying on hooks hung from a suspended ladder. A mouth-watering smell of roast beef hung in the air.

Chris stepped forward with an outstretched hand. "Hello, Mrs. Daniel. Morag's told me how special you are to her. I'm Chris Norman. I've the good fortune to be a friend of your daughter's."

Ailise took Chris's hand and held it, saying nothing as she caressed the back of it with her thumb. Then, without a word, she reached out her other hand and did the same to Morag. Still saying nothing, her bright eyes watched them both.

Chris forced himself to stay calm despite this unusual welcome. He noticed that Morag had dropped her head and was looking shy.

Ailise nodded slowly. As she did, Morag broke free and embraced her mother in a hug. "Mamma." The two women held each other, rocking slightly from side to side, murmuring endearments to each other in Gaelic.

Tears ran down Ailise's cheeks. "Ach, so that's the way of it, mo ghaoil." She stroked the back of Morag's hair, then leaned back to explore the edge of the bandage around her eyes. Seemingly satisfied, she reached out again and reclaimed Chris's hand.

Chris stole a glance at Morag to check that she was all right.

Ailise nodded. "And so it is with himself." She smiled at him. "You may call me Ailise, except when I am displeased with you." She turned back to Morag. "I knew you'd be arriving now. So dinner will be in just five minutes. Wash, and get yourselves ready. You and Christopher are on the top floor."

"But Mamma, my bedroom is on the second floor."

"Ach, but it's busy with my things at present. Both rooms at the top are made up for you."

Morag led the way to the top floor. Chris watched as she moved up the stairs ahead of him. She seemed relaxed and happy, almost glowing with contentment. She obviously felt very much at home in her parents' house. Morag spoke to him over her shoulder. "I think these top rooms must have originally been the servants' quarters. Dad had the bedrooms and bathroom renovated so that he could rent them out to uni students, but he's not yet brought himself to actually do it. I used them as my study area when I was at uni." She sat herself down on her bed as Chris placed her bag inside the door. As she sat, one of the feet of the bed wobbled slightly.

Chris stepped over, and examined it. "The bolt's come loose. I'll fix it for you later."

Dinner was an easy, pleasant affair. Much of the conversation centered on Ruan and on Chris's building plans. Curiously, no one mentioned why Morag's eyes were bandaged. It was as if James and Ailise dared not allow themselves to ask.

Back in their aerie on the third floor, Morag commandeered the bathroom, warning Chris that she would take ages because she needed to dry her hair and reposition her bandage. Chris took off his shoes, stripped off his top and waited. As he did, he caught sight of himself in the mirror. He smiled ruefully. A month of hard physical labor had certainly changed his shape.

Chris discovered that Ailise had put a cloth bag of herbs on his pillow. He sniffed it. One of the herbs was lavender. He moved it to one side and was about to lie down when he remembered that he needed to tighten the bolt on Morag's bed. He pulled out the combination pliers and screwdriver set from his rucksack, stepped across to Morag's room and set to work.

Chris looked up as the door banged open and Morag came in, pulling a brush through her hair. "Bathroom's free," she called. She was wrapped only in a large towel. Chris could see the beautiful complexion of her bare shoulders and a great deal of her slender legs. They rose up to very feminine thighs. He was awestruck.

Propriety eventually asserted itself, and he whispered in a hoarse voice, "Morag. I'm here... mending your bed. I'm sorry to..." He trailed to a stop. His heart yearned with the anguish of love. He instinctively reached out one hand to her and waited.

Morag stood still, holding her bandaged head high, regal, like the woman with the scales of justice.

Chris was desperate not to hurt her. She'd been so terribly wounded. But he now knew with savage certainty, that he loved her passionately. He was desperate to finally end his torment and enfold her with his arms. He wanted to caress, to explore, to delight in, and make passionate love to her. Dear God, she was beautiful.

Morag gave a start of surprise and then stood still. Motionless. Frozen in time. She'd heard Chris's voice coming from below her and surmised that he must be squatting on the floor at the foot of her bed. Instinctively, she moved an arm to protect herself. The specter of past terrors rose up in a shriek, bringing the memories that haunted her. She shivered. But it was Chris who was with her. Chris. She was intensely aware of his presence, and knew herself to be standing on the edge of something very dangerous.

She heard him say, "Morag, are you all right?"

The concern and anguish in his voice hushed her silent screams of fear. In its place, a new, more powerful feeling welled up. It was that most primal ache—the need for love. She needed to feel Chris's hands caressing her. She needed to release all that which had been repressed for so long. And yet... the fear... the terror...

The battle raged.

"I'd better go," Chris said.

No, no. Don't go. A silent voice screamed from deep within her soul. She needed his love...and she needed to show her love for him. It was just that she also needed time to make sense of the moment, a moment that she knew she had been heading toward for the last two months.

But there was no time.

Morag held up a hand to prevent Chris leaving. She carefully laid her hairbrush on the dressing table beside her. Then, very slowly, her hands went up to her chest. She undid the towel and let it fall to her feet.

Chapter 12

He that will not look forward must look behind
(Scottish proverb)

Morag entwined her fingers with Chris as she held his hand—restlessly exploring the novelty of love. The woman at the reception desk of the National Museum of Scotland said, "Ah, yes, Miss Daniel, I have a parcel waiting for you. Here it is."

Morag felt for the parcel, picked it up and thanked her. Still standing at the reception desk, she opened it, extracted the Celtic cross, and hung it around her neck. She hadn't wanted to part from it for longer than was absolutely necessary, so she had phoned that morning to see if she could pick it up. One of the curators, a Dr. Williamson, had assured her that the cross would be waiting for her at reception. He'd thanked her for bringing it in. "It is intriguing. We have used your cross to make a cast, so we can make a copy from pigmented polyresin. This will enable us to continue our research into its history. I'll be in touch when I've something to report."

"I'm glad to see you've got your wedding ring back," whispered Chris into her ear.

They walked out of the Museum and back to the car. Soon, they were threading their way through the Scottish mountains back toward Skye. They were easy in each other's company, if still a little shy about their love. Morag was both thrilled and bewildered by the strength of the passion she now felt. Somewhat disbelieving, she was reluctant to test its fragile newness too much. She was anxious not to presume, whilst desperately hoping that she could.

Morag laid a hand on his arm. "I love you Chris. You know that I do. But let's not complicate things with plans to live together until we are both very sure of what we want." She knew that she was already sure, but she wanted to be sure that Chris felt the same way.

Chris said nothing for a long time. Morag was wondering if he would respond. Then, with something like a sigh, she heard him say, "Okay, then. But promise me that you will tell me the moment, the instant, you are sure what you want." He paused. "I'll never be far away."

Morag dropped her head. She'd hoped, perhaps unreasonably, that Chris would protest, and insist on living together straight away. She would have agreed readily enough. Perhaps he was not yet ready to embrace the idea of a real marriage. "All right." She tried to hide the regret in her voice.

A welcome surprise greeted Chris as he pulled up at the building site next morning. Hamish had already built half the stone wall that was being extended to the front of the house. The man was, even now, already at work, laying out stones for the next course. When Chris voiced his appreciation, the old crofter brushed it aside. "Ach, it's easy enough when you've got plenty of stone to choose from, and Alsdair making the mud."

Chris could see that the McCormacks had organized the site ready for the next stage of building. Reinforcing rods had been cut, bent into right angles and laid next to each corner. Long rods lay beside each wall, next to packets of foam panels, plastic ties, and metal brackets. The position of the walls had been drawn on the concrete slab in chalk, and the metal base-track for the inside edge of each wall had already been fastened to the slab. As Chris inspected the site, Jack and Tom McCormack drove up in their battered van.

Chris immediately set to work. "Right, guys, let's lay some sealant along the metal base-plate and put the first layer of foam blocks in place. We need to begin at the corners."

And so the work began. Layers of hollow foam block began to be laid side by side. Plastic ties were then pushed into place to brace the foam walls so that they wouldn't move apart when concrete was poured into the middle. Finally, reinforcing rods were laid over the bracing and wired into place.

The routine of the work soon settled into place. Chris put the foam blocks into place like a giant Lego set. Jack placed a plastic tie every thirty inches along their length, and Tom pushed them into place. Both Jack and Tom expressed amazement at how quickly the foam walls rose into place. Strengthening brackets were added in the corners, and wooden blanks were put into place where the windows and doors occurred.

Ruan came to help them in the afternoon and took over the job of placing the plastic ties in position, ready to be pushed into place. By the time Chris called it a day, they had built up four feet of walling. He was delighted. "We'll be ready for the concrete to be poured in three days. You've done well." He turned to the McCor-macks. "Congratulations. You are now the island's experts on insulated concrete building. It's the most insulated building material around, and it will withstand a hurricane." He smiled. "You should corner the market with it. See you tomorrow." The McCormacks, however, did not go until they had again checked that all the walls were plum, square, and true. Chris was impressed.

Chris had worked with Ruan and the McCormacks, whilst Hamish and Alsdair had managed to build another three square yards of the stone wall. It was intense physical work.

Alsdair stretched wearily. "I'm knackered."

"I'm knackered, too," said Ruan.

Chris looked at the boy askance, but said nothing.

Hamish joined them. "Ach, now he's got himself another eye, he'll be wanting twice as much work, I ken." He hunted around to find where he'd left his pipe. Having locating it, he lit it, and drew on it with evident contentment. "Two days, and we should finish the stonework."

"A tie!"

"A tie," confirmed Morag. Chris couldn't remember the last time he wore a tie, probably not since school. "If you won't wear the MacLeod tartan, you've at least to look smart."

"I'm not sure why I'm going," grumbled Chris.

"Ach," Morag said, giving him a kiss, "you've yet to learn the island ways. The rules are simple. First, you need to be dead or a social pariah not to attend a ceilidh. And I'm weary of being a social pariah, so treat this as my 'coming out' party. I'm nervous enough myself, so I'm going to need your support." She grabbed him by the shoulders. "So you're coming, my wee mannie."

Chris kissed her on the end of her nose. "And the second rule?"

She turned away to escape his roving hands. "You've at least to arrive looking respectable, but it's considered poor form to look respectable when you leave."

"Strange. Very strange." He hugged her from behind, nuzzling her neck.

Morag giggled before she pushed him away. "Go and get changed."

Chris returned to the manse and did his best. When he walked out of the bedroom, he found that Peter had moved all the chairs against the wall and was laying out mugs and glasses on the table. "What's this for?"

"Ah, well, I'm expecting some visitors," said Peter evasively.

"Aren't you coming to the ceilidh, then?"

"Morag's asked me to attend the meeting, but I need to get back here straight afterward. But, you stay on and have a good time."

At six o' clock, Peter and Chris climbed into the car and made their way down the rough driveway.

At the gate, Chris was surprised to see a black hearse. A bunch of crofters stood around it chatting happily. Chris recognized Hamish standing among them. He was organizing the rest of them as they lifted the coffin out of the hearse. When Hamish saw Peter, he came over to the car.

"It's a strange time of day for a funeral, Hamish," Chris said.

"Aye, that it is. But death waits for no man."

"Whose funeral is it? Anyone I know?"

Hamish rubbed his whiskery chin. "Well, in a manner of speaking, you might."

"Who is it?"

Hamish leaned closer to the car window and whispered, "'Tis Mr. Percival."

Realization dawned. "Don't tell me you're going to bury a pig in the churchyard?"

"Ach, of course not," said Hamish. "He was not a Protestant. We've dug a hole for what's left of him outside the cemetery fence."

"I take it you'll be having a bit of pork at the wake, then?" Chris smiled.

Hamish grinned. "Indeed, that's the way of it. We've a spit set up behind the manse. Food helps the grieving process."

Chris glanced at Peter and was rewarded with a small smile.

Hamish trudged back to the funeral party, picked up a length of silk cord attached to the coffin, and began leading the funeral procession solemnly up the drive. Chris heard the occasional clink of bottles, as they filed past.

When Chris arrived at the front door of the White House, Morag was waiting. She was dressed in a loose, white shirt, and a tight blue waistcoat that showcased her figure. Her kilt was made from a blue, black, and green tartan with red and yellow lines running through it. She looked sensational.

"You look amazing," he said as he helped her into her coat.

She smiled, took hold of the lapels on his jacket and admonished him. "You're late. Elizabeth has already left with Alsdair."

The community hall was full by the time they arrived, so Morag's entrance attracted a lot of stares. Chris was quite glad she couldn't see them. Some were hostile. Others stared with curiosity at her bandaged eyes. A few looked with open admiration.

He guided Morag across the hall to the table where Alsdair and Elizabeth were seated.

On the rough wooden dais at the front of the hall, Jason Haines was scanning the crowd. Most of those present were gathered by two notice boards on which pictures and plans of the proposed development had been pinned.

Murdoch, leaning on the lectern, looked grim. He glanced at his watch and brought the meeting to order. After everyone was seated, he said, "Welcome to ye all. I'm instructed to tell you that our local Laird, Jason Haines, has supplied the food for the ceilidh afterward, but you buy your own whiskey." A ripple of laughter broke out.

"There will also be a dancing competition with the first prize being a two hundred pound voucher to spend at the Stein Inn at Loch Bay, again kindly supplied by Mr. Haines." He paused. "I've apologies from eight crofters who are attending a funeral. I now call on Mr. Jason Haines to outline the development that he is proposing for the Bluff. The issue at stake is whether you want to vote him the rights to five hectares of the common grazing land on the Bluff, together with an access road from the Manor gate." He turned to the Laird. "Thank you, Mr. Haines."

Jason Haines stood up, donned a winsome smile for the audience and launched into a slick, well-illustrated presentation of the proposed development. It failed to impress Chris. To him it looked plain tacky, like something transplanted from the Gold Coast in Australia. It was a tightly packed jumble of condominiums, function centers—concrete boxes with red roof tiles. Haines brought his presentation to a close. "So it will create jobs, increase wealth, and put us on the map as a place of significance."

"If I wanted to be on the map, I'd have lived in Edinburgh," grumbled an old crofter.

"Any questions for clarification?" Murdoch asked.

A middle-aged crofter's wife stood up. "How many of your proposed new jobs will go to locals like us rather than people on the mainland?"

Haines was obviously trying to look as if he were pleased to have the question. "I honestly can't say. But any jobs are better than none at all, wouldn't you say?"

There were no more questions.

Murdoch stood up and surveyed the room. "Only those with grazing rights to the common land can vote," he growled. "The issue will be decided by simple majority with Jason Haines, as Laird, having the casting vote." He paused and looked sternly at the audience. "You have a chance tonight to help define what you want your future to be. In making this choice, please understand that you will not only be making it for yourself but for the future generations of your families who will inherit the legacy of your decision. So let the decision you make be one you are proud to stand by. No one should feel bullied or coerced to vote in a way they don't want." Murdoch glared at the audience. "Is that clear?"

Many of the islanders dropped their heads and looked distinctly uncomfortable.

Jason Haines spoke up. "I propose that the vote not be secret but open with a show of hands."

The proposal was seconded and carried easily by six votes. Most abstained. Haines smiled.

Murdoch called out clearly, "How many vote for Mr. Haines to have the land on the Bluff to develop? Murdoch counted the hands. "I count eleven hands. Everyone agreed?"

There was a general chorus of "Aye." Haines leaned back in relief and rubbed his hands.

"Those against?" Murdoch called. The hands were counted. "I make that twelve hands."

Haines had been leaning across whispering to a pretty girl with a doll-like face. But the moment he realized what had been said, he jumped to his feet and roared, "What! Rubbish! I demand a recount!"

Murdoch, unmoved, said, "Those against, please raise your hands again."

Jason glared around the room. His eyes fell on Alsdair. "You disloyal fool," he hissed. Next, he noticed Chris, now with two eyes, looking at him with a hand raised. Chris saw hatred in his eyes. Jason continued to scan the room. On seeing Peter with his hand up, he protested volubly. "Why has that man got his hand up? He has no right to vote on this issue."

The room went very quiet. It went quieter still when Morag stood to her feet.

"Mr. Chairman," she said. "According to the legal advice from the Crofting Law Group at the University of Strathclyde, the resident cleric at the manse has the right to graze a cow on the common land. The church has had this right since 1628. Peter therefore has the right to vote. I've brought copies of the relevant documents from the Crofting Law Group for you to examine if you wish."

"Outrageous!" Jason was furious. He scanned the room for the twelfth person who voted against him. "Who the hell is the other person who voted against me?"

Morag was still on her feet. "That would be me, Mr. Haines. As the legal carer for Ruan Norman, the Crofting Law Group also assures me that I have the right to vote on his behalf. Again, I have documents to prove it."

Uproar followed. It was immediately evident that the crofters, who had largely been antagonistic toward Morag, now saw her as their champion. They clapped and cheered so much that few of them heard Murdoch shout, "The proposition has been defeated."

Amidst the bedlam around him, Chris could see Jason standing stock still, his face ashen. To his alarm, Jason began walking over to where he was standing with Morag.

As Jason came near Morag, Chris stepped in front of her and held him back with a hand to his chest. Ignoring Chris, Jason hissed at Morag. "Miss Daniel, I regret to say that I need the White House. You have, as your contract permits, one month to get out of my property."

Chris said evenly, "Jason, if you cause Miss Daniel any more hurt, I will drop on you like the angel of death, and destroy you." Chris looked him in the eyes. "Are you in any doubt about the truth of what I'm saying?" Chris continued to stare until Jason turned around and marched over to his girlfriend. The young girl put her arm around Jason in a gesture of sympathy, but he threw it off, sat down, and put his head in his hands.

Alsdair came up to Morag. "Brilliant! Absolutely fantastic, Morag. I had no idea you were going to spring that on us. You're an absolute champion."

Still keeping his eye on Jason, Chris nodded toward the young girl. "Tell me Alsdair, who is Jason's girlfriend?"

"She's his latest, temporary sweetheart—yet another one too young to be discerning." Alsdair sighed. "Jason likes to have a little showpiece by his side. However, I suspect that he particularly wanted to bring her here tonight because she happens to be a champion dancer. Jason expects to give her first prize. I suspect that is the only reason he's been so generous in offering to sponsor the ceilidh."

Morag put her hand out and found Alsdair's arm. "Alsdair," she said.

Chris glanced at her. Her face had a look of fierce determination. He understood the look well enough now to know that something was afoot.

"Alsdair," she continued. "Would you be kind enough to enter me into the dance competition?"

Alsdair gulped as he looked at Morag's bandaged eyes. "Are you sure, Morag?"

"Yes, quite sure."

Chris also began to protest, but she held up a hand to stop him. "This is my coming out party, remember?"

Sensing the steel in her resolve, Chris contented himself with a whisper in her ear. "Mrs. Daniel, I do declare that your dander is up. Just take care." He kissed her lightly on the cheek. "And know that whatever happens, I'm right behind you."

"Did I hear you say Mrs. Daniel, not Miss?" inquired Morag coyly.

"Mrs.," Chris confirmed.

"Hmm."

The dancing competition was to be held first, to kick off the ceilidh. Alsdair told Chris that they had learned from experience that it needed to happen whilst people were still sober.

"Ladies and gentlemen," called a portly MC with several missing teeth. "Our judges tonight are our usual experts; and they will judge our five contestants. Our first dance is, as usual, the victory dance of a Scottish warrior, who dances the strutting of a highland stag. I refer, of course, to the highland fling."

The crowd roared their approval and stomped their feet.

"The order our contestants will dance in will be decided by lot." The MC put his hand into a shoebox and pulled out a name. He appeared to look at it in some disbelief before he shouted, "Our first contestant will be Morag Daniel."

A murmur of surprise went around the room. After the names of the remaining contestants had been announced, the three-piece band played the introductory chord.

"Chris," whispered Morag, slipping out of her coat. "Lead me to the center of the dance floor."

Very unsure of what to expect, he did so.

Standing alone in the center of the room, Morag stood poised and ready. Her proud back was arched, and her arms were upraised. Alsdair leaned forward and explained, "Her arms need to represent the antlers of a mighty stag." He leaned back and smiled. "This could be interesting."

Consumed with anxiety, Chris could nonetheless appreciate that Morag's bearing and blindfold made her a compelling spectacle.

With a wail from the bagpipes, the band launched into action.

Everyone was mesmerized as they watched. Morag's heel and toe movements, grace and agility were breathtaking. It was quite obvious that she wasn't just going through the motions. She was dancing her passion for Scotland.

At the end of her dance, there was spontaneous applause. Chris let it continue for a few moments before he stepped forward to claim her, and kiss her in full view of everyone.

The other dancers followed. They were good—particularly Jason's girlfriend, but there was no doubt in Chris's mind that Morag was superior.

The MC again stepped into the center. "An outstanding display, as I'm sure you'll all agree. And now the final dance before the judges hand down their decision. This dance will be chosen by our benefactor tonight, Jason Haines."

There was muted applause as Jason came forward. He glanced briefly toward Morag and said, "Let's have *Gillie Callum*, the sword dance."

A few people clapped, but there was also a whisper among the crowd. Chris leaned forward to Alsdair. "What's going on?"

Alsdair sighed. "The blighter." He turned to Chris. "No blind person can dance the sword dance. It requires very precise placement of feet within the quarters of crossed swords laid on the floor." He reached over and laid his hand on Morag's arm. "I'm so sorry...'

Morag interrupted him. "Alsdair, it's all right. All I need is a drawing pin. Can you find me one from a notice board? I'll be able to feel it through my dancing shoes."

Chris instinctively drew Morag to his chest and wrapped an arm around her. "Do you know what you're doing, my love?"

Morag nodded, and kissed him on the cheek.

Lots were drawn again to decide the order in which the contestants would dance. Morag was drawn second-to-last, and Jason's girlfriend was again drawn last.

Once more, the MC introduced the dance. "Ladies and gentlemen. The Scottish sword dance has both a noble and a dark history. It was once used as a pretext by Scottish mercenaries to smuggle weapons into Stockholm Castle in an attempt to assassinate the king of Sweden. It is the dance of battle. So, let the battle commence. The *Gillie Callum*."

The first three dancers gave a competent, if unspectacular, performance. While they were dancing Alsdair got up in order to prize out a drawing pin from one of the notice boards. He returned and handed it to Morag. She nodded her thanks.

Then it was Morag's turn to dance. With some trepidation, Chris escorted her to the two swords lying crossed on the floor.

As he was about to leave her, a wag shouted, "Kiss yon lassie again, laddie. It did the trick last time." Laughter followed, and Chris was happy to oblige. As he backed away from her, Morag bent down, felt the position of the swords and pressed the drawing pin into one of the spaces between them. Standing up straight, she arched her back and put her hands on her hips.

She was ready to dance.

The music surged into life, and Morag began to move. She was light on her feet, and moved deftly and surely. Everyone sat spellbound, watching her intently. It was wonderful dancing. Impossible dancing. However, just as the closing bars were being played, Morag misjudged a footfall and trod on the edge of a sword, causing it to spin and clatter from under her feet. She fell to the floor.

A groan of sympathy came from the crowd.

Chris leaped forward and knelt by her side. "Are you okay?"

"I'm fine." Morag's voice was a little shaky. Chris enfolded her in his arms and carried her off the floor.

There was silence for a few seconds from the crowd, and then the applause began. It was thunderous.

Morag disentangled herself from Chris, stood up gingerly and smiled her thanks to the crowd.

Finally, it was the turn of Jason's girlfriend to dance. She too was good on her feet and very quick. It was evident, however, that, although technically perfect, she did not dance with Morag's verve and passion. Nonetheless, she was very good... and would have carried the day if she had not stopped dancing near the end, stood still, and then deliberately fallen over.

The crowd, realizing what she had done, gave her a rousing applause. The girl got to her feet and walked over to Morag. "Miss Daniel, you are an amazing dancer. I hope to see you dance again." She turned around, walked over to her chair, collected her coat and marched out the door, without acknowledging Jason. He watched her go, open-mouthed.

The MC again waddled to the center of the floor. "And now,

Ladies and Gentlemen, our Laird, Jason Haines, will present first prize to…" The band struck a dramatic, if slightly dissonant, chord. "…Morag Daniel!"

The crowd cheered.

Jason walked stiffly over to Morag and gave her a perfunctory handshake. As he thrust the voucher at her, Chris heard him hiss, "Four weeks, Miss Daniel," then he turned on his heel, and stalked out of the hall.

Later that night, Chris and Morag were curled up together on a sofa in the front room of the White House. Elizabeth and Alsdair had not yet returned, so they were alone. Morag had kicked off her shoes and was lying on the sofa with her head on Chris's lap. He was toying with her hair.

"Well, my love, when you were planning your debutante's coming out party, I certainly wasn't expecting this. I had no idea you could dance. Are you going to spring these surprises on me throughout our life?"

"Mmm," Morag said. "I can't even begin to tell you the things you don't know about me yet."

"You were a triumph."

"Do that head massage thing again. It's yum." Chris reached across and massaged gently. "Head, I said," she laughed. Chris feigned apology and obliged. She continued. "It did have its high-lights, but it also presents me with a massive problem."

"The need to find a new house to rent?"

"Yes. There's nothing in the village. Jason owns most of it, so I'll probably have to look in Dunvegan." She sighed. "The idea of moving from the village is horrible."

"We'll see…" Chris was still reveling in the memory of her triumph. "Tell me honestly—what was the best part of tonight?"

Morag smiled. "This part actually isn't too bad, but the best part…that would have to be when you called me Mrs. Daniel."

"Oh." Chris was silent for a while as he continued to run his fingers through Morag's hair. "I don't want to spook you, or rush you, or take advantage of a rotten situation, but you could always live with me."

Morag took a moment to respond. "In what capacity would I share your house, Chris? Would I be Miss Daniel or Mrs. Daniel?"

"Neither."

"Neither?" she said, surprised.

"No. What I want is for you to be Mrs. Norman, my wife." He reached for her hand. "I want you to be my wife in the fullest sense. The idea of me not sharing my life with you, of not rescuing remote controls from the fridge, of not having to remember where you've left your handbag, is appalling." Chris eased Morag's head up from the sofa, stood up, and then sank to one knee. He picked up her hands from her lap. "Miss Daniel, will you marry me…for real?"

She blinked. "Are you serious?"

"Deadly."

"Are you sure?"

"Morag, I have been sure for over a month, absolutely certain for a week, and never surer than tonight."

She started to smile. "Then yes, my wee mannie, a thousand times yes." She pushed him in the shoulder, laughing with joy and delight. "And why didn't you ask me earlier in Edinburgh?" She fell into his arms.

Once they had both settled down, Morag sat back and sighed. "But we have a problem. We have no house to move in to. Yours is still just a slab of concrete. It will take months to build."

"Actually…" Chris leaned back so that he could feel her hair on his cheek. "…with the building technique I'm using, I'll have the walls completed in three days' time. It's very quick."

"Really?"

"True. But it doesn't help us much. I'd need to employ a host of contractors to finish it in time, and my cash flow simply won't allow for it." Chris shrugged. "It's frustrating."

"How much would you need to really blitz the place and have it habitable in a month?"

"Too much." He reached up, took her hand and kissed her

fingers before laying them alongside his cheek. "I'd need teams for roofing, rendering, second fixings, plumbing, electricity, plastering, tiling, and fitting the kitchen. There's no way."

"How much?" Morag was insistent.

Chris sighed and mentally did the sums. "I suppose it would be about sixty-thousand."

"Give me your account details. I'll ring the bank in the morning and organize for sixty thousand to be transferred into your account."

"What?" said Chris, in disbelief.

Morag traced her forefinger across his brow. "One of the many things you don't know about me, mo ghaoil, is that I am actually a very rich woman."

In the small hours of the morning, Morag switched off her computer and sat back. She stretched languidly, warm with joy and still exulting in Chris's declaration of love. Deciding she was too wired to sleep, she switched her computer back on, paused to think for a moment and began to type:

Sweet, sweet surrender, I've given up the fight.
  Sweet, sweet surrender, I know now you were right.
  You chased me with your love,
  Changing what I was.
  I couldn't but surrender to its might.

Sweet, sweet surrender, so this is what it's like.
  Sweet, sweet surrender, your love has got me psyched.
  You've broken through my shell,
  Released me from my hell.
  Your loving is relentless when it strikes.

Sweet, sweet surrender…

Next morning, a voice message from Wozza was waiting for her on her computer.

Bleedin' hell, Raggy! Wot's this last song? You'll 'ave us singing bleedin' Bing Crosby next. How the hell am I goin' to turn this into rock and roll? Trouble is, I showed it to my girl, and she likes it, so we'll bleedin' have do it. It's just your bleedin' good fortune that I've got a voice like a corncrake, and the boys have got serious attitude. But toughen up, girl. Even though we can make 'Ave Maria' sound like an anarchist's anthem, seriously toughen up!

Morag laughed.

Chris decided it was time for a break. He had spent all morning at the building site. "Smoko!"

"An' what sort of language would you be speaking?" It was the first time he'd heard Hamish speak since arriving; he'd been distinctly taciturn all morning. Chris suspected that he was probably having to cope with the damage caused by his over-indulgence during the previous evening's festivities.

"That's Australian for morning smoko, smoke break, morning tea."

"Ach, why dinna ya say so? Speak proper, mon."

Alsdair joined Chris at the tailgate of the Jeep and reached for the vacuum flask. He nodded toward Hamish who was washing his trowel. "I'd say he's less than his usual ebullient self this morning." Alsdair picked up an iced bun and continued, "Do you realize that I've only had three glasses of whiskey in the last five weeks?"

"Are you blaming me for that, or the lovely Elizabeth?"

Alsdair smiled. "Well, let's just say that between the two of you, I've not had much of a chance."

"I only suggested that you help me here in the afternoons." Chris raised his eyebrows. "So, what's happened to your morning writing?"

"Leave off. I'm having fun. I'm off the hooch and growing

muscles to impress my girl." He flexed his arm. "Besides, who said our antics won't end up in my next book?"

"Don't even think of it," warned Chris.

Tom and Jack McCormack walked over to join them. They had been setting up trestles around the inside of the wall to enable them to begin the final three feet of walling. Chris handed them their mugs of tea. "Jack, supposing I had the finances to complete this house in four weeks, could it be done? Are the contractors for plumbing, electrics, and roofing available?"

"Everyone's available at a price. But you wouldn't want most of "em.""

"Is there a way?"

Jack took his woolen hat off and scratched his head. "If you offered ten per cent above the going rate, and let me pick the contractors, it might work."

"Which parts of the building work would you and Tom like to do?"

Jack looked at the half-built white foam walls of the house. "I'd like to render the walls so that I'm familiar with the whole ICF system of building. We can also do the plasterboard and the second fixings."

"Then those jobs are yours. I've got pre-made steel roof joists, corrugated iron, and high-grade insulation coming this afternoon. I'm putting two rooms in the roof with dormer windows. We'll need a team to put this up in three days' time, after we've poured the concrete into the walls. After that, we should at least be weather-proof. Can you be my project manager from this point on and orga-nize it?"

Jack thought it over. "Aye. I can."

They discussed terms and agreed on them with a handshake. Chris took the house plans out, and they pored over them together. Jack pointed to a ducting system shown on the plans. "What's this?"

"That's the ducting for the forced air system. The house is essen-tially airtight. Fresh air is forced through a heat exchange unit which recovers eighty per cent of the temperature of the expelled stale air."

Jack nodded. "What about your windows?" He stabbed at the plans. "They look mighty strange."

"They're from Canada."

"Canada!"

Chris smiled. "They understand cold in Canada. Those are triple-glazed windows. They have fifty per cent better insulation than double-glazing, and less condensation. The only trouble with them is their weight. That's why they need special frames."

"Ach, but will the frames need painting?"

"No. They're made of reinforced fiberglass and have foam insulation. Being fiberglass, they're strong, well insulated, and expand with temperature at the same rate as the glass."

Jack blinked, nodded, and continued to search the plans. "You've no fireplace."

"Don't need one."

Jack shook his head sadly. "If word gets out about this wee hoosie of yours, I dinna think building on Skye will ever be the same again."

It had become custom for Chris and Alsdair to have lunch at the White House. Annie grumbled, of course, but confessed, "At last it's finally worth getting the pan and the griddle blackened." When she saw him give Morag a quick kiss on the cheek, she smiled. "I saw how it was at the dancin'. About time, if you ask me—though no doubt she could have done better." She poked Chris in the midriff. "You've become scrawny." She turned to Morag, "Look after your man. It takes more than dancing to keep a man's slippers under ya bed."

Morag blushed.

Ruan was toying with his soup. JJ, ever hopeful, was by his feet. Chris noticed Ruan's disconsolate expression. "What's up, Half-Pint?"

"Ach. It's the Collins boys." He was swinging his legs, rhythmically kicking at the table leg. "They won't let me go ferreting with them this afternoon if I take JJ. They said JJ would spoil things. I said it wasn't fair, and I wouldn't go."

"But you wish you could," Chris finished for him.

Ruan nodded.

"Well, maybe in a year or so we can talk about you having a ferret of your own." Chris dimly remembered that a friend of his at school used to talk about ferreting. "Would you know how to look after a ferret? They need a lot of care. Would you know how to groom it, clean its ears, cage it, and train it?"

Ruan looked indignant. "Course. I help Ian Collins with his."

Chris couldn't help but think that what Ruan assumed was common knowledge did not relate to the experience of most other people. Ruan knew every type of fish, and how to catch it; could name almost every plant on the island; and understood much of what was required to be a crofter. However, he still needed to catch up on regular education if he was going to make the most of life's opportunities. Fortunately, thought Chris, he was bright, intensely curious, and learned quickly. "Well, if you can't go ferreting, we'll just have to bring forward your next science adventure. Are you up for it?"

Ruan brightened immediately. "Aye."

"Okay. We are going to make a rocket. What we need is a plastic bottle, partly filled with water; a bicycle pump with a needle attachment; and a cork. Do you reckon you can find all of that?"

Ruan signaled his reply by dashing out the door. JJ followed, barking at his heals.

Thirty minutes later he was back.

Chris led him into the back garden, and it wasn't long before the experiment reached its climax. The rocket's successful launch resulted in them both getting drenched.

After drying themselves, they headed off to join Alsdair at the building site.

That evening, Chris joined Peter for tea in the manse. Over the weeks, he'd learned to value these times. Quite often, not a lot was said. Peter seemed to exude an air of peace that made the use of words unnecessary. On this occasion, however, Chris recounted his antics with Ruan.

Peter laughed and then looked out of the window with his hands in the washing up tub. A moment later, he said, "It's sad when children stop collecting sea shells too soon…and it's sad when parents are too busy to watch them."

Having got Peter talking, Chris decided to broach the issue that he particularly wanted to discuss.

"Peter, do you think I should marry Morag for real?"

Peter grunted. "I don't think the scars of the past should have the power to rob us of the future."

"You mean I should live 'in the now,' like Ruan?"

Peter nodded.

"I married Morag in a civil ceremony in Edinburgh over a week ago, just so she could keep Ruan."

Peter said nothing.

"But it's not working. It was a sham of a ceremony, done for the wrong reasons." He shrugged. "And I don't want a sham of a marriage."

"Don't knock it too much. It served its purpose."

"What do you mean?" Chris said, surprised.

"I knew you were in love with Morag when you first proposed your preposterous scheme. You just weren't ready to recognize it. I rather suspected it would work out eventually." Peter paused. "What does Morag think?"

Chris smiled sheepishly. "I proposed to her properly last night."

"And you were accepted?"

"Yes."

"Congratulations."

"The thing is: could you marry us? The covenant thing you mentioned... I want that to be…" Chris searched for the right words. "…real for us."

"You do realize it's a God thing? I'm a Christian minister, not a civil celebrant."

"That's why I've asked. You've helped awaken something in me, that I had no idea existed." He shrugged. "I can't explain it."

Peter nodded. "That's good enough for me. Yes, of course I'll marry you. When?"

"In three weeks' time. The day we move into my house. There will just be a few of us: Alsdair, Elizabeth, Murdoch, and Morag's parents."

Further conversation was interrupted by the arrival of Murdoch in his Land Rover. Peter put the kettle on the hob and walked into the parlor to pull another chair up to the fire.

When the three of them were settled in front of the fire, Murdoch looked at Chris. "It's you I've come to see, Christopher."

Chris waited for him to say more.

"I've three questions," Murdoch growled.

"The first?" inquired Chris.

"What are your intentions with Morag? I saw the way it was between you at the ceilidh. I dinna want her hurt."

"You're the first person I'm inviting to our wedding in three weeks time."

Murdoch's grizzled features did not change. He simply nodded. "What is the meaning of the bandage around her eyes? Is something amiss?"

"Nothing's amiss. I'll tell you more in six weeks. And the third question?"

"Alsdair and Elizabeth are looking ower fond of each other. Are they right for each other?"

Chris looked at Murdoch and saw genuine concern.

He nodded. "I think they are. Alsdair has never been so motivated to get himself together. He's smitten. For her part, Elizabeth is generous and highly principled. She would have packed her bags and left by now if she was not fond of Alsdair." Chris shrugged. "That's as much as I can say."

Murdoch nodded and seemed to be lost in thought. After a moment, he pulled himself together and looked up. "So you're engaged, Christopher." He turned to Peter. "Peter, I think this calls for a whiskey."

Two days later, the giant boom of a concrete pump was delivering concrete through a four-inch nozzle into the foam wall cavities. Jack McCormack directed the nozzle whilst Tom walked behind, plunging a pencil vibrator into the concrete to get rid of any air cavities.

The big surprise of the day was the arrival of Professor Ewen Edmondson from St. Andrew's University. Chris had been emailing him each week to keep him informed of progress. But never for a moment had Chris expected the professor to travel the length of Scotland to view the building process for himself.

The Professor walked about the site, filming everything with an expensive camera. He was particularly taken by the beautiful stonework completed by Hamish and Alsdair.

By lunchtime, the concrete had been poured, and all the walls were finally complete. The McCormacks, however, didn't even pause for breath. They took advantage of the continuing good weather, and began to apply the adhesive and mesh to the outside of the walls in readiness for the synthetic stucco.

Hamish and Alsdair had both headed off home, and Chris was now beginning to feel a sense of anti-climax. At this point, Professor Edmondson walked up to him and asked if the two of them could talk.

Chris indicated the Jeep. "Hop in."

For a while, the professor looked out of the window at the loch. Chris could well understand why. The sea was looking sensational and uncharacteristically calm. Sunlight was playing on the water, causing it to sparkle. Occasionally, a 'cat's paw' of wind touched the sea, drawing dark patterns on its surface.

"Chris, one of the things I do at the College of Physical Sciences is run a postgraduate course on 'energy futures,' which is all about renewable energy. The course has a fieldwork component that, until now, has meant visiting one of the giant wind farms. We've never done what I really want to do, and that is to visit places where renewable energy is working well at a micro-level—the level of a croft." The professor pointed to the building site. "The geothermal heating, and the style of building you're showcasing here is very innovative. Can I ask what other renewable energy features you plan to incorporate in your building project?"

Chris wasn't entirely sure where the conversation was going, but began to describe his plans.

"The house is built on an east-west axis to catch the sun through the windows on the south. This will fall onto the stone flooring inside and aid heating. The thermal mass of the slab, and the old cottage walls on the inside, will even out temperature fluctuations."

"What about power and hot water?"

"I had hoped to put a water heating system on the roof, one made of borosilicate glass—vacuum tubes which heat up glycol. The glycol heats a coil in the hot water tank. The trouble is, the start-up costs are quite high."

Professor Edmondson nodded. "But at least these units are already available commercially. What about power?"

"I was simply going to use power from the grid."

"Might you be persuaded to install a vertical axis wind turbine? It will at least run the lighting."

"Not if it means installing a generator. My fiancée is sight-impaired, and I don't want her having to mess about with one of those." Chris glanced at the professor. "Why the questions? What's on your mind?"

The Professor ignored the question. "How much more power would you use beyond your need for lighting?"

Chris scratched his head. "Well, not very much. I'm planning to buy a German-made, bench-top cooker. It weighs, chops, grinds, cooks, and pretty much does everything. So we'll only have a small oven for baking. It will also have a hotplate on top. However, while we won't have a conventional oven, we will need a conventional fridge."

"I apologize for grilling you like this, Chris, but you'll find out why in a moment." He smiled. "How would you feel about part-nering with St. Andrews University and the Scottish Crofting Feder-ation to help run courses for postgraduates doing the Energy

Futures course, and courses for aspiring crofters? The courses would run for two weeks, and would involve about a dozen students. My hope is that our students could be billeted with local crofters, as it would all help their education."

Chris raised his eyebrows. "Wow!"

Professor Edmondson continued to speak. "Of course, we'd provide a staff member, but we'd like you to show students what you've done here, and teach them how to do it themselves. For this to happen, though, I'd want the students to also understand solar hot water systems and wind turbines." He looked at Chris. "What do you think? If could you handle up to eight courses a year, it would be a half-time job on a full lecturer's salary." He nodded toward the building. "We'd also pay most of the cost of your solar hot water system, and your wind turbine."

Chris was amazed. His natural instinct was to grab the opportunity. Here was guaranteed employment and a chance to bring significant economy to the village. However, he kept a poker face. He shook his head. "My concern is that you and the Crofting Federation may not be innovative enough."

The professor raised an eyebrow.

"Why not ask some of the local crofters, such as Hamish next door, to show students the old crafts of farming, fishing, and cutting peat? And why not ask Miss Daniel to teach the identification and uses of native plants? As a post-graduate who has studied the island's history, she could also give introductory sessions on island culture." He shrugged. "Why not make this place a true center for learning the culture and practice of crofting?"

The professor started to laugh. "I'll say this for you, Chris, you certainly don't lack courage. Tell you what: put your ideas down in an email, and send them to me. If you do it in the next hour, I'll have it in time for my meeting with the manager of the Scottish Federation in the Kyle of Lochalsh. Can you do it?"

"Sure."

Jason Haines' father, Aaron, was seated in a wing-backed chair. An oxygen bottle stood at the old Laird's side, and he was holding the mask to his mouth. The hand that held it was covered in blotchy skin—as thin and delicate as the skeletons of last winter's leaves.

The fool should be dead by now, Jason thought uncharitably.

Although Aaron Haines was shrunken and bent with age, he still retained his formal Scottish dress. Jason suspected that it was in defiance of the world in general—and death in particular. The old Laird removed the mask and glared at his son.

Jason had not been invited to sit.

The old Laird spoke with a quavering voice. "So, you took the crofters on with your greedy scheme, and came undone." He laughed harshly, wheezed, and reached for his mask. After regaining his breath, he continued. "I told you that crofters are an obdurate, bloody-minded lot. They've more tricks between them than a sack full of ferrets. But you wouldn't listen. How much are you in debt for?"

Jason told him. Just speaking the astronomical sum highlighted the appalling reality of his ruin.

"Then you are bankrupt, you fool. There is no way I can, or indeed want, to underwrite any of it. You began this venture through your own company, and not through the family trust, because you were greedy and thought you knew better. Fortunately, this means that your stupidity does not affect the estate."

Jason clenched and unclenched his fists. Rage and self-pity writhed within him like Hydra's serpents. He had known he would get no pity from his father. Indeed, he never had. Yet the old man's mocking was almost more than he could bear. But he could do nothing. His father's personal assistant, Penmann, was never far away. In all probability, his father had switched on the intercom, so that Penmann could hear every word that was being said.

The old man continued. "You will continue to manage the estate, and even continue with the title 'Laird,' but you will now simply be an employee of the trust. I will make arrangements for you to report to Penmann. I will withdraw all rights for you to sign checks against the family trust. You have shown yourself to be greedy, stupid, and untrustworthy. You will just be a manager, until you find a woman you can actually keep, someone who will give me an heir worthy of being Laird."

The old man raised a crooked finger at his son. "By God, if you only knew what I've had to do to ensure the posterity of the Haines estate, you would have treated it with more respect." He slumped back in his chair. "Now get out of my sight, and send Penmann in."

Chris despaired of the house being ready in time for his wedding. In truth, he knew it wasn't going to be. The plastering had only been completed downstairs, and none of the house had been painted. But other than that, the essentials were complete. The only rooms not completed were the dormer bedrooms upstairs. In fact, they had not even been begun. Chris reasoned that they could be built later, if and when the extra space was needed.

Two days before the wedding, a large parcel turned up at the manse for Chris. On the back of it was a company logo, 'Hector Russell.' Inside it, was a note from Morag.

> *My Darling. I cannot marry a man who is not Scottish. Inside is the tartan of the MacLeods of Harris, which any MacLeod, such as yourself, may wear. It is my gift to you to wear on our wedding day—for you have given so much to me.*
>
> *With all my love,*
> *Morag.*

Inside the package was a black jacket, waistcoat, sporran, and a kilt of the same blue, green and red tartan he remembered Morag wearing at the ceilidh. He fingered the gift with bewilderment, not really believing that he could wear such a thing. As he did, it dawned on him that this was his heritage. This was his story. He lifted out the kilt. It was surprisingly heavy. He could wear it and, what's more, he decided, he would wear it with his grandfather's kilt pin.

Chris could not believe anyone could look so beautiful in a simple white dress decorated with a MacLeod tartan sash. Morag looked so feminine—and so Scottish.

Peter stood in front of them, dressed in his brown habit. He beamed at them as he spoke.

Just as God invites us into a covenant relationship with himself, so God invites a man and a woman to enter into a covenant with each other.

Alsdair, as best man, had helped Chris with his unfamiliar garb.

As such, marriage is a way of life that should be honored and protected. It is a commitment that reflects the qualities of God's commitment to us.

Morag's curling hair fell freely over her shoulders.

We pray for Christopher and Morag as they pledge their lives to each other, asking that their love may continue to grow and be a true reflection of your love for us.

Murdoch was standing alongside Alsdair. He was clean-shaven for once, and looked very much at home in his kilt.

Will you love her, care for her, honor and protect her, and, forsaking all others, be faithful to her, as long as you both shall live?

Murdoch's hand was resting on Ruan's shoulder. Chris saw Ruan practice taking the rings from his pocket. They appeared momentarily in his hand, along with a piece of broken biscuit Chris suspected had something to do with JJ. Ruan would be spending the night with Annie. Annie must be at the wedding

I, Morag, in the presence of God, take you, Christopher, to be my husband. All that I am I give to you, and all that I have I share with you. Whatever the future holds, I will love you and stand by you, as long as we both shall live. This is my solemn vow.

Chris noticed Ailise Daniel sniff and fumble for her husband's hand. She had given Morag a special gift of herbs and ointments for her wedding night.

He turned his gaze back to Morag, and caressed her hand. Then he said the words that he had wanted to say for so long.

I, Christopher…

Moments later, Peter pronounced a blessing on them both.

The blessing of God Almighty, the Father, Son, and Holy Spirit, be upon you and remain with you always. Amen.

They left the church and drove to the Stein Inn at Loch Bay to enjoy a seafood dinner.

Following strict orders from Chris, Alsdair ensured that the bride and groom left at a reasonable hour for their new home.

It only took ten minutes to drive there. When they arrived, Chris carried Morag over the mud to the front door of his new cottage. The quagmire was, Chris knew, entirely due to the fact that he had labored with Murdoch and Alsdair earlier in the day, moving Morag's furniture from the White House into the new house. This had happened whilst she was spirited away by Elizabeth for a wedding day breakfast at Annie's house. Evidently, many of the neighboring women had gathered there to offer their best wishes, and to share some earthy wisdom for the wedding night.

He pushed his way through the door and gently put her down.

Morag stood quite still, as if feeling the place. Chris could understand. She'd not ever been inside it before. Eventually, she said, "It's beautifully warm…and amazingly quiet."

Chris led her through the doorway in Hamish's stone wall to the study. "This is your study, darling." With a lump in his throat, he added, "It has a wonderful view over the loch." He then led her into the bedroom, showing her the en-suite and the walk-in wardrobe.

"And where did you say the bed was?" she asked sweetly.

As the weeks passed, the plastering and painting were completed, the teething problems of the wind turbine were sorted out, and the outside garden was landscaped. Ruan was allowed to choose the paint color for his own room, resulting in alternate walls being painted yellow and red. Morag's response had simply been, "Just paint his furniture white. Then it will work."

Annie had agreed to come two mornings a week, "…if only to bring you some proper cooking." She'd been scandalized at Chris's minimalistic kitchen, and adamantly refused to use that 'newfangled cooking thing.'

The day of Ruan's educational assessment eventually arrived. It was not quite a glittering success.

"What's the capital of England?"

"I dunno."

"Where do Eskimos live?"

"I dunno."

Ruan did, nonetheless, impress the education officer who accompanied Ms. Eden with his knowledge of English and math. The dedicated efforts of Morag and Elizabeth had resulted in good progress in both areas. They were less impressed when Ruan enthusiastically recounted how he and Chris had made a gun for firing tennis balls, using a length of poly pipe, an aerosol can and a lighter.

At the end of the assessment, Ms. Eden pursed her lips. Chris suspected that she was about to air a litany of shortcomings, so he decided to forestall her. "Ms. Eden, as you can see, I now own a house. I am also married to Morag, and am in receipt of a generous pension. Later this year, it is expected that I will begin a half-time job with the Crofting Federation and St. Andrews University. Not only that, but I'm told the authorities foresee no difficulty in our application to formally adopt Ruan." He smiled at the social worker. "Notwithstanding this, Morag and I would very much appreciate your assessment of Ruan's educational standard. Is he at a stage where he can now fit in to his year group at school?"

The black Bentley edged its way along the rutted dirt track to the graveyard. It came to a halt.

The driver, in a somber gray suit, got out, unfurled an umbrella, and opened the back door. An elegant middle-aged woman stepped out and nodded to the driver. "*Merci, Francois.*" She was wrapped in a black cloak, and had pulled the hood over her head.

The woman took the umbrella from the driver and stepped delicately across the tussocks of grass to the far side of the graveyard. She stopped at one particular grave and knelt down. At the base of the lichen-encrusted headstone was a bunch of wildflowers. She picked them up, smelled them, and allowed the delicate petals to brush her lips.

The woman then extracted another bunch of flowers from inside her cloak. All of them were red. She laid them on the grave, and stared at them for some time.

Eventually, she picked up the wildflowers again and concealed them within her cloak. She reached out one more time to touch the red flowers—as if saying a benediction. She knew that next day they would be gone.

The woman rose to her feet and returned to the car.

"Now Morag, are you ready for this? I've dimmed the lights. Whenever you are ready, begin to open your eyes."

Morag squeezed Chris's hand fiercely. She kept her eyes shut. The only thing escaping from them were tears.

"What's the matter?" asked Dr. Hardy.

"Do you mind, Doctor, if Chris is the one standing in front of me. I…I'd like him to be the first one I see—if I can."

"Certainly. I quite understand." He moved aside to make room for Chris.

Chris took his place and gave Morag's hand a reassuring squeeze. "I must warn you, darling, that you did marry me sight unseen. Promise me you won't be too appalled."

"Ach, you're handsome enough, Chris Norman, my fingers tell me that."

Chris lowered his eyes to suppress his emotions. He failed, and found himself sobbing.

There was an intake of breath…a pause…and then Morag said, "You cut yourself shaving this morning."

Chapter 13

A crookit stick will throw a crookit shadow.
(Scottish proverb)

The grandeur of the Scottish mountains were on display in
their full glory. With childlike delight, Morag exclaimed at the
spectacular vistas as each unfolded. However, the sweetest view of
all was the sight of the man at the wheel of the car. The previous
night, they had again made love in the attic of her parents' town-
house. They'd done so in the dark. She'd found her sightedness so
overwhelming that she'd asked, shyly, for the light to be switched off.

Once they crossed the bridge to Skye, Morag twisted in her seat
to take in views that were once so familiar, and once so lost. She saw
Chris smiling at her. How could she explain what she felt? "It is my
home," she said simply.

"I know, Morag. You'll always be an island girl."

He understood.

She wasn't surprised.

They pulled up outside Annie's cottage where both Ruan and

Elizabeth were staying. Elizabeth was the first to come running out. On seeing Morag's gleeful face, she flung her arms around her—and the pair of them danced up and down. Annie and Ruan followed with JJ at their heels.

Morag knelt down and hugged Ruan, then held him at arm's length to inspect him. She gently touched his face in wonderment.

It didn't take long for Ruan to tire of her attention. He broke free and ran down to the beach with JJ.

Chris finally managed to disentangle Morag from both Elizabeth and Annie, and drove her the short distance to their new cottage.

Morag immediately set about exploring the house in minute detail. She ran her hands over the triple-glazed windows and the solid, insulated walls. Tears came to her eyes.

"What's wrong, darling?" Chris looked about him. "I know it's very Spartan, but we'll soon fix that. There'll be curtains and pictures and…"

Morag held up her hand to stop his flow. "I love it, Chris. Stop your fretting." She leaned back against the stone wall of what had once had been the old cottage. "I can see the whole loch through the front windows, even from here. It's beautiful."

Chris left her to explore, saying that he would make them both a cup of tea.

She moved through the house marveling at all Chris had managed to achieve. Finally, she sat at her study desk and gazed out the window. Some minutes later, she was roused from her reverie as she became aware of Chris leaning against the doorpost watching her.

That night, they made love to the light of a single candle.

She drifted off to sleep, but awoke a few hours later and relit the candle. Then she propped herself up on an elbow, and studied the details of Chris's face. After some time, he awoke.

She smiled at being caught out.

He reached out and enfolded her in his arms.

By the time she woke in the morning, Chris had already left. Faint noises from the kitchen told her that Ruan was having his morning school lesson with Elizabeth. She got out of bed and walked into the en-suite to brush her teeth. As she looked in the mirror, her eyes were drawn to the Celtic cross hanging around her neck. She studied its reflection closely. As she did, the untidy tangle of swirls at the center of the cross swam into focus to form two entwined letters, 'AC.'

Morag's jaw dropped open. The Celtic cross was not just a pectoral cross. It was a seal, designed to be pressed into hot wax. The stylized letters had been carved in mirror image at the center of the cross.

It took a moment for the significance of the two initials to sink in. The Celtic stone was none other than the seal of Angus Crenshaw, the old Laird—the man Lachlan Daniel had reputedly murdered!

Excitement rose up within her. She had to share her discovery with Chris.

Morag dressed quickly and joined Elizabeth, Ruan and Annie in the kitchen. Annie was baking biscuits. Seeing a roll of greaseproof paper on the edge of the bench, Morag tore off a sheet, placed it over the cross and rubbed Ruan's pencil over the paper to bring out the patterning. When she'd finished, she reversed the paper and held it up to the light. There was no doubt about it. The entwined letters 'AC' could be seen clearly, surrounded by restless Celtic patterning. The seal had been ingeniously designed.

She thought momentarily about telling Elizabeth and Annie about her discovery, but decided to share her discovery with Chris first.

Even as she pondered what she might do, her mobile phone rang. It was Chris. "I can only speak for a few seconds, darling. My battery's dying. I'm in Portree for the morning. I'll drop in to see Alsdair before coming home. He's just rung to say his mother's arrived from France." He chuckled. "Evidently, she came all the way in a chauffeur-driven car. Can you believe it?"

Morag smiled. She could believe it.

Chris continued. "Alsdair wants us to meet his mother, and is desperate for her to meet Elizabeth. As he's a bit spooked at having just the two of them to dinner at his place, I've invited them to have dinner with us tonight. I hope that's all right. Annie has agreed to stay on and do the cooking. I'm sorry that…"

Before she could utter a word about the Celtic cross, his phone died.

Morag rolled her eyes in frustration.

Back in the kitchen, Ruan was stuffing some freshly baked biscuits, wrapped untidily in greaseproof paper, into a plastic lunch-box. "Annie's told me to give some of these to Alsdair," he said.

"Ach, but I wonder why I bother," complained Annie. She glared at the tiny bench-top oven. "If the devil had an oven as small as this, we'd all be laughing."

Alsdair was surprised. His father had never visited his cottage before. He watched as Penmann helped the old Laird enter the threshold and step down into the parlor. Once inside, the old man instructed Penmann to wait for him in the car.

The Laird had a sling over his shoulder that held a small metal bottle. A plastic tube ran from the bottle to feed oxygen into his nostrils. Alsdair led him to a leather armchair.

"Can I make you a coffee, father?" he asked.

His father grimaced.

Alsdair went on to reassure him. "I've some freshly ground coffee and a coffee machine."

"Black," ordered the Laird.

The old man looked around the parlor that served as kitchen, lounge, office, and sitting room—and scowled. "I didn't raise you to live in a place like this. I don't know how you can do it."

"I'm comfortable enough, father. What brings you here?"

"Your fool brother, Jason, will shortly be declared bankrupt. His greed got the better of him, and I can no longer trust him to run the estate or operate the family trust." The old man stared into the fire burning in the hearth. "I've removed him as signatory for the trust, and told him he will remain simply as titular head."

"I'm sorry you felt the need to do that."

The old Laird grunted. "The thing is, Jason left this morning without telling anyone. I suspected that he'd done a runner, so I told Penmann to contact our travel agent. He's discovered that Jason is flying out to Malaysia this evening on a one-way ticket." The old man slapped the arm of his chair in frustration. "It looks as if he will be trying to dodge the stringencies of bankruptcy by hiding abroad with his low-life business cronies."

"Yes, it does," agreed Alsdair. He looked at the hunched figure of his father. Whilst it was impossible to feel sorry for the old tyrant, he could at least understand his frustration. "You must feel it badly."

"I need you as a signatory who is able to operate the family estate." The old man paused to catch his breath. "I'd like you to take over from Jason."

"You can't be serious. You've never made any secret of your... er..."

"...Disappointment in you. Don't for a moment think that has changed. You lack ambition, and you are altogether too frivolous. But you at least have some sort of commitment to the island."

"That's hardly a ringing endorsement." Alsdair forbore from explaining that he was in fact comfortably well off, and had achieved significant success as a writer—a field in which very few succeed.

"Will you agree to become a signatory to the Family Estate?"

Aldair massaged his temples. "Who are the other signatories?"

"Technically, your mother is, but in reality she is a sleeping partner. I am now the only other signatory." The old man again began to wheeze. After catching his breath, he gripped the side of his chair. His voice quivered with passion. "The family heritage and the estate must not be allowed to die with me."

Alsdair wanted to ask why, but knew it was futile. He leaned back and said slowly. "If I am to be a signatory, I will need to be fully involved with the decisions concerning the estate. I am not content to simply be your puppet."

The old Laird looked at him with derision. "Oh, so now you want to play Laird, do you?"

"No. You want me to play Laird. If I take this on, I want to meet with Murdoch and Penmann at least once a week."

The old man stared into the fire. Eventually, he said, "Tell Penmann to bring in the briefcase with the documents."

The papers were signed and were being returned to the briefcase when there was knock on the door. When Alsdair investigated, he was relieved to discover it was Chris.

Before Chris had a chance of entering the cottage, he heard a high-pitched yell behind him. "Oi! Wait up."

Ruan came running up, clutching a plastic lunchbox. The boy said, between gasps of breath, "Hey Chris, Mum's dead keen to chat with you. It's important, she says. I was meant to tell Alsdair, so he could tell you." He then pushed past Chris and thrust a lunchbox at Alsdair. "And Annie told me to give Alsdair some of her biscuits."

It took a moment for Chris to realize who 'Mum' was. *Morag! Mum!* He smiled. In his own way, Ruan was making his own decisions.

"Come in, both of you," said Alsdair.

Chris stepped into the parlor in time to see a short, barrel-chested man in a black leather jacket putting some documents into a briefcase. Beside him, an old man was seated in an armchair.

Alsdair introduced them. "Chris, meet my father, Aaron Haines, and his personal assistant, Mike Penmann."

Penmann shook Chris's hand, but the old Laird didn't offer his.

"Come and join us for a coffee," said Alsdair. He turned to Ruan. "What sort of biscuits have we got?"

"Ginger," said Ruan. The boy backed away into the kitchen, as if overawed by everyone's presence.

The old Laird turned to Chris. "So, you're the Norman boy."

Before Chris could stop himself, he found himself saying, "No, mate. That would be Ruan. I'm a married man." He held the old Laird's gaze without expression, and allowed the atmosphere, already chilly, to drop a few more degrees.

Alsdair jumped in and explained. "Chris married Morag about a month ago." He favored his father with a glare. "They are both very special friends of mine."

The old Laird nodded. "This would be Morag Daniel, the blind woman?"

Chris answered, "No. It would be Morag Norman, who can now see—thanks to the miracle of stem cell research."

There was an uncomfortable silence.

Alsdair handed round the box of biscuits. The Laird shook his head, but then snapped, "Wait!" Then he reached out and fingered the greaseproof paper that splayed up inside the edge of the box. Chris could see that there was some sort of penciled drawing on it. The Laird's face looked grim. With a pang of guilt, Chris hoped he hadn't pushed the old man too far.

"Take me home, Penmann," the old man wheezed.

When they had gone, Chris flopped down into the vacated chair. "Geez, mate, I hope I wasn't too rude to the old codger."

Alsdair handed Chris a coffee. "You do have a rather unique way of upsetting members of my family. But his behavior was inexcusable. The blighter may have chosen my genes, but he doesn't get to choose my friends."

"Spoken like a champion." Chris raised his coffee mug in salute, as Ruan crept out from behind the kitchen bench. Chris turned to him. "Ruan, mate. What's the matter?"

"I don't like the old Laird."

"What do you mean? You've hardly had anything to do with the bloke."

"Don't have to."

"Why don't you like him?"

"Da didn't. He had a fight with him. Da were right mad. Something Da thought was unfair to crofters. Something the old Laird were trying to hide. They had a right stramash."

Alsdair looked at Ruan with alarm. "Are you sure?"

"Sure as I'm standin' here," said Ruan indignantly.

"You're talking about the old Laird, not the new one?" asked Chris.

"Aye."

"When did this happen?"

Ruan dropped his head. "It were on the day of the fire. The day Da died."

Alsdair paced up and down the lounge as he waited for Chris. Eventually, Chris came down the stairs. Alsdair looked at him desperately. "I'd kill for a whiskey."

Chris raised an eyebrow at him.

"Purely medicinal," assured Alsdair. He stopped his pacing. "Will Ruan be all right tonight?"

Chris nodded. "He's had his tea and will be off to bed shortly. He's upstairs in the attic—which he seems to have commandeered for himself." He smiled. "I left him researching dinosaurs on my computer. The dogs are with him."

Chris stood in front of the mirror to adjust his attire. Both he and Alsdair were wearing jackets and kilts. "Isn't all this getup a bit over the top?"

Alsdair shook his head and gave him a rueful smile. "Wait 'til you meet my mother."

The bedroom door across the hallway opened. Alsdair could hear Morag saying. "No. You'll need no jewels, Liz." She lapsed into the patois of the islands. "You're beautiful, just."

Elizabeth whispered urgently inside. Alsdair couldn't make out what she said.

He did, however, hear Morag's reply as she stood in the doorway. "It's your heart she'll fall in love with, mo ghaoil, and you're pure gold." Morag pulled Elizabeth out of the bedroom into the hall. "Ach, now look at you," she continued. "You look wonderful." Morag smiled at Alsdair. "Isn't she now?"

Alsdair looked at Elizabeth. His mouth was open, and he hoped he wasn't salivating. Elizabeth was wearing a simple black cocktail dress, and had chosen to leave her hair down. The simplicity of her dress showed off her natural beauty to full effect.

"My darling…" Alsdair got no further.

Annie came in, carrying a tray of antipasto, complaining loudly. "There is no way that wee cooking gadget thingy will cook a meal for five." Setting down the tray, she put her hands on her hips. "You're going to need every bit of my apple pie to save the night from disaster." Having made her dire prediction, she sniffed and bustled back into the kitchen.

Alsdair tore his eyes away from Elizabeth, and accepted a sherry from Chris.

His mother arrived fifteen minutes late.

Alsdair and Chris went outside to greet her as her chauffeur opened the car door.

Alsdair smiled. Even with her beauty and careful dignity enshrouded in a black cloak, Marianne knew how to make a regal entrance.

He kissed her on both cheeks.

She inspected him briefly, turned and, without a word, held out her hand to Chris.

Alsdair's smile became a grin. It was clear that Chris was unsure whether to kiss her hand or shake it. In the end, he elected simply to take her fingers in his own and bow.

Alsdair nodded his approval.

His mother looked at Chris and smiled. "Christopher, I am pleased to meet you." Marianne's voice was a purr. She glanced at the two of them. "You both look very *formidable* in your tartan."

The triple-glazed door shut behind them with a gentle thud as they came indoors. Marianne looked around and pushed back her hood. "I think I will need to take both my cloak and jacket off. I had not expected the house to be so warm and comfortable."

Ruan, struggling to restrain both dogs, came bounding down the stairs.

Chris took control of Bess. "Marianne, this is Ruan. He…" Chris paused. "…he completes our family here."

Marianne shook him formally by the hand. "Good evening, Ruan."

Ruan seized the opportunity to air some of his newfound knowledge. "Did you know the largest dinosaur was as long as two school buses, and as tall as a four-story building? He'd be a big bugger, right enough, wouldn't he?"

"A monster," said Marianne, with creditable poise.

Alsdair saw Chris roll his eyes.

"Watch your language, Ruan," Chris said, and pointed to his bedroom. "To bed. Twenty minutes reading, and then lights out."

Ruan padded through the door into the lounge, kissed Morag and Elizabeth goodnight, and continued through to his bedroom.

As Chris hung up Marianne's cloak, Alsdair looked at his mother. She was dressed in a pewter colored silk dress and jacket. Strings of pearls hung around her neck. He took a deep breath. "Mother, come and meet two wonderful women, one of whom is very nervous."

Marianne looked at him and placed a hand on his cheek. She whispered. "You are sure, Alsdair?"

Alsdair smiled. "Yes, mother; very sure. Come and meet her."

As he shepherded her into the lounge, he saw Elizabeth and Morag glance at Marianne with ill-disguised awe.

Marianne, however, proved more than equal to the occasion. She rounded on Alsdair and scolded him. "Alsdair, you know that French women hate being introduced to beautiful women, but here are two of them. *Mon dieu*! Why have you done this to me?"

Morag stepped forward with a laugh. "I am Morag, and this…" She took Elizabeth by the arm. "…is my best friend, Elizabeth."

Marianne inspected her comprehensively in the milliseconds that followed. Elizabeth dropped her eyes shyly. "Welcome back to Scotland, Marianne. Alsdair has told me you are very special, and I can well believe it."

Marianne stepped forward and kissed her on both cheeks. "This is very frightening for you, and I'm glad. Mothers like their sons' girlfriends to be a little frightened of them. I will keep you frightened of me by asking you a question. Tell me, have you made love to my son yet?"

"Mother!" protested Alsdair.

"What is the matter?" Marianne affected all innocence. "She

would know if she had…and she would have told her best friend…who would have told her handsome husband on the pillow." She gave an elegant shrug. "So, I am the only one who does not know."

Elizabeth surprised everyone by saying, "I would very much like to make love to your son, Marianne, and have come dangerously close on a few occasions. It is just that we have this old-fashioned idea we'd like to keep lovemaking for the marriage bed—where there are no inhibitions, no doubts, and no regrets."

Marianne looked at Elizabeth and nodded. "Bravo, Elizabeth. I have provoked you, and seen your spirit. Mothers-in-law are never meant to say this to daughters-in-law, but I think you will be good for my son. Now, you can relax, *n'est-ce pas*?" She gave a soft laugh.

"Mother, you are incorrigible. I haven't even proposed yet."

"Why not? Why would you delay with such a beautiful woman?"

"I was waiting for your approval first."

"You have it. Now propose."

Marianne was being outrageous. Alsdair knew it and laughed. This was her way of making her approval of Elizabeth very public. In truth, although Alsdair was very much his own man, he couldn't resist making the most of the occasion.

Elizabeth, wide-eyed in disbelief at Marianne's comments, looked on open-mouthed as Alsdair knelt down in front of her.

He cleared his throat. "My darling Elizabeth. This wasn't meant to happen until we were alone tonight." Alsdair fished in his jacket pocket and produced a small box. He opened it to reveal a diamond ring set in gold, worked with a simple Celtic pattern. "Will you marry me? Will you marry me despite my mother? Will you marry me despite my unreasonable passion for remote, uncivilized corners of Scotland? Will you marry me despite my inability to organize a romantic engagement night?" He shrugged. "Will you marry me?"

Elizabeth looked at him for an eternity, her eyes soft with love. She lifted her head, and spoke. "If you promise that I will always enjoy your mother's company; and if you promise to teach me your love of Scotland; and surround me with friends such as I have tonight—and if you love me half as much as I love you, then, yes, Alsdair Haines, I will marry you."

Marianne turned to Chris and asked, "You have champagne?"

"Marianne!" Chris raised his hands. "This is Scotland! I have a single malt whiskey awaiting our attention. But first, risotto, Australian red wine, and then a famous Scottish tradition—Annie's apple pie."

Marianne raised an eyebrow. "Risotto, in Scotland? Things have indeed changed."

Dinner was a great success. Afterward, as they lingered over their drinks, the story of what had transpired at the ceilidh emerged. Alsdair experienced a moment of misgiving as to how Marianne would take this, given that Jason was her eldest son.

He need not have worried. Marianne laughed delightedly. "It will do him no harm to be bested by a woman. He is a bully, like... well, never mind. But tell me, are the interests of the crofters now safe. Will he try again, do you think?"

Alsdair shrugged. "That's just it. None of us can be sure."

Marianne gave him a considered look. "Alsdair, are you simply fighting your brother, or do you have real concerns for the crofters?"

"It is a good question." Alsdair played with the stem of his wine-glass, twirling it between his fingers. "I don't think I'm vindictive, but neither can I claim the virtue of Sir Galahad."

"Sir Galahad?" Marianne looked confused.

"Let's just say that it was wrong for the crofters to be tricked into debt, so that they could be manipulated. And it was wrong for Jason to vandalize Chris's cottage in order to protect himself against a potential vote against him." He twirled the glass again. "I've lived among the crofters for a few years now. They do it tough enough... and I like them. So yes, I do care."

Elizabeth leaned across and kissed him.

Marianne looked into Alsdair's gray eyes and smiled sadly. "My sons—so different. One championing the crofters' interest; the other wanting to exploit them." She sighed. "Who would be a mother?"

"The trouble is," said Morag, "Ruan remembers his father being concerned about something that he'd learned which he thought was unfair to crofters—something he discovered when your husband was looking at some documents he'd taken from his safe. We're just not sure what's afoot."

Everyone was silent for a while, lost in their respective thoughts.

"I would breathe a whole lot easier if I knew what was in that safe," Alsdair admitted.

"This is in the safe in his study, yes?" inquired Marianne.

"Yes."

"Then I will find out for you."

"Mother, you can't do that!" protested Alsdair.

"*Mon cheri*, I am old enough to pay you no attention. I think I have a good chance. Leave it to me." She smiled. "We are fellow conspirators, no?"

The old Laird stared at his wife. She looked as beautiful as ever with her delicate features and dark, bobbed hair. He sighed and remembered the times when she had responded to his love. No more, however. Her love for him had died many years ago. He had long since resigned himself to the reality of it, and was grateful that she did at least keep up appearances by visiting him from time to time— if only to see her sons. How he wished he could rewrite the past. His love for her burned as bright as ever.

The two of them were seated in his study, taking a brandy nightcap before retiring to their respective bedrooms. The ritual had been established over the years, and was the nearest thing to intimacy that Aaron now experienced with his estranged wife.

"Why don't you come back and live here with me, near your sons? With this emphysema, I only have a few more years to live. You could have an entire wing of this house to yourself."

"No, Aaron. Your sexual peccadilloes, and your cruelty do not make this possible. Please be grateful that I at least come and visit you from time to time." She gave a delicate yawn. "Now I will go to bed. But first, I will put my jewelry in your safe. Will you please open it for me?"

Bitter at himself, and tormented by his love, he got to his feet, crossed the room and opened the safe. Turning around, he looked at the striking figure of his wife, sighed, and made to return to his chair.

"I am wearing the gold chain you gave me around my waist, and I wish to remove it. I would ask you to wait outside until I call you to lock the safe again."

"You've kept the chain then?"

"I have."

Powerful images flooded into his mind. He had bought the chain after she laughed at seeing one whilst watching an old black and white film of a Middle-Eastern dancer. He had fixed it around her slim waist himself and then made love to her. Aaron breathed in his oxygen, and walked slowly out of the room.

Four minutes later, she opened the door, said goodnight, and made her way to her bedroom.

The old Laird stepped back into the study and crossed to the safe. Taking a set of keys from his pocket, he opened it. Marianne's clutch purse was lying inside it. He took it out and smelled it. A wave of anguish swept over him as the familiar perfume played on his senses. Opening the bag, he saw the earrings and the strings of pearls inside. There was also a lightweight gold chain, but it wasn't the gold chain he had given her. Was it a small lie to spare his feelings, or something more ominous? The events of the day had been deeply disturbing. He was not predisposed to give anyone, even Marianne, the benefit of the doubt. He reached past a stack of folders to a box file standing at the back of the safe. He withdrew it and walked to the desk with it. After sitting down, he extracted two old pieces of paper.

He looked at the familiar pages, hating them. So much of his life was controlled by those pages—and so much death. He picked up the first. It was a letter from his grandfather warning his son of the danger to his family if the personal seal of Laird Angus Crenshaw was ever found. The other piece of paper was a letter from Laird Angus. It was a call for crofters to gather together in protest at Haines's plans for the clearances. The Laird's personal seal at the bottom signified the authenticity and urgency of the call.

The rest of the story was told to him by his grandfather, who had impressed on him the need for secrecy. Way back in 1860, the local Laird, Angus Crenshaw, had been sympathetic to the plight of the crofters. He had instructed his estate manager, Lachlan Daniel, to make copies of the letter now sitting on the desk, and to affix his seal to the bottom of each copy. He was then to deliver them throughout the region, calling the crofters to action.

Luckily, the plan was discovered by his grandfather, Laird Haines. Haines was desperate to get the crofters off his land so that he could generate some income. He'd crept to the house of Crenshaw's estate manager one night and killed both him and his wife. However, whilst he was able to intercept the letter before it could be copied and sent out, he was not able to find Crenshaw's seal, the Celtic pectoral cross. The wily estate manager, mindful of its importance, had hidden it.

Having failed to find the seal, Haines set fire to the estate manager's cottage in order to remove all evidence of the murder. He'd then ridden over to the manor of his nemesis, Angus Crenshaw. Crenshaw let him inside, only to be forced at knifepoint to write a letter implicating himself and his estate manager in a secret scheme to dispossess the crofters of their land. Having extorted the letter, Haines killed Crenshaw with the dagger he'd taken from Lachlan Daniel.

Aaron Haines smiled. It was the perfect crime.

When the locals discovered the murder and the incriminating letter, they went off to confront Lachlan Daniel. They arrived to discover the house a smoldering ruin, and Lachlan and his wife dead inside it. Only the son, not yet returned from fishing, had escaped death. In their anger, the locals destroyed what was left of the Daniel cottage and voted to absorb the Daniel land into their own common grazing land.

Weeks later, the crofters voted to come under the authority of their neighboring Laird, Haines. It did them no good, however. Within five years, his grandfather had forced most of them off their land.

Aaron sat in his study and pondered the violence of his history.

He knew all too well that it was vital that Crenshaw's seal, and the letter in front of him, never be joined together. The seal would prove the authenticity of the letter.

There had been no real threat of this ever happening —until now.

Today he'd had the shock of seeing Crenshaw's seal impressed on, of all things, some greaseproof paper wrapped around some biscuits. The Daniel woman didn't know what she had. He shook his head in disbelief. *The fool.*

If the truth ever came out, the consequences would be... He shuddered. *I should have destroyed the letter years ago.* He knew why he hadn't. He'd been fascinated by it. The letter represented power, control and, above all, victory. It was intoxicating. But now was the time to end it, and protect the Haines heritage forever. He heaved himself up from the desk, picked up the two letters and crossed to the fireplace. With the regret of an alcoholic watching whiskey pour down a drain, he watched the two pieces of paper flare up momentarily and die.

The wind had risen during the night and was howling over the tops of the stumpy chimneys of the crofters' cottages. Alsdair needed to concentrate as the violent gusts dashed rain against the windscreen of the Subaru. He pulled up in front of Chris and Morag's house, fought his way to the front door and pushed the doorbell. Morag opened the door dressed in jeans, tee-shirt, and bare feet. As it closed, all evidence of the storm outside became muted. It was warm and peaceful inside.

Chris was in the kitchen having his morning cup of coffee. It being Saturday, there was no home schooling for Ruan. Alsdair could hear him bumping around upstairs, probably with the dogs.

"I can't stay for more than a moment," he said as he entered the kitchen. However, he allowed himself to be tempted by the smell and accepted a cup of coffee.

"My mother is amazing, he said as he flopped into a chair. "She emailed me photos of two documents from my father's safe last night. She took them with her Smartphone. Don't ask me how she managed it."

Alsdair produced a large yellow envelope and extracted two pieces of paper. He unfolded them, and smoothed them out on the kitchen table. "The good news is that I don't think the crofters need to worry about any skullduggery from Jason or my father. Take a look. Both documents appear to be quite old—one of them very old. They seem to be referring to the drama surrounding the clearances years ago."

Chris fingered the documents and shook his head. "Didn't all this happen way back in the nineteenth century?"

Alsdair nodded. "These documents suggest that old Angus Crenshaw was on the side of the crofters after all. The evidence would be incontrovertible if it was accompanied by his personal seal. It would be like having his signature on the bottom." He looked up at Morag. "I've been stewing over this all night, Morag. This has huge implications on what the true role of your ancestor was. It blows everything that has been popularly believed out of the water."

Morag took the documents from Chris and studied them. Alsdair noticed that she had turned very pale. He hoped the information he'd brought wasn't too upsetting for her. The last thing he wanted was to… He looked at his watch. "Good grief, I've got to run. I daren't be late."

Morag cut in. "Alsdair, you won't believe what I…"

But Alsdair was on his feet and heading for the door. "Sorry Morag. Must run. I overslept. What with all this intrigue, I didn't sleep much last night. I'm picking up Elizabeth in five minutes and taking her for lunch at Portree, and then to dinner at the Glenview Hotel." He smiled ruefully. "I need to make up for my lack of romance last night." He sketched a wave. "I'll see you tomorrow. You can tell me your news then."

With a 'whump' of the front door, Alsdair was gone.

Morag said nothing for a long time. She read and re-read the two documents that lay in front of her. Then, without a word, she reached up, unhooked the Celtic cross from around her neck, and placed it on the ancient letter from Angus Crenshaw.

Chris nodded slowly. "Alsdair has never seen the stone cross, and doesn't know we have it, does he?"

"No."

He whistled. "Wow!"

Morag stared into the middle distance. There was another disturbing significance to these documents that Chris didn't understand. It was evident that the Haines Lairds had known the truth of Crenshaw's loyalty for generations, yet had chosen to suppress it—presumably for their own interest. It was beginning to dawn on Morag what those interests were. The Haines family had benefited from Crenshaw's demise, and even more when he was branded a traitor. Lying in front of her was hard evidence that Crenshaw was organizing a political rally for the western part of the island, which would have had extraordinary significance for the island's society and politics. Contrary to popular belief, Crenshaw had been a supporter of the crofters. Her suspicions, formed while researching her thesis, had been well founded.

Tears welled up in her eyes. If Crenshaw was innocent, then it was likely his estate manager, Lachlan Daniel, was also innocent of wrongdoing. She thought of the generations of her family who had suffered scorn and derision from the close-knit community of islanders, and started to cry. She wept for the loneliness that it had caused her. She wept for her father. He'd remained stoic as he had continued to teach the island's children—until he could bear it no longer and left. She wept for her grandfather and all those who had gone before—each of them branded by shame.

Chris held her as she sobbed and sobbed against his chest.

The following morning, Morag stood at the window in her study, nursing a coffee. She could see some of the locals climbing over the rocks and walking the sands, beach-combing for any treasure thrown up by the sea. The storm that had raged through most of yesterday and continued into the night had now abated.

Her thoughts were interrupted by the ringing of her phone. She answered it, and was surprised to hear Marianne's voice.

"Is this my beautiful Scottish hostess, and co-conspirator?"

Morag's spirits lifted. "Hello, Marianne. It was so good to meet you the other evening. You were beautiful, outrageous, and awe-inspiring."

"I happily accept all three compliments. Now, *mon cheri*, I am ringing to thank you for a lovely evening, and also to say something important."

"Oh?"

"It is this. My bags are packed, and I will be spending the day with Elizabeth and Alsdair before I drive to France. I tell you this to let you know that you are free to tell Aaron you have seen the documents in his safe, if you feel it necessary to do so. Alsdair is greatly disturbed at the thought that his father may have obscured the truth about a matter that has so greatly affected your family. Although it will be impossible to prove this, I still think you can justly demand some sort of explanation, without worrying about the consequences for me. If you choose not to confront Aaron, know that Alsdair certainly will do so on your behalf. So, my lovely Morag, that is all I have to say. *Bonne chance.*"

"Thank you so much, Marianne. *Au revoir.*"

Morag continued to stare out of the window, deep in thought. Marianne had given her the opportunity of bringing closure to the issue that had tormented her family for so long. However, she was far from certain how she should proceed. She did not want the wrong people to be hurt. Certainly, she was reluctant to involve Chris, and put him in bad standing with the old Laird. She was equally reluctant for Alsdair to do it, since he was not in possession of all the evidence. A conviction grew within her that she needed to face Aaron Haines herself, and to look into his eyes when she confronted him with the evidence. The issue was personal—very, very personal.

Chris came into the study, walked up behind her, and put his arms around her.

"In all the excitement of yesterday, I forgot to tell you that St. Andrews and the Crofting Federation want us to run a crofting center. They want to expand their courses to include cultural studies, but that will depend on us finding a classroom that holds up to twelve people." He nuzzled her hair. "It suddenly occurred to me that we've got the attic here. It's a huge space—warm, light, and airy. Do you think we could use it, at least in the short term."

Whilst Morag luxuriated in his attention, her mind was on other things. "Do you suppose you can drop me off at the track running up to the Bluff? I need to do some thinking and sort some things out. I'll walk home. The exercise will do me good."

Chris kissed the side of her neck. "Where do you go to in that lovely, absent-minded head of yours, darling?"

"Did I miss something?" She tried to remember what Chris had been saying. She had heard his words, but they hadn't registered. *St. Andrews… crofting…*

"Yes, my darling, but it can wait. I'll get your coat."

Ten minutes later, she climbed out of the car and watched Chris drive back down to the village. Suddenly, she felt very alone and vulnerable. She hoped he would turn around and come back, but he didn't. Irritated by her own weakness, she shook her head and started walking. However, instead of turning left up the track to the Bluff, she turned right through the gates to the manor house.

Mr. Penmann opened the door to her. As he did, she saw him give a start of surprise. He recovered quickly and asked what her business was. On hearing her request to see Aaron Haines, he escorted her down a paneled corridor.

Penmann knocked on a door, and then opened it. "Mrs. Morag Norman to see you, sir."

There was a long silence before the old Laird replied. "Tell her to come in."

Aaron Haines was hunched behind his desk in the darkened

room. He was wearing formal Scottish dress. A glass banker's lamp reflected its light from the desk to the underside of his features, making him look grotesque. He stared at her, waiting for her to speak.

Without saying anything, she withdrew an envelope from inside her coat, removed the copies of the two letters, unfolded them and placed them on the desk.

Aaron Haines recognized them instantly, but did not allow even the faintest flicker of emotion to reach his face. Marianne had betrayed him in a way more damaging than she could possibly have realized. The image of Morag standing in front of his desk carried a sense of déjà vu. His mind recalled Ruan's father standing on exactly the same spot, years ago.

Magnus had been working on the estate to supplement his income. He'd discovered Jason's plans to develop the Bluff, and had stormed into the Laird's study to demand an explanation. The Laird returned from the bathroom to find Magnus stalking up and down his study. On the desk, in full view, had been the two same letters. The risk that he might have seen them had sealed Magnus's fate.

"What do you mean by this, young lady?"

"These documents are copies of letters you keep in your safe. Marianne was kind enough to supply them. They are clear evidence that Angus Crenshaw was supporting the interests of the crofters, and that your family knew it. They withheld this evidence, fearing its disclosure—presumably for reasons of self-interest." The Daniels woman fixed him with a steely look. "Why did you continue to perpetrate this injustice by withholding this information? You knew that doing so would have direct implications for my family."

The old Laird leaned forward. "You are rude, ignorant, and presumptive." He took a deep breath from his oxygen tank, and then stabbed at the papers. "These are no more than a hoax, probably put out by Crenshaw and your ancestor to fool the crofters. I simply kept them as an historical oddity—as proof of the desperate,

245

Machiavellian schemes Crenshaw and your odious ancestor were engaged in." He sneered at her. "On top of that; these letters were obtained illegally." He waved her away. "Now get out of my sight."

The Daniels woman did not move. "Intimidation and obfuscation. I had expected both, and you didn't disappoint."

She spoke with a calmness that disturbed him. Aaron lent back in his chair as she continued to speak.

"Firstly: You know full well that Crenshaw's organization of a public rally was not the action of someone conspiring against the crofters." She pointed to the letter. "This letter is concrete evidence of Crenshaw's total commitment to bringing hope to the crofters. Secondly: your story does not explain your family's fear that Crenshaw's seal, authenticating this document, might be found." She pointed to the two pieces of paper. "This evidence is totally consistent with the research I was doing for my Master's thesis. Your family have gained a great deal from withholding this evidence." She pointed at him. "But your family's credibility will be shattered if this goes public. It might even affect the legitimacy of your claim to be Laird of this region."

"Are you attempting to blackmail me, woman?"

"A thief that is caught by the law cannot claim that the law is blackmailing him. The simple fact is, you and your family have been caught out." She paused. "But I am prepared to compromise. I don't want any of your money, and—no thanks to you—my personal standing among the crofters is now high. My father, however, needs an apology from you in writing. If you do that, I will not raise the issue publicly unless you do anything to endanger the wellbeing of the village or the crofters. Is that clear enough?"

"Don't try to bluff me, Daniel. You know Crenshaw's letter is meaningless without his signature seal. It could just be a fake." Even as he spoke, he knew it was a desperate gamble—a forlorn hope that she didn't know the significance of the cross she had in her possession.

But he looked at her expression, and knew he had lost. With a dignity that was almost regal, she dashed his hopes. "Mr. Haines, I have Crenshaw's seal. I have the Celtic cross."

As she stood there, he couldn't help but wish Jason could find a woman like this to marry. She was everything any man could wish for. Outwardly, however, he remained impassive—schooling his eyes to remain as bleak as a winter fog. "Who knows you have the Celtic cross?"

"At this stage, only my husband and myself, unless you accede to my demands."

There was yet hope. The Old Laird stabbed at a button on the console in front of him.

"Penmann, get in here."

Fifteen minutes later, Penmann drove an ex-military Land Rover to the quarry. There, he unlocked the steel door to a safe that was embedded in a bank of soil. After lifting out a small box, he closed the steel door, and returned to the Land Rover. Moments later, he was threading his way down the narrow lanes to the estate's boat-shed. It was located in a tiny bay on the other side of the headland from the village.

A clinker-built workboat was moored beside a narrow stone jetty.

Penmann picked up his carryall, and went down to the boat. As he did, the familiar rush of adrenaline coursed through him. It was not just the danger; it was infinitely more heady than that. It was the sense of power—the divine power to end someone's life.

His mind went back to the time when he had been posted to Northern Ireland during 'the troubles.' In those days, he was a sergeant in the military unit commanded by Major Aaron Haines. It was there he'd learned to kill.

Although he was more familiar with military grenades, he'd seen often enough how the mine engineers used C4 plastic explosive in the quarry. All that was needed was a detonator and a blasting cap —simplicity itself.

He had five one-pound blocks of C4 in the box. It was more

than enough. Taking three blocks of the white putty, he taped them into place in the boat's engine bay.

Chris received the phone call an hour after he dropped Morag off. It was Penmann. "Mr. Norman, I have a message from your wife. She has made her way down the steps to the rock platform at the base of the Bluff. I saw her down there and shouted down to her to make sure she was okay. She's asked me to tell you she's fine, but doesn't want to climb back up the steps. She wants you to pick her up. I said I'd offer you the use of the estate boat. It's moored in Cullin Bay between the village and the Bluff. Do you know where that is?"

"I've been there, yes."

"I can't come with you, I'm afraid. I'm working here near the Bluff, but I can keep an eye on your wife from the top, if you like. You'll find the boat is fueled and ready to go. Just push the start button and operate the throttle beside the wheel. It's flat calm, so there shouldn't be any problems. I'll light a small fire at the top of the Bluff so that you know exactly where to come to."

"Thank you. I'd be grateful if you would continue to keep an eye on Morag. Her enthusiasm can sometimes run away with her."

Penmann laughed. "I'll do that. However, she said not to bother picking her up until one o'clock, as she's having lots of fun. High tide is not for another eight hours, so she'll be quite safe." He paused. "Oh, and one more thing. She asked if you would bring the stone cross, whatever that is. Evidently she's discovered a lobster creel and wants to show you something."

Chris was silent. A frisson of alarm ran through him.

"Are you all right?" Penmann asked. "Have you got all that?"

"Yes, thank you. Tell her I'll pick her up at one o'clock..." He looked at his watch. "...in three hours' time."

Chris bolted from the house to the Cherokee, ignoring the stab of pain in his left leg. He drove the short distance down the fore-shore track to Alsdair's cottage and found Marianne, Elizabeth and

Alsdair sitting outside, enjoying the mid-morning sun. He called out, "I think Morag is in trouble, and Penmann may be holding her against her will."

Alsdair stood up in an instant. "What! Tell me what's happened."

Chris couldn't conceal his bitterness. "I suspect it's all to do with this wretched crofters' thing, and the letters we saw."

"Damn and blast it," Alsdair said. "I'm so sorry, Chris. I'll ring my father straight away and put things straight with him."

"Perhaps wait for a bit—at least until I know a bit more of Morag's situation. I don't want to make a bad thing worse and panic people into doing silly things. Just keep your mobile handy."

"But Chris, how do you know something's wrong?" Elizabeth asked.

"Two things. Morag, as keen a naturalist as she is, would struggle to find things to do on a wave-cut platform for three hours."

"And the other reason?"

"She knows that she is wearing around her neck the very thing I've been asked to bring with me—the Celtic cross."

"Oh." Elizabeth's face went pale as she nodded in understanding.

"Anyway, I've got to go." Chris turned back to the car. I feel Marianne would have something to say in the above section

"What are you going to do?" Alsdair called after him.

"I plan to keep the appointment, although probably not quite as Penmann expects." He sketched an untidy wave. "I'll give you a ring."

Chris drove along the familiar track up the glen to Murdoch's cottage. No one was home. Going around to the side, he found the sleek sea kayak resting against the wall. Chris heaved it out of the grass, cleaned the worst of the leaves from the cockpit, and hefted it on top of the Jeep's roof rack. After throwing the paddle into the car, he drove back to the village and along the foreshore track as far as it went.

Chris parked, undid the kayak, and carried it down to the water.

Then, climbing in, he began paddling west along the base of the cliff toward the Bluff.

Chris was seeking to be both silent and unseen. He'd calculated that no one standing on the cliff tops above him would be able to see him if he kept within a few yards of the cliff base. However, he discovered this was not as easy as it sounded. The sea was calm, but the swells left over from the recent storm sloshed against the rocky wall and refracted off it, causing the water at the base of the cliff to be choppy and confused. On top of this, disturbed guillemots would occasionally dash out from rocky ledges and startle him. Despite these challenges, he made good progress. The sea kayak cut through the water well.

He had three miles to go—a little over half an hour's paddling.

Alsdair paced up and down inside his cottage. "Dammit!" he said. "There's got to be something I can do. I feel so responsible for all this."

Elizabeth stood up and blocked his way, halting him in mid-stride. "Relax, Alsdair. Chris will be in contact soon enough." She put her hands against his cheeks.

Alsdair grunted. "It's that Penmann character. I don't like him. Both Chris and Morag could be in real danger. Perhaps I should call the police." He flopped into a chair.

"There is danger?" inquired Marianne.

"Possibly." Alsdair put his head in his hands.

Suddenly, a thought occurred to him. He clicked his fingers and got to his feet. "I know what I can do. I'll go to the bluff instead of Chris. I'll get to the boat ahead of Chris and chug over to the Bluff myself. Penmann wouldn't dare try any funny business with me." He glanced at his watch. "Right, I've got a bit of time, I'll just get a few things together and be off. Chris can still contact me on my phone if he wants to."

Elizabeth looked at Alsdair with concern. "Do be careful, darling."

"I will." Alsdair kissed her on the forehead and strode outside.

Marianne excused herself and went to the front door. She opened it, but paused for a moment to lean on the doorpost and borrow its strength. *Penmann.* She'd known him for many years, and knew what he was like. She closed the door and stepped outside. Then, leaning on the stone wall, she put a hand over her stomach and bent over, trying to contain her anxiety. A moment later, she stood up, and reached into her handbag. She pulled out her mobile and dialed a number she knew oh so well—but had always tried to resist ringing.

"Hello," she said. "It is Marianne." She started to cry as soon as she heard his voice. Desperately trying to pull herself together, she sniffed and replied, "My darling, I long for you, too." Her breath caught on a sob.

She heard his alarm and concern.

"No, no. I am fine," she assured him. "But Murdoch, I am very afraid for our son." "Alsdair is in danger."

Chris reached the Bluff and could clearly see the steps carved into the rock-face soaring above him. They cut diagonally across the face of the cliff. The challenge now was to get out of the kayak and onto the apron of rock forming the wave-cut platform, without being seen. In the end, he solved the dilemma by capsizing the kayak, and swimming to the rock.

The rock platform spilled out from the cliff face like a giant, flat table. Morag was nowhere to be seen.

Chris hauled himself onto the rocks like a seal, and crept across to the lowest steps. The view above him was daunting. He forced his anxiety back under control and began to climb. It did not take long for the pain in his left leg to become excruciating, but he pressed on.

"Are you going to kill me?" Morag was lying against a rock with her hands bound together.

"Yes." Penmann appeared completely unruffled, and continued his task of gathering wood.

"Why?" Morag couldn't keep the tremor out of her voice.

"You're a threat to me and to my boss." He started to build a small bonfire.

"Why? What does he want?"

"He wants the Celtic stone—the cross."

"Then take it." Morag screamed. "It's hanging round my neck. Take it. Just let me go. No one needs to know, as long as this doesn't go any further."

Penmann looked up in surprise. He walked over to her and ripped open her blouse. There, between her breasts, hung the stone cross. He gripped hold of it and gave a savage jerk. The cord broke, but not before it cut into her neck. She watched, horrified, as Penmann inspected the cross, then walked to the edge of the cliff and threw it out to sea.

"You've got what you want, now let me go!" Morag yelled.

Penmann applied a match to the bonfire. "Not until I kill you and your husband."

On hearing this, Morag immediately flew into a violent, hysterical rage. She screamed and writhed, trying frantically to get to Penmann. The man merely stepped back and, without any expression, kicked her in the face.

Morag lay groggy and whimpering on the grass.

As her senses returned, she watched in terror as Penmann took a rope from the back of the Land Rover. He tied one end around the steel fender of the vehicle, and made a loop in the other. Walking back to her, he slipped the loop around her waist, and hauled her to the cliff edge. She screamed and tried to pull away, but she was no match for him. Penmann pulled a knife from his boot and sawed through the rope that bound her wrists.

Penmann smiled. "If they find you, we can't let them see you with your hands tied, can we?" With a brutal shove, he pushed her over the edge. She screamed, but Penmann didn't let her fall. He gripped the rope and began to ease her down until she was about twenty feet over the edge.

She hung there, helpless, with the rope biting under her arms. Above her, she heard Penmann call out, "I've got something for you to watch before you die."

When Alsdair drove his Subaru down the track to the boat shed, he was surprised to see Murdoch's Land Rover already there. Not only that, but the man himself was in the estate's workboat, just drifting clear of the stone jetty.

Alsdair shouted at Murdoch to stop, and sprinted down to the jetty. Murdoch slipped the engine into neutral and waited for him as he came panting to a stop.

"Wha…" Alsdair bent over to catch his breath. "What are you doing, Murdoch? I need this boat urgently."

Murdoch seemed utterly unperturbed. He looked at Alsdair and said, "No you don't, Alsdair. I'm going in your place."

"No, you're not," he said, still gasping for breath. "You don't know what's going on." Alsdair rushed on in desperation. "I need it to help a friend."

"Chris? The Bluff?"

Alsdair nodded. "How did you know?"

Murdoch looked at him with a curious intensity. "I'm proud of you, Alsdair." The grizzled gamekeeper turned away, and eased the throttle forward.

The boat began chugging its way through the water, out to sea.

Alsdair watched him go, totally confused. He was even more bewildered when he saw Murdoch look up to the headland at the end of the bay. A figure wrapped in a black cape was standing on the cliff top. As Murdoch passed below, the figure raised a hand in silent salute.

Morag put her feet on the rock-face and leaned back to ease the pressure from the rope under her arms. As she did so, Penmann shouted over the edge of the cliff, "If you look out to sea, you will see your husband coming to us in a boat. Now you can watch him die."

She kicked at the rock-face to turn herself around, appalled at the prospect. As Morag turned, she received a shock. Chris was only a few yards away, climbing up the stone steps. He was waving to attract her attention.

She was about to call out when she saw him place a finger to his lips.

Realizing that there was only one way to reach him, she pushed sideways on the rock, making herself swing like a pendulum. She ran against the rock-face to increase her swing. As the arc increased, she was forced to push herself out in a series of giant steps. Then —tragedy.

She miss-timed a push, crashed into the cliff and span out of control. As she was swept across the rock-face, she fought desperately to get back in control. She tried to twist toward the cliff and brace herself with her feet each time she collided with the rock. Eventually, she succeeded, but her momentum was gone.

She saw Chris looking at her with a look of horror on his face. His look was all the inducement she needed to try again.

Gradually, she swung higher and higher, closer and closer to him. She could see him bracing himself behind a rocky protrusion, getting ready to catch her. Conscious that her strength was beginning to fail, she leaped across the rock-face with a final burst of determination. For one tantalizing instant, their fingers touched. But gravity pulled her away. Every fiber of her being screamed in protest.

She began to swing back. As she did, she pushed toward him with a desperate lunge.

Chris caught her forearm and hauled her to himself.

She sobbed with relief, safe within his arms.

Chris was appalled at the sight of Morag. She was bloodied and bruised. He brushed her down, eased the rope loop from around her and let it drop away. The cruelty of what she had endured was beyond his imagining. He was all too well aware, however, that they were not out of danger. He whispered to her to stay where she was. Then, ignoring the pain in his leg, he continued his climb to the cliff top.

Eventually, he arrived at the top step. Taking great care, he peered over the edge. The gnarled rowan tree prevented him from seeing anything except the back of the Land Rover. He paused for a while to catch his breath, then he crawled under the tangled foliage as far as he dared.

Thirty yards away to his left, Penmann was standing near the cliff top holding what looked to be a radio controller.

"Daniel," he heard Penmann call out. "Four years ago, I contracted two idiots to stop you doing your research. But you just couldn't stop meddling, could you? So today, I'm going to finish it. But first your boyfriend dies."

From out to sea came a thunderous explosion.

Even from where Chris squatted on the ground, he could feel the pressure wave of the blast. Gulls and guillemots screamed and circled the cliffs in alarm.

Chris's jaw muscles tightened. One thing was sure: someone had just died. He tried not to think who it might be. Penmann was staring out to sea, punching the air in exhilaration.

Being careful to keep below a grassy hummock, Chris got to his feet and ran at a crouch to the Land Rover. He desperately needed to find something he could use as a weapon. If the keys were there, perhaps he could even drive off for help. *Please, Lord.*

He reached the vehicle, and risked a brief look into the cabin.

No keys.

Chris edged himself toward the back of the vehicle where he saw a carryall sitting on the tailgate. He lifted it down and explored inside it. He discovered a number of electrical items he didn't recognize, and two blocks of C4 plastic explosive.

He lifted his head to check on Penmann.

It was a mistake.

Penmann saw him. The man reached down and picked up a double-barreled shotgun. Chris knew there was no escape. It was time for a final roll of the dice. Taking a deep breath, he limped out from behind the Land Rover.

Penmann raised the shotgun.

Chris halted beside the bonfire and held his hands over it. He called out, "Do you know what this is, Penmann?" Not waiting for a reply, he added, "It's a kilogram of plastic explosive. You just killed my wife—and I don't care much if I live or die. So I'm going to drop this C4 into the fire." He paused. "Do you know what will happen then, Penmann?"

Penmann said nothing.

"I'll tell you. In four seconds, it will heat up to over two-hundred-and-fifty degrees Celsius, at which point it will explode, killing us both." He shrugged. "I used to work with this stuff in the mines in South Australia." Chris paused. "So, what do you reckon, Penmann? Will four seconds be enough for you to save your life by diving for that rope in order to escape the blast?" He shrugged. "Personally, I don't think you'll make it. Let's see, shall we?"

With that, he dropped the two pieces of C4 into the fire.

Penmann dived for the rope and flung himself over the edge of the cliff.

In its severely frayed state, the rope stood no chance of supporting his weight. It snapped.

Chris heard Penmann scream as he plummeted to the rocks below.

The gulls screeched again in alarm.

In the middle of the fire, the two blocks of plastic explosive burned demurely.

Chris stared at them with relief. He'd heard rumors of soldiers in Vietnam using C4 to cook their rations when no dry wood could be found—but it was only now he knew for certain that it would not explode in a fire. It had been a terrible gamble.

Morag!

As he limped toward the rowan tree, he saw Morag emerge from underneath it and stumble toward him.

He caught her in his arms and clung to her, sobbing with relief.

Aaron Haines had never seen Marianne wear this expression before. She was dressed in her black cape, and came into his study almost soundlessly. Her demeanor caused a stab of fear. She looked like the angel of death.

"The police will come for you very soon." Marianne spoke very slowly and deliberately. "You and Penmann will be tried for murder. You attempted to kill Chris Norman. But Penmann succeeded in murdering the wrong person." She looked at him without expression. "It may interest you to know you are not the father of Alsdair. He was fathered by the only man I have ever truly loved." She pointed at him. "You revolt me. And now you will have the rest of your life to reflect on the ignominy of your actions, and endure the contempt of all who know you."

It took a moment for Marianne's words to register. The news was shattering. It was impossible. The old Laird gasped for air—air that did not come quickly enough. His hands flailed in a desperate bid to help him breathe, but he succeeded only in dislodging his breathing tube. He pounded his chest to activate the medical alert button that he normally wore there, but realized he'd removed it whilst eating his soup. It was still on his desk, two feet from where Marianne was standing.

His hand clawed at the air. "Help. The button," he wheezed. Panic drove his body to use more oxygen—but there was none. Turning sweaty and pallid, he called again. "Please, please…"

Marianne didn't move.

As Aaron collapsed to the floor, Marianne turned and walked back into the entrance hall. She opened the front door and stepped outside to the waiting car.

She did not look back.

Chapter 14

May the blessing of the rain
be on you.
May it beat upon your Spirit
and wash it fair and clean,
And leave there a shining pool
where the blue of Heaven shines…
and sometimes a star.
(Celtic blessing)

M orag watched the raindrops trickle down the windowpane. They occasionally hesitated and changed direction.

Her window looked out over the gray roofs of the cottages that lined the foreshore of Loch Portree. It was a beautiful view, but she barely noticed it. She wanted to be home, not in Portree hospital under observation. She wanted Chris. She wanted to cry. She wanted…

Her head ached abominably, and she was sore from a dozen nasty cuts and grazes. She sighed. Chris had left an hour ago, and now she felt very alone. She had insisted that he return home to reassure Ruan. He'd left reluctantly, his face pinched with fatigue and gray with grief.

Morag thought back to the closing drama of the afternoon. Chris had rung the police from the Bluff, given them the essential details, and then commandeered Penmann's Land Rover. He'd taken her straight to hospital and stayed by her side until the police had arrived and asked to see him privately. When he returned to her bedside, he sat beside her and shared the news that it was Murdoch who had died in the terrible boat explosion. Morag had curled into a fetal position and wept in despair.

"No. Not Murdoch." It was impossible to think that his uncompromising strength and steadying hand were no more. "No." She shook her head in denial. Murdoch was the only one who had stood by her during those blighted years of loneliness. It couldn't be true. It mustn't be. He'd been her rock—indomitable like the Scottish mountains.

Morag held Chris's hand, seeking his strength, only to find that he too was crying his tears.

Not much was said in the next few hours. Eventually, she persuaded him to return to the village and check that all was well with Ruan. He'd gone under protest, promising to return as soon as he could.

It was now ten o'clock in the evening, but the lingering summer twilight was still reluctant to give way to night. Her room was in darkness, although her door was open to the lighted corridor beyond.

A small movement alerted her to the presence of someone standing in the doorway. She watched the dark silhouette, and said cautiously, "Hello."

"Did I wake you?"

It was Alsdair.

She smiled wanly. "No. They've given me a sedative, but it doesn't seem to be working. What are you doing here at this time of night?"

He walked in and sat himself in the chair beside her bed. Light from the corridor highlighted the planes of his face, making him look like... *But that was ridiculous. It's just grief playing with my mind.*

Alsdair's face was stricken with anguish. "You've heard about Murdoch?"

"Yes."

Alsdair nodded and closed his eyes. "But you probably haven't heard about my father. He died late this afternoon as well—from natural causes as far as anyone can make out."

"I'm so sorry Alsdair." Morag was shocked.

Silence followed. The voices of two nurses talking further down the corridor could be heard. One gave a brief laugh.

Alsdair, in contrast, had his head bowed and appeared to be wrestling with his own demons. Eventually, he looked up and blurted out. "It should have been me who died, not Murdoch. I was going to take the boat, but Marianne must have told him." He dropped his head. "He took my place."

"Oh."

Another lengthy silence followed.

Morag said tentatively, "You tried to go in Chris's place?"

"Yes."

"Why?"

"Because I thought I could make Penmann see reason." A vein in Alsdair's neck stood out, betraying the guilt and anger that he was feeling. He rushed on. "Morag, you must hate my family. I certainly do. I've finally pieced it together. My family has suppressed evidence over the years that proved Crenshaw's innocence, and the innocence of Lachlan Daniel. You and your family have endured generations of shame because of a lie perpetuated by my family. How on earth can you be civil to me?"

Morag realized that, although Alsdair had pieced much of the story together, he had no idea of the full extent of his father's involvement. She reached out and took hold of his hand. "You're a good man, Alsdair. You tried to go in Chris's place. I'll always be grateful."

Alsdair snatched his hand away. "Morag, my family has blighted yours for over one hundred years. I can't imagine the hurt that you have had to endure. And my father and Penmann have conspired to kill you in order to cover it all up."

"Alsdair, you don't know that your father was involved. Penmann might have heard of your father's fears, and decided to act on his own initiative." She reclaimed his hand and gave it a squeeze. "You don't know for sure. Give him the benefit of the doubt."

Alsdair looked at her, disbelief plain in his expression. Eventually, he nodded. "I think you're being very generous, Morag. I will insist, however, that the truth about Crenshaw and Lachlan Daniel be made public so that the Daniel name is vindicated. I owe you that at least."

Morag leaned back on the pillow and closed her eyes. "Alsdair, I have decided not to pursue my Master's degree, and will not dig any further into events now lost in history. There are no more Daniels living on the island, so let it go. I am now Mrs. Norman—a woman of good standing among the crofters. There is nothing to be gained."

"Morag, there is truth to be gained."

"Not at this cost." She opened her eyes and fixed him with a level gaze. "Believe me, I know what it is like to live with a family's shame. I would not wish that on anyone, least of all you." She dismissed his objections with a wave. "Think of it as my wedding present to you and Elizabeth. With your brother overseas, you will become Laird. So go and make beautiful babies. Continue the family line, and make your family proud."

"No," Alsdair protested. "It's not just. It's not fair to you."

"Ach, Alsdair, you know what Murdoch would say. We have no right to insist that life be fair, only some responsibility to live it well. So let's drop it." She paused. "If you can't accept it as my wedding gift to you, then think of it as your wedding gift to me."

Outside the window, the twilight dimmed, coloring the loch indigo blue.

Alsdair said gruffly, "I don't want anything to do with the Haines estate. I'm going to let it die." He banged the arm of his chair. "It should die."

Morag sighed. "That would be sad. You love the islands. You

respect the crofters, and care for them. Please, don't inflict an unknown Laird on us. You've got an opportunity—perhaps even an obligation—to be Laird; a good Laird."

Another long silence followed. Finally, Alsdair lifted his head and said, "I will stay on one condition."

Morag raised a questioning eyebrow.

Alsdair continued on. "The estate is currently run by the Haines family trust. It needs three signatories to run it. Marianne and I are signatories. My brother is another but he's absconded." He turned to her. "I'll stay on if you will be the other signatory. Will you share in the oversight of the estate?"

"That role should rightly be given to Elizabeth."

"No. She understands me, but she doesn't understand the islands. You do." He smiled. "I want to change the name of the trust, and run it in partnership with a Daniel. That is not only just, it's good management."

"Is this the only way to get you to stay on as Laird?"

"It is."

"Very well. I accept."

Alsdair nodded. He unfolded himself from the chair and walked slowly to the door. When he got there, he turned and said, "Chris is a very lucky man." And he was gone.

Morag lay still in her bed, trying to calm the storm of her emotions; trying to listen to the sound of tears falling on the window, but the rain had stopped. She turned her head to the pillow and began to cry her own.

Peter came into the gloom of the stone chapel an hour before the service to find the grizzled, nuggety form of Hamish standing beside Murdoch's coffin.

Hamish was the one who had found Murdoch's bloodied body. On hearing the explosion, he had immediately put out to sea in his boat and located it. The seagulls had shown him where it was floating.

Peter walked up beside him and put a hand on his shoulder. Hamish, squeezed into an ill-fitting, suit, sniffed and wiped a tear from his eye. Laying his rough hand on the coffin, he said, "Yon man were a bastard."

Peter said nothing.

"But he were an island man, right enough." Hamish sniffed again. "A good one."

Peter had long since stopped being surprised by what people said at funerals. That someone could be described as a bastard and a good man in the same breath was a fair summary of life's complexity. He simply nodded. "Yes."

"And the bastard has had the last laugh."

"How so?"

Hamish brushed away another tear with a thick, dirt-ingrained thumb. "Yesterday, Alsdair asked me to be the new gamekeeper."

Peter didn't even attempt to fit the village community into the chapel for the funeral. There were too many people. He wheeled the coffin to the front door of the chapel and conducted the service from the church steps.

In front of him, the crofting community stood on the rough, tussocky grass.

A stiff Atlantic breeze tugged at Peter's brown habit as he told the age-old story of a God who invaded our confusion with his very presence, someone who shared the grief of ordinary people, and who died on a cross to pay the price for the many creative ways human beings had discovered to disqualify themselves from his holy presence. He told the story of God's relentless love.

Peter read: "*Greater love has no one than that they lay down their life for their friend.*" He looked out over those standing on the rough pasture in front of him. "Murdoch was that friend."

Ruan, hanging on to Chris's leg, whispered up at him. "Chris, I want to be a gamekeeper when I grow up."

It was as good an accolade as any.

That evening, Chris and Morag stood on the foreshore in front of their cottage. A hundred yards away, Ruan was jumping between rocks, followed inevitably by JJ.

Morag's head rested on Chris's shoulder. "Sad?" he asked.

She nodded.

"Happy?"

She paused, then nodded again. "Hmm."

Morag smiled at her own contrariness and leaned back to give Chris a kiss. As she did, she noticed a movement high overhead. An eagle was soaring on an afternoon thermal. She pointed to it. "Look! That's a golden eagle."

As Chris looked up and watched, it circled slowly round and round, as if guarding them. Morag continued, "There are only thirty breeding pairs left on Skye."

"Go find a mate!" Chris yelled.

Morag laughed and rested her head back on his shoulder. "Speaking of which," she said. "Put your hand on my heart and tell me what you feel."

Chris looked at her in puzzlement, but complied.

Morag felt the warmth of his hand on her breast.

Chris frowned as his hand brushed against something hard. "The Celtic cross!" he stammered. "How...?"

"You don't think I was ever going to lose my wedding ring, do you?" She smiled. "The original is safe in the Scottish museum. This, like the one taken from me, is a polyresin replica. It arrived from the museum this morning in the post."

Chris laughed. "Morag Norman, you are full of surprises."

"Hmm," she added. "Have you thought about Alsdair's suggestion of using one wing of the manor for the crofting school?"

"Not much. Why?"

"I think you should, because we're going to need the space in the attic."

"Why?"

"We might need another bedroom."

"Another... what?"

"Bedroom."

"Why? Then realization dawned. He grinned. "You're not...?"

"Yes," she smiled. "I'm pregnant."

Note from the author

Thank you for reading *The Celtic Stone*. I hope you enjoyed it. Please consider leaving a review on Amazon for the benefit of other readers.

A lot of what you read was based on my personal experience of sailing a twenty-nine foot boat up to Scotland and exploring the mysteries of the Isle of Skye.

I'm pleased to be able to report that the "Stone Collection" of books is growing all the time. It includes:

The Atlantis Stone
The Peacock Stone
The Fire Stone
The Dragon Stone

Two more are in the process of being made available.

To be kept up to date on new releases, sign up to my mailing list at www.author-nick.com. New subscribers will receive an exclusive bonus novelette, *The Mystic Stone*, a complete story, six chapters (15,500 words) in length. It is an adventure that takes place on Caldey Island off the rugged Pembrokeshire coast. I hope you like it.

Glossary of terms

Native Australian terms

- *Ahakeye* = Bush plum
- *Anaty* = Bush yam
- *Atnongara* stones = Australites or tektites: glassy, aerodynamically shaped stones that fall back from orbit after a large meteoric explosion has sprayed melted rock into the atmosphere. They are considered magical.
- *Pitjuri* = A native bush with narcotic properties
- *Waluwara* = Eagle
- *Woomera* = A device used as a lever to throw a spear with more power. It is a narrow, elongated bowl with a hook at one end and a handle at the other. The hook notches into the back end of the spear.
- *Yirarra* = The Milky Way

Australian names

- The Adelaide Crows = An Australian Rules football team

- The Sydney Swans = An Australian Rules football team
- The Wallabies = The Australian Rugby Union team

Terms commonly used in Scotland

- Awful whiley = a long chat
- Carragheen = a dark purple edible seaweed
- Crack = chat
- A wee crack = a little chat
- Crowdie = soft, sour milk cheese
- Croft = a Scottish rural cottage on a smallholding leased from a landlord
- Dampty = damn
- Ding = catapult
- Dinna fash yerself = don't fret yourself
- Dulse = sea lettuce (a seaweed, *Ulva spp.*). It is edible and is used in salads and soups
- Gillie = an assistant who helps with hunting parties
- Haud yer whist = be quiet
- I doubt = no doubt
- Jimmy = a general term for 'man"
- Laird = Lord (Scottish gentry)
- Mannie = man
- Puggled = exhausted
- Royal = a 'royal' is a stag that has twelve or more points to its antlers
- Skart = a cormorant
- Strupack = cup of tea
- Whelks = the Hebridean name for winkles (small edible, marine, sea-snails)

Gaelic

- *Ceilidh* = a dance or party
- *Foileag* = potato

- *Mo ghaoil* = my darling
- *Slainte Mhath* = good health
- *S math sin* = terrific
- *Stramash* = commotion

About the Author

Nick Hawkes has lived in several countries of the world, and collected many an adventure. Along the way, he has earned degrees in both science and theology—and has written books on both. Since then, he has turned his hand to novels, writing romantic thrillers that feed the heart, mind, and soul.

His seven novels are known as, 'The Stone Collection.'

His first novel, *The Celtic Stone*, won the Australian Caleb Award in 2014.

Also by Nick Hawkes

The Atlantis Stone

Felicity discovers the 'Atlantis stone' whilst scuba diving on the south-east coast of Australia, in a treacherous area known as 'the ship's graveyard.' Her diving is part of her research into the fabled 'mahogany ship,' a wreck sighted on the beach by early white Australians.

She meets Benjamin as a result of her love of diving. He is an indigenous Australian, but past traumas have caused him to disown his aboriginal heritage. Benjamin is now struggling to find his identity in the Western world, and has retreated to his workshop where he ekes out a living as a wood-turner. An attempt on his life propels him into Felicity's world of historic mysteries…and a quest that takes them to an ancient city in Sardinia.

An anthropologist dying of cancer, and an ex-Special Forces soldier with post-traumatic stress, join them in an adventure that centers on a medieval treaty, a lust for gold, and an audacious plot to rewrite world history.

More details at www.author-nick.com

(See next page for more)

Also by Nick Hawkes

The Dragon Stone

Elliot is hiding in his world of boats from a past that has wounded him. He is anti-authoritarian, lacking direction and broke.

Emma is terrified of life outside the studious, ordered world of Oxford. But circumstances propel her into the dangerous world of international subterfuge.

Kai is a Chinese triad gang leader, who is all too familiar with violence. However, he is now questioning his life, and seeking redemption.

The three of them meet in Hong Kong, a place where money is king, corruption is rife, and the secret societies of the triads are flourishing. Somehow they need to band together to outwit the murderous intent of powerful corporations, and Hong Kong's ruthless triad societies.

More details at www.author-nick.com

Made in the USA
Monee, IL
14 August 2020